MANY MEN HAD DIED FOR IT . . .
DOUG STAVERS WOULD KILL

"Tell me what you know about this object," he said to de Luca.

"The Vatican is seeking it. Also the Israelis. The Americans, as well."

"They're working together?"

"To the best of our knowledge, they're not."

Stavers thought a moment. "Is there anything more definite you can tell me?"

"Only that all indications are that it may be carried by one person," Kovanowicz said. "It has bizarre powers. It affects people. We are fairly sure of that. It is not a device, as one would think of machinery. And it must involve people who have affected world events. People with power."

"You have someone in mind," Stavers said.

"Yes, I do," the former KGB man told him. "*Adolph Hitler.*"

Novels by Martin Caidin

THE MESSIAH STONE

MARTIN CAIDIN

BAEN
FICTION
BOOKS

THE MESSIAH STONE

Copyright © 1986 by Martin Caidin

A Baen Books Original

Baen Publishing Enterprises
260 Fifth Avenue
New York, N.Y. 10001

First printing, April 1986

10 9 8 7 6 5 4 3 2

ISBN: 0-671-65562-0

Cover art by David Mattingly

Printed in the United States of America

Distributed by
SIMON & SCHUSTER
TRADE PUBLISHING GROUP
1230 Avenue of the Americas
New York, N.Y. 10020

This book is for
Ken and his lady, Gwendolyn.

Chapter 1

He stepped out into wind howling at 140 miles an hour. One moment his skin felt only the cold air within the cabin, and then forty multi-colored forms shuffled toward the doorway and brought stinging cold back around their fluttering jumpsuits. He was anxious to go. He always felt this desperate need to *get out!* when he was so close to jumping into nothingness. A beautiful free fall from three miles high. If you fucked up you'd die. It made it all the sweeter, this diving through a freedom never found anywhere else on or off this world. Weightlessness couldn't touch it. Screw the astronauts and their zero-g. They had nowhere to fall. No risk, no bittersweet taste in the mouth. Death had you by the throat and you had Him by the balls all the way down and you weren't going to hurt each other, right? He laughed. Falling from three miles high and waiting until the last instant to pull the shiny metal ring was awesome separation from the world's bilious gravity and its billions of tiny souls.

Doug Stavers loved it and he hurled himself into it, six kids before him and thirty-three behind, and they all went out in a foot-shuffling, throat-straining chant and eagerness to be throat-and-balls with Death and then they were away, separating. The icy wind of an Antarctic typhoon smacked him cold and delicious in the face and he arched his back and spread his legs and arms and he stabilized in the invisible soft cushion of resisting air. About him bodies dove away or spun or held hands and circled, and almost immediately Stavers ignored them all, holding his arch, his suit whipping and crackling against his body. God, so free of scars and mind at this instant! His senses sang and reveled. He moved a hand; a magical twist of his wrist and his body turned. There swept the golden blue shining of the Atlantic Ocean, the white sands of Crescent Beach and St. Augustine, below him the St. John's River and pencil-thin roads and creeks, and downwind of his perfectly balanced body, playing its melodious windsong to the sky, was the waiting crisscrossing concrete and grassy spread of the airfield at Palatka.

Stavers saw nylon blossoming far below him, heard the thin cracking sounds of chutes opening. From the corner of his eye he saw a skydiver keeping pace with him, the grin wide beneath the goggles and helmet. The other skydiver waved. An old instinct tugged at him. Hunch, sixth sense, the prickling along the back of the neck. He moved his arms and legs, pivoted slowly and saw the other jumper closer now, arms together, hands clasped and—

The son of a bitch was shooting at him.

He heard the three muffled reports, saw smoke whipping away. He felt a sharp pain, glanced at his wrist, saw the shattered timepiece and the whipspray of blood and without taking time to think because he knew the other man was taking a bead on him again, Stavers snapped his arms back to his sides, legs and feet together, arrowheading away. He heard a slug whine close by his head and then he had speed, diving at 200 miles an hour and he knew that crazy bastard couldn't get another shot at him like this. He tried to figure out *who*, or what, or *why*, and he came up empty. What the hell; he wasn't even on assignment, he hadn't tied any tin cans to anyone's ass in months, and now he'd been targeted in a way he'd never anticipate. He pushed aside all thoughts save the ground. He aimed his body to track crosswind so as not to land anywhere near the drop zone. He didn't want company. *No witnesses.*

At the last moment, the earth scorching up at him, the trees perilously close, he released the big square chute. It boomed open with air, turning into a wing he flew as a glider. Immediately he hauled down on one riser to jerk the chute into a tight descending spiral. That made him a lousy target. He heard another chute crack open above him. That had to be his friendly visitor from the skies. No one else was near them. Stavers hauled his body into the wind, one leg extended, and he was already into a half-run as his sneaker hit soft earth and in a blur he was out of his harness, unencumbered, free of body and he ran, turning as he dashed toward the other man just touching down. The bastard was good. He stepped onto the ground in a perfect flare, but he needed both hands on his toggles and Stavers hit him at that instant when all his attention was on his landing.

He hit him almost hard enough to kill. But not quite. He still didn't know *why* this creep had made a target of him. Stavers slammed a fist into the ribcage of his still unknown assailant. He heard a cry of pain and the other jumper collapsed to one knee, retching, but he had one hand to his waist and Stavers didn't need to see the gun to know what was happening. A dedicated hit man was the last thing he needed. He hooked the fingers of his right hand beneath the other man's helmet, pressed hard against the opposite side of the helmet, and twisted savagely. The sharp snap of the breaking neck sounded like dry wood. The body fell limp beneath him. Stavers reached down, pulled the gun, a long-barreled .357 Magnum, from the dead man's waistband. He'd been luckier than he deserved; hard to miss with one of these mothers if you know what you're doing, and he *knew* this man was—*had been*, a pro. He took the extra few seconds to search for a wallet. People were running across the field. The gun and wallet disappeared within Stavers' jumpsuit. He picked up his chute and harness, started toward the people running toward him. He pointed to the crumpled figure. "He's hurt. Better get a doctor."

The jumpers hesitated only a second. One ran back toward the jump shed, the others to the body.

Stavers walked to his rental car, dumped his gear in the trunk and locked it. He stood by the car, lighting a thin cigar, watching. A crowd collected across the field with the usual milling about and an ambulance wailed along a runway. Good. No one was watching Doug Stavers. He slipped behind the wheel and drove away, taking the highway to Jacksonville. No one would look for him by name, no one would connect him to the dead man. He removed the blond wig he had worn at the jump center. The moustache came off and so did the horn-rimmed glasses with their flat dark-grey lenses.

He drove at 55 miles an hour, thinking hard. He simply couldn't place any attempt on his life. It wasn't a hit-or-miss proposition. Whoever wanted him dead also wanted the job done in a way that would close off all avenues back to the source. No one could be fingered, because the man with the gun would simply have landed in his chute and vanished. So the affair had been planned carefully, the man selected from a background of—of course; an ex-paratrooper or mercenary. Skydivers are a congenial bunch, not professional assassins, *unless* they entered civilian life with that particular skill well established from earlier times.

The more he considered the ramifications the less Doug Stavers liked his conclusions. He'd been tagged by a professional hit man with excellent qualifications. The bruise along his left wrist was aching proof of how close the man had come. But *why?* That question demanded an answer, because where there's one, there will be more. That had always been the rule in Stavers' life: No real pro—

and these folks were obviously pros—quits after one failed attempt. If they wanted him badly enough to set up the skydiver attack, then they would have backed it up with other moves.

The only other person who knew where Stavers had gone to resharpen his jumping skills was Tracy North, and Stavers didn't question Tracy's loyalty to him. That meant they'd been tailing him; and whoever they might be they had their best hit men (or women) poised to take advantage of any situation that might come up suddenly. *A group.* He smiled as mental gears began to synch and mesh. He needed to shift his thinking back to the old days when death was always a companion to whatever he did, wherever he might happen to be.

He shook his head at his own stupidity. Whoever fingered him had also judged his moves subsequent to the attempted killing when he fell to earth. So they were out to nail him *now*. If he survived the hit when he was skydiving he'd move like a well-trained dog as he made tracks through northeastern Florida. They'd have to nail him *before* he got out of Florida because the instant he got running room he'd be a wraith instead of a target. He'd shift safely to Indian's Bluff in Arizona, twenty miles outside Phoenix, the small dusty town he used as his headquarters. You can't beat a small desert town for security. Doug Stavers had made a great deal of money as a mercenary and he owned six businesses in Indian Bluff. Almost everybody in town either worked for him or benefited directly from his trade. From the sheriff and the local Indians on down to the town drunk, everyone looked out for Doug Stavers. Any stranger was tagged immediately on sight, followed, spied upon and, if any doubts arose, tossed into the local slammer by the sheriff until they decided what to do with him. The best security system in the world was made up of people who had virtually nothing else to do than to be suspicious.

His own suspicions were clamoring like a fire alarm. Whoever wanted him wasted also knew they were dealing with one of the most efficient and deadly mankillers on the loose—*himself.* So they'd do the unexpected. They knew that if Stavers escaped the killer in the sky he'd try to identify his assailant and start backtracking to the source. And how do you do that? No chance for fingerprints on an airfield milling about with excited skydivers and local cops. No way. *You take the man's identification with you and—*

He could amost feel the cold wind down his back. *Asshole!* He looked for a rest stop along the highway and pulled in slowly. He sat in the car, thinking, went to the trunk and opened a carryall bag. Old habits were his friends, and he always carried with him an oddball assortment of inoffensive items. Such as fishing line. He picked up the dead man's wallet, being absolutely certain not to open the leather fold. He could see a thick sheaf of hundred-dollar bills in the wallet. He smiled thinly. *Come into my den, said the spider to the fly . . .*

He went into the men's room. Good; it was empty. The toilet stalls had doors that pulled open; just what he needed. He stepped into a toilet stall, laid the wallet carefully on the floor behind the bowl. He wrapped the fishing line around one half of the wallet, extended the line carefully. With the door to the toilet open no more than a few inches he tied the fishing line to the lock on the inside of the door and then closed it slowly. He waited patiently in his car. Ten minutes went by and a station wagon pulled into the rest area. He watched a young couple separate to the rest rooms.

A bright flash speared the high small windows of the rest-room building, followed by smoking debris. Stavers thought he heard a shrill scream. It didn't matter. He shook his head. It had been a long time since he'd seen the booby-trap wallet. You opened the wallet, a tiny spring pulled to release a flat packet of acid, the acid touched plastique, and *blooey*. The stuff was about six times as powerful as dynamite, and just that little tab was enough to have blown that poor bastard who only wanted to take a crap, to bloody chunks. *Better thee than me*, Stavers mused as he drove off.

So that was the second attempt. One-two, just like that; if he survived the attempted murder in the air, then simply trying to discover *who* was also a lethal set-up. That meant, he thought carefully, that they'd figured he might escape both attempts on his life. *And that means they've got a dossier on you, old friend*.

He often held running conversations with himself, playing devil's advocate and antagonist in the mental exchange. You needed to have the fight inside your own head to see the opposition's point of view. He was coming less and less to appreciate what that really might be. He didn't have the *why* of all this yet, but he did have the *modus operandi*. No matter what he did, they—whoever the hell "they" were—would have the gaff out for him.

And he had an open-ticket flight on Eastern Airlines from Jacksonville to Phoenix. They didn't need a flight number to wait for him. He had to go through Jacksonville. He'd be turning in a rental car and he hadn't had any reason not to use his own name. That was a neat trap. The parking lot. The walk to the rental car counter. The walk to the terminal counter. Maybe a stop in the men's room. They could waste him anywhere along the way. Then he'd have to change planes in Atlanta. Once again he'd be naked. In a crowded airline terminal you could do just about anything you wanted to do.

So he stayed on I-95 going north through Jacksonville. He crossed the bridge across St. Mary's River that formed the Florida-Georgia border and continued eight miles north to Kingsland. There he left the highway and angled back to a remote airport on the edge of the town of St. Mary's. He parked and went inside to the small operations building. There he made arrangements for a charter flight in a twin-engined Baron to Orlando in Central Florida. He wasn't in any rush. He studied the usual crowd of student pilots hanging around the field and selected one, a husky youngster.

"I need a favor," he started the conversation. "Do you have a car?"

"Sure do. What kind of favor?"

"Nothing much. I'm late for an appointment in Orlando and I'm taking a charter down there. But I've got to turn in this car at the Avis counter, you know, at Jacksonville International. You'll need your car and someone to drive with you down there so you have a way back. There's a hundred bucks for the both of you if you can handle it."

"You got it, mister, uh—"

"It's right there on the rental agreement. It should cost about ninety or so for the car. I'll give you two hundred. Just turn the car in and pay cash. Use my name. That way it won't complicate matters because you're not twenty-five years old and Avis won't throw a fit. Deal?"

"It sure is, Mr. Stavers. How soon do you—"

"Now."

"I'll get my car. I got a buddy here who'll drive it down and I'll handle the rental car for you."

Stavers passed him two one-hundred-dollar bills, shook his hand. "Have a good trip, and thanks."

"Thank *you*. This is great, Mr. Stavers."

Stavers nodded, carried his gear into the waiting Baron and joined the pilot. "You got the route?" Stavers asked.

The pilot was young and bright-faced. "Yes, sir. The jetport at Orlando?"

"You got it. Let's fly, son."

They were flying over Gainesville when Stavers told the pilot to change their destination from Orlando to Tampa. Too many people knew he was going to Orlando. Only this pilot would know about Tampa and it didn't matter to him; it was only another ten minutes of flying time.

His parachute and other gear were jammed into a large duffel bag and he took it to the airlines counter where he booked a flight to Phoenix. He didn't want to carry anything with him. No hand baggage. He had thirty-five minutes before his flight left. He went to a phone booth and placed a person-to-person call to Sheriff Paul "Hoot" Gibson of Indian Bluff. Gibson was a three-hundred-pound mixed-breed Indian of enormous shoulders and equally enormous gut, and the two men were close friends.

"How you doing, cowboy?" Gibson shouted affably into the phone.

"Hoot, shut up and listen. I haven't much time and I'll be calling you back later, maybe two or three hours from now."

Gibson knew *that* particular tone. "Shoot."

"About an hour or so from now, use your position as sheriff and place a call to the security police of Jacksonville International Airport. Then—"

"Hold it. Jacksonville where? They's lots of them."

Stavers smiled in appreciation. "Jacksonville, Florida."

"Got it."

"Ask them if they have any reports of a missing person."

"For Christ's sake, *who?*"

"Me."

"*You?*"

"Yeah. Use my name but don't offer any information. Tell them anything. Got it, Indian?"

"You're crazy. I got it."

Stavers hung up, went casually to his flight. He didn't change planes in Atlanta. From Tampa he flew direct to Los Angeles with a no-change stop in New Orleans; there were plenty of airlines making the run out of Los Angeles back to Phoenix. He had twenty minutes between flights. He used the time to call Hoot Gibson again.

"Injun? It's me."

"Jesus *Khee-rihst*, but I'm glad to hear your voice!"

"You sound upset, Injun."

"They told me you were fucking *killed!*"

"You didn't let on that—'

"Hell, no. What's going on?"

"Let me guess. I was killed by a car."

"You're close. It was a bus. Ran you down in the parking lot. They said it was Avis."

"They're right. How'd they get the identification?"

"Car rental papers, they said."

"Very neat."

"What?"

"Never mind. Play it just like you heard it. There's an eleven o'clock arrival at the airport tonight. Pick me up."

"You can't miss me, white man. I'll be wearing silver spurs."

Doug Stavers didn't push the banter. His mind worked furiously. That was the third time! And all in one day, and he knew there'd been more of these little bushwhacking deals set up to nail his hide to the barn door. Again and again his mind kept pushing the *who*, and just as quickly each time he forced himself to ignore the identity of those people after him, because that was the kind of blind alley that interfered with survival. He knew now the game was getting deadlier all the time. He knew it by instinct and cunning and long experience, he knew it by the feel of the techniques being used against him. He also knew they were screwing up in some ways. That skydiver had been good. He'd fingered Stavers despite the perfectly fitting wig and the moustache and a false name at the airfield, and he'd almost done the job. Whoever was working with the skydiver had rigged the wallet, because if the skydiver was killed they'd need someone else to let the sources, the people who'd ordered all this, know what had happened. *They* were almost programming him. They figured he was better than good and a hell of a lot better than smart, because who's going to anticipate a wallet being set up to blow your head off? *He* had. He'd also escaped the bushwhacking he knew they'd arranged at Jacksonville Airport simply by driving *past* that airport.

But they'd screwed up because he'd anticipated what they would do. That was a critical error on their part. They were ready, waiting for him at Jacksonville. He slipped their noose by driving onward to St. Mary's. Somewhere along the line he'd been tailed, most likely the unidentified man who'd watched the skydiving scene and its aftermath. The tail had stayed with him all the way to St. Mary's, found out easily enough that Stavers had driven off to Jacksonville. That was the bad mistake. The tail hadn't gone into the operations office. He'd seen Stavers's rental car drive in, and from a distance he'd seen the same car drive off, with a man behind the wheel of about Stavers's size and build. Another error had been to ask one of the youngsters at the airport about the *car* and not the *driver*. He had also failed to inquire at the operations counter, or he would have known that Stavers had chartered a flight to Orlando. Too many mistakes ... of the kind a man commits when he's trying to keep a low profile. Of course,

Stavers hadn't gone to Orlando, but the man who'd watched the rental car and been told it was driving to Jacksonville had compounded his own stupidity. He'd made a phone call to Jacksonville, which meant that the people running this show had hired local soldiers to do their work for them. And that was the ultimately stupid mistake, because the locals didn't know Doug Stavers and had never seen a picture of him, and they'd killed the wrong man when they ran down that kid in the Avis parking lot.

There was a message in all this and he was trying to pick it out from all the debris about him. Two cracks at him; failure. A noose set up for him and he'd squeezed by without ruffling a feather. An abrupt change in his own plans they'd blown like rank amateurs. They were erratic. They also didn't know where he was right now. They really wouldn't be able to figure his flight to Los Angeles because he could have gone to a dozen different cities and then worked his way back to Indian Bluff—if, indeed, he was returning there. But they'd cover that possibility *because it was easy to do*. He felt better. He was starting to anticipate their moves. He had one other advantage. The big Indian might have been a fat, sweaty halfbreed, but Gibson had the mental characteristics of a steel beartrap. He didn't bother to ask any questions of Stavers, but the reported death of Stavers in Florida, and their casual dismissal of the incident, would have already galvanized Gibson into his own moves.

A strange dog couldn't move through Indian Bluff without Sheriff Hoot Gibson knowing his pedigree, and a man was a hell of a lot more visible than a dog. Every motel room would be checked, every strange car, every face, every road, every airplane movement into the Indian Bluff Airport. Because both Stavers and Gibson knew that, whoever was playing this game, they *must* make their next move on Stavers's home turf. And that was fine with him. He pushed his seat back and fell asleep.

Chapter   II

They gathered in the penthouse suite of Hotel El Cid on the neon-emblazoned Strip of Las Vegas. The Board of Directors. That was the only name by which they were ever identified as a group. No company name, no corporation, only hazy references to industry. Some people knew they had vast land holdings in Canada, were up to their armpits in oil and great supertankers, controlled powerful insurance companies, ruled the holdings of several hotel chains, a charter airline and the controlling interest in an independent car rental agency. And several travel agencies, and a chain of flower shops as well. The perfect covers for their income, the perfect and always justifiable reason for extensive traveling, and the perfect way—through the rental cars and delivery trucks and the small charter airliners—to move drugs at their own whim and absolute control. They were big business. Together they were worth in all their control and holdings more than six billion dollars. They were friends with the right people in OPEC and many other right people in the right political places.

Benito Gibraldi was small in stature, as taut as a bowstring stretched to its ultimate before releasing its arrowed shaft. Fifty-six years old, as healthy and strong as he had ever been as a survivor of the French Foreign Legion, where he had gone to change his name and obliterate a past that included a string of murders in Naples and Milan. Always impeccably dressed and courteous, with the manners of the Italian nobility, he was utterly impersonal in his business dealings. And absolutely loyal to those with whom he offered his hand. The others knew this and drew mutual strength from it. Gibraldi, like the other four, was so wealthy that mere greed no longer much motivated him.

Harold Metzbaum was as gross as Gibraldi was diminutive. A gross lumbering waddle of nearly 450 pounds, his face as round as the full moon, his legs of elephantine girth, his tailored suits costing him three thousand dollars each, his shoes made by hand, he was a man who moved with effort, who sat in chairs tailored and handcrafted to his terrible bulk. To lift himself from an easy chair was a Herculean effort. His skin reflected light with an unmistakable sheen of fatty tissue caused by hormonal imbalance. His bulk was not of his own choosing; he had spent a small fortune on medical disasters intended to trim his mass. But whatever imbalance issued from his pituitary and other glands defied the best of medical science. He was imprisoned within that terrible bulk.

So fleshy was his face his eyes seemed porcine, embedded within rolls of fatty tissue. Metzbaum had grown a beard to place his eyes in further retreat behind his thickened features. But if you looked deeply into the eyes you saw brightness, clarity, intelligence; you might even discern a steely purpose that had shaped his existence. What his body denied him of physical ability he found compensation for in mental agility, a ballet of seeking and manipulation of power. His was a strange throne, for he had not left this hotel for nearly two years. He had a private elevator to his apartment, where every piece of furniture was handcrafted to his unusual needs, where he could bathe without fear of drowning from a bulk too difficult to control on slippery marble. The hotel and its splendid gaming casino was his immediate world; the real world lay beyond, but always within reach of the power he controlled. He was trapped in his body but free in his mind. And when he won, he conquered. Conquest, to Harold Metzbaum, was as deep and satisfying as orgasm for any other human being. It gave him reason for living.

Alberto Grazzi, in his personal life, was the epitome of charm, a soft-spoken, kind husband and father who affected comfortable loafers and smooth silk shirts and slacks that wrapped his hips like slim leather gloves. He conquered nothing. He and Maria had nine children, a small ranch in the hills near Boulder City with horses and emerald-green grass and the sounds of children at play. Laughter was music to Alberto Grazzi. So were numbers. He was not a businessman and likely would have failed even in a haberdashery store. The man with the slim moustache might have been cast in life as a pleasant barber, surrounding himself with friends and relatives, celebrating the growth of his children and all Italian holidays with impromptu but neverending feasts. He was a gourmet and a splendid chef, attributes unnecessary as a member of the Board of Directors. What Alberto Grazzi gave the others was a memory that never erased numerals. Mention any number, of any triviality or enormous consequence, and it remained locked forever in his memory cells and always available for instant recall. The man who could not sell a suit of clothes to a customer could carry the contents of a huge warehouse in his head and, if asked ten years later what had been that warehouse supply all those previous years, would have related every digit and identification number in his pleasant, warm voice. He was the walking ledger, the instant memory computer, the ultimate bookkeeper where keeping written books was always dangerous. He had no aspirations beyond his family and his friends, he was generous, and he was blessed with that memory that defied biological or scientific explanation. He attended all meetings, studied all ledgers of the many corporations and organizations, and sat quietly at the meetings, speaking only when a request for numbers was presented to him. Only four people in the world knew of this extraordinary genius in an otherwise absolutely ordinary man, and it was agreed among them that this wonder should never be spoken of to any person beyond their own group. Who in a fiercely competitive world points to the secret Rosetta Stone?

Then there was Vernon Kovanowicz, on first sight the perfect candidate for a garbage collector. There was no earthly way in which this great stump of a man, stolid and square-jawed, might be considered to have intelligence greater than that required to tie his shoelaces. He presented thick, black, curly hair, a chin with a perpetual bluish stubble, fingers that might have been clamped to his hands from a sausage factory. His clothing was always rumpled, even within moments of donning a suit fresh from his tailor. His body, thickset and burly with tufts of hair sprouting from his ears and over his eyes and in great clumps along his shoulders, seemed lumpy and misshapen. As much as this was a natural condition for this man, it was and had been deliberately cultivated in a world where keen intelligence was not nearly as important as blind loyalty and uncompromising willingness to obey orders. Even if the order was to slit your mother's throat.

Vernon Kovanowicz was a rarity, a native-born Czechoslovakian with a brilliant mind, a man who dallied as easily with higher mathematics and chemistry as skillfully as he would torture an enemy agent. As the only non-Russian who had been high in the echelons of the KGB, the secret police arm of the Soviet Union, he was the perfect adept at survival. He survived Russian suspicions, Czechoslovakian hatred, American and British agents who cheerfully would have slit his throat. Above all, he survived his own intelligence by concealing it from his superiors and coworkers. He had also prepared a certain move for years. The first part was to collect a dossier on seventeen high Soviet officials that proved beyond all question their trafficking in political areas in which they had no reason to be concerned; skimming funds from factories, seeking luxuries by condemning certain affluent Russians to prison camps and insane asylums, and making secret deals for profit to agents of other countries. With these documents carefully concealed for use at the proper time, the stolid, unemotional Kovanowicz then proceeded with astonishing stealth to arrange a fire and explosion in a Prague museum. In the confusion that ensued, the Czech member of the KGB vanished with $140 million worth of jewels from the historical treasures of his country. Once copies of seventeen dossiers had been delivered to seventeen influential Russian government officials, the name of Vernon Kovanowicz was found on the identity papers of a KGB agent "killed in the performance of his duty in Berlin."

The Czech at that moment was in Algeria, where his meticulous plans for a chartered jet flight to the United States had gone awry in the midst of a savage, unplanned battle between local government forces and the hired mercenaries of the Foreign Legion. Retaining his composure, studying the Legionaires, Kovanowicz fixed his eye on a small wasp of a man with sergeant's stripes. This was his first meeting with Benito Gibraldi, who on shaking hands with the heavyset man found an astonishing diamond remaining in his palm.

"There is much more than this at our destination," the Czech had said.

"And this is worth?"

"In American currency, one hundred and seventy thousand dollars. It is a trifle. A gift."

Gibraldi never wasted a moment of a life that had been too many times perilously close to ending. "How do we go?"

"There is an American Boeing at the airfield over that hill. It is chartered in my name. It is fueled for a nonstop flight to Canada, after which another machine is ready for a flight into the United States. All arrangements have been made."

"And there are a thousand rebels between us and that plane."

"Yes."

"It would be wise if we broke through and seized the machine, I think."

"Yes."

Sergeant Gibraldi led his men on a devastating attack through rebel lines, captured the jetliner, ordered his men to stand guard as he boarded the Boeing with his new friend. Ten minutes later the Boeing lifted from the ground to disappear into a high grey overcast en route to a private Canadian airfield. Gibraldi and Kovanowicz had been inseperable ever since.

It was the Czech's responsibility with the Board of Directors to handle all business contacts behind that invisible but opaque Iron Curtain of the Communist bloc. Kovanowicz was more than simply familiar with methods and procedures. He had been a part of that system. He knew where certain critical materials were located and he knew whom to bribe. He knew how to divert merchant shipping and trains. He knew when, how, and where to make deals. He handled industrial merchandise and raw materials in silky fashion at prices shamefully below those available to competitors. He even had a long reach into China, where private trade agreements were negotiated in exchange for Vernon Kovanowicz's knowledge of secret agent apparatus in the Soviet Union. All in all, his was an eminently satisfying role in the activities of the Board of Directors.

Kovanowicz never bothered with the mundanities of life; marriage to him was both stupid and a sordid contract with restrictions reflecting on his duties as a KGB operator. Why bother? He had known nothing of strong family or friendship ties in a life where survival meant chameleon-like camouflage to meet situations. He did the next best; he kept a suite in the El Cid staffed with servants and three lovely young women, often rotated because of his unpredictable rages and fetish for striking out physically as well as verbally. Little matter. It met his needs. He consumed vast quantities of cognac, enjoyed gambling, knew no inhibitions sexually or personally, and soon found himself sliding into boredom. If nothing else, life within the KGB as a Czech had been constantly demanding of quick-wittedness. This demand did not exist now. Lack of challenge irritated him. He needed risk and penalty. Which is why he had an unusual respect and the only true fondness he had ever known for another human being in the person of the Chairman of the Board.

Of all things—a woman. Concetta de Luca, formerly of a family of Sicilian bandits who had hammered, pushed, blackmailed and murdered their way along a heroin-trafficking trail into the power elite of the Mediterranean. He didn't know the age of Concetta; the raven-haired beauty could have been twenty-eight or forty-five and he guessed the truth lay somewhere in between. When her organization was hard-pressed by its competition during a secret meeting on the island of Sardinia, Concetta de Luca's deepest fears were realized. The power groups from elsewhere in Italy had teamed with the Turks, the French, the Greeks, and a motley group of Arab freebooters. They believed that if the Sicilians could be broken up they would have a greater share of the drug market in their oval-shaped corner of the world. They were right, of course, and at the propitious moment automatic weapons fired in the meeting room. Concetta had anticipated the moment, and before the first shot and the blood bath, she slipped behind a heavy velvet drape into a tunnel of which only she and two young men who held her in total adoration were aware. Several hundred yards from the baronial estate where blood and gunpowder mingled freely, she turned to Filipo. "You have the heroin aboard the aircraft?"

"All is ready."

She smiled and stroked his groin gently. "The switch, Filipo. Where is the switch?"

He moved to several large rocks and lifted a flat slab, and pointed. "Ah. Good." The switch connected by power cables to four thousand pounds of dynamite, surrounded by several thousand gallons of gasoline, in the tunnels and basements of the estate. She smiled, dazzling in her beauty, and turned the switch handle to detonate the dynamite and the gasoline and she incinerated the one hundred and fifty-seven people, including the kitchen help and the servants, in the building. The towering flames lit their pathway to the airport where Dominic waited in the Learjet. Concetta de Luca stopped Filipo at the side of the runway. "Before we see Dominic," she said quietly, "one last kiss while we are alone."

He was still smiling, joyous, when the poison from her ring pricked his neck. He slid slowly from her body, arms trailing from about her neck like dead vines, to collapse at her feet, only seconds from death. She walked to the Learjet and climbed aboard. "Where's Filipo?" the other pilot queried.

"He will follow later. He wishes to be certain no one is left to talk about us," she told him. "There will be police, Dom. Waste no time." He nodded, closed the door and returned to the left seat. Before he busied himself in starting up she had a last-moment detail to confirm. "It is aboard?"

He gestured to the rear of the aircraft. "We removed two seats. Twelve suitcases, each hermetically sealed, each with one hundred pounds of the goods."

"It is good. Do what you must," she said, gesturing to the controls. Twelve suitcases each carrying one hundred pounds of pure heroin. It would guarantee her position across the Atlantic. They flew to Lisbon and refueled. The Learjet had extra tanks built into the wings and the aft fuselage and a very long range. The Portugese officials pocketed the envelopes with their "gifts" inside and the Learjet fled Europe to 49,000 feet to cross the Atlantic. Dominic had arranged everything. They were three hundred miles off the American coastline when another Learjet, painted exactly the same as their aircraft and bearing the same numbers, slid into tight formation. Aboard the second airplane were a man and a woman, each bearing the same identification as Concetta de Luca and Dominic Caglione. The second Learjet had filed its flight plan out of Newark, New Jersey for Huntsville, Alabama. The airplane carrying Concetta and Dominic had filed its international flight plan for landing in Savannah, Georgia. The two aircraft simply switched roles. No one would ever check the similarity of numbers, and the airplane that had left Lisbon was now also listed as having departed New Jersey for Alabama. There would be no reason to make queries. The airplane that landed in Savannah was as clean as a hound's tooth.

That night, in a Hilton hotel suite, Concetta de Luca met a man she knew only as Donald Simmonds. She wasted no time. "You are the man with whom I am to receive a recommendation," she said calmly.

"Yes. Your contact. His name is Benito Gibraldi—"

The Italian name caught her by surprise. "Is that wise?" she asked quickly.

"In this case, yes," he assured her. "Mr. Gibraldi is a businessman of unquestioned repute. He is in, ah, condominiums and apartment buildings. You have the entire top floor of the El Condor Apartments in Las Vegas. It is already furnished. You will have your choice of servants or you may provide your own." Simmonds shrugged. "That is not my province."

"All arrangements are made, then."

He nodded. "Yes. I will remain here until your aircraft leaves the ground. Then I will be gone."

"And your fee?"

"One percent of your goods."

"It would be stupid to carry such an amount."

"I understand. Please do not be concerned. Mr. Gibraldi has attended to that matter."

She raised an eyebrow. "So?"

"It is done," he reassured her.

"A generous man."

"No. A businessman."

She laughed and he smiled without humor, without involvement. "I will be in the room to your left. Your pilot is to the right."

She didn't even blink. "Dominic will spend the evening here."

"Of course. If you need me—"

She never could resist the barb. "Your need has been met. Dominic will meet mine. Good night, Mr. Simmonds."

Everything went smoothly. Dominic exhausted himself pleasing her, and she slipped into a deep and satisfied sleep. In the morning they left for a private airstrip outside Las Vegas. Benito Gibraldi met them in a car with two very large and quiet men. Beyond the car was a delivery truck for a flower shop. She knew it would attend to the suitcases. Gibraldi went through the amenities of greeting and led her to the car. "Everything is taken care of," he assured her.

"I am not concerned," she said, almost diffident in her attitude. It impressed Gibraldi. He recognized true quality. They drove to her apartment, his assistants bringing her personal luggage. She walked into a twelve-room suite with elegant furnishings. Excellent; she told him so.

Benito Gibraldi sat across a small coffee table of pure marble. "Your goods will bring two hundred million without questions. The amount will be delivered to you in nine individual accounts, negotiable bonds and other documents."

"When?"

"Eight hours from now."

"Good."

"What about your pilot? I must ask these questions. He knows too much. He is an excellent pilot and—"

"And a very good lover, and quite expendable. I assume it will not be connected in any way with—"

He looked almost hurt. "Please," he broke in, gesturing for her to end such questions.

"Then let us have a toast to our future relations, Mr. Gibraldi."

"I am Benito and you are Concetta."

"So. Is there champagne here?"

"I will bring it."

They drank their champagne. "Excellent, Benito. Now, one last item of business. Eight hours for the documents to be delivered, you said?"

"Yes, Concetta."

"That provides you enough of a safety margin. Your champagne, my dear Benito, contains a poison that becomes quite fatal twelve hours from now. Only I know the antidote, which you will of course receive upon such delivery."

His face whitened. "You wouldn't—"

"Benito, you know what happened in Sardinia?"

He nodded, speechless.

"One more does not matter. I will see you in eight hours. You may send the servants to me, if you please. I like you, Benito Gibraldi. Please, for your sake, hurry."

He left at once. She bathed and ate lightly and made telephone calls. Eight hours and seventeen minutes after he left, Benito Gibraldi returned to the apartment. He encountered Concetta with a stranger. "This is my attorncy, Gaspar Puzo," she told him. "He is also my father's brother. He will handle the papers, Benito."

Another thirty minutes went by as the expressionless stranger examined the financial papers. "Everything is in order," he told Concetta.

"Tomorrow, then," she said softly.

Benito waited until he was gone. "Everything has been done," he said. "I wish to have the antidote."

"In a moment, Benito. Tell me about Dominic."

"There was an accident. His aircraft lost its pressure seal somewhere above forty thousand feet."

"And his emergency oxygen mask?"

"Sleeping gas." He shrugged. "The airplane went into a steep dive, of course. He was asleep before it struck the ground and exploded."

"Then there are no connections to over there," she said, in reference to Italy.

"None. Now, if you please, the antidote."

She smiled, almost purring. "You may relax, my new friend. There never was any poison."

They gravitated slowly but surely into a single group. By combining their power structures they could wield many times the influence that could be produced simply by combining five fortunes and businesses. In the world of international industry, finance, and commerce, power squares itself rather than simply doubling. It is a fiscal law of physics that men learn as they go along, not difficult to grasp once there exists the first hint. Benito Gibraldi, Harold Metzbaum, Alberto Grazzi, Vernon Kovanowicz, and Concetta de Luca, who had emerged as their leader by the subtleties of interchange between and among them. They were, really, a most extraordinary group; for they were free, by their own personal characteristics, of the one attribute potentially most destructive to their unique assembly: greed. Greed for money, greed for power. All that spells willingness to destroy the structure, to lie and misrepresent and cheat and kill. But each of these five had emerged from a background where such characteristics were the norm. They had not simply fled those dangers; they had *escaped* them. Their unity was their best protection, and none had the need or the desire to undermine any other member of their group.

They shared little outside their membership in their Board of Directors, almost as if following an unspoken agreement not to taint their unique relationship. They did not share dinners or parties, they did not socialize. Their dealings were wholly within the structure of gaining ever more control in their economic, monetary, industrial, trade, and political activities. Power meant control and control meant ruling and ruling meant mastery, and these were the rungs beckoning always to them. For in the end, to people of such a breed, what else can there be but more power?

As effective as they were, with control in the several billions of dollars, they were also aware they remained something less than they desired. They could be crushed by military force. They still found it necessary to compromise and to trade and to bargain, no matter how great their strength. They had tried methods old and proven in Europe with their contacts in China and run into stone walls, for fanatics in ideology cannot be bought for any price save their own wants for power, and this it was not always possible to do. Their own strength was a sharp focus of their limitations, and it grated beneath the Board's skin, irritated them, kept them uncomfortable. Certainly they were expanding their control, but to them at only a snail's pace. They wanted an authority that would have meaningful global repercussions. That had become their sole purpose for being.

And they had found reason to believe they might attain this Holy Grail of world authority. It was, at first, a story they dismissed as nonsensical, a fairy tale spread by idiots who dabbled and grunted in astrology, who believed in magic potions and worshipped graven images made of clay and plaster. It was to be ranked with theories of ancient gods and the rubbish that brings thousands of people to rainy hillsides waiting for shining ships to descend from the skies to prove clearly the inferiority of the zestful worshippers.

Concetta de Luca electrified them with new words on the matter. She sat with them in the penthouse of El Cid, draped in black silk and an exquisite touch of diamonds, and she was as they had never before seen her. *Agitated.* That was the word. Something was beyond her grasp, tantalizing. Impossible to be sure. *But what if it were real?*

"There is *something* out there," she told them, frowning, and she did not often frown. "Our reports leave no question. There is a special group financed by, of all things, the Vatican itself. Unlimited support. Open warfare if necessary. Killing and torture on any scale. If needed, this special group has the authority to surpass even the Spanish Inquisition to find, to find—" She shook her head. "I don't know *what* it is they are attempting to find, but when it is discovered, it is to be obtained at any cost in money or lives and brought to the Vatican." She turned to Kovanowicz. "Have you made any progress, Vernon?"

The great head nodded slowly. "Not what I want or what we need, but more than before. The Russians have their agents in the Vatican. They are inner members. What you speak of is held in the greatest secrecy. What they are afraid of more than anything else is that the Israelis will reach this thing, whatever it may be, before they are successful in their endeavors."

Concetta's dark eyes widened. "The Israelis. They are not fools and dreamers."

"Nor is the Vatican," Kovanowicz chuckled. "They could teach even the KGB many things."

Concetta ignored the aside, although what Vernon said was another cog in the wheel she was building. She looked at Harold Metzbaum in the enormous chair especially made for him at this conference table. "You reported you have a lead," she said.

The fat on his neck quivered as he nodded. His

voice was strained, a product of vocal cords misshapen by obesity. "A colonel in the Air Force. A
homosexual whose private life is even more secret
than his position in Air Force Intelligence."

"Please, Harold, get on with it."

"You're too eager. You miss the fine points that
way. I would not believe this man if we didn't
have such a terrible hold on him. We have proof of
his homosexuality. It is the only price he would
ever pay. Not to be exposed, that is. And we do not
ask much of him."

Concetta sighed. She knew better than to interrupt his thought flow. Metzbaum was a corpulent
monstrosity, but he never spoke in such a manner
without meaning to his words. The huge man
shifted uncomfortably, the inevitable perspiration
glistening on his face. He farted. It could not be
controlled. It was a small price to pay for what he
could do.

"In essence, the good colonel confirms what you
have said about the Vatican, Concetta." A wrist as
thick as a man's leg gestured. "And Vernon, he
too, has done well. The Israelis have a special
team on this. It has unlimited funds and manpower."

Kovanowicz pounded the table with a hamlike
fist, quietly and slowly, proud of his sources, nodding to himself.

"The Americans also are involved," Harold
Metzbaum dropped in their midst.

"Can all these stories really be true?" Concetta
felt excitement rising within her, felt a vein puls-
ing along her neck.

"If they *are* true," Benito Gibraldi said quietly,

"then whoever believes them will spare nothing, no one, to achieve their goal."

Alberto Grazzi kept his silence. No one had asked for his language, and when no one asked for numbers, he had no reason to speak.

Concetta's laugh was barely higher than normal. "We are being asked to believe in magic."

"Why not?" Kovanowicz offered. "Can you imagine what it was like early in the second world war? The Americans built an industrial empire with hundreds of thousands of people and spent billions of dollars to build a bomb that worked on a process no one could see or prove. That is magic. No one ever saw an atom. It was the kind of magic that ended a war."

"That was science," Concetta snapped.

"Then this magic must also be science," came the unexpected retort. "You are not one given to labels, Concetta de Luca. That shows you are uneasy. You are not sure of yourself."

She held his gaze. "Granted. So we must assume, until we have better knowledge, that there is something substantial about these reports. Enough to involve three governments, and I consider the Vatican a government unto itself—into pouring an enormous effort to obtain something that obviously has unprecedented powers."

"If our fag colonel knows whereof he speaks," Metzbaum said, "its powers are real. By that I mean the American government considers this object, whatever it may be, to have more power than all their weapons. And they have enough weapons to turn this planet into a cinder. So what could be of more power than all their bombs? There can be only one answer."

"Something that controls minds," Concetta answered for him.

"We must join the search," Gibraldi said as a statement of fact. The others nodded.

"But not with an organization," Kovanowicz said heavily. "With so many already pursuing this mysterious object, a large organization is unwieldy. We need a very small group. A specialist. The best in his business."

"We need a miracle, I think," Metzbaum grunted.

"There is such a man," Gibraldi said to them, watching heads turn in his direction. "Even in the Legion we knew of him. He is a mercenary and yet he is more than that. He is a soldier of fortune but on the highest levels. He deals with governments. He has an uncanny ability to lead men, to bring men to follow him without reason, with blind faith."

"For this job he would have to be a killer," Metzbaum said.

"He is more than a killer. He is a devil," Gibraldi responded. "I have never known a man like him. Death is his friend. It never touches him. And he has a reputation of never having failed to get what he wants."

Kovanowicz was staring at his friend. "You speak uncomfortably close of a man I know like that."

"It could be the same," Gibraldi mused aloud. "Berlin?"

Kovanowicz sat upright, his eyes suddenly bright, a touch of excitement emerging from his stolid expression. "If it *is* the same, he is the man who killed the KGB's entire assassination team in Berlin. He was wounded several times but he would not die. Indeed, he seemed to get strength from his wounds. A modern Rasputin."

"You are talking like children," Concetta said, irritated.

Gibraldi laughed. "Only to you. You have not met this one."

"Will he work for us?"

"Only if he wishes to do so," Kovanowicz said flatly. "The lure must be greater than the price. He does not need money."

"Then we must entice him," Concetta reasoned.

Gibraldi nodded approval. "I agree. How?"

"Kill him," she said.

Gibraldi's face showed astonishment, but Concetta gave him no chance to speak. "If this devil is what you say he is, then our best efforts will *not* be able to kill him. If you are wrong, he will be dead and we will not waste any more time. And if you are not wrong, he is our man."

"He is no one's man," Kovanowicz warned.

"A figure of speech," Concetta responded lightly. "That will be our plan. We are agreed?"

They nodded. "We will put our best man on this assignment," Concetta went on, warming to the unexpected challenge. She pressed the intercom switch on the table. A secretary and several guards were always at the entrance to the conference room. "Get me Monte Hinyub," Concetta spoke to the concealed microphone. "Have him report here immediately."

Chapter III

"Okay, bad man. Tell me just what the hell is going on, will you?" The big Indian settled himself in the driver's seat of his pickup truck at Indian Bluff Airport. There were only three other arrivals and Sheriff Hoot Gibson recognized each of the three men. No problems there. This was the last commuter line flight of the night and the airport control tower would close in fifteen minutes. To add to the security blanket he was throwing up through and around the town, Gibson had left a man seated in a car with orders to remain there until daylight. He'd be able to hear and see anything that landed during the night.

Stavers related everything that had happened during the preceding thirty hours, the attempted killing while skydiving, the rigged wallet, his views on a bushwhacking setup at Jacksonville International Airport, and how he'd been tailed all the way to St. Mary's. "I paid a kid to turn in the car at Jacksonville. Same general body build as myself. Whoever's on my ass obviously hired some local talent by phone; they waited for the car and nailed him before he ever got inside the terminal."

"Well, they sure been asking lots of questions. Mistaken identity and all that."

"Bullshit. The moment they looked inside his wallet and saw his driver's license, *and* talked to the kid driving the other car, they knew what happened. There's no reason for the police to suspect anything, Hoot." He glanced at the big man by his side, who was nodding agreement. "Who's been asking?"

"Jacksonville security police. At the airport."

"The hell they are. This is too cut and dried. Could you verify the callers?"

"Yep. Checked them out through the sheriff's department for that county. Checked them out through the national crime computer. They're for real."

"Someone paid them to ask all those questions."

"That's what I figured. They wanted to know when you were coming back, where you lived, what your routine was. They was as subtle as a hog in heat. I also figured that no matter what went on with the phone, you're going to get company."

"Sure as God made little green apples. Pick up anything yet?"

"Uh uh. You mind if I ask you some questions of my own?"

"You? You never were the inquisitive type."

"And I ain't started now. Anything I ask is to help keep you alive. Someone wants you pretty bad. They had three cracks at you that you *know* about. Doug, you getting back into harness or something?"

"That's a strange question for you to ask."

"No, it ain't. I've never asked because it's none of my business. But you got more friends here in this town than you know." Gibson chuckled. "You might say we got a vested interest in your breathing."

"Thanks a heap," Stavers said drily. "Now tell me what you meant by getting back in harness."

Gibson sighed. "Look, Doug, I'm just a dumb old Indian with a badge—"

"That'll be the day," Stavers said quietly. "Three years in 'Nam. Strike forces in the bush. Silver Star with two clusters, four Purple Hearts, et cetera et cetera. Best point man in your whole division. You used to walk through Cong villages at night and they never knew you'd come and gone."

Gibson's jaw dropped in astonishment. "How the hell did you learn all *that?*"

Stavers shrugged. "Call it business."

"Sure, sure. I also know you didn't answer my question. You getting back in harness?"

Stavers didn't play games with Gibson. "It's been a long time," he said after a pause. "And I'm not evading your question. I've been out of harness for a year now. How much do you know?"

"Well, it's like this. I got a cousin in the Bureau of Indian Affairs in Washington. And he's got a sister who works at the National Security Agency.

And she's got clearance right on up to the top. They got one hell of a file on you, round-eyes."

"Interesting. That file is supposed to be in a vault."

"It *is*."

"So you know."

"I know."

"How much your Indian spies tell you?"

"Jesus, Doug, I knew a hell of a lot before I had that phone call from Washington. Now, I know that *you* know about the skeletons in my closet. It don't pay to let the locals know their fat old Indian sheriff killed a couple of hundred people in that Vietnam crap. I still got a guilty feeling about all that. Sort of like I was playing the white man shooting up the Indians, you know? I didn't have anything against them gooks. Shit, I felt like Custer at the Little Big Horn."

"Different ending to the story, though. What did you know that made you violate national security through your cousin's sister?"

"You're a professional killer, Doug. Not like me. I was good at it. Okay, okay; I was great at it. But you're the pro. That was your job. No, it was more than that. That's been your profession. A man in this business sees certain things. You ever know your wrists are blue?"

"I know."

"That comes from martial arts. I don't know how many black belts you got—in fact, if I know you, you've never bothered. Why leave your name on a lot of lists? But them blue wrists. That's training and a lot of use. The sides of your palms are like boards. I know hand-to-hand. Shit, I taught it. I know the signs. The way you walk. Things like that. We've gone hunting together, remember? I know the touch of the pro when he handles his weapon. *You* don't handle a piece. The goddamn thing becomes part of you. For Christ's sake, Doug, look at the list. You're a crack pilot and you flew in 'Nam and a couple of banana wars down in South and Central America. You earned your paratrooper wings when you were a kid and you were also in 'Nam with special forces. You went through underwater demolition school and qualified top in your group. You can take a machine gun apart and put it back together again in the dark. You're better than an Indian at creeping around. That told me something else. You trained at ninjitsu. I don't care how long the Japanese been doing that; we're the people who invented it. I know it when I see it. A knife is like an extension of your hands. I'll bet you're just as good with the shuriken throwing stars and nunchuks."

"Don't bet."

"I know. I'd lose." They approached the town center. "Again, do I get to know about you being back in harness?"

"Injun, all I know is that someone's trying to waste me."

"That's all. No reason?"

"Whoever it is knows the reason. I don't."

"They won't let up. I can *feel* that."

"For sure, Injun."

"Tough to bushwhack someone when we don't know who or what they are."

"We'll find out soon enough, won't we?"

"I hope it's in time."

"You're a cheery bastard."

They lapsed into silence, each with his own thoughts. Doug Stavers had never heard his background described as Gibson had just recited it. And that was only a part of it. He really didn't want a rundown of his own past, but he knew it would intrude on his thoughts no matter what he wanted. Because he'd have to shift mental gears to stay alive. Hoot Gibson was right. They'd be coming after him on his own turf. Whoever *they* were.

Chapter   IV

Tracy North knew what he was, better than anyone else in the world. Doug Stavers made love to her. Not as often as she liked or wanted, but enough to recognize when he'd slipped from the straight sexual-partner role into letting himself go. She'd watched him, studied his face while he slept, watched him do a thousand things during the two years they'd been together. She loved him without reservation, despite the fact she knew him to be the only real contempt machine she'd ever met in her life.

She thought about that stark, incredible contrast. *Contempt machine*. It had taken her a long time to reach that conclusion, and she was all the more astonished when she recognized she had drawn the final judgment without any criticisms attached.

It wasn't Doug's attitude toward other people; except with herself or the big Indian who was sheriff, he remained remote from his feelings with other people. He glided through such encounters as if all the bodies and minds about him were so much fog and he was a massive ship untroubled and unswayed. Thus relationships never came to pass. He couldn't be touched, by warmth or anger. He wasn't cold towards people, just massively and unstoppably indifferent.

Tracy North was beautiful. She knew it; the facts were impossible to dispute. She was grateful she had brains to go with that physical attraction. Not just smarts, but the kind of common sense that counted. She had been an army brat, and that had exposed her to a great deal of living at a young age. Her father often left home with little or no notice. A member of the Blue Light team of the army's special strike command, he was a paratrooper, ranger, commando, and specialist all rolled into one. Her world was filled with men who killed for their vocation. All kinds of men, gentle and kind to her, but always seeming to be restrained, as if held back by some leash or steel clamp on their personalities. She saw only the warm veneer and never the deadly creatures within, but she overheard them at night when they thought she was asleep and what she heard had often horrified her and chilled her to the bone. She had been "adopted" by the Blue Light warriors. Watched them in hand-to-hand combat training and the martial arts and she began to learn these herself. She could have had no better instructors than men who killed with silken effort, and by the time Tracy was seventeen she was deadlier than most trained men in the business. These were the men who taught her to shoot, to climb, to swim, to use bows and arrows and crossbows and knives. To escape from their world their urge was to reach out into the far country, hunting and fishing and living off the land. They could live off *anything*, and she learned by living with them. They never took rations with them, savoring the challenge of meeting all their worldly needs through crossbows or bows and arrows, or spears they cut themselves, or their incredible throwing stars. She'd seen her own father cut down a running rabbit at fifty feet with a snap of his wrist so fast his arm was a blur. She learned trapfalls and snares and falling rocks and how to catch fish without line or hooks, which grasses and berries and nuts to eat. They killed deer and other game animals for their food and feasted on trout and delighted in pheasant and goose and duck, and all the time they were on survival terms with the wilderness.

Accompanying this extraordinary growth was the unyielding insistence on her father's part for his daughter to specialize. "I don't care what it is you make your specialty," he told her, "just so long as you're the best in whatever you do." She had no question as to her choice. Simply being around her father and his friends had already convinced her that in the world that now existed and the one to come a linguist was the key to unlocking doors. Tracy North, beautiful and cutting a winning figure and five feet seven inches tall, dove into languages.

She had heard Vietnamese, Chinese, Japanese,

Russian, Polish, French, Spanish, German, Portugese and a dozen more languages in her own home. She learned quickly, starting with Spanish and its close derivatives in the Americas, and stepping quickly into Portugese and French. Her brilliant progress was as much due to her feeling that she was at home in languages as it was to her ardor; she had grown up in a welter of strange tongues, and had a perfect affinity for bridging the gaps in her mind. Russian, German, Norwegian, Finnish; all came quickly and with easily-given, intense effort on her part. When foreign visitors stayed with her family, she bedeviled them by insisting on conversing with them, no matter with what difficulty or balkiness, in their native tongue. Idioms and nuances and subtleties were an unexpected windfall.

Language brought her into touch with Doug Stavers. She had heard that name through her growing years. These men about her, professional killers and special forces and secret agents, either knew Stavers or knew of him, and she had never heard that name without approving nods or a glint of eye that said more than any words. And then he showed up one night. Or to be exact, just after four in the morning, unannounced, standing at the door to their home on an army camp, wearing paratrooper boots, bush clothing, and a dark beret, with a large duffel bag by his feet. Jack North opened the door and stared at Doug Stavers, Tracy watching from the shadows of the stairway, and for the first time in her life she saw her father embrace another man. Not a word passed between them, just that silent, powerful squeeze. The stranger who was not a stranger stood in the living room and Jack North poured a long shot to both of them and they drank fully of the brandy. Finally her father spoke, the usually loquacious man talking in clipped phrases.

"Rhodesia, wasn't it?"

Stavers nodded. He eased onto the couch like a cougar resting on a tree limb.

"Bad?" her father asked.

"We were slaughtered."

"What went wrong?"

"Nothing went wrong. My men were mediocre. I whipped them into shape. My men became the best. They had artillery, we didn't. They had Stalin Organs, we had popguns for mortars. They had tanks and flamethrowers, we had jeeps and pickup trucks. They had choppers, infrared systems; the works. And they outnumbered us six to one. The only reason our people didn't quit before it ever started was that they knew they'd be killed in prisons. They preferred to die like men, in the field." He shrugged. "They did that very well. They took a great many with them."

"I didn't think the blacks had that much equipment," her father remarked. "Or if they did, that they could handle it that well."

Stavers showed disdain. "Their blacks were idiots. One step out of their huts. You give me Senegalese and I'll show you black fighting men. Not the ones we faced. They were along for the ride. They had three Cuban divisions in the field against us and with Russian pilots and advisors."

Jack North nodded slowly, poured another drink

for them. "You sound like you have a score to settle."

To Tracy's surprise, Stavers shook his head. "Nothing personal. The Cubans were ordered there. They're good men and they did their job."

"Your men were good and they died."

Stavers raised his brows. "Nothing wrong with dying."

That was when Tracy first detected the quiet, indifferent contempt of Doug Stavers. She had taken her first step to knowing this man. She knew enough fighting men to recognize that, pound for pound, Doug Stavers was more killer than a panther. Not armed with weapons, either. In a fight to death with a panther, armed only with those attributes he had snatched from what life offered, the odds were against the creature with claws and fangs and total killing instinct. The naked man would have won. No matter that at first glance such a possibility seemed so ridiculous, that a man's hands and fingers are ludicrous against the slash of a great cat that in one sweep could disembowel a man.

The panther has greater speed, swifter reflexes, and is instinctively wholly committed to the struggle. But that would have been the animal's weakness, for Doug Stavers was committed only to himself. He lacked the sharp claws and tearing fangs, but he was as feral as any great cat, and he knew how to sidestep instinct, plan every movement ahead and take instant advantage of any opportunity, judge his enemy, and then use that most terrible of all weapons—his brain. His astonishing contempt for life, including his own, was an unspoken and overwhelming weapon greater than fang or claw or even cold steel. He could throw himself with utter objectivity and almost violent zest into a struggle with its outcome measured in life or death, for he suffered no inhibitions that he would not emerge the victor. Having none, he could not suffer from caution where it might slow him down. There was no hesitation on his part, *ever*, when events were brought to the point where direct physical action must replace all logic. To Stavers, those were the moments when total lethality *was* all logic and all reason. Thus, Tracy forced herself to reason along a convoluted path of trying to know this man, Stavers might well be not contemptuous of life, as she had judged when first meeting him, but rather aloof, separate, wholly apart from the wants and needs and fears of others. To onlookers, it was contempt on the part of Stavers. To Stavers, it was no more than unconsidered indifference. Only that which interested or pleased or affected him was accepted as the interface with other life. All else could be disregarded. As the average man exhibits disinterest in the life of an insect, so Doug Stavers was disinterested in all other men except where their lives touched, and at such moments it was Stavers, and no one else, who set the rules for the relationship.

Tracy had come to know him slowly. Whatever had happened in Rhodesia, or wherever else he had been, he had returned to the states with its scars still livid across his body, flesh still healing. He had decided to camp out in the Rockies. Something she didn't understand compelled an urgency

within her to confront her father. "I want to go
with him," she said, her eyes pleading.

"You're nineteen years old, Tracy. Six times three
and one more to boot," he told her. "It's not for
me to say."

"Dad, I'm not begging permission. I want your
approval."

"Why do you want to go? You don't even know
him."

"But I do! Oh, not in terms of time or even
talking that much to him, and there's no little girl
in me enchanted by the scarred prince, but—I don't
know. Something inside me *tells* me to go."

He thought long and hard, sucking on a pipe.
"Then do it. I know Doug as well as any man alive.
There's a lot of things about that man many people
don't like. They fear him. I don't. If the world had
more of him, it would be a—well, never mind. The
decision is his. You'll have to ask him."

"Will you ask him for me?" Her eyes were bright.

"The hell I will. You're going to step into water
over your head, damned if I'll push you in."

To her surprise, and his, Stavers agreed. It wasn't
a sexual thing. She didn't even think of Stavers—of
Doug—that way. Not yet. And she was woman
enough to recognize at once that he didn't *care*,
that way. Not yet. If it was there it would come in
its own due time. Her father flew them in an army
plane to a military camp at the foothills of the
Colorado Rockies, and then they were on their
own, living from the packs they carried. She was
strong and hardened, yet she felt like a helpless
pink animal against this extraordinary creature.
He never showed physical exertion. He was a ma-

chine of limitless energy. He glided on difficult trails without sleep for days and nights and she was ashamed to discover on their fourth day he'd been pacing himself slowly to take into account her own limitations.

She had heard much about the hands of this man; when he offered her assistance along a climb she felt as if she had placed her own in a robot's grip. His hands were scarred; bones had been broken and the sides of his palms were as rough-hewn wood. A single slashing blow, fingers extended and barely curving, could break a man's neck. Or crack the skull of an animal. His grip, with those huge fingers, was beyond anything she had ever known, and she never doubted the tales of how he had squeezed the wrists of other men and cracked bones while his opponent screamed with agony. Yet for her there was only a gentle strength.

They exchanged no false modesty in their travels. He afforded her every courtesy of her toilet, but when they came to a cold lake, without hesitation he would strip and dive into the icy water. He didn't make a fetish of his nakedness or pointedly ignore it. It simply didn't matter. Nor did it matter if she saw him nude and chose to retain her own clothing, or if she wished to be alone when she bathed. She sat quietly, legs drawn up, her chin resting on her knees, fascinated with the sight of him. His muscles rippled with an incredible hardness and flex. She recognized the tight scars of bullet punctures and thin white lines of knife scars. *And*, my God, *whip* burns across his back. One day when he was in a mountain pool, she slipped from her clothes and with a bar of soap in her hand joined him in the water. "Turn around," she said, and began to work a lather into his back and neck muscles. He was as comfortable as a child, and she shook her head in quiet amazement at the feel of him. His skin was tough and leathery, yet; then she knew. Like good leather well kneaded. She had never felt like that before, and here, in the water, her own body glistening wet, her nipples erect from the icy water and her growing desire, he studied her.

"It's time," he said simply.

She felt for him beneath the water. *My God.* "Yes," she said. He carried her from the pool as if she were a young child and he made love to her, standing, her body weightless in those powerful arms, lifted by him and sent soaring by the incredible feelings, and she had *never* known anything like this and when she climaxed she swooned, not regaining her senses until she came to on the ground, opening her eyes to see him still naked, seated on a flat rock, smoking one of those thin cigars and regarding her with a warmth she had never suspected in him. Of a sudden he was a gentle giant, all six feet two inches and two hundred fifteen pounds of raw sinew and muscle, and she had to force herself to remember all the other things about him.

The professional soldier. The man who killed without feeling. The man her father respected, but for many things *she* found repelling. And fascinating. She put it aside. As well that she did, for she sensed the first deliberate intrusion on her part into his mind would have closed a steel door permanently between them. Whatever happened must

be on his terms. And she found a way unexpected.
She murmured a feeling of pleasure, but in Japanese. He answered her in kind and her eyes widened. They agreed to talk the rest of that day only
in Japanese. It became a game of unexpected laughter, and by the look on his face she knew Doug was
looking beyond the body and into the real her.

She was astonished at his command of language.
"It can save your life," he explained. "Knowing
what other people are saying in other languages
keeps you from being a stranger." He spoke fluent
Italian and Spanish, he was very good at French
and Portugese. He was comfortable in Vietnamese
and could get along in Chinese and Korean. He
had a working grasp of most European languages,
and to her delight he showed his pleasure at learning her fluency in languages and dialects. She was
also the first woman he had ever met who spoke
the tribal tongues of the American Indian, which
had come from living in the west in remote army
bases.

He had a deep scar along the third finger of his
left hand. One night, after roasting venison over
an open fire, she tread dangerous waters. "It was
from a gold ring," he answered simply. "I was face
down in mud. Angola. Half unconscious from a
grenade. I came to with some crazy native trying
to cut the finger from my hand to get the ring."
She didn't need to ask if that native was still alive;
it was obvious he had cut deeply, likely to the
bone, before he faced sudden death emerging from
the mud.

"You're not married," she said openly.

"You seem certain of that."

"You're my father's best friend. You wouldn't be making love to his daughter if you were married."

"You think like a man sometimes, Tracy."

"I grew up with men. Real men," she said.

"Yes. Your father is that, all right." He studied her. "You haven't asked about my wife."

"You'll have to tell me without asking, I suppose."

"I might not want to do that."

She shrugged, waiting.

"Her name was Helena. Tall, striking, blonde. Swedish. She was the only woman I've ever loved. We met in Berne, in Switzerland, and were married ten days later. I don't know how it happened, what magic there was. But it happened. It was as natural as breathing. We were together four months. I suppose hell visits you when you're unprepared for it, when you can't protect yourself. It's really a simple story. We were on a commercial flight from Los Angeles to Reno. We flew into a thunderstorm. We crashed. The plane burned. I got out through the back. The fuselage was broken. I kicked it open, carrying Helena with me. But she was already dead, from a broken neck when we'd hit."

He didn't say any more for a while and she didn't dare to ask. After a long stare into the twilight, he picked it up again. She had the feeling he'd never said this to anyone before. "I didn't know what to do. I was never so helpless in all my life. I saw the pilot. He'd made it. He had a broken arm but that was all. I guess, after they covered Helena with a blanket, that I wanted to know what the hell had happened. I went up to him. I smelled alcohol on his breath. But there was no doctor there, no way for anyone to give him anything since we'd hit. The bastard had been drinking before we ever left the ground. Now he stood there with his broken arm and he was going to be a fucking hero because some of his passengers had lived." Again he lapsed into silence. "It wouldn't bring back my wife but I couldn't let it pass. I hit him. Killed him. It was like stepping on a bug."

That had been years before. She knew what sex had been to him since then. Likely no women for a long time. Then his own physical needs and instincts would crowd back into his being. He would be distant, that brand of true inner contempt that drove women crazy. What *real* woman could be insensitive to this animal maleness? This man could have anyone he wanted. His love-making was extraordinary; intense pleasure along with pain he offered indifferently, and often a frenzied mixture of the two. He hurt Tracy but was never aware of those moments and she would have died before allowing him to know. She knew sex with Doug Stavers could be raw and unbridled, with even an element of assault a woman would find marvelous, but she had never known his body without compassion on his part. For this she was very, very grateful.

They returned from their mountain trip three weeks after they'd left, deeply tanned and her body in better shape than she'd ever believed was possible. Something had happened within her. She couldn't explain it in words but her father knew at first glance. "I watched my kid leave," he told her huskily, "and I see a woman come home."

"I'm going to work for Doug," she said.

"*No.*"

She stared in surprise at her father. "Work *with* him, Tracy. With him, but never *for* him."

That's the way it had been. Doug Stavers worked under contract anywhere in the world. He was incredible at a game played since the term bounty hunter was coined. He worked for companies, for individuals, and for governments. Sometimes he killed, but only when he had no other avenue to follow. Tracy went with him everywhere and a meaningful partnership began to emerge from what started as an association, which was all Doug Stavers would allow. He was excellent in languages, but she was everything he could do many times over. The world was their beat. She was mistress to him, but only on equal terms. They never discussed their relationship, or financial arrangements. He took her to his bank and she was given power of attorney and check-signing privileges and the rest of the legalistic nonsense. It freed his mind for other details, such as considering the offers and requests that came his way. There was a hell of a lot of work for a man with his unique qualifications and record of *never* having failed an assignment. Tracy came to understand that one of the keys to such success was exhaustively researching the job to be done and not accepting the contract until he knew enough to make a meaningful decision.

She went with him to France. The directors of a bank met with him secretly. The private vaults had been stripped clean, and while the bank officers knew much of the contents they could not operate through the authorities, either French or through Interpol. They had a lead, they wanted recovery of cash, drugs, millions in jewels. The job was too big for one man. Stavers called Jack North, recently discharged from the army but with no intentions of retiring. "Get four good men and meet me in three days at the St. George Hotel in Paris. Your rooms will be ready and waiting. Make sure your people speak French and Italian."

They found their quarry in a mountain retreat close to the Swiss border. Tracy regretted being along. The suspects were flushed from hiding and brought to a large room, where all the doors were locked. No one had weapons. Six men faced Doug Stavers, who depended on psychological factors even more strongly than he on his own body as a weapon.

"None of you will tell us where you concealed the contents of the vault. So we have decided to give you a fair chance. The six of you against me. No weapons. I assure you that until one of you tells me what I want to know, you will die one by one." His voice would have frozen salt water. But these were men of the streets and the gutter. At six-to-one odds they did not fear Stavers, which was their mistake. Tracy watched with her father and the other four men through concealed windows looking down into the room, and she held her hand to her mouth as they formed a circle about the man she loved.

"This is going to be interesting," her father murmured. "Every one of those mothers is a murderer."

"But why is he taking them on *alone!*" she protested.

"They're a strange breed. We'd have to torture them to make them talk, and torturing a man for baubles isn't our way. Or his," he referred to

Stavers. "This way they've got a chance. If they can't take him, six men against one unarmed man, then whoever's left alive will sing like a canary with his ass on fire."

She couldn't believe what was happening. The men before Doug held back as the three behind him moved in. A hand grasped Doug's shoulder to spin him about. That was the signal for the others to make their move. To their surprise, Stavers didn't resist the man pulling him around. He went with the pull, much faster than expected, pivoting on a toe and heel and bending his body. His right hand blurred through the air as he delivered a backhanded smash to the man who had grabbed him. Blood flew out in a spray as the man's ear tore open and his cheek split to the bone. He tumbled away unconscious. Tracy thought of those terrible scarred hands and she understood.

The others rushed Doug. That was an error on which he had counted. A man dodges a fist; that's to be expected. Doug didn't mind being hit. He took a blow to the head, ignored it, stepped quickly forward and with one hand grasped the man by the armpit, with the other the groin and swung him high in the air. More fists thudded into him and again he ignored the blows. The man above his head came down in a wicked arc as Doug slammed the base of the man's spine against his knee. A limp rag doll fell to the floor.

"Well, he's dead," her father said quietly, amusement showing on his face. My God, was this man her *father*?

The others hesitated when the sound of the cracking spine echoed through the room. It was a bad mistake. Doug's hand shot out, knuckles protruding, into a man's upper lip, just beneath his nose. It was like being struck with a tire iron. Skin tore, pulped, and the man was on his knees, choking on his teeth. Doug wanted him alive; he ignored him.

An arm gripped about his neck and a boot thudded into his groin. He wore a protective steel cup; that had always been lesson number one. His own boot smashed a groin and an animal scream tore through the room; the victim fell onto his side, hands clasping his testicles, vomiting wildly. The man behind Doug found himself flying through the air; as he came over Doug's head Stavers grasped a wrist, twisting it violently. The attacker was now helpless on the floor, arm twisted and extended, and he took a terrific kick to the kidneys.

"That's two. He won't live. His kidney's ruptured," she heard her father's voice.

A third man died from a sweeping blow of Doug Stavers' hand to his neck. But another man had managed a good position and smashed a heavy fist into Doug's mouth. Blood ran from a split lip. Doug reached forward and caught the attacker's fist in his enormous hand. He squeezed. Through the walls they heard the other screaming as Doug tightened the pressure and bones cracked and protruded whitely through skin.

"Well, that's it," Jack North said. "Let's go in. Who's got the video recorder? That's part of the deal."

They recorded everything and left two men to guard the pitiful remains in the room. Tracy cleaned Doug's lip. "You watched it?" he asked. She nodded. She was still sick to her stomach. "You shouldn't have," he rebuked her mildly.

"You're wrong. I love *you*. Not any false or partial pictures of you."

He shrugged; that was the end of that. "What happens to them now?" she asked. "This is business, Doug. I need to know."

"We call the bank and talk to their people. They come down here and we give them all the information. While the bank people are here, within our reach, they pony up. When we confirm that our payment is deposited to accounts we specify—which I expect you to do—we leave. That way the bank people know they're not going to get the same treatment."

"And the men in the room?"

"I suppose they'll kill them. It's the system. They're trash. They'll make sure photos of the bodies are distributed throughout the banking world. That kind of reliability for secret depositors is great for business. Okay, okay, quit with the Florence Nightingale bit. I'm fine."

Chapter V

Sheriff Hoot Gibson drove slowly through Indian Bluff to an all-night Texaco station and convenience store. Cal's Catch-All fit its name well, supplying repair work, rentals, box lunches, hunting and fishing licenses, and concealed video cameras that provided a day-and-night scan of any strangers in town. It stayed open twenty-four hours a day. It was a real piece of shit store, and Doug Stavers lived there.

Gibson stopped by a service ramp and pressed a radio switch to open a garage door, drove inside, watched the door close behind until the SECURE light flashed on. The wall before them pivoted smoothly to reveal a ramp leading downward. Soft lights came on and Gibson eased along the concrete ramp to his left. He stopped the pickup truck in a deeply buried chamber with cars and trucks parked about it. He and Stavers left the truck, walked past Tracy's gold Corvette, and stood before a concrete wall. Nothing happened; nothing *seemed* to be happening. They saw a glimpse of red as they were scanned by ultraviolet, infrared retinal beams, and other sensing devices. Tracy's voice greeted them warmly. "Welcome home, lover," she said to Stavers. Concrete slid aside and they entered the subterranean chambers of sprawling apartments and an elaborate command and operations center concealed from the world above. His communications systems connected through computer-run satellite links to most of the world and especially to other fully secure comm centers, all of it code-functional and as close to impossible to break down as cryptographic science could make the system. He had a full ordnance and machine shop facility, a major electronics workshop, gym and training center, and a host of other amenities Stavers had personally designed as necessary to his good business and continued health.

Tracy greeted him with a vodka martini on the rocks. He sipped slowly, aware she had a talent for sensing his mood for a particular drink. This one even had Suntory vodka. She waited a moment, greeted him with a long and shuddering embrace, and withdrew quickly. For just an instant he tensed, but she showed no dewy eyes or maudlin expressions. She knew all that had happened to him; the Indian always kept her up to the moment. She never interfered with the thought processes of Stavers when he was a target. In his business that was easily a fatal error, and if ever he found his woman's company to be a female disturbance she'd be out of his life instantly. That's all it took for Doug. He turned some switch in his mind and whoever he wanted dismissed simply became a nonperson.

He finished his drink and she took the glass. "Coffee?"

He nodded. "And some iron rations, please."

Another sign. Coffee and iron rations from the army. Fast energy food; no drugs. He wanted energy but without a full stomach. He turned to Gibson. "Injun, I figured out something I don't like. Our security for the town stinks."

Gibson eyed him carefully. "That's a come-on if ever I heard one."

Stavers grinned toothily. "I meant it to be. I've said, Self, if you knew they'd be sleeping with one eye open in Indian Bluff and you wanted to get in there, what would you do? Self said to me, man, why, that's easy."

"Okay. Tell whoever it is you're talking to inside your head to tell me."

Stavers pointed a finger straight up. "From there."

"We *got* someone at the airport, remember? And a chopper would be too noisy. I've already thought of parachutes. Not enough time to get all that ready, and it's tricky landing in desert country in the dark. Unless they creep across the desert, and I got all four of our dogs working tonight with my deputies, I don't see *how*."

Stavers lit a cigar. "They'll come, tonight. And by air."

"*How*, damnit!"

"The same way I would: without making any noise."

Hoot Gibson was paying strict attention. "Now you're getting interesting."

"First, call your man at the airport. Tell him to get up in that control tower and stay there. Tell him not to smoke. Even a cigarette glow could give him away. Also, tell him to bar the door behind him at the tower entrance. I'll explain later, Hoot. Just do it."

Stavers waited for Gibson to make the call. When the Indian replaced the phone on its cradle, he saw Stavers sipping coffee and eating his rations. Tracy brought him his own steaming mug.

"Next, activate the radar. Not the airport system. That's set up to get a response from a transponder aboard an airplane. We want to skin-track. We'll get our best return from a prop, anyway. We'll use the radar atop the telephone building." That would work, Gibson agreed to himself. It looked like telephone microwave equipment. It wasn't. It was military skin-tracking radar, the same type used in the field to set up mobile runway control. Gibson sent two men to the telephone building, just to be sure.

"If you get a target coming in here to this airport," he instructed his men, "first you let the tower know and then you call this number. Got it? Good. Shove off."

He looked at Stavers across his coffee mug. "Now what?"

"Now you call the state police. You got a tip on a smuggler run of cocaine into Indian Bluff tonight, by plane. Tell them you've got the stakeout all set, you don't need any help, but you're just putting them on alert and you'll let them know the moment anything happens."

Gibson made the call. Normally, by now he would have been one jump ahead, but he was still behind the game. "Next?" he asked.

"Three cars, two men in each. Riot guns. Use the cars set up not to show dome lights or brake lights. Send them to the airport and wait alongside the runway. No smoking, no lights, stay out of sight. If a plane comes in without lights, let it land and then shoot out its tires."

"Just like that? You sound awfully sure of yourself."

"I am," Stavers agreed. "Now, we'll take the pickup with anti-tank launchers. The best for this job would be the wire-guided goodie. It's small and the flash is minimal, and the fire will be gone by the time it leaves the tube."

"A goddamned *missile?*"

"Yeah. You'll see."

"I'll get my jacket," Tracy said.

"You stay here," Stavers told her. "Call your old man as soon as we leave. Brief him. Tell him to get his tail here from Los Angeles *fast*. Use the Lear. I'll talk with you later."

She almost told him to be careful. She bit her tongue in time.

Stavers and Gibson arrived at the airport only two minutes before the tower phone rang. Radar had a small target at high altitude, descending along a steady line to Indian Bluff, estimated speed eighty miles an hour. Gibson shook his head. "Okay, round eyes. Tell me your secret."

"It's so simple," Stavers told him. "We've got a good moon tonight and a concrete runway. Stands out real well from the air. The plane coming in probably is modified for short-field landings. The guy starts at ten thousand feet. He kills the engines, drops gear and flaps, and down he comes on a steep slant. He'll aim five hundred feet from the approach end. The only noise is the wind. No lights, no sound, no transponder making signals to any radar. If our lookout is the slightest bit loose, he won't see the plane and he won't hear it. He'd be expecting lights, engine noises. *Normal* sights and sounds. These people come in like a ghost, come to a stop in only a few hundred feet. One or two get out, they have silencers, and they nail our lookout, and without anyone the wiser they're on their way into town."

"How come you know so much about how they think?"

"Because I used to do the same thing in Vietnam, *and* in Egypt and a few other places. Okay, look over there. About thirty degrees above the horizon, off the end of the runway. You may be able to see moonlight reflecting off the wings."

"I got it."

"Damn, did we bring the cocaine?"

"Got it."

Stavers squeezed Gibson's shoulder. The dumb old Indian never forgot a thing. He had already brought the infrared night scope to his eye. Beneath the scope was a special .357 high-velocity, flat-trajectory hunting rifle. "You don't fire unless the other people screw up," Stavers cautioned. "If they miss the tires, or that guy tries to take off even with his tires shot away—and some planes can do that—kill the pilot. I don't want to have to use this thing if I can help it."

He made out the plane now. A Cessna 340 from the looks of it, modified with high-lift devices to give it slow-flight capability. They were pros. The twin-engine plane ghosted down from the sky, its only sound a sighing of wind. They heard the thin squeak of rubber on concrete as the pilot dropped it on with a perfect landing. It rolled no more than six hundred feet in the night breeze and came to a stop still shrouded in silence. So much the better; those props weren't turning. They waited. The cabin door opened and three men climbed out quickly. Hoot Gibson had a perfect view through the infra-red telescopic sight. "Shit, they're carrying automatic weapons. Big stuff."

Almost at the same moment, gunfire erupted from the drainage ditch at the side of the runway. Two deputies, shooting at the airplane's tires. The three men flattened onto the concrete and returned a murderous fire of their own. They heard a man scream and the sound came from the ditch. Everything happened in a blur. The left engine coughed into life and roared suddenly. The three men threw themselves back into the cabin as the right engine thundered.

"Get the fucking pilot!" Stavers yelled.

"He's not there!"

Stavers knew what had happened. The pilot had

dropped sideways on his seat and no doubt the lower part of the cabin had armor plating. "Shoot anyway," Stavers snapped.

Four shots banged out. Gibson was right on. The bullets spanged off the curving windshield. Armored glass, for Christ's sake. The Cessna screamed with its engines at full throttle and started off in a rush. Stavers sighed. He stood erect, taking his time, aiming just ahead of the moving plane and fired. He saw the glow behind him, heard the whooshing roar of the small rocket firing at full thrust. Then the finned missile was well ahead of him, glowing, and he kept the launcher aimed at the plane, which in turn sent signals along the trailing wire to the missile. The small warhead blew the Cessna in two. The rear half scraped along the runway in a shower of sparks, tumbling end over end, throwing a dark form from the wreckage. The front half, engines howling, lifted like a maddened bird in the air, spinning around, throwing the nose up, and dropped heavily back to the runway, exploding on impact. A great fireball boomed upward.

"Let's *move*," Stavers ordered. "Get to the tail assembly. Toss the cocaine in there and we've got a bona fide drug bust on our hands."

There was no chance of survival for the three men in the forward part of the Cessna. It was a huge mass of flames. Anyone in there had already been cremated. They reached the aft cabin and Gibson threw several packages of cocaine into the baggage section. He'd let the state police pick that up for evidence. They looked for the body. "I don't believe it," Gibson said. "The son of a bitch is still alive." A crumpled figure on the runway stirred and an automatic rifle turned toward Gibson. His own rifle cracked twice, the figure jerked and then lay still. "Sorry about that," the Indian said. "For a moment I thought we might have a private conversation with that fella."

Stavers leaned over the body. Big man, the side of his face raw meat where he'd scraped the runway. Had to be somebody special to be alive after that, and he was still trying to shoot. Stavers went carefully through his pockets. Nothing. Then he checked the inside pocket of the jacket. He stood up slowly, holding a large sealed envelope. He held it out to Gibson.

"Hoot, this is one for the record books."

Gibson looked at the envelope. Printed neatly on its face was a name. *Mr. Douglas Stavers.*

"Get a flashlight here, Hoot."

"I wouldn't open that mother so fast. They tried the wallet gimmick on you. You've heard of letter bombs," Gibson warned.

Stavers shook his head. "No sweat. The danger is all behind us. They mean for me to read this thing."

He tore it open. Inside the envelope were ten one-thousand-dollar bills. And a note.

> *We would be grateful if you would accept our invitation for a meeting Tuesday night at nine o'clock at the El Cid Hotel in Las Vegas. Please ask for Mr. Monte Hinyub. Dispose of this note at once.*

"What the hell does that mean?" Gibson asked.

Stavers crumpled the paper and tossed it to the runway. "It means that once this paper is exposed to open air it undergoes a chemical reaction and—" He didn't need to finish. The paper burst into flames.

"Neat," Gibson said with admiration.

Chapter VI

The Bell Jetranger slid from the sky on a steady angle to the rooftop helipad of El Cid. No one knew just how Doug Stavers would attend the meeting and he wasn't sending out free road maps. Bill Elliott at the controls was a master at handling a chopper; he regarded with contempt the red lights flashing frantically at them from the hotel roof. "They don't want us to land," he said stoically.

"True, true," Stavers mused. "Can you hack it?"

"Bet your momma, boss."

"Do it. When we're down, cut the power, get outside and start tying down with *our* ropes."

"Hey, man, I'm bananas over safety. That's wind up here. Trust only our own."

"Down, boy."

The Jetranger settled onto the roof. A dozen men

were waiting for them: large men in suits and three uniformed guards. None looked happy, and the guards rested their hands on holstered guns. That pleased Stavers. Only assholes stood in threatening gestures like that; they were unsure of themselves. They were down and Elliott killed the switches when another man walked rapidly toward them.

By the manner in which the waiting men stepped aside for him, Stavers knew this one ran the security operation. He confirmed his feelings: Monte Hinyub. Canuck. Tough whipsaw from the word go. Canadian special forces. His record showed he'd tangled with the Russians on those extreme northern borders. If he worked for these people using El Cid as their business headquarters that meant he was very, very good. Hinyub was deceptive. Five feet ten, Stavers judged, but a good 200 pounds compacted beneath his business suit. The neatly trimmed beard and dark curly hair helped disguise the professional killer beneath. Stavers grinned. You could always recognize one of your own.

Stavers forced a standoff. He sat in the helicopter as Elliott moved quickly outside, tying nylon line from the tiedown rings of the chopper to rings set in the rooftop flooring. Then he stretched several lines from the gear to the sides of the landing area. A beefy man tried to wave him off. "You don't need to do that," he said unpleasantly.

Bill Elliott looked up as he continued working with the security lines. "Friend, I do three things. I fly that machine, I tie it down very securely when it's not flying, and I mind my own business. Why don't you take up number three for yourself?" The man started forward impulsively and Elliott stood tall and quiet. "You can't be that stupid. Hinyub will cut your heart out himself if you touch anything here."

The impulsive move became a statue. Elliott ignored him and went back to his safety lines.

Monte Hinyub stood outside the helicopter door, waiting. Doug Stavers smiled at him and came out slowly, carrying an attaché case in his left hand. He knew Hinyub was set to give him hell—but then he studied Stavers' face and recognition became obvious. "We figured you for downstairs," he said. "Welcome, Mr. Stavers."

"Ah, the temperature is going up," Stavers remarked. They didn't bother to shake hands. It was already standoff.

"I'll have to examine your attaché case before you meet the others," Hinyub told him. He extended a hand, not to grasp, but to be offered the case. His face went through open surprise when Stavers shook his head.

"You don't examine the case," Stavers told him quietly. "I was invited here. What you're suggesting is rude. Very rude. You stay up here and I go downstairs. I don't believe I saw your name on the invitation card. Did you lose many friends during delivery?"

It showed as Hinyub fought down his emotions. He was very good, Stavers granted him. Stavers stood rooted. "This is a standoff?" he asked.

"That it is," Hinyub smiled.

"Then you lose, asshole."

Hinyub gaped.

Stavers gestured to the helicopter. "Take a very good look at those tiedown ropes," he instructed Hinyub. "They're not ropes. They're primer cord. There's enough of that cord spread across this roof, plus what's inside that chopper, to remove the top three floors of this building. Get out of my way. *Don't follow me.* You leave this roof, my pilot releases that dead-man's grip he has on a detonator and that sets off the primer cord and it's goodbye, Aunt Molly."

"He wouldn't do it." Hinyub ran his tongue over dry lips. "You'd both go up with us."

Stavers smiled. "Try him. If he relaxes his grip on that detonator—" He let it hang. A minute went by.

"Goddamnit, I don't believe you," Hinyub said hoarsely.

"But you know about me, right? And I may just be telling you the truth. So stop this nonsense right now or we do our thing. That man's got terminal cancer and I don't give a shit." He walked past Hinyub without even glancing at him, and stopped at the door leading down to the penthouse. A big man barred the way.

"Open it," Stavers ordered. He knew the guard was watching Hinyub and he knew Hinyub was nodding. The guard opened the door and held it wide. Stavers went down the stairs and stopped by a steel door. He looked up at the TV scanner. "This is getting tedious," he said.

"You're quite right," said a woman's voice through a concealed speaker. "Welcome, Mr. Stavers." The door slid aside and Stavers walked slowly into the enormous room. A hundred feet by sev-

enty, floor-to-ceiling glass walls on two sides over-
looking the neon river of the Strip in one direction
and McCarran Field and mountains in the other.
Everything in superb design of rich woods, foun-
tains, lighting. But then, he already knew that.
He'd had almost three days to find out what he
needed to know. The fact that it had been tougher
than he expected told him almost as much as the
actual discovery of information. He went up to the
end of the oval conference table with its six deeply
upholstered chairs. The one directly before him
was empty, awaiting his presence. He laid the
attaché case gently on the table, remained standing, moving his eyes from one person to another.
He bowed slightly and the names rolled from him
as he shifted his gaze around the table.

"Ah, Concetta de Luca. A pleasure. And you, sir,
are Harold Metzbaum. Benito Gibraldi. You carry
a splendid record as a Legionaire. And there is a
man I have not seen since a certain surveillance in
Berlin. Vernon Kovanowicz, a true professional. And
Mr. Alberto Grazzi. The man who never forgets."

They were astonished. He had dropped just
enough to let them know he knew a great deal
more. Concetta de Luca knew he was carrying the
ball and she moved swiftly. "Please. Do sit down.
Name your pleasure, Mr. Stavers."

"Cognac. It was cold on the roof."

No one ordered the drink. A waiter appeared
almost immediately with a snifter and what Stavers
knew would be superb cognac. He tested the moment. He lit a cigar. No ash tray before him. It
was there in moments with a gold Dunhill lighter
by its side. He liked their touch.

"We heard your conversation with Mr. Hinyub," Metzbaum said.

"I didn't think you were asleep down here," Stavers said.

"Then you must have something very special in that case. Do you still mind if it is opened?" Thick fingers drummed lightly on the table.

"I do mind. But I will tell you. It contains a tape recorder that runs for three hours, more than this meeting will last. It has a combination lock on the outside. It is most important that the lock be opened with the proper combination."

"There is a reason for that?" Kovanowicz asked, already knowing the answer. After all, they were fellow professionals.

"Of course," Stavers said amiably. "If it is opened any other way it will detonate the fourteen pounds of plastique within."

Gibraldi leaned forward, elbows on the table, fingers clasped together. He was actually grinning. "You fascinate me. What you said about the helicopter on the roof. All that is true?"

"It is."

"You have style, Mr. Stavers, you have style."

Stavers sipped the cognac. It wasn't superb; he'd never tasted anything like it. It was incredible.

Concetta recognized his response. "We will send a case of the cognac to the roof. A gift."

"Tell your men to be careful not to trip over any ropes."

Kovanowicz burst into laughter. Stavers lifted his glass to the Czech. "I presume you intend for me to drink that cognac in good health."

"Of course!" Kovanowicz boomed.

"I must say," Stavers said slowly between sips, "that your greeting card was hardly on the friendly side. Beginning," he added slowly, "with that friend I encountered at fourteen thousand feet."

"He was good!" Kovanowicz said with open enthusiasm. "In fact, I will tell you something, Mr. Stavers. I won a bet of twenty thousand dollars that he would *fail.*" Kovanowicz leaned back in his seat, beaming. "Very few people truly understand—what shall I call it—our closed circle? I knew of you in Berlin. *That* was an episode. So what is one man falling through the air?"

"And the wallet?"

"Crude, amateurish. I told that to Hinyub. Once you were alerted, it would fail. It was wasted motion."

"What about that idiot you hired in Jacksonville?"

Gibraldi gestured lightly. "He is a dead idiot."

"No loss," Stavers murmured. "It's too bad you had to lose the others in Arizona."

"The only one that mattered was the pilot," Metzbaum broke in. "The others were garbage men, dolts. The pilot was very good."

"I'll testify to that. I watched him coming in."

Metzbaum was fascinated. "How could you have known so quickly?"

Stavers shrugged. "We knew long before he arrived."

"That is not an answer," Metzbaum said pointedly.

"And you're accustomed to answers."

"Yes. I am."

"Figure it out for yourself."

The first touch away from the circle of pleasantries. The woman laughed lightly, enjoying Metz-baum's discomfiture, the flush that moved up from his neck.

Stavers looked not at Concetta de Luca, but to Gibraldi. "Why the ten thousand dollars in the envelope?"

"A courtesy," said the waspish Italian. "One should always pay the taxicab."

"The cab is paid." Stavers looked at each person, one after the other, allowing the silence to fill the long moment. "It's time," he said finally. "We all have precious little of it. There's no need to fence with one another. Let us get to it."

Metzbaum pointed to the attaché case. "Turn off your machine."

"You're not recording this?" Stavers said with sarcasm. "You're not filming everything in color? You haven't already checked my voiceprint against your computer records? You didn't check my body mass when I stood outside the door? Or even right now, in this seat?" Again his eyes swept the table. "Concetta de Luca. Gentlemen. Waste any more of my time and I leave at once."

They looked at one another and the woman shifted position in her chair. She had changed expression. Her eyes flashed. Doug Stavers knew the look. She had professional interests, business at mind, but she had begun to consider him as a man. As a male. He knew she would; she must. Women of such intelligence and power all too rarely find men to whom they can and *want* to surrender physically and emotionally. A woman who doesn't surrender to making love never receives her complete release, and the frustration becomes monumental. Concetta de Luca was such a woman, and in that sudden smouldering glance between them, she understood that he *knew*.

"We wish to retain your services, Mr. Stavers."

"I know that."

"It is for a most unusual assignment."

"Madame, you are being obvious."

Her eyes took on a sharp look of daggers. "Please don't make this a contest, Mr. Stavers."

"Then you stop setting it up in that manner. With all due respect, Miss de Luca, get to the point."

"It is difficult." He knew she wasn't staging that remark. "We have little to go on. Rumors, myths, stories, reports, perhaps fairy tales. We are searching for some specific object, we believe, that has a most unusual characteristic. We do know that other groups, and governments as well, believe enough in this object to be devoting an enormous amount of money, effort, and personnel to the task of finding this object. That will either let them reap its benefits or prevent others from obtaining possession. Even if they are wrong, the potential *appears* to be so great they're willing to make this enormous expenditure simply to confirm whether or not they're right. Or, equally as important, if they are wrong."

Stavers believed her implicitly. Not so much what she said but her manner of expression. Metzbaum wasn't a liar; he didn't need to be. And if Kovanowicz were involved in a sham *he* would be talking. He knew about Alberto Grazzi; he was only here because he was *always* at these meetings. Benito Gibraldi was too intense, much too interested in this object, whatever it was, being real. He would have relaxed with his cognac. There were many signs to read along this trail, and he knew how to do his tracking. *This is for real*, he reassured himself.

"Tell me what else you know," he said to de Luca.

"The Vatican is involved. We have a name. Rosa Montini. Her family is extremely high in Church circles. Perhaps the name Montini strikes a chord within you?"

He nodded. "Joseph Montini was Pope Paul. His brother, Lodovici, a Roman senator."

Gibraldi applauded softly. "Bravo. This Rosa is of the same family. We have discovered she is part of a massive effort to locate this object. It's most curious the Church should have such an intense interest. They have free rein to do *anything* to achieve their goal."

"As do the Israelis," Metzbaum said. "They also are involved."

"Nazis?" Stavers asked. He gestured to stop the reply. "No, it wouldn't be any of the old war criminals. The Vatican helped many of them flee to South America and other parts of the world. That doesn't fit."

"The Americans, as well," Concetta de Luca added.

"They're working together?" Stavers queried.

"To the best of our knowledge they are not," came the immediate reply.

"Is there anything more definite about this object?"

"Only that all indications are that it may be carried by one person," de Luca told him.

"Its characteristics?"

"We are guessing. It has bizarre powers. We regard such stories with a grain of salt, so to speak."

Stavers nodded. "And your interest?"

"We are very wealthy, Mr. Stavers," the woman said openly, without attempt to impress. "More wealth will come to us without much effort. To go to so much trouble simply for money would be a terrible waste of time and talent. We are intrigued by the tremendous effort others are placing in this object, whatever it may be. If it deserves such attention on their parts we can be no less interested. We attracted your attention because a small, private team has the best opportunities in this quest. *Your* team, obviously."

He threw a question from well out in left field. "Do you represent the Syndicate?"

No immediate reply, but he was aware they were not concealing anything or searching for an inconclusive response. The question *was* unexpected. Vernon Kovanowicz answered for them. "You know my name, my background, Mr. Stavers. Unequivocally, the answer is no. We are not linked directly to what so many call the Mafiosa, the Mob, the Syndicate. We have no need. In fact, in many areas they find us dangerous competition."

"I am very glad to hear you say that," Stavers told him.

"You surprise me," Concetta de Luca spoke. "I would not have thought *you* would be concerned about any syndicate."

"I'm not," he told her frankly. "What pleases me is to have you confirm openly what I already knew."

"Then we should stop sparring," Gibraldi announced. "We require mutual trust in our relationship, Mr. Stavers. Any arrangement we make cannot possibly exist if suspicion and distrust walks with us."

"Agreed. Go on, please."

"Using your own methods, keeping us free of involvement in your effort, we wish for you to seek this object," Concetta said, slipping into control again. "We are aware you may not be successful, and for a number of reasons. The object may not exist. Others may reach it before you, if it *does* exist. We would expect you at such time to continue your pursuit of this object. We do not care what means you employ on our behalf. We also expect in this arrangement your word of honor, and we place more reliance in that than you may be aware, that you will abide by whatever agreement we reach at this meeting."

Stavers nodded. "Fair enough."

"Is that all, Mr. Stavers? You do not ask why we wish this object and are so anxious to confirm and possibly seek its possession?"

"The answer is obvious. It goes beyond money. After a certain point, money becomes meaningless. It needs to be translated, to be transformed. Ultimately, money becomes an expression of political, military, diplomatic power. That's always been the name of the game ever since men held their first meeting like this. In a cave," he added as an afterthought. "Nothing has really changed."

Kovanowicz leaned forward. His eyes were intent. "And do you know why we're so willing to trust *you?*" he asked.

"I know why," Stavers said with a smile. "The question is whether or not we hold the same opinion."

Harold Metzbaum sighed with a great wet, hissing sound. "You're a free man, Stavers," he said in his strained, high voice, "one of the really free men I have ever known. You're at home in the field and in the environs of the most crowded city. You can be alone on an ice floe or in the midst of thousands, but you are a man who is never lonely. You are your own man. You do not need money for its own sake, but you appreciate its value and the ease and advantages it brings. Most of all, Stavers, we know your intense, deep desire and determination to maintain what I believe you would describe as a low profile in life. *That* is why we trust you. We are not so blind as to believe you are afflicted with myopia. Power, control, call it what you will. That is what we seek. If this mysterious object is what the rumors make it out to be, we— all of us you now face—have a most admirable goal before us."

"It is also why," Kovanowicz said in his deep rumbling voice, "we do not fear you will break any pact with us. *Your word is everything to you.* You have never been known to break it. You've staked your life on it." The Czech lifted his arm in a sweeping gesture. "Strange as it may seem, Mr. Stavers, we trust you to keep your part of the bargain. That if this object exists and it falls within your grasp, we will be the recipients of your effort. You may not succeed in your quest, but you will not break your word to us. If, of course," he said slowly, "we receive that word."

"You think highly of me," Stavers said carefully.

"That is true," Kovanowicz laughed. "You are bound by your morality to yourself. It is a powerful chain, the strongest I have ever known."

"Fair enough," Stavers murmured. He returned his attention to Concetta de Luca. "It will be expensive."

"We are prepared to commit to numbers," she said coolly.

"Specifics in this instance are impossible," he responded in the same businesslike tone. "I will require several teams, travel, research—our KGB man here can fill you in on those sort of details. And if this is as far-reaching as I'm convinced it is, then the cost is immaterial."

The woman waited. "True," she agreed.

"First, an advance of three million dollars. No receipts, none of that nonsense. No accounting, no—"

He never had the opportunity to finish. "Agreed," she said. She didn't even bother to look at the others for confirmation.

"The advance will total ten million dollars. The remaining seven million will be kept in an account where I draw on it, when and if needed, without question."

"We agree."

He hadn't expected such compliance with these numbers. It sobered him more than he'd anticipated.

"One hundred million dollars to be placed in an account with a third party, acceptable to both of us, and its issuance to be decided upon by that third party at such time as the object you seek is delivered."

"And if it is not delivered?" Gibraldi said softly.

"Then the funds are returned to you. I will not have earned them and they have no interest to me," Doug Stavers said, and knew they were accepting his terms.

"We agree," Concetta de Luca said. "I speak for the five of us."

Stavers saw agreement in their faces. No one even blinked when the numbers were discussed. "There is one more matter to be settled," he said slowly.

"Which is?" Gibraldi asked.

"Don't ever try to tail me again." Stavers was unaware that a steely tone had slipped into his voice. "I mean that. Don't check up on me, don't tail me. That could screw up everything I'm doing, give me false leads, and it would be tantamount to absolute proof you do *not* trust me."

"That will not happen," de Luca told him. "My oath upon it."

"That is good. I will give you *my oath*, Madame, that if that happens I will not waste my time on those people playing stupid games with me. I will come after you. All of you. And you will never know who, besides myself, will keep you permanently in mind as a target. Please, be assured that with all your strength, with the extent of your organization, you may all be eliminated with relative ease."

"Then," Metzbaum said with a measure of discomfort in his voice, "we will never provide you with such incentive."

And that acceptance told Stavers more than everything else put together. Whatever it was they wanted, it must be earth-shaking.

"Then we have a deal," he told them.

"I am pleased," Concetta de Luca said quietly. The others nodded. "How do you wish the initial payment of three million to be accomplished?"

"You will receive a telephone call and then a visit directly from a man called Jack North."

"Oho! I know him," Kovanowicz said with a broad smile. "An excellent choice."

"North will make the arrangements. He speaks for me."

"As you wish," the woman said.

"Now, what else can you tell me? *Anything*, no matter how outlandish or far-fetched or trivial it may seem, may help."

"You have already been given the name of Rosa Montini," Gibraldi said. "That is a start."

"It is," Stavers said. "What else?"

"We are involved with something relatively small and powerful," Kovanowicz said, suddenly all business. "It affects people. We are fairly sure of that. It is not a device, as one would think of machinery. That is what you would call a hunch. It must involve people who have affected world events. People with power. With great ability."

"You have someone in mind," Stavers said after digesting the Czech's remarks.

"Yes, I do," the former KGB man told him. For one of the few times in his life he could recall, Stavers was caught completely by surprise.

"*Adolph Hitler.*"

Chapter   VII

Think.

Assemble, correlate and coordinate data.

Identify your opposition and the obstacles between yourself and your enemies.

Select your objectives.

Be relentless. Never forget the rule of warmth of heart. It's more important and has deeper import than all the weapons ever made. If you love someone, then let them go.

If they don't come back, hunt them down and kill them.

Doug Stavers pursued his rules with icy fanaticism. They were the checklist chiseled deeply into the structure of his brain. To say he moved carefully was to beggar description. An element that had for years been a stranger to him intruded now into his daily awareness. He both welcomed the stranger and found its presence unnerving because of its emotional touch.

This whole goddamn thing excites me. He made the self-admission in a moment of introspective wonder. Excited? *Him?* For a long time he'd thought such a feeling impossible. Far beyond his killer grasp. Something subtle, this new sense of excitement, for it reached far beyond the thrill of danger or even the simple risk of life. Intuitively he knew he had returned, sure-footed and glistening with self-confidence, to the gladitorial arena. His nostrils flared with heady thoughts of life-fighting. Women were stunned with the musk-awareness of his power. He smelled of danger, masculinity, barbarian lovemaking. His own pleasure went through him in near-orgasmic waves, and the dimly-recalled smell of blood assailed his memory senses with the heady aroma of oversweet roses. He laughed with the thought, delighted the small touches of remembrance had remained with him.

Roses. How marvelous that so delicate a creature could invoke so great a storm of memories and realizations.

If it ain't got thorns, buddy, it can't be a rose.

He remembered that lesson all too well. But there was another. The strongest scent of the rose never came at full bloom. That marvelous fragrance, that gush of perfume to the world within reach, came only from a *dying* rose. It was never sweeter than when it had yielded life and was about to offer a withering embrace to death. Somehow, that fit quite well with his thoughts, for with every passing moment he tread ever more carefully the minefields of the chase on which he had already embarked.

He planned each move with consummate care and along several parallel tracks. He began culling the top men who'd served covert agencies of many governments, as well as calling to memory the best of the mercenaries he knew could be trusted to serve to the ultimate of their given word. And there was another, ceaseless search he ran again and again through his mind for knowledge of *past* events, as if he knew he must match thousands of tiny interlocking pieces he would inevitably encounter. The best way to obtain these clues and hints and nuances was to use the piercing steel of *his* own memory to slice back through the thickening sludge of history that had been so deliberately confused by so many.

Jack North ran his international team of investigators. Jack had unlimited funds and carte blanche in a most dangerous way. He exercised life and death over many of the aged individuals they queried, because asking questions and leaving behind people eager to talk to the wrong parties could be exceedingly dangerous. Very bad news, indeed. Unencumbered by clumsy conscience or government restrictions, especially if they recognized North or Stavers, those who refused cooperation were executed swiftly. Swiftly and methodically and always "accidentally." Such a theme produces flourishing cooperation.

Germany beckoned as their first area of detailed search. It was a ground scoured by thousands of military and intelligence operatives, political teams, refugee organizations, seekers of vengeance against former military or political masters, and hordes of historians. The latter proved of enormous benefit; much of Stavers's work had been done, and people long dead remained able to tell their tales through what had been placed on paper, recorded on film and on tape. There were still some of the older party members alive, just as there still remained aged but mentally alert men and women who had fought Hitler and his power mania. They were in declining numbers and often concealed by the distance they sustained between their own pasts and the present. And it didn't help Stavers *not* knowing just what it was he sought.

Something that gave power to men. To a man. It could be singular. It might not be. This was an invisible needle in a towering haystack. They would have to feel their way through. They had help from a source that had not existed in the aftermath of the second world war. Historical information had in detail been committed to computer records. To Stavers and Tracy, those computers were a time machine. They could electronically cull millions of words of memoirs, the Nuremburg trials, the hundreds of books written on Adolf Hitler. Not the normal biographies, but long-forgotten documents that existed now only in unlisted files or libraries or, in the computers.

Out of their vast study there emerged an enigma lacking a definite answer: Hitler's ability to control, dominate, awe and frighten almost every human being with whom he came in direct contact. The realization was hardly new. What stood out,

Stavers emphasized to the others, was that no one had ever come up with an answer. Hitler had been a gutter bum, a failure, denied admission to schools he wanted desperately to attend. He leeched off friends and relatives. Often he sulked and nearly starved in flophouses. He had even failed tests in the German language. He lacked any higher education. He had been a brave soldier in the first world war, unquestionably had earned his Iron Cross while serving as a messenger for his unit. He had almost sacrificed his life to save a superior officer. He had also been gassed and was hysterically blind for several weeks; was again struck by blindness through emotional grief and rage in the '30s.

"So something doesn't fit," Stavers said to Tracy as he had so many times in their frustrating search. "How the hell did he manage to so completely dominate his generals, the political leaders about him; how could he frighten so many people? *What did he have going for him?*"

"Can astrology help?" Tracy asked.

Stavers was stunned. "What the hell are you talking about?"

"Most of the histories," Tracy related, "insist that Hitler thought astrologers were charlatans, fakes, mystics, idiots. The historical records, especially the memoirs of his top political cronies and his generals, all insist on that. I don't believe it's true." She had his interest, and he called in Jack North and their top computer specialist, Steve Georgieff.

"Hitler was *not* a good speaker in his early days,"

Tracy said. "Oh, he harangued and he shouted a lot, but Germany in the days after the first world war was filled with starving and desperate men, and Hitler was one shrill voice among many screeching sounds. Somewhere along the way he learned how to change that. He came to study his audience, to feel them out, to judge them well. If nothing else, with all his ranting and raving, he commanded their attention. It wasn't an accident, of course."

Georgieff nodded. "You're referring to Erik Jan Hanussen, aren't you?"

"Partially." Tracy looked at Stavers and her father. "Erik Hanussen was a seer, an astrologer, a dabbler in the satanic arts, and a man who prophesized the future. Most people who knew him considered him an expert in parlor magic. Hitler was fascinated with him. It's been rumored, but never confirmed, that Hitler became a pupil of Hanussen, and—"

"Oh come on, Tracy, are you asking us to believe that Adolf Hitler gained his mesmerizing powers through black magic!" Stavers was surprised with his own strong reaction, but this was asinine.

Tracy shook her head, amused with his response. "You, of all people, not hearing me out?"

He squeezed her hand. "You nailed me on that one. Chalk it up to the frustrations of chasing phantoms and ghosts."

"Mesmer had a part in this, but not through Hitler," Tracy went on. "Hanussen had been fascinated by Mesmer, studied him; and what he learned most of all was that Mesmer was able to place his subjects into a hypnotic trance by movements of his hands, the way he used his eyes, things like that. Did you know, Doug, that Adolf Hitler *was* Erik Hanussen's student for many months? That the one thing the old seer and mystic taught Hitler was *body language?* The arts and secrets of dominating an audience through both subtle and major movements of hands and torso, the tilt of the head, the glare of the eyes; well, whatever it was, it seemed to work. It was *after* this period of training that Hitler's effectiveness as an orater became positively unbelievable."

"What happened to Hanussen? Did he leave anything behind that could help us?" Stavers queried.

"He never had the chance," Georgieff broke in. The scholarly man with horn-rimmed glasses and huge bushy white eyebrows, as always puffing a pipe, leaned back and studied Stavers. "Imagine the scene, Doug. Hitler is coming out of nowhere. He has cursed and ridiculed astrologers, sworn to do away with the gypsies whom, incidentally, he hated even more than the Jews. The gypsies were his first target and they were marked for eradication long before Hitler came up with his Final Solution for the Jews. Now, here's Erik Jan Hanussen, known all through Europe as a seer and a mystic, from whom Hitler has learned elements and behavior critical to his future. Does he dare leave Hanussen around to tell this to other people? Of course not. He can't take the chance, because then his opponents could make a lot of hay by claiming Hitler dabbled in black magic and he was under the direct influence of Hanussen. It could wreck the political career he was after. However it happened, Hitler became aware of these possibilities. He has Hanussen brought to Nazi party headquarters, sweet-talks the old man into undying friendship, and the next day Hanussen is found mysteriously shot to death. No one wants to ask questions that would bring the Brownshirts down on them, and the whole thing is forgotten or swept under the rug. Besides, seers and astrologers don't matter."

"Do we chalk that up as a dead end, then?" Stavers asked.

"No," Tracy said with unusual emphasis. "There was more to it than that. Hitler had no need to bring Hanussen to his headquarters. All he had to do was to snap his fingers and the old man was as good as dead. He had some reason, some *need*, to see Hanussen personally, on a face-to-face basis. From what we've been able to learn, Hitler *tested* himself on Hanussen. He went through a madman's speech, shouting and pounding his desk, reviling Hanussen. The old man was too smart not to miss the point, of course. Hitler was testing himself out on his former teacher. What has us so intrigued is that there have been strange references to another factor in all this."

"That factor is the X we're seeking," Georgieff added. "I'm absolutely certain of it. Because Hitler for a time sat absolutely silent with Hanussen. There were several other people in the room. They said that even before Hitler started shouting at Hanussen, the seer was agitated, perspiring. He wasn't afraid of Hitler. There was something else.

We've had vague reports that there might have been some sort of amulet involved. We draw a blank there."

"Amulet," Stavers repeated. "That doesn't fit at all. From everything we've learned, Hitler never wore personal jewelry of any kind."

"Not true," Tracy disputed. "In his early days as a rising figure of power he would wear gold badges. Then, at about the time that he eliminated Hanussen, he gave them all away as gifts. Except for what *appeared* on his tunic or uniforms, he was never seen or known to wear jewelry again. There are reports that he wore something beneath his clothing. But once again," she shrugged, "we get into that grey area. We spoke to a former transport pilot of the German air force who flew a transport in the Holland invasion. He was captured there and went to Canada as a prisoner for the rest of the war. He lives in Florida now."

"Name?"

"Frankel. He recalls that just before they left for Holland, their outfit had a visit and inspection by Hitler. He was in a jovial mood, absolutely convinced of his forthcoming success. And as best as this Karl Frankel can recall, Hitler mentioned something about golden fire. The fire of ice, I believe. It all gets rather confusing from that point. But the pilot was quite definite about Hitler referring to something that was out of the ordinary as being very important to him. The trail gets cold there."

"Well, it's better than nothing," Stavers said doubtfully. "That mean anything to you, George?"

"Could. Might. Perhaps. Maybe."

"Thanks a hell of a lot."

"We ran it through the computer. The terms. Golden fire. Fire of ice. There are Norse meanings. The old gods, that sort of thing. *They* simply fade out. But that second phrase about the fire of ice. There *is* a meaningful description involving that phrase."

Stavers nodded. "That's how some diamonds are described. Icy fire. Flashing brilliantly. Never warm, but always the term fire."

Georgieff nodded. "That's what Tracy and I have been working on. We've come to a few conclusions. They're tentative, however," he warned Stavers.

"Let's have them."

"We have to jump forward. Span the time between Hanussen's murder, on to the Holland invasion in 1940. From there we get a leap of five years. Right to the end of wartime Germany. The bunker is what I'm referring to. Hitler's last holdout in Berlin."

"Why the bunker?" Stavers asked. His curiosity was piqued. "That territory's been gone over with a thousand fine-toothed combs. The Russians sifted every ash, bone, rock, piece of metal. Every bit of it. British intelligence was in there all the way. We've all seen the reports. Hitler died there. Poison, shot, cremated. The works."

Tracy nodded. "And in the last few days, just before Hitler died—and a day or two *after* he was dead—several planes flew into the highway near the bunker, and a few of them flew *out* again. We *know* at least one of those planes was carrying diamonds. We *know* that Hitler gave one of his men a bag filled with diamonds that he always kept with him for Germany's highest awards for valor."

"Nothing about golden fire? I mean, specifically?"

"No," Tracy admitted. "There were even more diamonds involved. One of Hitler's most trusted officers was shot for treason. *He* had diamonds. Some of them vanished when his mistress, who was also working as a British agent, escaped Berlin, with diamonds, even as the Russians were closing in."

"Christ, it seems that every time we uncover something," Stavers said wearily, "we get three more leads that end up in smoke."

"It's the first time we have a direct correlation," Georgieff reminded him. "Hanussen and the events involving him. Hitler talking with his pilots, especially Frensch, and what he recalls. Then diamonds in the bunker, and pilots running for their lives, known to be carrying diamonds. It's wisps of smoke only, perhaps, but there's that correlation, and we've got to follow it through."

"That means," Tracy suggested, "we should go to the bunker. Maybe we won't learn anything by being there, but sometimes, well, just being at a place can give you a *feeling* you can't get any other way. Maybe we'll get some ideas. Besides, there are people we need to talk to in Berlin and also in West Germany. East Germany, too. We don't know yet. But we may get some leads."

"Getting to the bunker is bad enough," Georgieff noted, shaking his head. "Wandering around East Germany in the open is impossible."

"Not," Stavers said, smiling, "when you have certain friends who also have certain friends in high places." An hour later he hung up the telephone after a long talk with Vernon Kovanowicz.

"Who was that?" North asked.

"That was Vern Baby," Stavers told them. "He says we can go anywhere we want to in Berlin or East Germany."

"Just like that?" Georgieff asked.

Stavers snapped his fingers. "Just like that."

Chapter VIII

They moved through what had been the final stronghold of Adolf Hitler and the last gasp of the Third Reich, down the winding stairways and into the concrete bastion the Russians still kept as a sign of crushing the remnants of the men who had savaged the Russian homeland. It was more than an eerie feeling; they had to remind themselves again and again that this was where Hitler and Eva Braun had died, where the Goebbels family met death from guns and poison, where men and women drowned their fears, where some yielded to fear and cowardice and others remained unstintingly true to Hitler even *after* his death. They were accompanied by an old German, Kurt Mueller, who had known Adolf Hitler and his top military and political staff; an old man of 84 years, but with a barrel chest and astonishing strength for his age. He had been found by Kovanowicz for them, for he might tell them more than all the history books together. He had been in this bunker until the Russians were in sight and had fled through underground sewers, wounded and burned, to American lines to surrender.

"You knew Hitler," Stavers said quietly to the old man. "I know you've been asked this many times, but we would be grateful for whatever you can tell us again. We are not searching for war criminals and we are not the police."

"I know that," Mueller said testily, and his command of English told Tracy North that the aged German was master of many languages. Inflections and nuances always give that away. "We are sick to death of such searches. I am here only because the Russians let me be here. You should know that. Also, I was informed by a certain party that all I need do was remember and answer your questions, and a thousand dollars American would be in my hands."

Georgieff handed him a brown envelope. "Not a thousand, grandfather. Three thousand. We know of your family."

A shaking hand accepted the envelope. "On the black market this is worth twice this amount." The envelope disappeared within his shirt. "Thank you. What do you want to know?"

They discussed with Mueller the many reports of the comings and goings from the bunker in the last days of the war. Many intimate details of the period with names, activities, events, all leading to the specific questions and whatever information they could glean from the old German.

"Many of us begged Hitler not to remain here," Mueller told them. "We knew he could escape, that he would survive. He could carry on the Reich, could rearm. We were all convinced the Americans would fight the Russians, and soon enough, and that resurgence for Germany was very much in our future. You know that Hitler was not a well man, of course. He had a palsy condition. His left arm shook badly, and his skin had a strange yellow pallor. Often he would be seized by shaking. Somehow, he always fought it off. We would believe he had met his end, and then he would play with the dogs, or work at his maps and issue orders for hours on end, and when he emerged he would be incredibly revived, filled with energy, his voice again vibrant, his grasp of the situation clear beyond all question. At such moments, who could *not* believe his greatness would know no end! When he chose to lift his head and his strength filled him he was undaunted, invincible. We would follow him anywhere. Ach, those eyes, and that *feeling* he gave forth. It was astonishing. Men died gladly for him." Mueller's face grew reflective. "Too many, of course. Germany's finest. But for those of us who knew him, no sacrifice was too great."

Stavers was fascinated. He had heard and read so much of this extraordinary aspect of Hitler, and now he was talking with a man who had experienced it many times. Mueller related how he had been still a youth in glider training when he first met Hitler, when he became a transport pilot and on several occasions personally flew Hitler about Germany and to the Polish and Russian fronts.

There were occasions on the ground, between flights, when he could talk directly with Germany's leaders. There were others when he was in conference and meeting rooms, standing on the side, waiting as ordered, and Hitler would confront either his own generals or foreign dignitaries.

"For many people, meeting with Hitler was the most startling experience of their lives. I saw it happen many, many times. A man entering the room with Hitler waiting was like walking into a million needles pricking at the skin. Those who faced him directly often looked as if they had been struck a physical blow. They stammered, they could not think clearly. Hitler toyed with them as if they were children. This did not always happen, of course, but it was the dominant theme with almost all those he encountered. If he wanted to press home a point there was almost no way to contest his magnetism. It was an aura that filled a room, a religious experience. When one encountered Hitler's wrath, it was to be drained emotionally and spiritually, to be left as weak as a kitten."

Kurt Mueller sat down on a concrete bench, as if recalling those moments could exhaust him even now. Georgieff handed him a flask with brandy and the old man sipped gratefully. Color returned to his face. "Thank you. I did not mean to run on like that."

"Was there any time when Hitler ever used expressions such as the 'fire of ice' or the 'golden fire' in your presence?" Tracy asked.

Mueller looked at her with astonishment. "Never, *never* in all these years have I heard any other person ever say something like that to me!"

Stavers and Georgieff exchanged glances. Tracy had hit something, and Kurt Mueller seemed more relaxed talking with her than to them. They let Tracy run with the sudden opening.

"I am sorry if I said something wrong, Herr Mueller—"

"Wrong? No, no; it is not wrong! But no one has ever known of such an expression from Adolf Hitler except a very few of us, and perhaps I am the only one left alive who heard such words. I am overwhelmed. You bring moments to mind, young lady, that I have not thought of for many, many years."

"Then . . . you did hear Hitler talk about a golden fire?"

"Nein, nein. Not a golden fire. There was an occasion when those words, words like them, that is, came up.

"I remember it because I had been ordered personally by Hitler to go to Tempelhof Airfield, to greet a special group arriving by plane from Roumania. I was to bring them to Hitler's office. I had twenty guards with me. They were to talk with no one, they were to be brought to see Hitler directly, and he gave strict orders not to be disturbed during that visit."

"You are that certain after all these years, Herr Mueller?"

"I am certain because small things stand out in memory forever. I was surprised to see the Roumanian aircraft. It was flown by Bibesco himself. That is Prince Antoine Bibesco. I remember so well because I did not expect the Roumanians to arrive in their own Junkers 52 machine. And I was a Ju-52 pilot, if you recall."

He had never stated any airplane specifically, but Tracy dared not interrupt this unexpectedly sharp recall. "I remember the airplane because it had a double tail wheel. I had never seen any Junkers like that before. A double tail wheel. It stuck in my mind. Also, the machine had strange engines that were not on any German Junkers of this type. So, I talked with people about the airplane. That's why I remember it."

"You brought Bibesco to Hitler?"

"What? *Ja.* I followed my orders. We had several big cars and we gave them full honors and brought them to headquarters. I recall that Bibesco and two others went into Hitler's office and the doors were closed. We all expected to hear a great deal of shouting, an uproar, you know, because Hitler knew the Roumanians were flirting with the Bolsheviks. They were being much too friendly with the Russians, and Hitler was upset about this. Many times we had heard him threaten to sweep through Roumania and take it over completely."

Mueller became reflective. "That did not happen. I mean at the meeting. All was quiet from inside the room. We were all surprised at this. They were together maybe two hours, then they came out, Hitler with his arm through that of the prince, this Bibesco fellow, and they were smiling and laughing at something Hitler said to them. I was ordered to return them to Tempelhof, to remain there until I saw personally that they had made a safe departure. I did this, and I reported to

Herr Hitler that his orders were carried out to the letter."

Tracy maneuvered very carefully. If the old German lost this memory train it might never be available to them again. "When did he speak with you about the golden fire, Herr Mueller?"

"Golden fire? Did I say golden fire? I thought ..." His voice began to fade as he searched his memory. "Ach, I recall now. *You* asked me about golden fire. Hitler did not say that."

Tracy's heart sank. *So close!*

"He said something about a great yellow fire of ice." He tried to find more in the dusty attic of his memories but he had drawn a blank.

"Did you know what he meant, Herr Mueller?"

"*Nein*. I did not know. To this day I do not know! I never understood what he meant. I just recall the words, and they are yet in my mind because of the Roumanians."

Stavers was almost chewing his tongue. "Herr Mueller. Please. You said you didn't understand what he meant. You did not ask him?"

Mueller looked with surprise at Stavers. "Do you all speak such fluent German? I wonder who you people are. The Russians seemed quite anxious that you should be pleased."

"That doesn't matter, sir. Did you ever ask Adolf Hitler what he meant by his words about yellow fire? And, what he said about ice?"

"Herr Stavers." Mueller's eyes bored deeply into his. "One did *not* ask Adolf Hitler what he meant."

"Of course, sir."

Tracy almost shoved Stavers aside. She knew that this blessing of recall might be gone at any moment. "Herr Mueller, you were here in the bunker, you said. At the end."

"*Ja.* I was here."

"And you told us you, and the others, did everything you could to get Hitler to leave before the Russians stormed the bunker. How could he have done that?"

"Young woman, we had people coming and going for days before the end. We had planes coming and going. We had a machine waiting even to fly Hitler nonstop all the way to South America. He could have gone. We absolutely did not believe he would die. We believed he could *not* die. You know he took his own life. Otherwise he would be alive *now.*"

"He was nearly killed several times, if I recall my history," Georgieff said quietly.

"Aha! *Nearly* killed, indeed! You all know of the bombing attempt on his life, of course. The terrible moment of the twentieth of July. That was in 1944."

"Yes, of course," Stavers said for them all.

"That was the attempt that received so much publicity," Mueller recounted. "And because Germany's leader was wounded in that bomb explosion. Are you aware that the bomb did *not* miss? It went off close to Hitler? It tore apart the room and wrecked heavy furniture and it blew down walls and killed several people, and Hitler was directly in the force of the explosion. It tore his trousers to shreds, left them rags, it did many other things, and it was impossible, but he survived, he went on without hesitation leading Germany against her enemies." A light not present before had come into Mueller's eyes as he recalled incredible events of his past. "There were *so many* attempts on his life. We all believed at first that he was charmed, he had been selected by fate to accomplish his works. Somehow he escaped every treachery, every greedy reach for power by others. There were more than thirty attempts to kill Adolf Hitler."

Mueller sighed, and instantly Georgieff presented the brandy flask again to him. The old man wiped his mouth and nodded. "The miracle is *how* Hitler survived. It was at the beginning of the big wars, when Germany made its move in the Balkans and prepared for Russia, that his life became beyond the reach of any power on earth. I recall that time because it was right after Bibesco came to see Hitler. Did you people ever know Joachim Fest? No? You should talk with him. Fest knows better than anyone else the truly miraculous ability of Hitler to survive *anything* but his own decision to die. If you can, talk with him. I think he is alive."

He was starting to ramble and they kept prodding Mueller back to his direct recollections. Stavers was making a very sharp mental note about one factor that kept recurring. The Roumanians. History had little enough to spell out for Bibesco or anyone else from Roumania affecting Hitler's moves or exercise of power, yet this old man who had known Hitler personally over a span of years kept returning to the visit of a Roumanian group, secretly, with Hitler. Stavers forced his attention back to Mueller's words.

"Somehow, no matter what these *schwein* tried,

nothing worked. They did everything to kill our leader. Everything! There has been much talk of technical failure. Joachim Fest has all the records. How is it that in wartime Germany, when our science was the best in the world, when we were building weapons and systems other countries could hardly believe, that detonators failed to work? That radio mechanisms strangely jammed? That simple mechanical devices broke down? Again and again, everything the plotters tried to do failed them. And then, then, there was above all else the uncanny sense of our leader in detecting danger. There was nothing to tell him except something from *within* him. He could smell danger! Or so it seemed. Sometimes it had to be, or so we all reasoned, that fate itself was protecting him. Impossible things would happen. Hitler was aboard his transport plane when he had one of those strange feelings of his. His eyes would shine. On this particular flight he ordered Braun, his pilot, to land at once. They were still far from their destination. Hitler and his staff proceeded by motorcar, *ja?* Even the pilot, at Hitler's orders, drove with him. The airplane was flown by another crew to its destination. They did not arrive."

Mueller showed a strange, enigmatic smile. "And you know why? Because there was a bomb aboard that plane. It had been there from takeoff with Hitler aboard. It exploded and killed everyone, *after* Hitler had followed his hunch. One time he refused to enter a building that had been prepared for a secret meeting. The Gestapo, as always, had examined the building. It was declared safe. Hitler went to a nearby inn. While he was there, the building, with the Gestapo still inside, was destroyed by an explosion."

Mueller sighed. "They never stopped trying, those men who wanted to destroy Hitler. Finally they resorted to suicidal methods. Since the mechanisms they used would not work, they decided to sacrifice themselves. I was there, myself, when one of these attempts was made. It was in the Chancellory. We were waiting for a message to be delivered personally from the front by Cavalry Captain von Breitenbuch—"

"Excuse me, Herr Mueller," Georgieff broke in softly. "I know of the incident with von Breitenbuch. Was it not at the Berghof instead of the Chancellory?"

Mueller stabbed a gnarled finger at Georgieff. "Of course! You are correct. Forgive me; my memory, sometimes it mixes up places. The Berghof, that is true. Anyway, von Breitenbuch arrived with the dispatch. He was about to enter the main conference room when Hitler had one of his premonitions. *I saw this*. He lifted his eyes from the maps he was studying, and he told the SS guards to bar the doors, that no one, *especially* von Breitenbuch, was to enter. The captain was stopped at the entrance to the great hall. Do you know what they found? The traitor had twenty sticks of dynamite taped to his body! He was going to blow himself into little pieces just to kill Hitler. The Gestapo did their best but they were too eager. Captain von Breitenbuch died from his interrogation before we got much information from him."

Mueller fell into a deep, reflective mood. They let him rest, then decided it was too damp and cold for him to remain in the bunker. They had learned from their visit here all that they could. Georgieff drove to a restaurant where they could sit comfortably to learn whatever else Kurt Mueller might have to tell them. "We've got company," he said. "I have them in the rearview mirror. Two cars."

Stavers nodded. "Kovanowicz said they'd be with us all the time we were in Berlin. They're KGB in one car and German police in the other."

"Will they bother us?" Tracy asked. A touch of nervousness showed.

"You don't know Kovanowicz," Stavers smiled. "They're not here to tail us. *We're* here because they set it up, remember? No, they won't bother us. They're here to make sure nothing happens to us." He didn't spell that out any further, and Tracy let it drop.

In the restaurant, with a long glass of cognac and some cheese to refresh him, Mueller regained his composure and his strength. "Herr Mueller," Georgieff began easily, "you were in the bunker until the end, weren't you?"

"*Nein.* The end to me was when Hitler brought on his own death. I was there for some days afterward, and when the Russian troops began to close in, I escaped."

"We understand several aircraft landed near the bunker and took off again during this period," Georgieff prompted gently.

Mueller nodded. "That is true. The Russians were close. Artillery shells and rockets had been falling all about the area of the bunker. It was dangerous to be above ground. Yet, it was late in April, the twenty-sixth of the month, I am sure, when Colonel-General von Greim and Hanna Reitsch landed on the East-West Axis. That is the highway we just rode on that goes east and west through Berlin. They flew there and landed in a Feisler Storch. It was an incredible thing to do. At the eastern end of the Axis, you have seen it, stands the Brandenburg Gate. In fact, it was the woman, Reitsch, who had to land the plane. Von Greim was hit in the leg, very badly, by Russian gunfire. After they landed, an armored car rushed them to the bunker. I saw them come in. Hitler was overjoyed to see them. They had proven their courage and loyalty under the most trying of conditions.

"But that was not all. On the next day another pilot, and this one was most incredible of them all, landed one of the big Junkers on the same highway! Imagine, a great three-engined machine with all the Russians firing at it, still coming in to land safely. It had been sent for one purpose. The Ju-52 was heavily armored, and it had been sent to the bunker to remove Hitler, von Greim, Reitsch and other people, along with most valuable documents, from Berlin."

Mueller searched their faces. "Do you not understand?" he asked, almost in a whisper. "*He was free to go*. Hitler refused. He sent secret papers and several large packages from the bunker to the big transport. Von Greim refused to leave Hitler, and Hanna Reitsch said that she would remain always at von Greim's side. I believe they were lovers.

Anyway, the Junkers transport that had been sent
to retrieve Hitler landed safely, loaded people and
documents and other materials, and flew out safely.
Hitler should have been on that airplane!"

Mueller sighed deeply. "Colonel-General von
Greim did everything he could to persuade Hitler
to leave, but he refused. The day after the Junkers
left they kept trying. Hitler, very warmly, turned
them down. He told von Greim that another plane
would soon land. And it did. A small plane came
in that night. A little training plane, an Arado,
that holds only two people normally. Hitler gave
secret documents and an oilskin packet to von
Greim. He ordered them to leave in the Arado
immediately, while it was still dark. I went with
them by armored car from the bunker. We passed
through the Tiergarten to the Victory Column,
which was still in German hands. We had to almost stuff them in the airplane, von Greim with
his leg all shot up. Hanna Reitsch was a little
woman and that helped. So the three of them took
off at night, the air filled with exploding Russian
shells. They had maybe four hundred yards for
room in which to get into the air. They barely
made it. I saw them pass the Brandenburg Gate
and fly into low clouds. That saved them."

"Where did they go?" Georgieff inquired. He
already knew, but it was vital to let Mueller thread
these events together.

"Why, to Rechlin. Where else would they go?"
Mueller asked, surprised. "We had four machines
there. I know, because I was on the planning group
for those machines. One was a Kurier, the big

Focke-Wulf. It had special tanks and a small pressurized cabin for the crew and a few passengers. It could fly eight thousand miles without stopping. We also had a captured Lancaster bomber, a British machine. Our engineers had built in tanks for this aircraft and we knew it could fly six thousand miles. We had not yet decided whether to use a German aircraft or the Lancaster, which could have escaped fighters who caught sight of it. Then there were two machines of which the Allies knew nothing. They were real giants. Junkers 390 transports. Very special. A pressurized compartment, also, for the crew and passengers in each aircraft. They could fly twelve thousand miles. Straight from Rechlin to South America. We had already sent many submarines there. The submarines are no secret. What is his name? Ladislas Farago, yes. He has written of those U-boats. Serial numbers, the names of the captains. Argentina and Paraguay. All was held in readiness for Hitler to regroup his strength, to wait for the Americans and the Russians to fight, and then Hitler would offer all his renewed strength to the Americans in the holy war against Communism." Mueller fell into a fit of coughing. He was played out, Stavers judged. It was enough for the moment.

They drove Mueller back to a small apartment house. He waved off their offers for assistance. Two old women came down the steps, nodding to the Americans, and took Mueller inside. If they wanted to talk to him again, he would be available.

That night, in the West Berlin Hilton, they had time to review everything they'd heard and discussed during the day. Tracy had taped their conversation with Kurt Mueller with a recorder built into her purse. An open microphone or even scratching on pads would have thrown the elderly German off-balance. He must have had hundreds, perhaps even thousands of interrogations by the Russians and the Americans and the British and God knew who else, and the slightest untoward event would have closed him up like a clam. The phone call that induced the Russians to permit Mueller to join them had been absolutely indispensable; Mueller knew then he could talk freely. And at his advanced age there was little with which to threaten him directly, even if they had anything worth their concern. But Mueller felt for elder members of his own family, distant relatives, perhaps, and the three thousand dollars in cash, slipped into his shirt, was perhaps the final touch to free both his memory and his tongue.

"What do you make of it all?" Stavers asked Georgieff. "You're the expert on the Germans and especially on Hitler."

"Strangely enough, I already knew most of what he had to say," Georgieff said.

"Not so strange, George," Tracy said by way of compliment. "You've been collating records on the phenomenon of Hitler for twenty years, haven't you?"

Georgieff nodded. "And I hadn't learned *anything* new for fifteen of those years," he acknowledged, "until today."

Stavers and Tracy sat up straighter. Their table was along the edge of the penthouse dining room and they looked out across the brilliant and lusty night face of West Berlin. It was almost impossible to equate the Berlin recalled by Mueller and this beautiful and wealthy city now spread before them. In East Berlin the past had seemed so much closer, dreary and grey and oppressive. Well, this was tonight, here, *now*.

"There were a few things I hadn't known, either," Stavers said. "I've been a history buff a long time. With special interests, of course. And you can't do in-depth research on the SS and the panzers and German paratrooper forces without running into Hitler. Everything the old man had to say about Hitler's uncanny knack for avoiding disasters, for heading off assassination attempts; all of it is true, and I'm sure there are more we don't know about."

"Well, one thing you two geniuses haven't told me," Tracy noted.

"Which is?" Georgieff asked.

"*How* did he do it? It wasn't the SS or the Gestapo or the spies, although they probably stopped their own share of would-be assassins. All those other things, some of which Mueller talked about. *How* did he manage to *know?*"

"I don't believe he knew," Georgieff said quietly. "In fact, *it's impossible for him to have known*. Some other factor was involved."

"Are you referring to ESP?" Stavers asked. "Something paranormal?"

"That's one possibility," Georgieff replied. "And I don't want to hear counterarguments on that issue, because you'll be expressing opinion only."

Stavers grew very quiet. "George, I'm the last man you'll ever hear argue against what you call 'hunch.' I wouldn't be alive today if I didn't listen to some sort of voice inside my head, even when I can't tell what's being said. It's a warning of some kind. So I won't throw that aside too quickly."

"I don't believe ESP had a thing to do with it," Tracy announced. They looked at her with surprise. "Haven't you two seen the missing link? *The Germans never claimed anything paranormal for Hitler.* Charmed life, instinct, hunch; all phrases, but one thing holds sway all through those comments. They just don't *know.* It's one of the elements that's kindling this new fascination with Hitler. Hitler the monster, Hitler the wonderful, Hitler the leader of the masses, Hitler the stupid, Hitler the genius. There are a thousand Hitlers all around us and the ghosts are not only *not* laid to rest, they're gaining strength all the time, the good and the bad."

"What did you find today that was that new to you?" Stavers asked Georgieff in a sudden shift.

"I've never heard of Hitler having any conversation about golden fire, yellow fire, fire of ice or anything like that," Georgieff replied.

"I have," Stavers told him and saw Georgieff's eyes widen. "I got it directly from Vernon Kovanowicz, and his sources go everywhere. He didn't know what it meant. He speculated, as we are doing right now, that there's a reference to diamonds there, but he drew the blank at that point. And one other matter that won't go away."

"I know," Georgieff said. "The Roumanians."

"Exactly," Stavers confirmed. "Until today, when the old man told us about Bibesco flying into Tempelhof and having that secret gathering with Hitler, the Roumanians have always been way down on the totem pole of people and events in the history of Germany and Adolf Hitler."

"He was so specific about that airplane," Tracy offered. "I listened to the tape again. He kept talking about the double tail wheel and the unusual engines. Is that supposed to mean something?"

Georgieff nodded to Stavers. "You're the pilot. You tell us."

Stavers shook his head. "I don't know. We can go to Munich to the Deutches Museum to see what we can dig up there, if anything. Or we can go to Dessau, where the Junkers company had its production line for their Ju-52 transports. If the airplane came to Berlin before Roumania got involved as an ally of Germany, then it was built well before 1941. Back in the '30s, I'd say."

"Do we need to talk with Mueller anymore?" Tracy asked.

Stavers shook his head. "No. We've pulled everything we can from him that's meaningful. All he can do now is to share memories and there's no need to put him on the grill again."

"Oh, I don't know about that," Tracy retorted. "For a while there today I had the uneasy feeling he was lecturing us on the glories of the Third Reich rather than our grilling him."

"You, too, huh?" Georgieff grinned. "That bunker has its ghosts."

"I'm going to our room for a few moments,"

Stavers told them. "I'll call our Russian contact, thank him for today and let him know we don't need the old man anymore. If you leave things hanging with the Russians they become paranoid. This way all the loose ends are tidied up."

Anyone interested in Doug Stavers knew he was having dinner at that moment in the penthouse dining room with Tracy North and George Georgieff. So they didn't expect him to return at any time soon to his hotel room. And they would have known about it by listening for any sounds of a key opening the door. Old habits keep a man in Stavers's business alive, and it was habit that brought him quietly into Georgieff's room so that he would enter his and Tracy's room through the adjoining door. And heard noises from within their room. He played it smart.

He called the hotel clerk, gave the room number across the hall from his own room, said someone was trying to break in, and hung up at once. He slipped into the hallway. Less than thirty seconds later two burly men came running down the hall to find the intruder. "In there! In there!" Stavers shouted, pointing to his own room. No one stops at such a moment, and the two men went crashing through the door with guns drawn. Stavers stepped back into Georgieff's room and waited. An explosive roar of gunfire and thudding sounds came from his own room and the door between the two rooms burst open. Stavers was waiting slightly to the side of the door, and he brought the side of his palm whipping into the man's throat. He dropped like a poled steer and Stavers went into his own room, low and fast. One hotel detective was sprawled on the floor with half his head blown away and the other lay against the couch, shoulder pumping blood. He looked up and nodded weakly. "Thank you. There is another on the window ledge outside. My gun. On the floor, over there."

"Don't need it." Stavers went to the bar, opened a bottle of cognac, and poured it onto a small towel. He went to the window, standing away from the opening, and flicked his lighter. The flames curled up slowly and then mushroomed. Stavers stepped to the window, still keeping his body to the side and his arm bent as he flung the blazing towel along the ledge. He heard a thin wailing scream as his would-be killer flailed against the sudden flames and lost his balance. Seventeen stories straight down. That would do it.

He went to the phone and called for an ambulance. The house doctor would get there first. He examined the detective's wound, stuffed a towel against it and bound the shoulder tightly with a belt. "You'll make it," he told the man.

"Heineman," the detective murmured through a haze of pain. "Thank you. You had better watch out for that one you hit."

"Unfortunately, I don't need to. I wanted to ask him some questions, but he's dead," Stavers said quietly.

Heineman nodded, hazy with pain. Stavers waited for the doctor and ambulance crew, the police and the undercover police of the government. He didn't need to ask how much they knew about his trip to Berlin, and they didn't need to ask him. They knew. But why that trip, his visit with the old man, Mueller, should result in an attempted killing by two professionals, baffled them. Stavers could have told him about the Board of Directors in Las Vegas and given them names like Concetta de Luca and Vernon Kovanowicz, but that would only have intrigued them and that was the last thing he wanted. They asked a great many questions and they talked also with Tracy and Georgieff, but when it ended they were as baffled as when they'd answered the frantic call to the hotel. They had nothing to hang on Stavers. He hadn't entered the room to precipitate the shootout—*the hotel detectives had done that.*

"How long will you be in West Berlin?" they asked him.

"We had planned to leave tomorrow morning," he answered.

"To where, if you please?" The man asking the question was quiet, thorough, courteous. The pros are like that, Stavers knew, so he didn't play games with Wolfgang Harttman.

"Dessau. Specifically, to the Junkers factory."

"It is not called that any longer."

"Yes, I know. We're not interested in what they're building now. We'd like to study some historical records on Ju-52 production."

Harttman showed a touch of perplexity. "The Ju-52? That is an ancient machine."

Stavers shrugged. "I like old airplanes."

Harttman nodded. "As you wish. Please report in to the police headquarters there when you arrive. A formality only. We will be able to reach you quickly that way. We may have some questions to ask."

"For Christ's sake, Harttman, ask them now. We haven't anything to hide about what happened here tonight."

Harttman lit a cigarette, calm again. "No, no, you misunderstand me, Herr Stavers. We had a call on our private line from the other side. The police in East Berlin. They are curious, that is all. They wish to know if *you* know why a man named Kurt Mueller was strangled to death earlier tonight."

Chapter IX

Stavers spent the next several hours placing calls to Las Vegas, Indian Bluff, and New York. Many ducks waited to be placed in a neat row. First there was Kovanowicz, and they both knew the call was monitored. The Berlin police, even in West Berlin, were hardly so amateurish as to dismiss as closed the events of the evening. Three dead men and a wounded hotel detective, plus a possibly related murder in East Berlin, all revolving about one man who a long time ago had been in the same city when it was *not* ruled by the Germans.

At the least, intensely interesting. And this Stavers; ah, but he posed disturbing questions. He was a former American agent. He was the very man who had destroyed the top Russian assassination team in Berlin, and now he was back and cooperating *with* the Russians! And they with him!

Too many questions and too few answers always leave government agents upset and *very* suspicious. And hungry for more information.

Stavers's call to Las Vegas was not made directly to Vernon Kovanowicz. He spoke to Gibraldi because he knew the little Italian was swift on his mental feet. When he asked Gibraldi to put him through to the accountant who handled his checking balance, it took only a few moments for Gibraldi to make the connection, keep Stavers on hold, and then put him through to the forewarned Kovanowicz. Stavers had no doubt but that the Czech would interpret apparently innocent remarks. "Would you be certain my contract with the Bertellsman publishing group has gone through? The one for the history on German civil and military transports. We are going to Dessau to check the production records and get what pictures we can, and then we will arrange for a flight to study the records of Charlie Victor Frank Alpha Item. Can you take care of that? The information must be on file by the beginning of the workday. Good. I am very pleased. Goodbye."

Tracy stared at Stavers, absolutely baffled. Before she could voice a question, he scribbled a note to her. "The place is bugged. Burn this note and flush it." She read the note, nodded, went into the bathroom, and closed the door behind her. Stavers's next call roused Hoot Gibson from a sound sleep. He talked with the dumfounded Indian about police armament, told him he could get a really good buy on small and deadly submachine guns for the county department. Gibson didn't tumble to everything Stavers was saying, but since he recorded every incoming call he could replay the tape enough times to get the drift of Stavers's mystifying message. A third call went to Jack North in Los Angeles, and questions were asked about the market for Roumanian wool, custom jewelry, and artifacts from Transylvania. Stavers talked about the current cult wave in Dracula movies and souvenirs, and Jack North assured him they could handle anything he might pick up in Europe.

They took a cab in the morning to Tempelhof. Georgieff left for Dessau as planned, but at the last moment Stavers and Tracy boarded a flight for Rome. The police were at the scene immediately and Stavers greeted Harttman cordially. "Your plans have changed," the police official said curtly.

"Not really. Mr. Georgieff is on his way to Dessau and he'll check in with police headquarters as soon as he arrives, as requested. *We* are going to the Vatican."

"Perhaps you expect to find some of those old transport planes there?" Harttman said.

"Not the planes, of course," Stavers told him. "But Italy flew several dozen of the Junkers trimotors as a major commercial airliner, and we will take the opportunity to mix a vacation with our work, after which we will fly to Dessau where Mr. Georgieff will be waiting for us."

"And who did you say was the publisher for this book, Mr. Stavers?"

"I didn't. But if you want to know that badly, it's the Bertellsman group. They own several major publishing houses in the United States, and here in Germany they own—"

"I know, I know," Harttman said testily. "But I

do not like your leaving Berlin without having notified us of your destination."

"Then arrest us."

"What did you say?"

"Arrest us or stop this silly charade, Major Harttman."

The German studied him carefully. "I never told you my rank," he said coldly.

"We're even. I never told you my publisher. Now, are you refusing us permission to go to Italy? Our papers are in order, and I do *not* want to miss our plane."

The confused police official waved them through. Aboard the DC-10 on its way to Rome, Tracy confessed she was even more in the dark than the Germans he had so thoroughly confused. "Just take notes," Stavers said to her, reclining his seat and falling asleep almost immediately.

They *did* go to the Vatican, to Tracy's astonishment, because Stavers went simply as a tourist, rubbernecking, enjoying everything he saw, and it wasn't until most of their first day was behind them did Tracy realize that not once had the man with her asked directions of anyone or consulted any printed guide. He knew where to go, where everything was located. *He was at home here.* She had no idea he'd been here before. At any moment she expected him to meet someone in the Vatican area, but the day went by and they returned to their hotel. That night, in a small restaurant on a side street she would never have found in a hundred years on her own, they were joined by a very large man wearing a dark blue suit and white tie. He was immense, not portly as she had first considered him. She had also thought him to be fat until she noticed that his enormous chest simply sloped down to an equally enormous stomach, and something told her that beneath that silk suit was a very powerful and dangerous man. That did not make her uneasy; Tracy had grown up surrounded by dangerous men.

"Tony, this is Tracy North. Tracy, let me introduce you to an old friend, Tony Casarotto." Casarotto took a seat and declined dinner. "Cheese and wine," he told her. "It is good for my figure, no?"

"It is good for your figure, yes," she answered in flawless Italian. His eyes widened slightly and he responded in his native tongue. His smile grew broader and with a gallant flourish he took her hand in his and kissed her fingers lightly. She sighed. "I guess I should have known," she said. "You're both in the same business."

Casarotto looked blankly at her. Stavers laughed. "Tony, you don't know her but you know her father, and she can spot us a mile away."

"You said her name was— Of course! Jack North. Yes, I know him well, and the last pictures I saw of you were when you were but a little girl." He was genuinely pleased.

"How did you know my father?" she asked.

"If anyone else asked me that question I would be suspicious," he said, his eyes twinkling. "Would you believe he was once an instructor of mine?" Casarotto turned back to Stavers. "I received your message." He looked around him. "You picked this place well. Like the old days. Very much out of the way. No tourists. And the *policia*, they do not bother anyone here. So long as it is quiet, of course."

"I'd like to keep it quiet," Stavers said.

Casarotto's face changed. The pleasant look faded and his eyes grew hard. There was no unfriendliness in his expression but he had slipped from the warm old friend into his professional rôle. Again it was something most people would never have seen, but, Tracy shrugged to herself, living with Doug and all those maniacs who poured into her home for so many years, she couldn't miss it.

"You have always been a strange man," Casarotto retorted. "How could you wish to keep things quiet when you left dead men in Berlin, changed flights at the last moment—and *knew* that Harttman would notify the local police through Interpol—and then you wandered about the Holy City like a pilgrim who'd made the visit many times. Do you have any idea of how many people had you under surveillance today?"

"Couple," Stavers said with a grin.

"You drove them crazy. You met with no one, you talked with no one, and tomorrow—"

"Tomorrow I visit with the Ministry of Air. As I told Harttman. To look up old records of Ju-52's that flew commercially with Italian air lines before the second world war. I'm doing a book on the airplane. It's really quite a marvelous machine."

"You expect me to believe you are writing a book on an old airplane?" Casarotto was incredulous.

"I never said anything about *you*," Stavers told him as he refilled their wine glasses. "But the story will hold. For the record, everything is true."

"Is that why Georgieff was in Dessau today?"

"What do you mean, *was*," Stavers said sharply.

"He was there, he talked with people, he sent out some telegrams and he left. To Amsterdam, I believe."

"That doesn't figure," Stavers said quietly, "unless George found something we didn't anticipate. Well, I'll know soon enough."

"All right, all right," Casarotto sighed. "Let us get down to what you call the nitty-gritty. What do you need of me besides my charming company?"

"Information."

"Of course."

"On a woman."

Casarotto glanced admiringly at Tracy. "With this one at your side, you are interested in other women?" Tracy flushed him a smile.

"This one is serious, Tony."

"Then I listen carefully."

"Rosa Montini."

He swore he saw Casarotto blanch slightly. There was a sharp intake of breath by the big Italian, who made an instinctive move by looking about him. He signalled to two musicians, placed a high-denomination note in the hand of the mandolin player. "You two. Make music. Loudly."

They knew Casarotto, which meant they knew not to question and also to play loudly. No one would hear anything except at their table.

"You tread in dangerous waters, my friend. You know who she is?"

"She's of the Montini family. I know enough about Joseph Montini. The pope. And his brother, Senato Lodovici Montini, and—"

"Never mind the family tree. What do you know of her now?"

"Just enough to want a great deal more."

The big man leaned forward and his voice lowered. "Tell me what you know."

"That's a condition, Tony. You've never asked that of me before. I wouldn't have liked it then and I don't like it now. Better run a memory tape of things past."

"It is *not* a condition!" the big Italian hissed. "Damn you, Doug, *tell me*. You should know I have a reason!"

Stavers considered his words, the agitation he'd never seen in Casarotto before. "She's part of a paramilitary group supported by the Vatican," Stavers said quietly. Casarotto's eyes widened. "Go on, go on," he pressed.

"The Vatican is very uptight about some unidentified object. No one seems to know what it is or even if it's real. It has powers that have been described as magic, sorcery, impossible, unquestionable, hypnotic, emotional and quackery. Yet there is so much in the way of possibilities that the Vatican appears determined, at any costs, to get its hands on the object which, again, seems to defy description. Rosa Montini is part of a very special group that has been assigned to—"

"The Six Hundred." Casarotto barely breathed the words. "How in God did you learn of them?"

"Ask God."

"Do not toy with me!"

"I'm not, Tony. That's the truth. But what I don't tell you, you can't repeat. True?"

Casarotto nodded. "Yes, yes; of course."

"Tony, for Christ's sake, you're sweating like a pig," Stavers told his friend. He was right. Beads of perspiration had appeared on the big man's upper lip.

"They have greater powers than the torturers of the Inquisition," Casarotto said hoarsely.

"I already knew that about them," Stavers lied. He had hit an incredibly lucky return when he used certain magic words, when he'd said that Rosa Montini was part of a "very special group that has been assigned to—" Tony cut him short there because he'd leaped to conclusions and the expression, *The Six Hundred*, had leaped unbidden to his lips. Which meant he knew a very great deal about Rosa Montini and others like her who were part of whatever this group might be. The Six Hundred. It spelled out its own name and place and organization. A few more or less than Six Hundred wouldn't alter its basic composition. He could guess a lot of it. A paramilitary force had been an educated guess, and bingo, it struck a responsive chord in Tony. His expression, the flaring of nostrils, the tightening of lips, the appearance of perspiration: these were all signal flags to a man who knew what to look for. He knew something else. He and Tony were old friends from a small but savage war. He'd saved Tony's life on at least four occasions. Jack North had taken the young Italian under his wing and saved his life again and molded Tony Casarotto into a splendid fighting machine and one of the best undercover operators ever in the business.

And it all wouldn't mean a thing if he, Stavers, kept pushing. Tony was already walking a line sharper than a razor. Something greater than friendship was involved here. Stavers didn't know what it was, but he knew when to stop pushing, because very quickly Tony would have no room to maneuver and he would have to choose sides. What Doug Stavers didn't like was that he would *not* be on the winning side. Time to disarm the big man, because whatever it was the Vatican had on the front burners, it was bigger than friendship and bigger than life or honor. He had to give Tony Casarotto something to take back to whoever it was, or *whatever* it was, that so dominated his very existence.

"Tell me more," Casarotto said, much too easily. He had regained his composure and of a sudden he was too slick. He was back in his invisible uniform. Stavers had to give him *something*.

"Tony, I've been out of the business for more than a year now," Stavers said. "It's just that when you've been in it for so long you can't miss seeing certain things. This whole book gimmick is just that. A gimmick. There's a real contract, and I *am* doing the book because it's a perfect cover for traveling around the world. I can claim everything on expenses for internal revenue. And I—"

"Why did you go to Kurt Mueller?"

"I'll tell you that if you'll answer a question for me," Stavers parried.

"You will speak first," Casarotto said quietly.

"The answer is easy enough. Kurt Mueller had been a Ju-52 pilot. He flew Hitler several times in one of those planes. He's one of six pilots I've been interviewing."

"And he was with Hitler in the bunker until he died," Casarotto said with a bare touch of acid in his voice.

"*That* is hardly a secret," Stavers said lightly. "It's only in about a hundred books." He counted on the patently obvious to throw Tony off stride for a few moments. One conclusion Stavers had already drawn and that was not to mention *anything* that referred to *yellow fire* or *icy flame*. Some deep instinct told him those words would also spell *death*. He didn't know why, but he tucked it away in the back of his mind for later reference. Now it was time to trip Tony, let him stumble.

"I answered your question." Casarotto nodded. "Now I've got one for you to answer." Casarotto nodded again.

"Why did Montini's group kill Kurt Mueller?"

Tony Casarotto covered himself swiftly, but there had been that fractional lapse, and it was enough for Stavers to detect.

"They did not kill the old man," Casarotto protested. "He was a Nazi. The Israelis—"

"Could have killed him every day of every year for the past twenty years," Stavers said sharply. "The Israelis didn't have a goddamned thing to do with it, and you, my old and dear friend, *are a lying sack of shit.*"

Casarotto paled, anger coming into his eyes. "Don't crap *me*," Stavers said harshly. "I haven't the faintest idea whether Montini or her group had anything at all to do with Mueller being strangled, *but you claimed to know.* And unless you did know something, how the hell could you make the statement that they *didn't*? Oh, you know, all right, and you also know the Israelis, whatever the hell they have to do with this, and *I* sure don't know, didn't kill Mueller. What the hell for? He was never charged as a war criminal—the Russians even look after him, for Christ's sake—so it was someone else. Either Montini's group or some other group, I don't know."

"You really do not know, do you?" Casarotto said cautiously.

"Tony, on my oath, I not only do not know, but I don't know why *anyone* would want him dead."

Casarotto considered the statement and the manner in which he had been offered the words. He was fighting a battle with himself. "Maybe we should let down our hair, Doug," he said finally, sidestepping Stavers's remark.

Stavers nodded. "Okay, take your best shot," he offered.

"I know the so-called publishing adventure of yours is true," the Italian said. "I also know how easy it is to arrange such things."

"You mean Harttman played you the tape by phone?"

Casarotto blinked, then burst into laughter. "Yes, yes, only he believes the book is real."

"He's supposed to believe that. I've already told *you* it was a cover. I hope you'll keep that little conversation to yourself."

Casarotto emptied a wine glass. "As my favorite American television character, Baretta, says, you may put that in the bank." He refilled the glass, slowly, carefully, stalling for time for another question—which in itself must be based on a decision, for the question might reveal too much to Stavers. He held his eyes steady on the American.

"There was a telegram for you at your hotel today," he started off.

"If there was it's news to me," Stavers told him flatly.

"I have it with me."

"Jesus, Tony, that's a crappy way to—"

"No, no; don't be angry. I will give it to you. And then perhaps you will reveal to me your code."

Stavers reached for the paper, unfolded the telegram, let Tracy read it with him. He started to laugh, nearly choked and swallowed wine instead. He tapped the paper. "You really mean to tell me your cryptographic people can't figure this out?"

Casarotto was not smiling. "They cannot. *I* cannot, and I know you and I know Georgieff."

Stavers read the telegram again. JULIETT UNIFORM DASH FIVER DEUCE SLASH THREE LITTLE MIKE SLASH BRAVO ALPHA CONFIRMED WUN NINER THUREE DEUCE STOP HISSO IRON WORKS AND FANS STOP SERIAL FOUR ZIP WUN SIX AND CONFIRMED CHARLIE VICTOR DASH FOXTROT ALPHA INDIA STOP DOUBLE TAIL SLIDE PRINCE CHARMING STOP EXTRA WIDE SHOES STOP DESSAU CONFIRMS STOP OFF TO THE ICE PALACE STOP SAYONARA.

"You're not kidding me, Tony, are you?"

The big man's face grew dark. He shoved a notepad and pen at Stavers. "Write it out, then," he said testily.

"Sure thing." Stavers wrote it down.

JU-52/3m/ba CONFIRMED 1932. HISPANO SUIZA ENGINES AND PROPELLERS. SERIAL NUMBER 4016 AND CONFIRMED REGISTRATION CV-FAI. DOUBLE TAIL WHEEL. PRINCE ANTOINE BIBESCO. EXTRA WIDE TIRES. DESSAU CONFIRMS

THIS INFORMATION. AM OFF TO AMSTERDAM.
GOODBYE.

He shoved it back to Casarotto, who read the
message with growing dismay. "It is about one of
those stupid German machines!" he said. He
banged his head against the paper. "There is nothing secret here!"

Stavers shrugged. "All George was telling me
was that one particular airplane we wanted confirmed *is* confirmed. A Ju-52 modified in 1932 for
Bibesco of Roumania. There's the factory work
number and we would expect the registration to
be what it is. CV stands for Roumania. Do you
know what FAI is? It stands for Federation Aero-
nautique Internationale. Antoine Bibesco was the
president of the FAI, the world group that certifies
speed and distance and other world records as
being accurate or false. The airplane had a double
tail wheel system and wide tires, which was common in those days, and it had three engines made
in Spain. For Christ's sake, Tony, that's our message to continue on to Roumania to get pictures of
that plane and some of its records. We'll go tomorrow. To Bucharest."

Casarotto pushed the telegram back to Stavers
and folded the translation and slipped it into a
shirt pocket. "You are sticking to your story about
the book? I can hardly believe that is the reason
for—"

"We're buying automatic weapons for the Ari-
zona highway patrol and Indian Bluff County. The
Roumanians have the best deal going. And while
I'm at it I'm buying a few hundred thousand dol-

lars worth of cult crap about vampires from Transylvania. They get shipped to Los Angeles. We can buy them in Roumania for a fraction of the price it would cost us to make them in the states."

Casarotto shook his head slowly. He knew Stavers had covered everything, so he quit peeking around corners and threw the next one from dead ahead. "One more question. My last. I swear it."

"Go."

"Who are you really working for?"

Stavers let him have right in the groin, the answer that would *never* be expected. "I really thought you knew. Concetta de Luca."

Casarotto coughed and choked as Tracy slapped him repeatedly on that huge back. Finally he got down some wine. He wiped tears from his eyes and looked with open admiration at Stavers.

"I would have bet a year's pay you would never admit to that. I apologize, my friend! There's no question that you have answered me truthfully."

"That's right, *paisano*. Now you lay one on me. A two-parter." Casarotto nodded for him to continue. "Who really killed Kurt Mueller, and, why?"

Casarotto reversed the tables.

"Your CIA killed him and none of us know why."

Chapter   X

Tracy plied him with questions all the way on the plane to Bucharest. Uppermost among them was the name of Concetta de Luca. "But *who* is she?"

"Obviously, someone Tony knows quite well. By name or reputation. I don't know. But you saw his reaction."

"Where does she figure in all this?"

"You already know."

"I do?"

"You've just learned her *name*, that's all. That was part of my trip to Vegas."

"But why tell Casarotto about her!"

"I make it a habit to tell people the answers to questions when they already know them," Stavers said, smiling.

"And the telegram from George?"

"All real. The only part of that I don't like is his going off to Amsterdam without letting us know. George is a genius and about as careful of his safety as a drunk staggering through a minefield."

She did not ask the next question lightly. "Is George in danger?"

"Based on facts, no. Based on the feeling along the back of my neck, *yes*."

"Same as what killed Mueller?"

Stavers shook his head. "The CIA didn't kill the old man. It was set up to make it look like that. If the Company wanted Mueller eliminated there'd be no way for anyone, let alone Tony Casarotto, to know about it. The whole thing was a finger-pointing job."

"Was it even American, Doug?"

"I hate to think so." He squeezed her hand. "Unfortunately that could be true."

She had nothing else to ask, but Stavers had things to say. "Tracy, I don't like the stink of all this. I like even less having you along with me."

"Try to get rid of me," she said grimly.

"I won't try. I feel better having you in sight in Bucharest than out of sight. No, damnit, don't go sloppy on me. There's trouble there somehow. If I knew what George was doing I'd have a better grip on it."

"Amsterdam spells many things," Tracy said quietly, "but most of all it spells diamonds."

"I know. Fire, ice, yellow flame; somehow they're all connected. George knows that too. He's jumped the gun, gone to Amsterdam without cover. It's much too fast. Berlin to Dessau to Amsterdam, one shot after the other. He's bound to attract atten-

tion and we still have to contact him there. Jack
has sent several people there already. I hope they're
in time. We'll also have some people meet us in
Bucharest. I don't know how but we'll find out
soon enough. Whatever you do, stick to me like
glue."

She slipped her arm through his and squeezed.
"That's easy."

The Roumanian government, like so many political assemblies in the Communist bloc, presented
an old but formidable obstacle. Either you got
nowhere in what you sought or the skids had been
greased and they fell all over themselves to please
you. Someone had laid a great deal of grease on
the rails. True to the stories he had disseminated,
Stavers bought two hundred thousand dollars American of souvenirs to be sold through the United
States as novelty items. Dracula masks, games,
photographs; the usual sort of gimmickry that follows every cult before it finally wanes. And again,
in keeping with the watchful eyes on him, he bought
one hundred and thirty Roumanian-manufactured
Uzi submachine guns, which had been produced
in shameless disregard of the Israeli origin. The
weapons would be shipped with the souvenirs,
palms felt heavy with payment in gold through an
international business agent, and after wasting two
days of this nonsense spending the money of the
Board of Directors, Stavers was able to get down
to his true reason for his visit.

No one ever would have believed he was truly
seeking information on Junkers Ju-52/3m/ba, Werke
Number 4016, Roumanian national registration CV-
FAI. He had made certain an agent of the Bertells-

man publishing organization had alerted the proper keepers of the historical archives to cooperate to the fullest with Stavers. Not too difficult. Roumania's star had waned drastically ever since her leaders fell in with Hitler and sent division after division to be hacked to pieces on the Russian front. And she had remained a Soviet vassal ever since. That accomplished two purposes for Stavers. Being within the Communist bloc, it didn't require much for Vernon Kovanowicz to pass on the word that historical archives must be opened freely to the American who was spending so much money in Bucharest. What counted was the small fortune he had already spent, the very good chance he would spend much more; if the man wanted to indulge in a personal passion of history for old airplanes, cooperate to the fullest. There were a few "or elses" in that message, Stavers was certain, but then so much the better. He had one more thing going for him. If Roumania had little enough of which to be proud in contemporary times, there were those moments when the Roumanian star glittered in international social and political circles. And the brightest of those moments were in the skies, when Prince Antoine Bibesco had been voted by a world group to be president of the FAI.

Stavers and Tracy were met at their hotel by Yevdokia Budilova, a heavyset official with a bristling beard, a fierce smile, and old but carefully mended clothing, clearly a treasured memento of better times long past. "We will go to the archives," he said proudly, "the museum of our history. I understand you are interested in the royal family of the '30s?"

Stavers nodded. "Especially the Bibesco family and their special activities in flying."

"Ah, of course!" Budilova nodded with pleasure. "The two princes and their sister, the princess of Roumania. They were all involved and were famous throughout the world. You are in great good luck, my friends. There is an old woman, an ancient woman, really, at our museum who is in charge of historical records. Her name, my friends, is Simeon Tuleca. She knows more here," he tapped the side of his head, "than you will ever find in the files. She is our living treasure. I think one day we should just let her talk and talk and talk into a recorder. When Simeon dies, a great part of our history will be buried with her frail old body."

"How old is Simeon?" Tracy asked.

"Eighty-seven years old. But she looks not a day over seventy. She is remarkable," Budilova said with obvious pride.

Simeon Tuleca was the art of preservation applied several times over. Instantly she struck them as a rare human being compounded of deep and quiet dignity, a royal grace, and a voice that rustled like the wind in high grass. She was small and surprisingly slender, her hair silvery and kept neatly in a bun. Her only yield to age and tired bones was a cane of intricate hand-worked silver.

Stavers discussed with her his research into the history of the entire lineage of the Junkers Ju-52, famed during the second world war by the name conferred on the rugged machine by German troops: Iron Annie. She nodded, her eyes twinkling. "They also called her *Tante Ju*, for Aunti Junkers." Madame Tuleca spoke with impeccable English, a clear reflection of times when she had worked for the Roumanian diplomatic office in London for twelve years. It made matters much easier.

"You are interested, I believe, in one particular machine?"

"Yes," Stavers told her. "It had the Dessau Werke Number of 4016, and—"

"Speak no further, Mr. Stavers. I know that machine better than any in the world. The designation, I am sure, you also know?"

"Yes, ma'am. CV-FAI. When Prince Antoine Bibesco was the president of the international group."

"Very true. The airplane was named after the country. The spelling painted on the side in large letters was ROMANIA." She sniffed at some almost-forgotten argument. "I personally preferred it should be Roumania. But then," she smiled, "I was still a young woman and had no say in such matters."

"Didn't Bibesco and his party fly the airplane to Germany several times?" Tracy asked, following her agreement with Stavers to split the questions.

Madame Tuleca shook her head. "That would be an answer of both yes and no. You see, the airplane came off the Dessau production line in 1932. Special modifications were ordered for it by Prince Bibesco. Instead of using the engines then available, he shipped three engines from Spain to Germany. Here, let me show you some pictures of the airplane." She displayed them on the table about which they sat. "See? Those are liquid-cooled engines. The German machines for Lufthansa and other customers used either American or German engines, what they called radials."

"Yes, ma'am," Stavers said politely.

"These were unusual. Here, I have some numbers. I will give them to you for your book work. But there is a difference in the engines. Those in the wings were quite powerful, but the one in the nose was especially so. You can see how the exhaust stacks were built to carry the exhaust well behind the engines and below the wings. The prince wanted the airplane as quiet as possible. He even had the cabin heavily soundproofed. See the generators here? They were driven by the wind in flight and they charged special batteries. This machine was like a small train for royalty. It had a kitchen and sleeping quarters, the most powerful radios in the world for its time and, you can see here? These round things? They were special mounts through which automatic weapons were held. Several were for machine guns."

Stavers looked up in honest surprise. "Machine guns? Madame Tuleca, what on earth for? This was a civil machine."

She nodded. "Of course. In fact, in 1937 the prince returned the airplane from his personal use to the main airlines of our country, and these special modifications were removed so it could go into commercial service. But for five years it served on very special flights through North Africa, and down through that continent to the South African areas."

Something was starting to ring a bell in the far recesses of Stavers's mind. He couldn't grasp it, couldn't get a handle on the nagging conviction that pieces were falling into place for him, but he knew something was opening for him like a flower spreading wide its petals. Tracy noticed his sudden introspection and picked up the conversation. "Madame, you speak as if you were very familiar with flying."

Simeon Tuleca smiled and patted Tracy's hand. "My dear, when I was your age I had been a pilot for years. I flew gliders and airplanes and I had made more than a hundred parachute jumps. It was that experience that brought Prince Bibesco to retain me for some time as the manager here in Bucharest for his African flights. That was how I was able to coordinate the ground support for this machine when it landed far from any cities or airfields. My job was to send ground parties ahead by ship and train, from where they would journey in a motor convoy with gasoline, spare parts, and the necessities Bibesco and his crew would require to keep operating in the bush."

Stavers nodded. "Then that's the reason for the heavy gear, the wide tires, and that double wheel for the tail gear."

"Precisely," the old woman beamed. "Mr. Stavers, you are a pilot?"

"Yes, ma'am. And like yourself, a skydiver."

"Excellent. Only we did not have that word then. We were jumpers. Or, as most people called us, we were crazy." She smiled at the memory.

Stavers kept those memories moving. He didn't dare slack off now. "Can you tell me when Prince Bibesco flew into the south part of Africa?"

"Of course. In 1933 and 1934. Remember, I sent ahead the ground parties."

"I do remember, Madame. Could the airplane fly there nonstop?"

"Oh, not at all. It stopped in Cairo, then flew south to the Sudan, always taking on fuel and supplies where they were available."

"Why were these flights made?"

"There were always good reasons. One was to show the Roumanian flag, to present evidence we were a modern nation. Far better to do that with the world's best airliner than with stories about vampires, I must say." They shared the laugh with her and she continued. "Also, Roumania was interested in airline routes. We had many dreams then. And, finally, Prince Bibesco was a great hunter. *Romania* was a flying arsenal. He hunted everything from lions to elephants. That was why the machine was modified with its special engines, the wide tires and that tail gear. It could land on grass fields, riverbeds, almost anywhere. It was truly remarkable." She leaned back in her seat and smiled at them. "You must forgive me. Rare gifts are more rare today than ever before in history. So why should I tell you more about this?"

Stavers glanced at the others and then back to Madame Tuleca. "Please forgive me. I don't understand."

"We were methodical in those days, young man. We kept the best records possible. So instead of wearing out this old voice, I will take you back into the past with me. Yevdokia," she said with a nod to the man who'd brought Stavers and Tracy here, "please see if everything is ready. It is in the next room." She rose to her feet, Tracy's hand out instantly to steady her. "Thank you, child. Now, we will have sweetcakes and coffee, yes? And then I will show you even better than what I can say.

You see, we kept a film record of almost everything we did then. Motion picture films. In black and white, of course, but still excellent. I took some of those films myself. The others were taken by people of the ground teams in Africa, and some by the crewmen of the prince's airplane. Yevdokia will help me identify what you see."

It was incredible, a stroke of luck far beyond anything they had dared to find here in Bucharest. The Roumanians had indeed filmed just about everything they could about the special airplane for their cherished prince. They watched films of the Ju-52 being rolled out of its factory at Dessau, the first test flights, the handshakes and backslapping of the Roumanians accepting official delivery of the airplane, the exuberant crew en route from Dessau to Bucharest. The film changed from that taken aboard the airplane to the people on the ground watching the three-engined transport landing and taxiing up to its hangar. There was the usual pomp and circumstance of the Roumanian royal family, handshaking, hugs and kisses, and then Doug Stavers was sitting very attentively as the film rolled.

The next scenes within the hangar showed further modifications to *Romania*. Bulky radio sets and provisions for long trailing antennas in flight. Kitchen, toilet, work, sleeping facilities. *And the guns;* powerful hunting rifles and ammunition stores. Then a white space flashed to show a splice, and he heard Simeon Tuleca's voice behind him. "What you see now was hidden from the world for forty years and more. When the Germans came to Bucharest in 1941 they searched for this film. It was kept buried in a vault. The Germans believed the film to be in the storage building above the buried vault. The building caught fire and burned to the ground. All the film was destroyed. That is the report given to the German government."

"Forgive me if I seem impertinent," Stavers said. "You do not seem reluctant to show *me* this film. Is there a reason?"

Her smile was wispy. "Because you are here by invitation, my dear. That is why."

"Thank you."

"Look at the film," she said.

They saw the cross-bracing of tubular metal and the sockets to hold lightweight machine guns. "Seven point nine millimeter," Budilova related. "Lightweight, air-cooled, drum fed. Very easy to handle, minimum recoil, fast to reload. A hundred rounds per drum."

Stavers gave no answer. Yevdokia Budilova could just as easily have been testing him for comment. Then Stavers decided too much silence could be misinterpreted. "I've never seen a piece like that. Is it Roumanian?" He already knew it wasn't.

"No. Czechoslovakian. The best in the world at the time. You can see in the film that a mount was placed along the top rim of the cockpit windshield. It took only a moment to drop the gun into position. They did the same in a turret position very far back in the fuselage. There was a metal plate that hinged, a man stood up, dropped the piece into place, and it was ready for use. There were also two side windows on each side of the fuselage through which the rifles could be used."

Stavers glanced from the film to Budilova. "I'm

afraid you've lost me somewhere. I simply don't understand the reason for the automatic weapons. Surely the prince didn't use *those* to—"

Budilova laughed. "Prince Bibesco? No, no, of course not! He would look an elephant in the eye at thirty feet before he fired a shot, and that would be from a bolt-action rifle. He was, what you would call it—"

"Sportsman," Tracy offered.

"Yes, that is it. If there was no risk, he had no interest. The automatic weapons, well, you did not know Africa in those days. The natives were mostly wild tribesmen. They owed loyalty only to themselves. Superstitious children of the jungle and the veldt, headhunters, inflamed easily, striking out at anything strange that frightened them. That is why those weapons were there. If they were ever attacked in the field, in the grassy plains or the dry beds of rivers, they had only one defense. Even superstitious natives will not charge twice into machine guns when they have only spears and arrows."

The film rolled and Simeon Tuleca spoke. "That is the takeoff for their flight well into the southern portion of Africa. The film shows some flight scenes along the Mediterranean, as you can see." She paused, her descriptions more staccato now, matching film scenes. Stavers watched in fascination. That feeling in the recesses of his mind was growing, had been fueled by Budilova's remarks. "They are landing at a desert strip now, taking on fuel and replenishing supplies." He watched trucks driving up, men loading fuel by hand from five-gallon cans, others carrying food and water jugs to the airplane. Bibesco and several men lounged to the side. Stavers noticed they all wore sidearms. The screen showed the takeoff from within the Junkers. There were long breaks between scenes. "They are over jungle now. Bibesco knew what he was doing. He took the coastal route so he could be assured of fuel which could be brought in by barge." More scenes on the ground, each airfield seemingly more primitive.

"They used sound equipment once they reached their destination," Madame Tuleca explained.

Little talking now. The camera was being handled by someone in the back turret so that they could sight forward along the top fuselage of the airplane, see as did the pilot. Grassy plains rolled on forever broken by clumps of trees. Obviously Bibesco was searching for something, and had found it. Black smoke on the horizon. The airplane headed for the smoke, flew low over a band of men and a motor convoy, the men waving. Bibesco used the smoke for his wind indicator and the big airplane settled to the ground, the camera bouncing in the hands of the man doing the filming. Motion stopped and the cameraman recorded veldt on three sides. The last view showed gentle hills and beyond that rock-studded and tree-carpeted confusion. The camera panned back to the trucks and men and for the first time Stavers saw several tall dark natives, *with their hands and legs tied together*. The film ended and the markings of additional splicing showed on the screen.

"Who are those natives?" Stavers asked.

"The Manturu tribe," Budilova explained. "Very fierce and independent. The convoy ran into them earlier and they attacked without warning. They killed four of the truck party." The next scene showed the natives in the camp. A native guide, obviously part of a police group hired by the Roumanians, was questioning the bound natives. The film, old and scratchy, was incredible. The feelings grew stronger; Stavers was straining at some mental leash. He watched the questioning become angry, the bound native spat at the guide, who struck out viciously with a whip that tore open the helpless native's face.

There it is. What I've been looking for, Stavers thought. *There aren't any animals. No head, no skins; nothing. That isn't a goddamned hunting expedition. They're after something else.*

The pattern began to emerge. Bibesco showed intense interest in the interrogation. He slashed at a second native with a whip. *The great sportsman in action*, Stavers thought acidly. The film ended, darkened by the setting sun.

It picked up again the next morning, a long shot from outside the perimeter of the camp, showing the truck convoy loading crates, men checking their rifles. Stavers kept looking for signs that would tell him what— *There it is. They've got all four machine guns ready for business.*

Brief scenes showed the convoy driving off, Bibesco himself in the lead truck. The cameraman started rolling again as the convoy approached a village and the trucks formed a wedge, driving with full speed into the startled natives. If they were fierce warriors, they showed none of it in the blurred, jerky film. Stavers couldn't believe it. They were tossing hand grenades into huts. Booming

explosions tore the huts to shreds, bodies flew
through the air. The film panned wildly from one
scene to another and then stopped at a large building. The leader of the Manturu, dressed in finery
and feathery headgear, came to the building entrance. He stood proud and unafraid, not saying a
word. The shooting and destruction ended abruptly.
It was awesome. The tall, regal native simply standing, then pointing a long, bony finger at Bibesco.

"As you can see," Budilova intoned, "that animal was giving an order for the others to attack
the prince and his party."

"I see," Stavers agreed. *And you're a lying son of
a bitch*, he said to himself, because none of the
natives in sight had weapons at their disposal.
Bibesco started forward several times, stopped,
went forward again, put a hand by his forehead as
if trying to shut out some blinding light and then,
in an act that seemed born of desperation, he lifted
his rifle and cut down the unarmed man before
him. The film showed Bibesco darting forward. He
tore a chain from about the dead man's neck and
turned to rush back to his truck. The film washed
out and ended in the splice.

"There is one more scene," the old woman said.
Stavers already knew what to expect: the camera-
man aboard the airplane, filming the crew tossing
everything not necessary to flight out of the doors.
Kitchen equipment, food, bunks, seats; everything.
"They are emptying the aircraft to reduce its weight.
They know they have a long way to fly. They need
all the range they can get."

Stavers didn't answer. The film seemed to tremble, the camera panned to the engines starting

with great clouds of smoke. Shouts were heard over the engine roar and the camera panned jerkily about to show a solid phalanx of natives rushing toward the camp and the Junkers. More vibration as the machine guns opened fire, sweeping the forward ranks of the natives like a scythe. Then movement, the natives receding as the airplane accelerated steadily. The last scene of the film showed the men of the convoy inundated by black bodies stabbing with spears and slashing with long knives.

"As I said," Budilova went on, "they were worse than animals. Not a single member of the Roumanian ground team survived." The film ended and the room lights came on.

Madame Simeon Tuleca served more cakes and strong coffee. She was the perfect, charming hostess. Stavers understood that to this final remnant clinging to some old and musty glory of Roumania when it stood proudly in the crystalled halls of European splendor, the natives being killed in great numbers, being beaten and whipped, and then falling finally upon their tormentors, were to be dismissed as no more than subhumans. There was not the first indication of compassion, the first sign of regret, in any eye expression or facial reflection. She had before and still to this day simply eliminated them from her thinking, as one might use a shovel to clean a gutter of a decaying rodent. For a while that had thrown him. He was unable to link the seeming honesty of Simeon Tuleca with the complete disregard of the events he'd just seen on the film. The more he dwelled on the matter the better he understood. Roumania's prewar fears of a glowering communism on her borders, her last-moment attempt to select the future victor in the war between the Reich and the Soviets, had culminated in a desperate prostitution of Roumanian principles by allying the country with Naziism. They had paid most dearly for that decision. Roumanian loyalty was ground into the muddy horror of the Russian front when Soviet steel and unforgiving judgement had pulverized the Roumanians on the battlefield and destroyed the survivors in forced marches and slave labor camps. Behind that came the crushing boot of Russian occupation and, ever since those days, living *with* the Russians, who seemed to promise to remain with Roumania for eternity.

What else to cling to but memory? That could also be worked to his advantage, Stavers judged, just as the willingness to display the finest linen from the Roumanian closet had found its expression in revealing this film and its remarkable scenes. So now, with the second round of cakes and coffee, was the time to dig even more deeply. He recalled a film scene and worked *around* it.

"Madame Tuleca, when did Prince Bibesco and his group travel to Amsterdam? I had talked with the Dutch and they recalled that the Bibescos, especially the princess, were exceptional judges of quality gems. Didn't they seek out many of the precious stones for the Roumanian family?"

The old woman nodded serenely. "Everything you say is true. They traveled often. Of course, Antoine's excuse, and it was quite legitimate, was his position with the international body on aviation, the FAI. It took him everywhere. They went all through Europe, from Vladivostok to Lisbon, from the Riviera to Oslo and beyond. They obtained some of the most remarkable jewels, which are still in our state museum. I hope you will see them."

"Of course," Stavers smiled as he replied. He took a deep inner breath. He had stabbed in the dark and it had worked. The elderly woman was infused with the glory of the past; reveling in ancient wonders, she thought and spoke freely. There would never be a better moment than this. He had guessed about the Bibescos and Amsterdam; he had been right. Now to take his next shot.

"What did the prince do with the great jewel he brought back from Africa? When he barely escaped with his life from the Manturu?"

Her eyes lifted as in supplication to heavenly memory. "Ah, the magnificent yellow." Her voice trailed a dusky whisper across the years. "Have you ever seen the perfect yellow of a purebred canary? Not true yellow or gold or copper or bronze or any of these, but a yellow as if the sun were frozen in an instant of time, utterly magnificent, frozen to ice and yet with its fire still pure and raging within? That was the most beautiful, the most stunning crystalled egg of Prometheus, as if he had personally torn it free from the heart of the sun itself. It—"

She didn't complete whatever it was she intended to add as she waxed rhapsodical. Yevdokia Budilova stood before her. "Aged mother, you know you are to take your nap every afternoon." Budilova turned to Stavers and Tracy. "Forgive me, if you will. We love Madame Tuleca most dearly, and we must be certain her health is never strained."

"Of course," Tracy said at once, moving to the side of the older woman. "May I help, Mr. Budilova?"

The coiled-spring wariness that had moved into the room with them eased. "Why, thank you, Miss North, but we shall manage. After the Madame is rested, we may continue this conversation. Now, if you will excuse us, please?"

They waited in the room. Tracy started to query Stavers on the abrupt removal of Simeon Tuleca by her escort, but Stavers smiled at her and gestured for her to hold her words. "Remember when Alice took her trip? It was a real wonderland. This building is magnificent. Cheshires everywhere." She gave no sign of understanding but Doug's point was unmistakable. She had to keep reminding herself she was now in a world where everyone was watched at all times. Alice of course referred to *Alice in Wonderland*, and any trip she took was through a looking glass. So they *were* under observation. "Cheshires everywhere" could only mean that those doing the watching were convinced their presence and activities were not suspected by the Americans.

Yevdokia Budilova returned fifteen minutes later in the company of a very large, thickset man with deep set eyes and a massive set of shoulders seemingly stuffed within a dark blue suit. "Mr. Stavers, Miss North, may I introduce to you one of our finest historians? Mr. Andre Gardescu, at your service."

Gardescu was as much a historian as Doug

Stavers was Peter Pan. The big Roumanian should never have worn three rings on one hand and two on another, especially when the bands had sharp rims and edges that gave them away as fighting rings. They were almost as effective as brass knuckles. It was a favorite ploy of the Portuguese secret police. A man could be devastating with those on his hands. And Andre Gardescu was secret police. Roumanian—which also meant, Russian. The old woman *had* talked too much, then. Now Stavers had to be certain he allayed whatever suspicions had been aroused.

"You are a pilot, Mr. Stavers?" Gardescu would play it cute.

"Yes. For most of my life, in fact."

"You are still active?"

"You mean do I keep my hand in? Certainly. My company has several planes. A Baron, a Rockwell Turbo Commander, and two Learjets. Then we have some machines for fun."

"For fun? I do not understand, Mr. Stavers."

"Warbirds are a big thing in the United States. You know, what we call heavy iron."

Gardescu was puzzled and didn't bother to conceal the fact. "I have never heard of heavy iron."

"That's the way most pilots refer to the warbirds. Fighters, bombers, trainers, that sort of aircraft. The types that were used in the second world war. For example, we keep two Mustang fighters in Arizona—"

"Mustangs," Gardescu mused. "They flew over this country during the war against the Hitlerites. Escorts for the bombers that attacked the Ploesti oil fields."

"That's them."

"And you fly a Mustang," he hesitated, "for *fun?*"

"Yes. There's a Heinkel He-111 bomber at Shiloh Field in Florida that I've flown. And one you may be more familiar with. A friend of mine has an Antonov AN-2 in Virginia. The Russian biplane. A most unusual machine. They use it for dropping parachute jumpers."

Andre Gardescu was way over his head and he struggled to return to the subject that had brought this man and woman together with Simeon Tuleca. "But you are writing a book about a German machine, I understand?"

"The Junkers Ju-52," Stavers said pleasantly. "I'm going to Gainesville—"

"Where?"

"That's in north-central Florida. Gainesville. A friend of mine has a German-built Ju-52 there. The same type of plane that Prince Bibesco flew to Africa and to Germany before he turned it over to your national airlines in 1937. I believe that's the date."

Budilova nodded. "That is correct."

"You say a friend has a German Ju-52, whatever this place is in Florida?" said Gardescu. "However did he find such a thing?"

"In South America. In the Ecuadorian jungle, in fact. It was brought to South America after the second world war, and was used as a Nazi courier there for some time before it was abandoned. After my friend found it, they worked for a year to get it flying again and then brought it to the United States, where they rebuilt the airplane until it was better than new."

"Remarkable," Gardescu mused aloud. "Truly remarkable." He forced himself back into the area where he felt more comfortable. "You made remarkable purchases—excuse my repetition, but the word fits you so well—while you have been here. Especially those automatic weapons."

"Yes," Stavers said.

"You have experiences with these, uh, things, Mr. Stavers?" He was as subtle as a bulldozer in a lily field.

"Of course, Mr. Gardescu!" Stavers came back with a broad smile. "You should know that. After all, we're in the same business, aren't we?"

Andre Gardescu blinked. "What business is that?" He wasn't smiling.

"Why, I thought Mr. Budilova might have told you by now. The secret police, of course."

Andre Gardescu was struck dumb.

Chapter XI

They flew to Amsterdam to meet Georgieff. Jack North and two men were en route from Tel Aviv and they planned to coordinate their activities in the bustling Dutch city. The meeting did not go as planned. Georgieff hadn't checked out of his hotel. But no one had seen the man for more than two days. "It stinks," Stavers said to the others. "This is one of the best-protected cities in the world. Every other pedestrian is the law. They've *got* to be because of the diamond market here. Every police officer in this city is qualified to fill in on any SWAT or commando team in the world. So how the hell did George just *disappear?*"

"Just as important a question," Jack North said quietly, "is *why* he disappeared. Unless he shows up soon, we have to accept that George was either kidnapped or he's dead."

Jesús Ferrer was a dark brooding man of exceptional judgement in affairs of life and death. "If George was kidnapped, it was to get information from him," he added to the conversation.

"What the hell would anyone want to snatch George for? He doesn't know anything worth a kidnapping or a murder," North said angrily.

"We don't know that," Stavers told him. "Look, we talked to Kurt Mueller in Berlin. Nobody had any reason since Hitler blew out his brains to harm Mueller. But he talks to us, and they strangle him. It's big enough for the German paramilitary police through Harttman to notify a lot of people through Interpol. We meet with Casarotto in Rome, and he's already got a file on us and what we're doing as long as your arm. If I hadn't leveled with him about a great many things, and we didn't know one another as long as we do, then Tracy and I would never have gotten out of Rome. Next we go to Bucharest, after finding out that Georgieff has gone to Amsterdam. Obviously someone is tying us in together. Before Mueller's body is even cold it's been blamed on the CIA, and we all know that's so much crap. In Bucharest we get the red carpet. Not too strange after you've laid out some three hundred thousand dollars American with the promise of more. A lot of palms got greased down there. Then we meet with the old woman, Tuleca, and she's straight arrow."

"Tracy? You agree about the old woman?" her father asked her.

Tracy nodded. "There was too much pride involved there for her to be anything but honest. Also, she still had open contempt for the natives we saw in that film, and—"

"Tracy, let that hang for a moment," Stavers broke in. "I want to get back to George and some other pieces. We know that Antoine Bibesco flew to the south of Africa in the '30s. We saw the film, we saw them in action. I don't know how many elephants that man killed, but in the film we saw that the last thing in the world that interested him was ivory. He was after something much more important.

"A few things have already fallen into place. Bibesco was an expert on precious gems. He was also a cold-blooded murderer. I don't know beans about the Manturu, and we'll have to find out fast, but that was a peaceful tribe. I still can't figure one thing. When they hit that village, Bibesco, who was armed, was facing their tribal leader and Bibesco looked like he'd been hit with an axe right between the eyes. Every time that old black pointed his finger at Bibesco he actually staggered. Finally he got that rifle of his up level and he blew the old man away. I *saw* him rush to the body, tear a chain with something attached from the man's neck, and then run like hell back for his truck. They'd already set half the native huts and buildings on fire with grenades. They high-tailed it back to the airplane and took off like a raped ape. In the meantime the village comes after them, a couple of hundred natives, and they massacre everybody in the ground party. The old woman, Simeon Tuleca, sniffs through her nose at all this because those blacks are still animals to her. She's floating through time and space in her memories and I get one crack at her when her guard's down to ask about the object. There should have been violins playing in the background. She talked about something that was the purest yellow, like the sun frozen in an instant of time, a fire of ice, as if Prometheus himself had snatched it from the heart of the sun."

Stavers took a deep breath. "The poetry lesson is just getting going full steam when this Budilova cat gets stiff bristles in his beard, breaks up the romance, and waltzes the old dame off for a nap. When he comes back he's got this Andre Gardescu with him and tries to pass him off as an historian. He's strictly Murder, Incorporated."

"We checked him out," said Jesús Ferrer. "He's their number-two man for Soviet state security in Roumania."

"That's hardly news," Stavers said with more disdain than he wanted to show. "Okay, pieces are coming together. The only two times I ever heard mentioned this stuff about yellow flame and fire from ice was in Vegas, when I met the dead-end kids in the El Cid, and from Kurt Mueller, and *he* didn't know what the hell it meant. But now I've heard it *three* times, and I'm starting to fit pieces together. We all know how dangerous it is to form a final picture from just a few pieces of the puzzle. Was that thing Bibesco yanked from the tribal leader's neck a jewel of some kind? We don't know, but it's a good possibility. *However*, let's suppose it was a diamond. That would mean a rough diamond, and diamonds in the rough don't shine with fire or even sparkle. They've got some sort of film over them. They're dull to the eye and sort of greasy to the touch, and the natives, the Manturu or anybody else, didn't have the tools to work

diamonds as they do here in Amsterdam. So whatever it was that got under Bibesco's skin, it had to
do with more than appearances." He looked around
at the others. "We need to learn more about the
Manturu."

"I've already got that under way," North said.
"Charlie Erickson was in London all day. The Im-
perial Museum has the best records of the African
tribes. He's coming here directly by helicopter."

"Good. Can we make any more pieces fit?"

"I have one," Tracy offered. She turned to the
others. "Before we left Bucharest we toured their
national museum. We saw the jewels of the Roumanian state. Madame Tuleca spoke of a magnificent canary-yellow stone, to put it all together.
Large pure canary-colored diamonds are extremely
rare. The way she spoke of that gem, or whatever
it was, it would have to be flawless, or close to it,
anyway. There weren't any large yellow diamonds
in that collection. I looked for it very carefully."
She shuddered. "I would have asked about it, but
not with that ape Gardescu hovering over my
shoulder."

"A wise decision," her father commended her.

"Well," she shrugged, "that's all I got from that
little tour."

"It may be more than any of us thought," Stavers
said, still fighting to fit pieces together. "The
Bibescos came here to Amsterdam often. Their last
trip here was in 1938, because by then Hitler was
already chewing up Austria and Czechoslovakia
and it was getting decidedly unhealthy for Bibesco
and his group to be traipsing about Europe. But
they didn't quit traveling, if you'll remember. Kurt

Mueller described very clearly that *he* was personally sent by Hitler to meet Bibesco and his group at Tempelhof, in 1940, and escort them to Hitler's headquarters. They had a meeting minus the usual uproar Hitler generated, and then the Roumanians went home. They were still in the Russian camp and then, presto, at the worst possible moment for Stalin, Antonescu and the Roumanian government welcomed German troops with open arms and they rolled a whole swarm of armored divisions into the country. Anybody else care to add to all this?"

"Sure," Jack North offered. "Who killed Mueller? We're full circle and no answer on that one."

"We won't find out *here*," Stavers promised him. "And what do we do about Georgieff?"

Jesús Ferrer gestured. "We have every cop in this town looking for him, Doug."

Stavers nodded. "I know, Jesús, I know."

The phone rang and Tracy took the call. They waited, silent. "That was the airport manager in London. Charlie Erickson's on his way. He'll be landing at the heliport downtown."

"Jesús, you meet that chopper," Stavers directed. "You carrying?"

Ferrer nodded. "It's legal, Doug. Special permit from the locals."

"Good. Take four of them with you when you meet Charlie and bring him right here."

"Four?"

"Yeah. Any more would attract too much attention. I've got a rotten feeling in my belly. A lot of people are paying attention to us. Some of them are Italians and some of them are Israelis, and that's something, Jack, we have to talk about. Jesús, get cracking. Tracy, get on the horn. Get us a flight about nine tonight to London. Everybody in our group. Charter a helicopter or whatever." He slipped her a note and she read it quietly.

Charter the helicopter and then book seats for us on a scheduled flight to London. Use aliases and keep quiet about it. Have the chopper scheduled for takeoff about five minutes after the commercial job leaves with us on it.

Tracy left for the lobby. The restrooms had telephones and that was the safest way to play the calls.

Stavers turned back to Jack North. "You take the part of George. He gets information at Dessau. He confirms everything about that airplane built under order for Bibesco. Christ, it's no secret. It's in historical documents everywhere. He sends me a telegram designed to attract attention, and it does, because everybody thinks it's some code. It's not. He was tweaking a lot of noses, that's all. But he comes to Amsterdam to find *something*. You're George. What in the devil are you looking for?"

"Bibesco and precious gems go together," North said. "So the thing to do is to tie them together in a meaningful relationship, *but in 1938*, because he never came back here to the best of our knowledge."

"So far, so good. What else?"

"Let's assume, just *assume*, you understand, that what Bibesco found in Africa really was a rare diamond. If he did, it was, as you said before, a diamond in the rough. Nothing to look at, but it had something special going for it. If Bibesco wanted it to be something more than a hunk of rock, where would he go to have that diamond cut?"

"Two plus two equal four," Stavers said slowly. "Right here at home plate. The diamond center of the world."

"And the only place to find someone with the skill to cut that stone. Here, or even more likely, in Antwerp."

"*If* it was a diamond," Stavers said, his teeth set hard.

"True," North confirmed. "We don't *know* that yet."

"And we need to find out. Okay, Jack, you're George again. You're here alone, you've found some information that burns the fingers, and you know people are on your ass and they mean business. You're not sure *why* they want to do you in, but you know they're likely to try. They've already done a number on Kurt Mueller. You have this information. What do you do with it? Wait, now. You know we're coming into town after you, but you don't dare keep the information on your person or in your bags or anything like that. You don't even want to be caught with it. You've got to put it in a safe place. What would you do?"

"The most obvious, which is often invisible. And the safest."

"Are you thinking what I'm thinking, Jack?"

"Like Casarotto always said from his TV scripts, you can put it in the bank. He mailed it to the American Embassy with *your* name on the letter."

"Bingo. I'm off to the Embassy."

"Alone? Not smart, Doug. You need eyes in the back of your head. Ferrer's gone for a while, and Tracy's doing her thing. I should go with you."

"How about the hotel security people? You know them?"

"Pretty well."

"Get Tracy up here and then get at least four of those people. A thousand a head. Two outside the door and two inside the room with Tracy until we get back. In fact, they stay with us from then on. Pick people you can trust, Jack. We're right on the edge of nasty."

"Got it."

Forty minutes later they were in the Embassy, discussing the letter with an aide to the ambassador, Sylvia Green. She had the letter that arrived the day before. Stavers identified himself with his passport. "Mrs. Green, may we have the private use of a room for a short while here?"

"That's a strange request, Mr. Stavers."

Jack North presented his credentials. She studied them. "Yes, Colonel North. Of course. Right this way, please." There were no more questions.

Alone, they opened the letter and read with growing excitement. "Bingo," Stavers said softly.

Doug: I have the feeling time is running out on me. Even if I can't pick them out, I'm being followed. I think I've put a lot of missing pieces together. Antoine Bibesco returned from an African trip with what apparently was a very rare gem. It was what is known in diamond circles as a pure canary yellow, one of the most extraordinary diamonds to exist. Bibesco was here in 1938 and on that visit he was closeted with some of the top people in this business. To make a long story short, records indicate they retained the best diamond cutter in the world at that time. His name was Frederik Neilsen. Now, some things don't fit. Amsterdam was *not* the diamond center of the world at all. That was Antwerp. If you wanted diamonds cut you went to Antwerp and that was that. Bibesco figured he would attract too much attention there so he had Neilsen and all his tools and equipment brought by train to this city, and he was kept in complete secrecy within the Roumanian embassy. It must have been a pretty good dodge, because I've discovered that some of our "friends" have been turning Antwerp upside down looking for the information that's been right here in Amsterdam all this time. Bibesco came to this city with a rough diamond of approximately 300 carats. He wanted the diamond cut to a perfect stone, but in a way it had never been cut before. It's called the radiant cut. I've made a rough sketch of it. Anyway, it was a tremendous gamble and it worked. There are no further records of that diamond after it was cut, but I did learn that on his way back to Bucharest, Bibesco and his party stopped off in Geneva. They went to see a man, Theodoreus Horovitz, where he appraised the finest gems for customers around the world. There are no records here in Amsterdam, and certainly none in Antwerp, of that diamond. *But they had the records in Geneva.* They're still doing business at the same address: 3, quai du Mont-Blanc. They don't know a thing about all the smoke we've been raising, and since I was calling from a diamond merchant's office, they were quite free with their information. And here it is. The diamond as it was cut was in what is known now, at least, as a radiant, or by its official terminology, a "cushion octagon modified brilliant." Its measurements were approximately

28.65 × 22.27 × 15.80 mm and, now catch this, it came in at 81.12 carats, *and it was absolutely flawless*! I got some more details. They listed the depth perception at 70.9%, the table diameter percentage at 60%, girdle thickness as medium, and the official rarity grade is flawless. Magnified up to ten times it was still flawless, so that should tell you something. The rather tame description of the diamond is "fancy yellow, natural color, and hue under ultraviolet exposure is faint yellow." Another way of saying all this is that the diamond is absolutely flawless, the rarest stone of its kind in existence, and it is about two and a half times the size of the infamous Hope Diamond. The Horovitz appraisers at the time, that's 1938, placed a value for that year on the diamond as something on the order of $800,000, and their estimate today would be on the order of four to six million dollars. They couldn't say any more because the diamond was never seen again, even to this day, to their knowledge. One more thing. They made mention of their old records, that the diamond was referred to by Bibesco as the "fire of Prometheus frozen," whatever that means, and I recall old Kurt Mueller using some rather fancy descriptions like that, or at least what he recalled from his conversations with Hitler. There was also something obscure about the diamond having a most extraordinary history at some time in its past, but Bibesco apparently clammed up, changing his mind about saying anything more. That's it for now. I'm going to post this immediately because I have the strangest feeling my time is limited. I'll get this mailed and I'll try to leave the city by rental car. I won't check out of the hotel; too obvious that way. Cheerio. George.

"Jesus," North said quietly.

"Yeah. And I think we know what happened to George. Driving a car alone was a stupid mistake. I think it was fatal. We'll call the police and ask them for records of a car accident in which the car and its occupant burned."

North studied him carefully. "You're that certain, Doug?"

"Like it was written in a script. It was the perfect setup. He might as well have painted a bullseye on his forehead. *Damn!*"

North sighed. "Well, if he did, then we're the only ones with this information," he said, tapping the letter.

"Use that colonel routine with Sylvia Green. Have this sent back in a diplomatic pouch. We'll pick it up in Washington."

"Okay. I can use my connections as a consultant with NATO."

"*No.* Jesus, Jack, you can buy almost anyone or anything in NATO. Ask the woman to send it back in some obscure medical or trade reports, just so long as it's buried in the transfer."

They didn't remain the night through in Amsterdam. A shaken Charlie Erickson was waiting for them at the hotel, holding a tall drink in both hands. Jesús Ferrer stood by his side. "They tried to nail him on the way over. We don't know who or why. They were over the Channel in the helicopter when a plane pulled alongside them and sprayed the chopper with gunfire. They killed two people in the cabin."

"Charlie, you get hit?" Stavers queried.

"I was shaking too much. No; no damage, Doug."

"How'd you get away?"

"Rain. Heavy showers to our right. The pilot swung straight into the stuff or I wouldn't be talking to you right now. And I've got plenty to talk about. That group in Africa. They—"

"Stow it for now. Everybody listen to me," Stavers said grimly. "Whoever it is out there is pulling out the plugs and making some very heavy moves. Tracy has everything lined up for us. Grab just what you need and let's go. Keep your eyes and ears open, kids. They're playing this one for keeps."

They made it to the airport without any problems. The helicopter was waiting to fly them to London. Tracy also had reservations for their party of five on a scheduled flight to London. Doug Stavers went to the customer relations office of Qantas Airways. Not even their best people, whoever these people were on their tail, would expect him to parlay with an Australian airlines. "You're Mr. Greg Crewdson?" Stavers asked.

"Right. What can I do for you, sir?"

"First, don't waste my time with silly questions after you hear what I have to say. You fly DC-10's to the States. How many seats?"

"Two hundred and twelve. That's first class and coach."

"What's your average load?"

"Eighty-seven percent. I must say—"

"Don't, please. If you fill all the seats, what's the fare for the aircraft?"

"Um, that would work out at an average of $590 per seat, or, just a bit over $125,000."

"I want a chartered DC-10 to Philadelphia. We'll buy all the seats."

"You can have a special rate for that, sir."

"Never mind."

"Yes, sir. When do you want the flight?"

"One hour from now at the outside."

"You're joking, of course."

"Goddamnit, I am *not* joking. Give me your phone. I'll have the entire amount transferred and confirmed to Qantas in twenty minutes. That leaves only forty minutes more before I want that thing to leave the gate. One more thing, Crewdson. Not a word about this *to anyone* or the deal's off."

"Sir, there's customs and—"

"We're not breaking laws or hiding. We're buying privacy. We're willing to pay for it. Do you have the aircraft and we have a deal or do I go to Pan Am or whoever else knows how to make money?"

Crewdson handed him a telephone. "Make your call. Our people will confirm directly with me. How many will there be in your group, sir?"

"Five."

"*Five?*"

"There must be an echo in here. Just make sure there's plenty of good brandy aboard."

"Yes, *sir.*"

Chapter XII

Jesús Ferrer leaned back in a plush seat of the private salon of the Qantas DC-10, smoking a Cuban Uppman cigar that had made a roundabout trip from Moscow. He held a tall scotch loosely in one hand. The others weren't as relaxed as Ferrer. Charlie Erickson was still wound tighter than a watchspring, and Jack North was worried sick over Georgieff. Stavers already knew by that unmistakable hunch machine he carried between his ears that Georgieff was dead. His only concern was finding out *who* and *why*, and then doing something very bad to the people who'd done in George. Tracy completed the circle; *she* was so obviously in love with Stavers that her concern went in that direction only. Funny, Ferrer mused. Her own father is one of the best professionals in the business, and Jack is still a few steps down the ladder from Stavers, but it's the real killer among them over whom she fretted. Jesús Ferrer didn't like being madly in love. It blinded you, he ruminated. So he did the next best thing. He loved them all and he kept his head clear. He glanced at Erickson. Charlie was coming out of his funk. They needed some information from him. Ferrer had an opener; anything to break this grim mood of silence.

They could have been in a huge opera house with not another soul near them, except for the crew flying and servicing the great trijet. They'd had some food and plenty of drinks, and the girls were told not to show up again until their call signals rang. "One thing about having your own bird on charter," Ferrer said lightly. "You can carry your hardware aboard." He patted his jacket.

Erickson looked at him and sniffed with disbelief. "Crap, man. I went with you through the security gate. You didn't ring any bells or even stir a breeze."

Ferrer grinned. "You're right. I bought some souvenirs, had them marked for the charter flight, dropped the hardware in with the rest of the goodies, and had Qantas personally bring the stuff aboard. With the bird chartered all the way to Philly, who's worried about a hijacking?"

Despite his mood, Erickson grinned. "Neat."

Ferrer slipped right into the opening, noting that Stavers hadn't missed a bit of it. "Speaking of neat, how'd you do in London?"

Charlie Erickson didn't *want* to come back to an issue that had nearly killed him, that had killed a close friend—Georgieff—and several other people he'd never even met. Yet he was also as puzzled as any of the people with him on the big jetliner, because what in the hell there could be in a tribe *now deceased* that was worth all this fuss and all these lives lay beyond his grasp. He sighed and pushed it all aside. That would be for Doug to solve, not him.

"In essence, I can't figure it," Erickson said finally. He sipped on straight vodka. "The Manturu covered a lot of veldt area of South Africa and had their villages and towns mainly in the hilly country. The main library in London has a special section with all sorts of drawn-out reports in incredible detail of visits, colonies, exploration groups. You name it in any language in which it was written and they've got it."

He sipped slowly from his drink, chain-smoking as he talked. "To save all your ears a great deal of battering," he went on, "much of what there is on the Manturu is really a gathering of data. Reports of missionaries, of hunting parties; that sort of stuff. It was all put together and they have, wonder of wonders, a computer system to sniff out any references by name, group, geographical area—"

"Shit, get to the point," Ferrer said impatiently.

Erickson stared into his drink. "Sorry," he mumbled. "Anyway, what I was trying to say is that anything I tell you is really a collection of stories and reports. There's no single authority and we can't ask anyone about them or even go down there for a look ourselves."

Tracy looked blank. "Why not?"

"They don't exist any more."

"Are you serious?" she pushed.

Stavers held up a hand. "Let him spell it out, hon." He nodded at Erickson to continue.

"The Manturu lived in a part of Africa where tribal warfare was commonplace. Everyone did it," Erickson explained. "That was their way of life. One tribe would raid the other tribe to steal wives, cattle, gold—whatever. The mumbo-jumbo about the Manturu, which is the way an English hunter described the stories, is that despite their being surrounded by a lot of bloodthirsty neighbors, no one ever attacked the Manturu."

"You're sure of that?" Stavers asked, surprisingly intent.

Erickson nodded. "No question. That fact, *if* it is a fact, keeps being repeated through all the reports. Everyone about them hacked and chewed and killed and raided, but the Manturu seemed to live in some sort of splendid isolation. And *they* didn't bother attacking anyone else, because they apparently didn't see the need."

"Anyone tie in a reason for all this?" Jack North asked.

"I was surprised to find that an explanation *was* given. All the old tribes, and many of the ones still existing as tribal units, had what was called a magic stone, or a lucky stone. It was always in the control of the chief medicine man or the chief or whoever ran the show for any one tribe. It was kept in sacred places. Caves, buildings; whatever. The Manturu had one of these magic stones, but it seemed they really had some powerful magic on their hands. Not only do the reports on the Manturu refer again and again to their magic or lucky stone, but reports on *other* tribes keep referring to the Manturu and their big medicine.

"You see, most of the tribes in that part of the world would grow to major strength and then over-extend themselves in wars, or be unlucky enough to be invested by powerful white slaving or colonizing groups and had to build up again from scratch. But not the Manturu. Their records apparently go back for about two thousand years when, like everybody else down there, they were an obscure tribe. Then their fortunes turned for the better and they started climbing to the top of the heap and they *stayed* there."

"But without fighting," Stavers said to reconfirm what he had heard.

"Without fighting," Erickson echoed. "That theme also went solidly through the references. They started out in mud and grass huts and little by little they gained strength. What put them in the lead finally was that they didn't go through the winning-losing-winning phases. They kept what they had. Finally the other tribes recognized that something very special was going on with the Manturu and they began to use them as an arbiter of disputes, almost as if everyone had agreed the Manturu were best fitted to be judges for all the tribes."

"But what the hell does all this *mean?*" Ferrer broke in testily.

"It means," Erickson retorted, "that we have a little shitpot of a tribe running around naked until about two thousand years ago, and then that same tribe, in the middle of bloodthirsty neighbors who slaughter one another just for the kicks, manages to stay out of all the wars and battles. In terms of history, that's impossible."

"Any hard explanations?" Jack North said easily.

Erickson shook his head. "Only that magic stone or rock or whatever it is they had. Everything fell apart about forty-five years ago. The exact time is tough to pin down, but that's close enough."

Tracy felt Stavers stiffen at her side. She also knew he was holding back a growing excitement.

"What happened then?" Stavers asked. "That would be about the early '30s or a little later, wouldn't it?"

Erickson showed his surprise. "How the hell did you know that?" he asked. "I never even heard of these people and you're telling me when they started coming unglued."

"*You* told him," Ferrer said impatiently. "Forty-five years ago, remember?"

"Jesús, shut up," Stavers snapped. He turned back to Erickson. "What happened to them at that time?"

"From what the reports say—and none of this adds up," Erickson emphasized to indicate his own disbelief, "the Manturu were visited by a strange race of white men who descended from the sky in a great dragon that could spit death in many directions at one time. The leader of the whites, who lived inside the dragon and carried with him the same kind of magic death the dragon had, visited the leader of the Manturu. He spread terrible fire and death all about him and then he did what no one else had done in nearly two thousand years. He faced the leader of the Manturu. The fables say their battle of the eyes was an occasion of lightning and thunder. The medicine of the white man, which some say was dragon's blood he drank, proved stronger than that of the Manturu, and the white man struck dead the leader of the Manturu. He took the magic stone and fled in a huge animal that rushed back to the dragon. When the natives, the Manturu and a neighboring tribe, found out what had happened, they went mad and raced to reach the dragon to kill the beast and its white masters. Well, they *tried*. When they got to where the dragon was waiting, it roared with a thousand great voices and spat its terrible thunder and flame and more than a thousand brave warriors were slain like wheat before a knife."

"And I suppose," Ferrer said acidly, "that the dragon then flew into the sky and vanished. Charlie, where the hell did you dig up this Disney horror story, anyway?"

Stavers moved his hand abruptly to distract their attention. Even the mild-mannered Erickson had bought too much needling from his own friend, and Stavers knew the next step was Charlie's drink in Ferrer's face and a wild melee on their hands. He wasn't at all concerned about weapons, but both men were so uptight they'd welcome a slugfest. Jesús Ferrer was a vicious street fighter who'd honed his talents in commando teams and mercenary wars, but the mild-mannered Charlie Erickson had been part of an underwater demolition and sabotage team, and his quiet demeanor was all part of his killing pattern. Either man could have seriously hurt the other. Stavers's hand gesture caught their eyes and it served its purpose in distracting them. Stavers clapped Ferrer on the shoulder and laughed.

"Jesús, you're not going to believe this, but everything Charlie just said is absolutely, historically accurate," Stavers told him. Charlie sat quiet, blinking his eyes and not really believing what he had heard. He'd been convinced he sounded like a fool with his oddball story and he was content to be removed from hot water even if he still stung a bit. Jack North said nothing; the old pro always waits to find out more. Tracy *knew*, and since Stavers was carrying the ball, she went along without a word. But Ferrer had a lifetime behind him of utter disbelief and suspicion, which had managed to drag him safely if battered through the worst ghettos and fights of a young and orphaned life. It was one thing being Hispanic; it was another to be the worst kind of bastard greaser who was always told he was less than shit. That kind of survivor is very pliable in continuing the survival pattern, and disbelief of fairy tales is near the top of the list.

"You, too?" Ferrer said finally, still uncertain if Stavers was pulling his leg. Ferrer would rather take a fist to the mouth than be teased by something just beyond his intellectual grasp. Doug Stavers knew that.

"Hey, this is *me*," he said very quietly, and because that was enough for him, Ferrer nodded. That signalled the end of the heat that had risen between them. When Stavers said something straight it was gospel. Stavers had almost made the deci-

sion *not* to spell out the details that were starting
to define the shape of the puzzle. What Charlie
Erickson had told them seemingly made no sense
at all ... unless you had spoken with Simeon
Tuleca and seen those films of Bibesco and his
cutthroats on their African flight and spoken with
Kurt Mueller in the bunker where Hitler died. And
a few other things. But all the pieces weren't yet
visible.

Who killed Kurt Mueller? And why?

And who killed George Georgieff? Stavers was
certain he was dead, but despite the letter from
George, which also began to link certain other
patterns, there seemed no reason to *kill* the man.

And then there was the attempt to shoot down
the leased helicopter bringing Charlie Erickson from
London to Amsterdam. That didn't fit. All Charlie
had done was look up some history on native tribes
in Africa. The point could no longer be ignored:
whoever was behind all this represented major
organizational capabilities and operations. Everything that had happened, the deaths of Mueller
and Georgieff and the near-death of Erickson, all
the other events, were linked through one way or
another. There had been the sharp reactions in
Berlin from the paramilitary police when still further murder had been attempted, and deaths had
abounded, but not where they were intended. Tony
Casarotto, a very good cop and an old friend, acted
as if the devil himself had been breathing down
his shoulder. The sudden suspicions of the Roumanians, representing Soviet intelligence, had flared
when the old woman waxed of historical, treasured moments.

Now Erickson had forged another link from the past. The Manturu had a link with Bibesco and Bibesco had a link with Hitler, and Hitler had nearly ruled the goddamned world, and Mueller had been with Hitler when he died, and now whoever was following those same links had killed Mueller and—

And tried to kill anyone else who was on the trail of the mystery that led inexorably to the last days of the bunker in Berlin.

Through it all, at first always hovering like a floating phantom in the background, had been those vague references to icy yellow flame. Somewhere in this convoluted twisting and turning hid a presence that seemed even now to be affecting everyone involved. A fiery, icy, magnificent yellow. Where could the connections be in the past beyond physical references?

The Manturu had prospered without weapons in the midst of tribes that bathed in blood and gore. *How?* Again and again, Stavers kept returning to the stories of the magic stone, the lucky stone, the tribal amulet or whatever the hell it was. Bibesco had killed the leader of the Manturu and gone to Amsterdam where he imported a diamond cutter and emerged, as the Swiss had related, with the most extraordinary diamond in the world. The trail went cold there except for the Bibesco meeting in 1940 with Hitler—and that madman, with his German forces outnumbered more than ten to one, had nearly conquered a planet. Everything ended in 1945 with Hitler choosing poison and a gunshot *if* those stories of his death were true, and there wasn't any real reason to ignore the facts as presented.

Diamonds had been removed from the bunker before the Russians moved in. Planes flew into the main highway of the bunker and flew out again beneath the muzzles of a few thousand Russian guns. With those planes, Stavers was certain, went the diamonds. The trail ended there. Well, almost; but if it wasn't ended it was damned close to being extinct. Next question: *Who* had left the bunker? Question to follow: Who had what with them, and where did they go? And the next question: Where were they now and how did all this tie in together? And how big was it that the Board of Directors in Las Vegas was willing to lay a cool hundred million dollars on the line for whatever-it-is? Why were people being knocked off? Where the hell did the Vatican fit in here with the name of Rosa Montini? And how were the Israelis involved?

Well, he would find some answers now, he hoped. That was why he'd sent Jack North to Israel. Who else would know more about the location of Nazis who had fled Germany during its death throes?

"The key man is Stan Havorth. He's a fiery Sabra. Deep eyes, constantly hyper, cleft chin, curly blond hair, the muscles of the trained acrobat. But Havorth is a hell of a lot more than an acrobat. He was weaned on guns and knives and fighting for his life. He saw his mother raped and killed by desert Arabs when he was a child, and for the capper they made his father rape his dead wife anally. You might say he's got a roaring abundance of hatred in him. They selected him very well. The world's convinced the Israelis have really slacked off in their hunt for the old Nazis. They got Eichmann, the stories about Martin Bormann are meaningless because even if he survived he would be in his nineties now. So who's left, really?" Jack North paused to light a cigarette and get a fresh drink.

Doug Stavers studied his friend and took advantage of the pause to think of an old airplane now in Florida that had been found abandoned on a jungle road in Ecuador, an airplane that had once carried ex-members of the Third Reich and the new members of the Fourth Reich taking seed throughout South America. Maybe the connection wasn't there. Maybe.

"Who's he after?" Stavers asked North.

"Ever hear of Patschke? Colonel-General Ernst Patschke."

Stavers searched his memory. The name Patschke rang a dim bell, but that could have been nothing more than similarity in names. He looked at Tracy, but she shook her head. Then something came to life. "Hold one. Patschke. Tall, blond, Aryan; archtypical of Hitler's dream soldier. He fought a delaying action against the Russians in Berlin. He had a hundred and thirty soldiers under his command and they killed over four thousand Russians."

"That's him," Jack confirmed.

"But he was a young captain," Stavers recalled.

"Until they told Hitler what he'd done. If you recall your history, Hitler found everyone turning into traitors because they wouldn't fight valiantly and ultimately. He accused Goering of treason and ordered him shot. He was shooting people everywhere, and here's this tall and courageous symbol of German fighting man taking on the Soviet subhumans and killing them left and right. Hitler made him a Colonel-General on the spot. Patschke was just as smart as he was brave. He knew what was happening and he didn't relish being anyone's prisoner. With Hitler backing him and his new rank he could do just about anything he wanted to do. He was close friends with some of Hitler's aides, especially Kurt Mueller, and—"

"*Say that again.*"

"He was friends with Kurt Mueller, and . . ." North's voice trailed off. "Are we talking about the one and the same Mueller? Freshly nailed into his coffin?"

"The one and the same," Stavers said. "Sorry to break in. Go on."

Jack brushed aside any interruption. "To tie it all together, Ernst Patschke was one of the people aboard that Ju-52 that landed outside the bunker, that was intended to carry Hitler to Reichlin where they had those long-range transports waiting to fly him out of Europe. Patschke went into Berlin, went to the bunker, met with Hitler and Mueller and, after Hitler decided to end it all in Berlin, he ordered Patschke out. This is what Stan Havorth believes beyond any question."

"And Patschke got out?"

"That he did. One of those transports, the big Ju-390 with a range of twelve thousand miles, *did* fly out of Germany. They went out at night in poor weather and they climbed to what we know was their operational ceiling of well above forty thousand feet, where there wouldn't be any Allied fighters, and they left for South America. Nonstop all the way."

"And they made it, right?"

"According to our fiery young Israeli, they made it."

"What did Patschke take with him?"

"Anybody's guess. Not much in the way of weight, because of the constraints on load for that big airplane. Most of its weight was fuel, as you might guess. He could have taken anything. Documents, scientific formulas, precious gems—" North studied his friend. "Did I say something dirty?"

"No. You just forged another link in the chain. Let me take a different angle on this for a moment. Stan Havorth is a Sabra, a trained killer, a special agent—I assume he has all the qualifications?"

"We'd be glad to have him on our team, Doug."

"Okay, that's good enough for me. He's a dedicated chaser of old Nazis. Still right?"

"You're still right."

"And he's after Ernst Patschke?"

"He's not only after Patschke, he's got a small goddamned army assigned to him. That surprised me, by the way. Money's tight with Israel. Their defense budget; that sort of familiar story. But they want Patschke *very* bad. Havorth has unlimited funds at his disposal. All the rules for not making enemies for Israel have been suspended if they interfere with his finding that old German and nailing him to the cross, as it were."

"Shit."

They looked with surprise at Stavers. He had pushed himself back with obvious anger in his chair, almost biting his cigar in two. "Goddamnit," he growled again.

"What in the hell did I *say?*" Jack North asked.

"It doesn't fit, Jack, that's what," Stavers said after a long pause. "It doesn't fit and it doesn't compute. Stan Havorth fed you, *you*, of all people, a line of tripe and you bought it, and until this moment, even *I* bought the same story. But it's so much crap."

"You mean Havorth?"

"I damned well do mean Havorth," Stavers snapped.

"Well, then I'll tell you you're wrong," he got back. "That young firebrand is for *real.*"

"You still don't get the point," Stavers told him.

"*I* do." They turned to Tracy. "It's been right in front of us ever since Dad described Ernst Patschke."

"Well, then, perhaps you'd better help your poor old Dad through this mystery," Jack told his daughter.

"Dad, how old was Patschke when the war ended?"

"I don't know exactly, but—" North stopped his own words. "By God, you're *right!*"

"She's right about what?" Erickson asked, almost pleading for the answer.

"Patschke *couldn't* have been more than twenty or twenty-one years old when the war was over," Stavers explained. "That's not much time to be a leading Nazi, is it? And it's not the rôle for a man to play as a mass murderer, or anything that would interest the Israelis *now*. What the hell do they want with someone who was still one step ahead of being a kid when Hitler choked to death? Patschke isn't a war criminal *and he never was*."

North gestured clumsily, reflecting his conflicting thoughts. "And yet," he said quietly, "the Israelis have pulled out all the stops to grab him."

"Wrong," Stavers said with another unexpected diversion. "They don't care about Ernst Patschke."

"Then they're sure going to a hell of a lot of trouble for nothing," Jack said sarcastically. "Unless, of course, they—"

"That's right," Tracy finished for him. "Unless they want what Patschke took with him when he left Germany."

Jesús Ferrer had a cold smile on his face. The search held real promise now. "Could that be the same thing that Georgieff was looking for in Amsterdam?"

"How'd you figure that?" Stavers asked, honestly interested.

"I grew up a thief," Ferrer said with a shrug. "If you are after a man and you don't care if he is dead or alive, then you want something else. His wife, maybe. That does not come into this. Patschke is old. Maybe his late sixties, no? So his wife would be an old woman, too. Not for *Playboy*, anyway. So what else he have with him? Gold? There is too much time between then and now. Money? It would be gone. Diamonds? Like the gold, it would not be kept this long. I know something about the old Nazis in Argentina and Paraguay. Some of my family come from there. They pressed the old Nazis, bled them white. So if Patschke is still around he is smart, tough, and has something very special going for him, and the Hebes, they want it bad. I wonder what it is."

"Give the man a cigar," Stavers said with admiration. "Very well done for a spastic spick who can't put ten right words in a row."

"Careful," Ferrer grinned at him. "I might resemble that remark."

Jack North pushed back to the subject. "The more I think about what went on in Israel, the more pissed I get at myself," he said.

"Why?" Stavers demanded.

"Because I was stupid not to see what I recognize *now*. They knew about you, Doug. They knew you were searching for something that connects with Patschke. *And there was no reason for them to know about that unless you and Haworth are searching for the same thing.*"

"Which begins to explain Mueller's death in Berlin," Erickson offered.

"Maybe," Stavers cautioned. "Just maybe. All of it doesn't figure. Why try to kill *me* without finding out first what I already know? What I might know? It would be a stupid thing to do if I had information they didn't."

"And it might not be them at all," Tracy offered.

"Then who would it be?" her father asked. "Who else *could* it be?"

"Would you believe the Pope?" Tracy asked. She couldn't resist the smile.

"Very funny," her father said acidly.

"That's a nice touch," Jesús Ferrer said. "The Pope. He's got a whole army, maybe. All them good Catholics, they going around spying on everybody and they killing people all over the place, yes? Maybe they should stay with real estate. They rich enough now to buy out half the world. So why would this bring in the Pope, my friend Doug?"

"Maybe it's something worth more than money," Stavers told him.

"More than money? What is worth more than money? That is crazy," Ferrer retorted, sticking to straight-line thinking.

"You ever bribe a priest?"

"What? Most of the priests I know never talk the truth. They screw in the confessional, no? They drink and they fuck and they lie and they use money and—"

"That's horseshit time," Stavers broke in. "Did you ever bribe a priest to sell out the church? To sell his ass and soul for money?"

Jesús Ferrer scratched his chest. "When you put it like that, I guess the answer is no." His face brightened. "But what good would that do anyway? What can a priest want from life?" He laughed as he answered his own question. "To make himself a bigger priest, that is all."

Stavers smiled at him. "Don't stop now, man. You're with it."

"Me? What did I say? A priest wants to be a bigger priest. He wants to get up in the world. He can be a bishop, and maybe even a cardinal, and then they got to make *someone* the Pope."

"And what does the Pope want?"

"Why, everyone knows that, Doug."

"Do they? If the Pope had unlimited power, my friend Jesús, what would he do with it? Rule the world?"

"No. I don't believe that. He would spread the word. He would make everybody listen as to why they should all be good Catholics. They would *have* to listen."

"Right on," Stavers said quietly. "They would have to listen, *or else.* You do remember the Inquisition, don't you?"

Chapter XIII

Cardinal Butto Giovanni was a large man with a face of dead-white skin. The flesh hung leathery from a big-boned frame that now was only a shadow of its former bulk and once-enormous strength, for Butto Giovanni, who once weighed nearly three hundred pounds without any fat on his body, was dying of terminal cancer. He weighed barely a hundred and sixty and the skin draped over his bones where once solid flesh had pulled that same skin taut. Much of his hair had fallen from radiation treatments until he had refused them. To die was not to be refused. It was his message from God. Why prolong the inevitable by causing pain and suffering? It was one thing to endure for his Lord if that was His wish. It was ultimate folly to deny what was there before his eyes, within his body.

Giovanni wanted only to live long enough to realize his dream. His Holiness had assigned *him*, Butto Giovanni, the man from high in the mountains where life remained simple, to head the holy mission of the Six Hundred. That was his assurance of Heaven. He knew his fate, he knew his place above. But to share the inner circle above all else! His eyes shone when he thought of such wonders, and his pale, almost translucent skin seemed to glow as it swayed on his bony frame when he walked. He had a look of death, cadaverous, because his eyebrows were gone and the skin was sunken on withdrawn cheeks and pulled back along his lips until his yellowed teeth stamped a skulled horsiness to his expression. Yet he was not unhappy. His was the ultimate of missions. He walked slowly in his small cell that adjoined the larger meeting room, set all about in thick stone blocks, where the only light in the dark hours came from thick candles, where a man could be closer to God. Here he planned and he worked and he coordinated. Here, now, he waited for Rosa Montini. The ways of the Lord were strange and wonderful, indeed.

Rosa. He had known this stunning woman ever since she was a child of four years. Giovanni had known Joseph who became Pope Pius XII, and her uncle, Lodovici, who held such powerful sway as *senato* in the halls of Roman politics. Rosa Montini of the purest blood, the family known all the way back to the great caesars. Regal. Five feet six inches. Womanly with a full bosom for the children she would one day nurse. Strong hips. Royal blood. Utter devotion, total dedication. A Catholic among

Catholics. Truly chosen. The red lips and dazzling white smile and jet-black hair and a mind that knew only one purpose above all others.

Butto Giovanni looked back and remembered the selection process, the secret naming of the Six Hundred, the promised place of Rosa Montini. A woman could not be Pope, but she could serve as no one else might serve, because no one would ever suspect a woman to challenge this strange and terrifying new world of utter destruction. Sodom and Gomorrah had been obliterated by the sweep of God's hand. Could anyone doubt that Hiroshima and Nagasaki reflected all those centuries before? The glare of a million suns that incinerated two hundred thousand souls, the fires that soared to the upper skies and spat lightning and darkened the earth ... they were a warning, and the Church prepared to survive in this world of imminent nuclear holocaust. There would be a sign, a challenge to be met, a test.

And then the way was opened to them. A most extraordinary event had taken place two thousand years before, and from that event there emerged an object of holiness that would stand even higher than the chalice from which Our Lord drank His wine at the Last Supper. How marvelous that the Church in its own infinite wisdom should prepare for its existence in a world rife with terrorism never before known. A few men today could hold in their grasp the same destructive powers that had been beyond the reach of emperors and kings of yore. Nuclear proliferation was the new abode of Satan, and if the Church was to survive in this world it must meet the tests daily put to it, and it

must fight fire with something *other* than nuclear
fire. With the weapon of Christ Himself: *persuasion*.

They would watch for Christ to give His sign.
For years they had heard the strange tales of a
mighty but subdued power sustained for century
after century in the barbarism of African natives
that had never even known the enlightenment of
the Lord's own ways. Rumor and myth given sub-
stance by an alarming mission of the Hebrews.
Not the ancient ones who muttered and caterwauled
and died for their unforgivable sins, but the new
breed, the fierce Sabra. They had forged a special
team of agents skilled in searching and killing.
The Church became alarmed and His Holiness
sorely agitated to learn the old myths might indeed be true, and that the ancient enemies of the
Church, the Jews seeking their own power, were
hard after what *must* be brought to Rome!

Cassocks, and crucifixes held aloft, were piti-
fully inadequate now. The Lord called, and His
test was plain to see. What had been in the darkest
of Africa must be held by the Papacy. If Rome
failed, the Church would surely fail. Thus the Six
Hundred, selected from the best of a global con-
gregation, taken in childhood to the mountain fast-
ness of Italy and trained for years in every mode of
guerrilla war and instant killing, in espionage and
languages and science, technology and weaponry,
history and psychology.

Rosa Montini and the others bore the touch of
the Holy Spirit. His Holiness had personally given
them final dispensation. In the name of the Ultimate Search they were absolved from all sin, for
in seeking the Holy Grail there could be no sin.

And now Butto Giovanni paced slowly, dragging his feet with enormous effort in his room of stone blocks and stone floor and hard tables and benches and the flickering light of thick candles all about him, waiting for Rosa herself, who had sent word that history had sustained the myths. Giovanni could scarcely contain himself, and he squeezed his bony hands about his crucifix of purest gold, and he prayed for patience and—

The angels themselves must have shaped that face. Rosa Montini came quietly into the room draped in black silk, a slim gold chain and cross resting on her high, full bosom. She kissed the hand of Butto Giovanni, took the seat he pointed out to her, and they sat across from one another. There was wine and bread and cheese, but Giovanni needed food for his soul and not his wracked, cancer-strewn belly.

"I have little time to waste," he said with a brusqueness that caught her by surprise. "Forgive this old bag of bones, child, but it is the word I seek."

She nodded. "As you command, Father." She took a deep breath, her bosom rising with the love of life before subsiding slowly.

"It is real," she said quietly. She heard Giovanni gasp, his intake of breath a dry whistling sound past cracked lips and tormented throat.

"You are certain, then," he said, and she knew he was forcing the words through an overwhelming emotion.

"I am certain," she said, nodding. "You have little time. I will not waste it with the details of our search. But it has been most thorough. We have used computers and agents everywhere. The soldiers of the Church have been busy."

"Never mind that," he snapped.

"Forgive me," she said quickly, reminding herself to stay only with what would interest this dying old man. "The diamond is real. It is not *adamas* as the world knows gemstones. It is not born of fires deep with the Earth's belly. We know that for certain. There is no other stone on this planet like this one."

"How strange to hear a young woman tell this ancient of such things," he said, smiling. Again he remembered his brief remaining tenure in this life and he hurried on. "Rosa, these computers. They answer the question that has defied us all these centuries?"

"They do, Father." He saw the hard fire of certainty in her eyes. "The stone has carried different names. To some it is the Star of Bethlehem." She paused. "I prefer the other name."

He cocked his head to one side, watching her, waiting. She continued.

The Messiah Stone."

"Sacrilege!" he cried. His face paled and she heard the death rattle in his throat. Instantly her hand shot out to grasp his skeletal limb, his skin feeling astonishingly like parchment.

"A stone of *God* among the heathens . . ." His head seemed to loll like that of a rag doll. She steadied him.

"Old Father, please. Be not concerned by the stories of simple savages. God has His own ways. This stone *is* the *adamas*, the holiest of holies." Her eyes lifted heavenward and she spoke now as much to herself as to this relic wheezing air into creaky lungs. "Butto Giovanni," she said tenderly, returning her eyes to look directly into his so that he had the overwhelming sensation he was looking into the face of a saint, "listen to me. It is perhaps the Second Coming."

His lungs gave a great rattle, leathery folds within his chest rustling together, and the almost transparent skin over his gums and teeth stretched in what she knew was a smile. "We have left nothing to chance," Rosa Montini said in a voice that would have gladdened the heart of a statue. "Computers, men, histories, even cave drawings; everything. Old Father, there is no question. There is a way the Lord made clear to us, to turn back time itself—"

She paused. Perhaps he lived only long enough to hear her words. She must not wait. "Butto Giovanni," she told him, squeezing his hands tenderly, "The Messiah Stone, this Star of Bethlehem, *was not a star.*"

He nodded. Something terrible was happening within this man. A tear squeezed from eyes dry for years.

Rosa hurried on. "No one can know from where it came," she said, trying to keep it simple for the old man's comprehension, "but as a messenger from far out in space it collided with our world. It heated from friction and burned, just as you have seen lights in the night sky." He nodded repeatedly, the movement urging her to keep on. "We are certain from historical studies that the object exploded in the air, an enormous bolide that cast its holy light of green over much of the world. The pieces scattered: some into the oceans, others buried forever."

He squeezed her hand in a sudden spasm. "Yes, yes; *go on.*"

"I must say all these things, Father." He gave her an agonzing look. "The temperatures were hundreds of thousands of degrees. The stone from space smashed against a rock outcropping in the deeps of southern Africa. There was another explosion seen all across the continent. The records are clear about this. And this second collossal blow created the stone like none other on this world."

He swallowed to force air through his throat. "It is the sacred stone of the heathens?"

She nodded. "Yes. The Manturu. The tribe that lived without war for nearly two thousand years."

"Do you believe the stone could do this?" he croaked.

"There is no question, Father."

"What else do you believe, child?"

"There is all justification for faith, holy one." Her face took on a glow of purity. "I think of this incredible stone hurtling through the void for eons untold, destined to meet our world *just* at that time our Saviour was born. How can this be an accident, a mere coincidence? Impossible! Our Creator moved all in time and space so that the star would flare in the heavens at precisely that moment of birth. The star that blazed in the heavens was no distant celestial orb, Father. It was God's message."

"The great diamond . . . the heathens, they used this to protect themselves," he said slowly, foam at the corners of his mouth. "While they had this

God-given star, no one could stand against them. Ah! The gem that softens the hardest steel by making the enemies of the holder unable to heft their weapons." His eyes contracted in pain. *"Bring the gem to Rome!"*

"Others also pursue this stone," Rosa whispered, unwilling to upset the old man.

"We *are* Christianity. The *only* true Church. We must have the diamond!" He spat up bloody bile, and alarm filled her. "With full humility and steadfastness, child, this stone will renew God's work on this world. The Papacy must reign supreme or all will be lost." The coughing subsided. "You say there are others who seek the holy stone?"

She knew his memory had yawning spaces. "Yes, Father. The Israelis. An American group, supported by their government."

"Ah, the bastards. Their bombs are not enough." More coughing.

"There is another group. No government is involved. We believe they seek the holy stone for profit," she said slowly.

"Judas reincarnated," he snarled. "Where is the holy stone now?"

That was what she had been trying to learn for more than a year. But some answer was needed. "We look for a German. Ernst Patschke. Somewhere, we believe, in South America."

The old man startled her. Butto Giovanni met her eyes. "He is there. You will talk with Joseph Bonoveccio who keeps the records. Tell him he is to withhold nothing from you. Ernst Patschke fled Germany and went to South America. Later, we sent him a passport and documents behind which he could hide for the rest of his life."

Rosa felt uncomfortable. She was utterly devoted to her cause, to bring to Rome the startling jewel sought with such desperation. But to hear Butto Giovanni, as she had heard others like him, speak so off-handedly about providing passports and documents to the most infamous of Nazi sadists and butchers was still beyond her pale. She chose emotional security in telling herself that such matters lay beyond her understanding, but she had never been able to completely dismiss the uneasy sensations when the matter came up. Well enough, then. If Patschke was the one she sought, she would welcome the chance to wipe *that* slate clean. The life of the old German was no more than a piece of crusty bread. What was one more life in a history dripping sodden and heavy with the blood of saints and martyrs?

"What about the filth who try to steal the diamond?" Giovanni's rasping tones snapped her back to the moment.

"There is that powerful organization in the United States desperate to obtain the holy jewel. They have hired a man. His name is—"

"You disposed of the German?" Giovanni broke in.

"Yes. Kurt Mueller. We discovered he was talking with this American, Stavers." She sighed lightly. "But we could bring on his death only after he had met with Stavers. The police blame the CIA."

"I care nothing about that. Why is the American still alive?"

"He is unbelievable. The most thorough and professional man in this business. We have killed several of his people. We are certain that if we eliminate him, the organization he represents will be of no further concern to us."

Butto Giovanni shuddered until Rosa could almost hear his bones creaking. "Child, listen to me. Find your most dangerous opponent and kill him. And if you cannot kill him, *use* him. Never forget you are joined in the holiest of crusades, you are—"

Wind rushed through his throat and blood poured from his nostrils. The old hand squeezed hers painfully and became stone.

Rosa disengaged her hand slowly. She bowed in respect to the old form and the grandeur now departed. Then she left to meet with Joseph Bonoveccio, who knew where Ernst Patschke lived.

So she could kill him.

Chapter XIV

The huge DC-10 slid down from forty-three thousand feet with hardly a tremble. Far beneath them the moon sprayed cold silver along a deck of thick clouds, a pale alien world. The pilots checked the details attending their descent from the stratosphere to a stretch of concrete glistening with rain and barely three hundred feet below the clouds. The Qantas jet with Stavers and his group followed the invisible electronic pathways unerringly through those clouds to the Philadelphia runway. Everything went as smoothly as any routine approach. The DC-10 followed the three-degree descent slope to the long runway. A quarter-mile from the concrete span the crew began to see the ragged edges of the clouds and the flashing lights beckoning them true to earth. They crossed the threshold in exactly the right position, the airliner flared its main gear, and as the nose wheel met wet concrete a large fuel truck hurtled from an access road directly into the path of the right landing gear.

The long strut extending beneath the great jetliner smashed into the curving metal of the fuel tanker, tore through and sprayed volatile kerosene outward in a mushroom of imminent disaster. It took only a split-second more as the gear buckled, a wing dropped, and metal scraped violently against concrete. Only for a moment did the dinosaur scream of metal tearing into concrete sound above the thunder of the jet engines. Sparks flew, the fuel ignited, and a great booming roar punched across the airport.

A moment later the fuel tanks of the jetliner's right wing also exploded, tearing open the fuselage, sending a sheet of flame through the cavernous body. The DC-10 ripped in two, twisting at the break where the wings met the fuselage. The passenger cabin floor buckled, twisted, wrenched violently. Seat fastenings broke free under enormous pressure, and Doug Stavers felt his own seat snap loose. He had a crazy view of the world spinning end over end and only dimly realized it was he doing the spinning. He saw a river of blazing fuel spear through the cabin of the airplane with its thrumming explosive roar. He knew the blazing torrent now plunged into that same area where he'd been seated. Then the world went crazy with bone-bruising acceleration and deceleration. He heard metal screech close to hand, above the sound of roaring flames . . . and then he jerked to a stop. *The screeching metal had been his seat sliding along*

the wet runway, and he was now lying on concrete a
hundred yards in front of the blazing mountain be-
hind him. He released the belt holding him to the
crumpled seat. He didn't believe it; everything in
his body moved in response to command. He was
on his knees, shaky but competent, and then on his
feet and his eyes were wide with horror as he
screamed Tracy's name again and again until his
voice faded away and only his mouth worked without sound as his beloved vanished from all human
form in that terrible crematorium. The battered
nose of the DC-10 was close by with the decapi-
tated torso of the pilot, and next to him a hand
moved against a pane of bloodstained glass. He
galvanized himself to run, not thinking. The flames
were curling up into the broken-off nose section,
but he pushed his way through torn metal, ignoring the cuts and gashes, to reach the copilot. He
released the seat belt and shoulder harness, grasped
the unconscious man under his arms, and dragged
him with enormous effort back from the mangled
cockpit. Stavers heard sharp crackling sounds and
knew fuel was still pouring into the huge cabin.
The inferno about him could instantly become an
all-engulfing holocaust. He forced himself to keep
moving and managed his way outside the crumpled nose. Now he could pick up the man and
move on to a safe distance from the burning plane.

The copilot made a strangling sound and died in
his arms. Stavers stared at him, hollow-eyed and
disbelieving. A moment later savage fire howled
and heat struck him with physical force.

Instinct now ruled every move. Stavers *knew* he
was now the only survivor; behind the cockpit the

aircraft was thick with roaring flames. He heard sirens and saw the flashing lights rolling so slowly and ponderously and utterly uselessly, to the flaming sheets painting everything in ghastly bright firelight. He didn't think any more; deep survival instincts ruled his actions. He'd seen that fuel truck. He knew what had happened, even if details and clear thinking were yet to come in the days ahead. He was marked for killing. He reached down and removed the wallet from the copilot's pocket, replaced it with his own. He bent down again, tore the wings from the dead man's shirt, ripped the copilot's epaulets from his shoulders. He was now as much a dead passenger as he was a crewmember. Flames snapped angrily at him like demons demanding their final victim. Startled, he saw blazing fuel pouring from the aircraft in darting rivers. Fire licked at his feet, washed about him. He covered his eyes and ran blindly from the holocaust, flames already curling along his clothes. Suddenly he felt impact, heard voices shouting at him. Icy cold smashed against him as a fire extinguisher reached him with full force, he felt and saw a thermal blanket wrapped about him and felt himself being dragged away. Moments later a huge gushing *whoomp!* hit his back and the rescuers' as the final explosion lifted the burning wreckage and then stamped on it with a mighty boot. The gear collapsed completely and wreckage sank down into its own pool of fire.

He knew rescuers were between him, between his own body and the ultimate consuming flames. His brain seemed to work in pieces and sections, one corner knowing he could no longer move his limbs under command, another brain section telling him to let go, let go, let it all go, man, they've got you now and you're safe, they'll take care of you, *just let it go, Stavers*, and another very cool and logical part of his mind told him that there's a time when even the toughest and the meanest of us *must* yield. He did. He let it all hang out, gave up body and soul to the unknown hands saving his life, and then *the other* barriers that raised automatically in his mind came crashing down and he knew what a Godawful mistake he had made.

He knew it when he heard the scream, a scream nearby so loud, so filled with torment and agony it burned his own soul and ripped at the muscles of his own throat and not until he felt his body twitching and his muscles going *snap!* and *jerk!* and *bang!* did he realize the scream was his own voice and what he heard was himself calling out to and for Tracy. The realization swept through him as though he were another person and it came through all in one ultimate shriek of pain and love and hate and longing. Tracy was dead. The finest part of him, the human part, the part that could love and even verbalize it without caution danced its fiery end in roiling, flame-destroying flesh. At that moment his own subconscious knew that Doug Stavers must have surcease or the mind would snap. Mercifully, the lights went out and Stavers slipped into total unconsciousness.

Paul "Hoot" Gibson drove into Philadelphia with a heavy heart and a face drained of life. He still couldn't believe it had happened. Doug could survive anything thrown at him. People had been trying to kill that son of a bitch for years. People who were professionals, and they'd failed; the trail was littered with uncounted bodies of the professionals who'd paid the price of failure against Doug Stavers. And then a stupid fucking truck driver didn't think and an enormous machine tore apart and—

Christ, what a way for someone like Doug to go. And with him the girl, that lovely incredible woman he'd known since she was a laughing, happy child. As bad as it was about Doug, at least death had been part of his life. But not Tracy! And Jack, and Jesús, and Charlie. What the hell was going on? Georgieff was missing and presumed dead. Other bodies had been strewn in all directions. He'd read of the old German being strangled in Berlin and knew that Doug had been there, but that wasn't Doug's way of— *Shit! Just shut up, Indian, and do what you came to do. Pick up the coffin with what's left of your best friend and take him home. Take him out into the mountains of the desert and bury him with your ancestors. Doug will like that.*

He drove to the mortician's building. Why the hell did places for dead bodies have to be so goddamned manicured with perfect grounds and trees and everything so goddamned neat? It bothered him. Death was more than mowing lawns and stuffing bodies into boxes. He grumbled as he heaved his great bulk from the motor home. He was going to bring a truck, but he felt better about Doug's ashes riding inside the motor home with him. They'd be together a bit longer that way. He went inside the office, identified himself, asked for the coffin. "Don't tell me no stories or how sorry you are," he said in a gravelly voice to the breathing zombie in the office. "I got a vehicle outside. All I want to do is back it up and load the coffin, and I'll be on my way."

The zombie had been through this and every other known variation of dealing with death. "Yes, sir," he said. He placed a form before Gibson. "Sign here, please. Receipt for the body and coffin. All expenses have been taken care of by the airlines, sir."

"That's fucking great of them," Gibson growled.

"Right around in back, sir. There'll be someone to assist you."

Gibson pulled into the service entryway, opened the emergency exit for the motor home. They knew what to do, anyway. A man in a dark suit was pushing hard against a wheeled platform with a coffin resting on top. Fucking hippy type with long hair and one of those stupid moustaches drooping down the sides of his chin. He didn't want the bastard even touching the coffin, but he needed help. Together they pushed and heaved the coffin into the motor home. The creep rolled the platform back into the mortuary and Gibson stood quietly for several moments, breathing deeply. He climbed into the driver's seat and started the engine, looking up in surprise as the long-haired mortician climbed into the front right seat.

"Get the fuck out," Gibson said menacingly. He didn't know who this creep was or what he wanted and he didn't care. He even hoped there'd be trouble. He had a lot built up inside him and he wanted to feel bones breaking under his hamlike fists. The other man coughed into a handkerchief, spitting and hacking, and mumbling something about getting off just outside the gate.

"You don't get off I'll kill you," Gibson said, starting out of his seat.

"Drive the goddamned thing," the other man said quietly, and Hoot Gibson's heart stopped beating and he *knew* he was going to die. *It was Doug's voice!* Gibson sat stupidly behind the wheel and drove through the gate and the stranger beside him removed the wig and the false moustache and Gibson stared at Doug Stavers and drove into a ditch. Stavers yanked the wheel to pull the motor home back onto the road. "Drive. I'll talk," Stavers said.

"I had to do it this way, Hoot. Sorry. But a lot of people want me dead. Only one of those people matters. She believes I'm dead because she thinks everybody but the copilot died in that crash she arranged. Her name is Rosa Montini and she's the sweetest, most beautiful, utterly devoted Catholic you ever met, and she set up that crash. Don't leave your mouth open like that. The copilot died in my arms. I switched wallets with him. We're carrying *his* ashes back there. He did me a favor. We'll bury him in the hills, except that everybody but us, and maybe a few other people, will think you're burying your old asshole buddy."

"You son of a bitch," Gibson told him. He was crying.

Chapter XV

This time Doug Stavers went in through the lobby entrance of El Cid Hotel. No dramatic rooftop landing, no need to impress anyone. He attracted curious glances, not because of his own presence, but because of the fat old woman with scraggly hair and shuffling gait who kept hurrying to keep up with his long stride. He was expected. The woman who ran the computer complex deep beneath the garage in Indian Bluff had made a call directly to Concetta de Luca. "A meeting is required," Kathy Sloan told the woman who ran the Board of Directors.

"Required by whom?" came the icy response.

"The holy spirit." That was all Kathy had to say; understanding was immediate. "*He* will be there with an old woman."

"Why would he—never mind," de Luca snapped. "When?"

"Three hours from now. Thank you for your attention, madame." As instructed, Kathy hung up.

Stavers knew the flap that would ensue. Concetta de Luca and the other four members of their private council *knew* Doug Stavers was dead. News reports, pictures of the crash, the identification, the burial ceremonies; all of it. They'd written him off. Monte Hinyub smiled when they discussed the matter. "You went too far with Stavers," he told them. "You've retained me as your director of security. You got yourself a mythical hero who sells himself to the highest bidder. I warned you about him."

"Shut up," Harold Metzbaum told him with utter indifference. "I notice *you* danced to *his* tune on the rooftop. That makes you a great deal of mouth and very little action, so until I request your opinion, keep quiet. I'm not interested in your gloating or your recriminations."

Hinyub kept a cool face to the sudden thrust against him. They paid him very, very well. It was worth eating what the fat toad offered. "Yes, sir," he said. Metzbaum nodded with satisfaction. "However, you do remain aware of your position with us. Do *you* believe he's alive?"

Hinyub was impressed with his own importance but he was no fool. "I don't believe he is. However, there's no way to know. That accident could have been set up."

"Are you serious?" Benito Gibraldi said with scorn. "He arranged an accident that exploded and burned an airliner landing in stinking weather, and he *arranged* for his seat to break loose and be catapulted out of the exploding wreckage? What kind of idiot are you?"

"The seat was found. Stavers wasn't in it. Only the copilot lived," Hinyub said in a careful monotone.

"You see only to the end of your nose," Vernon Kovanowicz said impatiently. "A passenger seat is found on the runway, there is no body found by the seat, and the man in the cockpit is the only survivor. *Think*, you clod." Kovanowicz turned to the others. "There's no question that accident was caused deliberately. But it was intended to *kill* Stavers. Once again he's proved he remains an icy chameleon even in the fires of hell."

Concetta de Luca studied him carefully. "*You* believe he is alive?"

Kovanowicz laughed. "Believe it? I *know* it! If not by facts, then by faith alone. I know this man, Concetta, I know this *type* of man. He does not succumb easily. And it will be he who walks through the door." He glanced at his watch. "In three minutes. He will be punctual."

"What's this business about an old woman with him?" Gibraldi asked.

Kovanowicz shrugged. "As soon figure out the devil."

"I'll meet him downstairs at the elevator," Hinyub told them. He started for the private elevator door.

"Stay here," Kovanowicz ordered. "The last time Stavers was with us you dawdled on the roof. And don't remind me about what he did up there. I know, and it was real. So this time *be here* when he arrives. You've informed the guards to let him through without delay? Good. A cognac will whittle away the last moments."

His glass was barely on the table when a wall speaker chimed and a voice announced the private elevator with a man and a women was on its way. The doors opened and they stared, hardly believing their eyes. *Stavers.* No question of it. Kovanowicz couldn't restrain himself. He rose to his feet and met Stavers directly, shaking his hand with an iron grip. "I know this is crazy, but I *am* very pleased to see you here."

Stavers met his eyes. "I'll tell you something just as crazy. I know it. Thank you."

"You had no problems with the, ah, arrangements in Berlin and Roumania?"

"None. Your presence is undiminished."

Kovanowicz slapped him on the shoulder. "We should have worked together. Thank you. Please, your seat." He looked at the waddling dump of a woman with her dirty clothes and stringy hair. "My God, why did you bring her? I can smell her all the way from here." Then he remembered with whom he was talking. "I'm sorry, Stavers. Anything she wants. I'll have a chair brought for her."

"No. She'll stay by Hinyub. He's your security. She's mine."

Disbelief showed in their expressions. Kovanowicz chuckled and returned to his chair as Stavers took the same seat he'd occupied the last time he was in this room. The Indian woman shuffled close to Hinyub. She rocked back and forth on her feet, nervously twisting a strand of braided leather in her stubby fingers.

Stavers looked at the group. "I don't have much

time. Certainly no time for amenities. Very soon I'll leave here with a special team. You don't know who they are and there's no need for you to be informed. However, you're paying the bill for many things and I'm prepared to tell you certain information. Understand, it is not *everything* I know. I decide what's told and what is not. Do we agree?"

Concetta de Luca leaned back in her chair and smiled. "We made our agreement the last time," she said, almost purring. "Please continue."

"What you seek is real," Stavers announced. Except for the computerized Alberto Grazzi, who never showed emotion in this room, his words struck them all with visible force. Gibraldi leaned forward, hands pressed so hard against the conference table that they were dead-white.

"There is no question?" he asked, his voice shaking.

"Please don't waste my time by having me *repeat* things. It *is* real. I know where to look, and I'm going after the diamond. What the Vatican calls The Messiah Stone."

"Then it *is* a diamond!" Kovanowicz cried in triumph.

"I know *of* the jewel. There's nothing else in the world like it. It's more than a jewel, as you already suspected. I don't believe it's a gem in the sense that we know diamonds. There's more for me to find out, but what matters is that it really does have extraordinary powers. Many people have already died for or because of it. Kovanowicz, here, was right. The Israelis are after it. The Papacy itself is pursuing the diamond, although in a different way and for different reasons. The two forces have already clashed. And there's an American team actively in pursuit of the stone. All those are facts I've now confirmed to you."

"You give us much to hope for," Metzbaum said in his forced voice.

"I haven't delivered *yet*. I came here to tell you what I've already said, and also to tell you that the woman I love died in that plane crash. Tracy North. Her father along with her. And two other very close friends. I do not take that lightly. Kurt Mueller is dead. My friend Georgieff is dead. People I know have died. All this is behind me, but the lesson is implicit. The CIA didn't kill Mueller, *or* Georgieff, or anyone else. The strongest of the groups after the diamond, the Godstone, is responsible. Kovanowicz warned me; he was right. The Six Hundred. I confirmed that in Rome. Rosa Montini is a name I've burned into my mind."

He reached within his jacket. Five people watching him from their seats stiffened. Hinyub started forward and then stopped as Stavers withdrew a slim cigar and lit up slowly and deliberately, allowing the seconds to pass by almost audibly. He watched the cigar tip glow red, then pointed it casually at Concetta de Luca. "Madame, this Montini woman. Do you know her?"

Concetta de Luca smiled. "Should I?"

"You are being clever and above all else you're now a fool," Stavers said, deceptively calm. "We have a business arrangement, de Luca. We are *not* in business together; I don't work for you. Perhaps you don't understand these things, so I will—" Concetta de Luca rose to her feet, face contorted in fury. Her voice was almost a hiss.

"No man, *no man*, talks to me in that tone!"

"Concetta de Luca, I don't give a shit if you stand or you sit. But I'll tell you this. Your life depends on your answer."

She whitened, returning slowly to her seat. As much as this man frightened her, the broad grin on Kovanowicz's face frightened her even more. He was enjoying the moment, and that meant to de Luca that her life was indeed threatened. She had the feeling that if she misled this incredible man before her she would never leave the room still breathing.

"No. I do not know her. I know of her family. That is all. Now, you answer a question."

Stavers nodded.

"Why do you ask me your question?"

"Because someone in this room led Rosa Montini and her band of killers to me. That same someone knew of our earlier meeting. They knew everything about it."

"None of us have revealed a thing!" Gibraldi protested.

"Do you know Rosa Montini?"

Gibraldi shook his head. "Only by her name."

"Metzbaum?"

The fat man chuckled. "*Me?* Unless she came here—" He shrugged to dismiss the idea.

"Alberto Grazzi. How about you?"

Grazzi shook his head. "Don't stay dummy with me," Stavers warned. For the first time he heard Grazzi speak.

"I do not know her. She's not of my affairs."

"Then there's only Kovanowicz, isn't there?" Stavers said.

The Czech was not frightened, which told everything to Stavers. "If I didn't know you better," Kovanowicz said, "I would think you were serious." He scratched his chin. "We were the only people at that meeting. *I* am the only one who really knew of Rosa Montini and the Six Hundred, and certainly I don't want the Catholic bitch to succeed. Then who would have led her to you? No one else here knew her. And no one outside of this room at that time—save perhaps yourself, Mr. Stavers—could have revealed your presence, your purpose, to the Papacy."

"You're wrong."

"Am I indeed? Then who was it?"

"You've just told me. Your security man. Your own trusted, faithful Monte Hinyub."

"He's lying!" Hinyub stepped forward, the gun leaping into his hand from a spring shoulder holster. Stavers didn't bother defending himself. The old woman sidestepped behind Hinyub and in a blur the braided leather jerked tightly about the man's neck. A powerful knee slammed into the small of Hinyub's back, freezing him as the leather cut cruelly into his neck. His tongue protruded and he choked and gasped, but the grip on him was inexorable. The gun fell from his hand and his face began turning purple, eyes bulging. The old woman's hat fell away and they saw her more clearly now. The muscles straining powerfully told them the sham. "No one move, no one interfere," Stavers warned.

He waited until Hoot Gibson held a dead man by the leather knotted within his fingers. Gibson let the body fall. He flung away the wig and stepped

free of the dress over his buckskin clothes beneath.
Before a word could be said, a Bowie knife ap-
peared in his hand and he dropped to one knee.
Steel flashed, blood splashed on the carpet, and
Gibson stood with a crimson scalp in his hand.
"You don't mind, do you?" he said to the group.
Alberto Grazzi threw up.

"What's this all about?" Gibraldi asked in a
hoarse whisper.

"Let Kovanowicz tell you," Stavers answered.

The former KGB man sighed. "I must never forget my own lessons. Hinyub knew everything that
went on in this room. The tapes, the films. He
played them back. He must have sold his information for a very high price. *He* made the contact
with Rosa Montini."

"But why?" Concetta de Luca asked in protest.
"He had no need for the money! And if he did, we
would have met that need!"

Kovanowicz looked at her as if she were a child.
"He was mad for you. You rule all the men in your
life. Except this one," he finished, nodding at
Stavers. "Hinyub couldn't take that. He couldn't
live with the way he was made to stand like a
child on the roof when Stavers came here by helicopter. So he struck back. What we wanted most
of all he was prepared to prevent. Stavers, thank
you. I never liked rodents."

Stavers stood before them. "I will have a list
sent to you. Names and addresses. Mueller, North,
Georgieff, Ferrer; others. Every one of them was
murdered by Hinyub, even if indirectly. See to it
that each family receives three hundred thousand
dollars. The money comes out of your funds."

"Agreed," Gibraldi said at once. He stared, fascinated, as Gibson dropped the scalp into a leather pouch at his side, and then carefully wiped the knife clean on the dead man's clothes.

"What now?" Kovanowicz asked Stavers.

"Now? I have a job to do." He went directly to the elevator, the big Indian following. Neither man looked back.

Chapter XVI

Killing Hinyub didn't erase Tracy from his mind. He had believed it would. Having the Indian perform the rite was almost ceremonial. Stavers also knew the danger in vengeance fulfillment on too intense a personal, emotional level. Oh, Hinyub would—*must*—die. No questions there. He would have died in a particularly grotesque and extremely prolonged horror except for Tracy's face hovering within the shadows of Stavers's mind. He knew she would never have wanted that. *Just do it.* He swore he could hear her voice and not for herself. *He killed my father. Get it over with.* Stavers came as close to praying as he ever had, that time would shroud Tracy and diminish her presence within him. She deserved her own peace. He swore he'd give her that final rest. As a start, he left the country.

Stavers took four of his most efficient killing machines with him to South America. Hoot Gibson was especially important. He had intense personal reasons for going, and an emotional charge could add greatly to the job before them.

He called in three other men. He'd fought battles and wars with all three at different times and in different countries, and he *knew* their qualifications. When they committed to a cause they gave their all. They were an international legion who might sell their talents and skills, but when they *offered* it formed a pact of unmoving steel. None held allegiance to any political entity. Their world was what they made of their code of honor.

Toshio Matsumara flew in from the still-virulent jungle wars of southeast Asia. He had fought in Vietnam and Thailand and in Cambodia *and* in wars unannounced in Burma; he had soldiered in Malaysia. He was friends with war. That he was still alive said everything. Toshio was a chemical warfare expert with jelly mines, poison gas, and every type of incendiary and explosive device one might imagine, including those he could cook up on the spot from seemingly innocuous materials. He was, it seemed, made of barbed wire and steel cables woven tightly together. He had been weaned in martial arts and the dirtiest kind of street and knife fighting. He had lived through a dozen bullets and assorted bayonets and nearby-exploding shells and bombs, and he'd come through it all with the scars to make him tougher than he'd been before. He was pure killing machine.

Skip Marden was a different breed with all the attributes Stavers required: skilled in close combat, expert with weapons, and an absolute lover of fighting. Even more than of whoring, at which he had established his own unsavory and yet enviable reputation. Skip towered six feet seven inches tall. His idea of fun was to climb into a wrestling ring, unknown to the other wrestlers before his appearance, and rid himself of pent-up emotions by battering a man half to death. And it was legal; he liked that neat touch. He didn't look his weight of 270 pounds because he was solid knotted muscle. All this served to conceal the fact that he was the best pilot Stavers had ever known. He flew helicopters to jets to airliners to fighter planes. It didn't matter. If the damned thing could fly, then Skip Marden could fly it like a demon. He was deadlier in a combat ship than ten ordinary men. He took chances that defied the laws of gravity and survival. Like the others he'd been bombed, shot, burned, and stabbed. He even had numbers tattooed by his scars. He liked that. The numbers were climbing. It was a race. He wondered if he'd run out of numbers or years first.

Joshua Logan completed the group. Josh was a Mormon who'd been thrown out of his church, unceremoniously dumped. He'd objected to certain scripture or perhaps the way it had been presented to him. He mumbled "Shit, just shit," in church and his father smacked him on his ear. There had been years of youthful protest in Josh, who wanted to join the marines and get the hell away from this saintly mumbo-jumbo. His father was a big man and Josh was only seventeen but the family was of good stock. Josh climbed to his feet and smiled and then he hit his father in the mouth and about his face at least thirty times in a blur of stone-hard fists before the old man even had a chance to defend himself. His father fell bloody and unconscious and neighbors interfered, and the whooping Josh leveled at least another dozen before he went down beneath fists and boots and sheer weight of numbers.

He came to in a hospital, skin scraped and torn, a tooth loose, and amazed that he didn't hurt. That was when he discovered his amazing tolerance to pain and injury. He was almost insensitive to it. He *liked* to fight and he laughed when he was hit. He left the hospital and he joined the marines, and because he was both amused and fascinated with what made people willing slaves of high temple priests, he studied religions and was delighted to find just how really bloodthirsty were the powerful, dominant faiths. He also became a marine paratrooper and then a special warfare expert, and he gained proficiency in the fighting weapons of every country where such weapons were made. He had an affinity for weapons. He caressed them, took them apart and put them back together in darkness, knew instantly by the heft and touch of a weapon what it could do. When he fought it was with exuberance and style and he didn't give a damn if he was killed. Which adds a touch of charm to that kind of man.

Doug Stavers took them by company jet to Brazil. No one would expect them to land *beyond* his intended goal in Ecuador. For that was where Colonel-General Ernst Patschke, or whatever he called himself now, remained hidden from the world. Stavers flew to Brazil and sent the jetliner back to the States. Then, loaded with equipment marked as a surveying team searching for minerals and ores, he flew with his men in an old Convair airliner of a Brazilian mining company to Talara on the Peruvian coast. Talara was a hotbed of thieves and smugglers and a key waypoint for drugs flowing northward to the United States. Talara had a very specific law. You paid the going rate for what you wanted, and nobody knew you'd ever been there.

In Talara they moved into an aircraft hangar at the far end of the sprawling airfield, on the edge of jungle and well concealed by trees. They waited for a night of clouds and rain and Stavers passed the word to a freighter cruising slowly off the coast. The message was to have Bill Elliott fly their Nighthawk helicopter to Saraguro. It was a shitty little town across the Peruvian border within Colombia. The right people had already been paid to ignore anything they heard about anything going on at Saraguro. Even the natives would recall nothing. They would be too busy counting more money than they'd ever seen in their lives.

Stavers and his team drove in a Peruvian army truck convoy to the border and then beyond to Saraguro. They unloaded their equipment and moved into a ramshackle building to wait. The army trucks left and no one knew they'd ever been there. "Everyone is always armed," Stavers told his team. "*Always*. And always keep one in the chamber ready to use." They nodded; they understood. "Injun, you go down there and you talk to the people in this outhouse they call a town. You hunker down with them and you do it in their lingo. They're already scared to death of us and they know we can wipe out their whole place in thirty seconds. They'll be glad to know you're human. Find out what you can. Some of the equipment we're carrying didn't seem to surprise them too much, and that can only mean other people, *like us*, have been in this area before."

Gibson slipped away into the night. He was gone for three hours, and by the time he returned Stavers was almost ready to go after him with flamethrowers. Hoot came back with his clothes rumpled and stains on his shirt and trousers. He shook his head to an offered bottle of scotch. "If I have anything more to drink on top of this native hooch I'll be dead before sunup." He sat on the floor with his back against the wall of the shack. "You were right," he told Stavers. "It paid off. I'm not a white devil, and they think I'm from a town upriver. They didn't figure on Arizona and I didn't tell them different, because when they accepted that we were blood brothers, their tongues got loose. We must have killed three jugs of their local brew. My God. My head is splitting."

"Goddamnit, get to it. That chopper is going to be here in an hour and I don't want to waste any more time. I'm not sure where we're going to find our wandering Kraut, and—"

"*Pasaja.*"

Heads turned to Gibson. "What?" Stavers asked.

"*Pasaja,*" he repeated. "It's taboo country, or whatever the hell they call forbidden territory down here. My Spanish lingo isn't the same as theirs, but I got the drift of it."

"Pasaja," Stavers said, echoing the name. For an instant he almost described the huge flattened mountain he knew so well. But that could be self-defeating. If your men believe implicitly that you know the ground better than the man who's leading them, they go quiet and you lose all the advantages of their own feelings and knowledge. Stavers blinked and shook his head.

"Pasaja," he repeated. "It just doesn't figure. First off, where is it?"

"Thirty miles in a generally north direction. Mountain country, but not like the high Andes," Gibson told him.

"That's why it doesn't figure," Stavers explained to his group. "Every indication we have, and I know the Montini group, and probably the Israelis as well—"

"You're forgetting the American task force," Skip Marden interjected.

"Sure. They could be following the same leads," Stavers agreed. "But that points overwhelmingly to some kind of eagle's nest high in the Andes. A high mountain stronghold. Top of steep cliffs. Barely accessible. And there's nothing like that where you're pointing, Hoot."

"There's one advantage to being an Indian who fought the roundeyes for so many years," Gibson said smugly. "And one of those advantages is to have learned what defensive positions worked against the cavalry. A real high point was for shit. You had the high ground, but much too often you couldn't get off the damn place. You had to carry all your food and all your water and when you ran low, because they had thousands of troops ringing the place, you were in deep shit. The women and children started to die. You had to get out. You discovered your mountain fortress had become a prison and you were caught. So why shouldn't Patschke figure the same way? He was a top soldier. He fought some of the toughest battles of the war. The *last* thing he'd do is let himself be bottled up with no way down. Then, with the stuff that could be thrown at him, a real mountain fortress makes a hell of a beautiful target. I think the Pope's legions or whoever they are, and the Israelis *and* the Americans, don't believe he's done that, either. The Israelis have been hunting the old Nazis more than forty years. They'd know better."

"He makes sense," Skip Marden said. "Any eagle's nest today isn't a defense. You can't live there without generating some kind of heat. That means a thermal signature that stands out like crazy to infrared scan. *If* this American group is as well equipped as I think they are, they've been searching this whole area with U-2's or some birds like that, at night, looking for infrared giveaways. They've got satellites and everything else going for them. Patschke would have to live like a mole and eat cold refried beans and I don't believe he's been doing *that*. If I had something going for me I sure as hell would go first-class. Wouldn't you?"

"We're not talking about you or me," Stavers criticized him.

"All the more," Marden grinned back. "You and me, what the hell, we're happy with beer *or* champagne. Don't matter. I never knew a German, *any*

German, who wouldn't go for the brass ring when he had his shot. Patschke will follow the mold."

"That has validity to it," Stavers admitted.

"Well, whoop-de-do for you," Marden told him. "You sound like a talking machine. You forget your gut feelings? We're on a manhunt, baby, pure and simple."

"No. It's a manhunt, but it's not pure and simple. Patschke has more than thirty years of surviving behind him. I've done a lot of homework on this Kraut. All of you, listen to me. This man was a superb soldier: dedicated, courageous, everything. And a hell of a fighter. He didn't stay in the lowly ranks. Even if it was a last-ditch move, Hitler recognized him for all time. That's a lot of confidence building. He also made it out of Germany when all the wolves were tearing open its belly. He's been in several countries in South America and he's still alive and well. He's been hunted by bounty hunters, drug dealers, local military, and mercenaries. He's survived double-dealings, even by overzealous Israelis when they went after the war criminals. A lot of other people have been after him. He's kept up with modern weaponry. He's done all this without major forces backing him up. So he's better than smart, he has a survivability index that's out of sight, and he can withstand just about everything thrown at him. All this means, people, is that he has *something extra* going for him, which is why everybody is now after his ass."

"You tell me what that something is," Josh Logan said quietly. He smelled a weapon here, a force, whatever; he didn't like weapons about which he was kept guessing. Once you understood a weapon you could beat it. A rock would pulverize you if you didn't know it was coming.

"The best I can tell you," Stavers said to his four men, "is that Patschke escaped from Germany carrying some kind of huge yellow diamond. We're *not* after the diamond for its monetary value. That would be crazy, even if the thing is worth millions."

"How big? Description, please," Matsumara requested.

"Good point. No one knows who'll come across it." He described the gem to them, described the reports of the incredible flashing incandescence that poured from the stone, the past words of icy yellow fire. "Let me make something else clear. From what we've learned, the diamond has strange powers. That goes back to when it was in the hands of the Manturu a couple of thousand years ago. To cross a lot of history, it was brought to Hitler, and supposedly it was responsible for keeping in line his generals and politicians who didn't agree with him. In some way it increased the dominance of his personality. It's never been described as a *control*, but more for its effect, and the longer you're around the damned thing the more effective it becomes on the people within visual reach of the man wearing or carrying the diamond. That's what we're after."

The men shifted their body positions, glancing at one another. Finally Josh Logan gestured. "Well, you just blew one beautiful theory, old buddy."

"Do tell." Stavers waited.

"A question keeps popping up in my simple Mormon mind," Josh said to Stavers and the others. "It's so simple, no one seems to have thought of it. You say this Patschke cat was never a war criminal."

"Right."

"So no one's really been looking for him."

"I didn't say *that*. The refugee organizations, different governments, headhunters like us. Patschke was known to have left the bunker in Berlin with diamonds. That big transport could carry a lot of stuff. There could have been all sorts of industrial papers aboard that plane. The Germans used coal and tar to make a beautiful refined kerosene that let them fly their jet fighters at six hundred miles an hour. No petroleum of any kind. They did a lot of stuff like that. Someone left Germany with those papers. They've never been found. They could be worth billions in today's world."

"It's all too pat," Logan said, sticking to his position. "Even if everything you say is true, why the hell would a man like Patschke stay in outhouse country like this? He doesn't have to *hide*, for Christ's sake. This place is for jaguar assholes, not for someone who has some kind of powerful personal magnetism and diamonds and may be sitting on a fortune of industrial secrets. Damnit, Doug, it doesn't add up. He's got to be here for other reasons as well."

"Jack North had a theory," Stavers replied.

"Hell, tell *us*, man."

"His theory was that Patschke was rebuilding

what Germany had built in South America before the war. That he's been training people for his final day of judgement, when he'll make his move to consolidate all the governments of South America. At that time, with everybody neatly in a row, he'd become their super-potentate. Not a ruler, but the man behind the throne who pulls the strings. Patschke has stayed in South America to establish clearly he's got his heart, mind, body, and soul with these people, that he's not the white devil here to exploit them. *If* he had those industrial papers, he has something to offer; and *if* that diamond can do what we believe it does, he can make it work. Maybe that's why the Israelis are so hot to nab his ass and that diamond. That could well be. As for the Six Hundred behind Rosa Montini, it's pretty clear they see the diamond as critical for the church, that it's from God and they're sworn to bring it to Rome."

"What about the American government?" Matsumara asked.

"Shit, our people would sell their souls and a left testicle to get *real* synthetic fuels, Toshio," Marden answered. "The long-term question in Washington is, if we can't get a synfuel program going, where do we start the next war?"

Josh Logan waved for attention. "Doug, this is turning into a roundtable, which is a bunch of shit when the safety's off your weapons."

The others nodded as Josh looked from one to the other. "So the big question is this," he went on. "*How* has Patschke held off everybody all this time? *What* has he got going for him? Defenses,

scouts, systems—*what?* I know you, old buddy.
You didn' t come waltzing down here in the blind.
There's five of us and he could have three thousand
working for him, all *very* well equipped, and he
could have something on the order of Gibralter
behind which he waxes fat and comfortable. Apparently he's not worried. I mean, what the hell,
we can take on five hundred people and we can do
them in. That still leaves the odds in his favor. He
knows who's after him. He's got the Israelis and
that bunch of super Catholics *and* now an American government that wouldn't hesitate to blow
away where he's holed up. After all, not even
Gibralter can take a hydrogen bomb in its belly.
All you got left is slag. He can't defend himself
against *that*."

"Agreed," Stavers said. "Anything else?"

"Yeah. Do you really believe this crap about
some sort of supernational government in South
America? Sounds pretty far out to me."

"That's exactly what they said about Hitler's
dreams for a Third Reich, back in 1932," Stavers
said quietly.

"Yield, yield," Josh said, gesturing to dismiss
his question.

"Anybody else? Anything else?" Stavers asked
again.

Hoot Gibson looked up from where he still
sprawled on the dirt floor of the shack. "You look
like the cat's about to be dragged kicking and
screaming from the bag, roundeyes."

"True." Stavers glanced at his watch. "Bill should
be here with the chopper in about twenty minutes.

Okay, here's what I've set up. We've got to be the guys who are on top of the hill, where there's a very big dam. We face odds down below of a couple thousand to one. It's no use just getting inside, like investing a fortress, because our goal isn't to kill everybody in the place and blow it up. *That's always been Patschke's real defense.* They can't afford wanton killing and destruction, because it would eliminate everything they're after. And 'they' includes anyone like us or Montini who want Patschke alive, or, at least, everything he's been hanging onto all this time. Let's get back to the top of the hill and the dam. We're too few and too small to move the mountain. But if we uncork the dam, what happens? We start dumping a few billion gallons of water. They have to scramble and they start blaming one another. We watch and we wait. It's a bit of an around-the-corner metaphor, but I think you get the general idea."

They nodded their agreement.

"Hoot, old friend," Stavers said directly to Gibson, "I owe you an apology. I sent you down into that village to collect fleas on your carcass and drink the native rotgut not because I needed information about Pasaja, but because I wanted to confirm something."

"You knew about Pasaja?" Hoot asked.

"It's an old secret military field from the second world war. Built when we figured the Germans were going to invade Brazil from Dakar in North Africa. Pasaja was a staging base the Germans wouldn't be able to crack."

"What's so special about it?" Marden asked. "And how come no one knows about it now?"

"You said yourself our people have probably combed this whole area with U-2's and satellites, using infrared scanners, remember?" Marden nodded. "Well, infrared isn't worth beans looking down through a perpetual cloud deck. Too much moisture and soaking up of thermal signatures. Still with me? Good. Pasaja is more than a town. It's a plateau twelve thousand feet high. It lies atop a huge swamp around its base to the west. The prevailing winds come in from the ocean full of moisture and they pick up more heat and moisture from the swamps and up the stuff goes to meet cold air on the top of the plateau. If there was ever a case of perpetual cloud cover, Pasaja has got it. The winds blow across the plateau with a lot of strength, and they're consistent. So despite the high altitude for operating aircraft, you've got a built-in wind factor of twenty to thirty knots, and you can operate at that height for landing and taking off with no sweat. The *big* trick isn't getting off, it's landing. With a ceiling of always three or four hundred feet at the most, you've got to come in under radar or an advanced instrument system. From everything we've learned, Patschke operates throughout South America from Pasaja, using local radar for GCA. The people on the ground just work him in all the time. I wouldn't be surprised if his teams have the new radar-bounce system. It's like ground-controlled approach managed from the cockpit. But all that doesn't matter as much as what Hoot told me, that confirms that's where we'll find Patschke. In a bowl of fog atop a plateau two and a half miles high."

"What are the approaches like?" Logan asked.

"Steep, covered with heavy growth."

"Neat. If you're on top."

"He probably has the place honeycombed with tunnels," Toshio Matsumara suggested.

"Wouldn't you?" Marden said to him, and his friend grinned.

"So how are we going in?" Logan persisted. "You said Elliott was bringing in the Nighthawk. What's its operating ceiling?"

"Twin turbofans," Stavers replied. "It'll hover with a full load at twenty thousand."

"It's a beaut," Marden said. "I've flown it."

"That's why you're here, sweetheart," Stavers told him. "Among other reasons."

"So we got this super chopper," Toshio said quietly. "What good does it do us? They could pick off anything with the right missiles from your mountain, Doug. Including us."

"True. That's why we set up everybody else."

"How do you mean that?"

"I've made certain that the right people know where they can find Patschke. The group under Montini has been working its way down from the eastern side of the high plateau. That's river country. They probably have a few hundred people all ready to die in the glory of the all-high, which is fine by me. They know about a loading shaft. It's almost vertical, six feet by six feet, that goes up the eastern slope. They brought supplies up that way by winch during the war. To our Catholic friends, that's their way up and inside. They're *very* good and they're ready to die if that's what it takes to get Rosa Montini's hands on Patschke's throat and get that holy grail from him. They'll be carrying enough explosives to blow away the top of the place if that's the only way to do it."

"That's the Montini group," Hoot said. "What about Havorth and the Israelis?"

"They're going to meet head-on in the river country," Stavers said quietly.

Marden whooped with laughter. "Beautiful! And they'll cut themselves to pieces. That leaves one winner, the one we have to deal with later."

"Wouldn't it be wiser to let them attack that place *and then* chew on one another, like dogs fighting over a dead cow?" Gibson would always think in terms of Indian fighting, but there was nothing wrong with that. This might be South America, but it *was* Indian country.

"Ordinarily, yes. I see your point, Hoot. The more dead bodies down in the river country, the less firepower against the plateau."

"You got it," Gibson said, waiting, for he knew there'd be more.

"You all knew Jack North was CIA?" Stavers asked his men.

"Who isn't at one time or another?" Marden asked with sarcasm.

"That was his cover. Jack was part of an international organization, headed by our government, to hold down the lid on nuclear proliferation. You know the routine: building nukes in your back yard, or stealing them, or whatever. The whole idea is to keep the bandit governments and terrorists from using nukes for blackmail or wholesale slaughter or even starting a nuclear war between the big boys. When they get hard information about any such nukes they put together a strike team and they go in, fast and hard, and to hell with the casualties."

"Oh-oh, I can smell this one coming," Logan murmured.

"All Mormons have clever and devious minds," Matsumara cracked.

"What did you do?" Logan asked.

"Before we left Europe, and it's fortunate we did it at that time, Jack North filed a Class One emergency report with this group. It's code-named 'Trinity.' A touch of whimsy for the first bomb in 1945, I guess. Anyway, Jack got direct input with the computer. While we're here jawing with one another, there's a hell of a Trinity strike force on the way down to Pasaja plateau, every man jack among them convinced there's three or four nuclear warheads concealed within that mountaintop."

Matsumara winced. "*Ooph*. Talk about Pearl Harbor."

"When do they move in?" Skip Marden was suddenly all business. This was his meat.

"They've been told a Communist force from Venezuela is also after those warheads," Stavers explained.

"Holy shit," Matsumara said with disbelief. "Did you write this whole scenario yourself?"

"I had some help from Jack," Stavers smiled.

"Goddamnit, forget the fucking credits," Marden snapped. "What's the rest of the drill?"

"Force Trinity is coming in with forty chopper

gunships loaded for bear. They plan to put two hundred men onto that mountainside and atop the plateau. They're going inside for those bombs. And Patschke, of course."

"Do we get the Trinity force and the people in the river country to tangle?" Logan questioned.

"Yep."

"How?"

Stavers lifted his head as he heard the Night-hawk approaching.

"You'll see," he promised.

Chapter   XVII

Two helicopters; that was all Stavers needed. Nighthawk was a deadly bitch with a Vulcan cannon that spat 2,400 rounds of explosive shells a minute. She hauled sixteen rocket pods plus incendiary and chemical launchers. Forty-eight small missiles each not much bigger than a good cigar but with micro-electronic guidance and the new RX7 plastique explosives that made them the deadliest shooting gallery in *any* town. The second chopper was a Bell Viper with Colombian Air Force markings. It would come in and get out as quickly as possible to the northeast with Elliott and a second pilot aboard.

They'd be Stavers's skyhook alarm bell, with onboard radar to alert them to the first sign of Force Trinity. The American strike team would work from a big carrier off the coast, but they'd have to climb high enough to give the Viper a sharp echo on the alert radar. The moment he had them confirmed, Elliott would radio Stavers that company was on its way.

Stavers and the others watched the Viper swing away and start its long climb, shrinking to a tiny dot over the thick jungle. Stavers turned to his men.

"Josh, Toshio, Skip; set up point around this area. Now that our bird has come home to roost, I don't want any surprises. Hoot, you and I have something to do."

The three men moved into flanking positions to cover all approaches to the cleared area at the edge of the little town. Stavers went to the Nighthawk, Hoot by his side, machine gun cradled in his arm. Stavers stood by the wide nose. "See that?"

"I see it. It's black paper on the fuselage. What for?"

Stavers grinned and removed the paper. Hoot stared at a brilliant yellow Star of David. He saw five all told by the time Stavers was through, two on each side of the fuselage, two fore and aft, and one beneath the belly. "Not trying to attract attention, are you?" Hoot asked.

"Warpaint," Stavers said smugly. "Get inside that thing and turn on the avionics power. I don't want to miss the call from Elliott."

It came exactly twenty-three minutes later. "Little David from Lone Ranger."

Hoot waved to Stavers as he replied. "Little David's got you five by five, Lone Ranger. Let's have it." Hoot glanced at Stavers, listening on another headset.

"Bingo, Little David. Repeat, bingo. Multiple returns, estimate four zero at five two nautical from destination. You copy?"

"Got it, Lone Ranger. We copy you four zero targets five two nautical from target. Reconfirm, please."

"On the money, Little David."

"Roger, Lone Ranger. It's time to get lost. Beat it, you guys."

"So long." The Viper would fly on up to Panama, where it had been scheduled originally to land. Everything neat, proper, and as filed by flight plan. Stavers leaned outside the Nighthawk, gave a short blast on a steel whistle. The three men came running.

"The show's on. Skip, crank up. Everybody to their positions." Skip Marden slid into the pilot's seat with Stavers by his side. The other men took weapons stations. Skip fed power to the big jet engines and the Nighthawk trembled to life. Everyone was already on his headset-and-mike system.

"Here's the scoop," Stavers said brusquely. "Elliott called in with a radar bingo, estimated forty choppers on their way to Pasaja. Their position a few minutes ago was fifty-two nautical from the plateau. They're in formation so that will slow them down a bit. We crank up and reach Pasaja a few minutes before they arrive. The timing ought to be about perfect."

As he spoke, Skip Marden had the Nighthawk fully wound up. Dust whirled madly outside the machine and the Nighthawk lifted, rocking in the bounce of ground winds. "Keep her down to two hundred above the deck," Stavers directed. "That'll eliminate any chance of someone getting radar on us until we're on top of them. Everybody have the script worked out?"

"We got it," Matsumara said. "But how do we tell the Jews from the Catholics? They all look the same."

"Funny, funny," Marden told him. "It's simple. If we work this right, the Catholics will be doing everything they can to blow your good head right off your shoulders."

"That's one way," Matsumara admitted.

They raced over jungle, Marden flying an even two hundred feet by radar altimeter over the treetops. They checked their weapons. Everything was ready. When they made their move, it would be timed perfectly. Get in hard and fast, tear up what was in front of them, and break away.

They saw the Pasaja mountain from a distance; there was no mistaking that towering monolith. It looked like Devil's Tower in the Dakotas but expanded enormously in size, with the top of the plateau shrouded in blowing mists. "You got the river in sight?" Stavers asked Marden. "You should see the gorge where it cuts along the east flank of the slope."

"Got it." Marden was terse, completely in his element, flying a killing machine.

"Okay, that's where the Montini forces should be right now, working directly to the west, taking the slope before them. They'll try to use that cargo elevator chute I told you about."

"Okay."

"The Israeli team should be just to the north. They'll be coming downriver. Fly east of the Montini group. Keep it low. They'll use binoculars and they'll see the stars on this thing. When they make us out, we'll be just over their horizon. They'll be wondering what the hell is going on, but they won't be too worried about us. Keep going to the north until we see the Israelis. I don't know how big their force will be. Anywhere from twenty to a hundred, I'd guess. Fly just off to one side of them. I want them to see the Star of David on this thing. When they have a good look, we take it right down to the trees and we hit the Montini group. Time for one good pass and then break out to the east again. Everybody with me?"

"Hello, General Custer," Gibson said quietly.

Talk fell away. No time now to waste words or divert attention from what lay ahead. The mountain kept growing in size as they sped over the jungle at better than a hundred and forty miles an hour. "I got the first group in sight," Marden said quietly. "Eleven o'clock our position. See them? Just to the left of the nose."

"Got them," Stavers confirmed. "Take her down to a hundred feet and keep on trucking."

They nosed down, picked up speed. So long as he could see the combat force by the river and on its west bank, Marden knew they could see them. They pounded through choppy, steaming air and then they were away from the first combat group in the heavy forest.

"Logan here. There's the other group. Damn, we're almost on top of them."

"Bring her around," Stavers ordered.

The Nighthawk clawed around in a steep bank until Marden saw the second group below and to his right as he headed south. They saw men pointing at them. There could be no mistaking the bright yellow stars on the helicopter. "They'll be wondering who the hell we are," Stavers said crisply, "and if they have any doubts about our being friendly, we'll take care of that right now."

He looked ahead. They were rushing back toward the Montini forces, which were well up from the river now. "They're still puzzled down there. Let's wake 'em up," Stavers snapped.

They went in like a demon flying straight out of hell. Three hundred yards out Marden opened up the Vulcan cannon. Explosive shells ripped forward of the speeding Nighthawk with devastating effect. He walked the chopper nose slightly from side to side and a hailstorm of exploding cannon shells sprayed through the shocked troops of the Montini force. Men were tossed about like rag dolls being torn into bloody chunks. "Toshio! Give them a few gas rockets!" Above the thunder of their engines and the *BRRRRRT!* of the Vulcan cannon they heard the whistling shriek of rockets leaving the Nighthawk. Sixteen rockets raced in a loose cluster toward the stunned forces now closer to them. Green Ring Three, a devastating nerve gas. In ten minutes its effect would be gone, but anyone who took a single lungful of that stuff would be dead in thirty seconds. There was just enough gas to demoralize those people below and take a few of them out for good. They rushed over the combat forces they'd nailed with such devastating surprise. They were good. People were firing back at them, machine guns and small heat-seeking missiles. They'd come ready for anything.

"Flares!" Stavers shouted.

Logan fired the flares from the Nighthawk. Small parachutes blossomed and thermite incendiaries burned with a savage glare, diverting the small homing missiles from the Nighthawk. Stavers aimed at a point on the slope two hundred yards above the Montini troops and let fly with two heavy rockets. They tore into the steep slope and exploded, starting a minor avalanche of rock, mud, and smashed trees. *"Go!"* Stavers yelled and Marden hit full power, skimming trees as he raced off to the east. "Turn her around five miles out, stay low and just cruise above the trees," he ordered.

"Man, they're a bunch of pissed people back there," Matsumara reported. "I think it's working, Doug. They're firing mortars and rockets back at the Israelis." He paused. "That does it. They're getting return fire now. They're going to chew hell out of each other."

"Here's hoping they don't have the chance," Stavers said grimly. Everything now depended on timing.

And there they were. Forty of the deadliest combat choppers in the world, the Trinity strike force, swinging in to approach the flames and smoke erupting from the jungle along the eastern flank of Pasaja. They flew within range—and all hell broke loose. The Israelis *had* to figure the American helicopters, which were without markings, as Patschke's defenses; and the Montini group, badly mauled by the slashing strike of the Nighthawk, knew that anything flying was enemy. *They* let loose with everything they had at the Trinity helicopters. Within a few seconds three of the big Sikorsky choppers were blown out of the air, trailing flames and smoke as they thundered into the jungle, killing all on board.

Stavers held his breath. *It was working.* The Trinity commander split his forces. Twenty of the big helicopters lifted steadily and went for the plateau far above them. The others threw everything they had at the unknown troops along the mountain flank that had opened up with such murderous fire, and the casualties on all sides began to mount. In the distance, literally lurking at treetop level, Stavers smiled with grim satisfaction. Rosa Montini was starting to pay dearly for her murderous actions in the immediate past. The Trinity helicopters poured screaming hurricanes of explosive shells into the Papacy force, shredding what was left of the stunned Italians into gory pulp. Four American helicopters, their men thoroughly enraged by this time, swung around to maul the hopelessly outgunned Israeli commandos.

It wasn't quite where he wanted it yet. Not by a long shot, Stavers knew. Somewhere atop that plateau, Colonel-General Ernst Patschke still had his own cards to play. There was every chance that Patschke's defensive leaders would make the mistake—and it was to be expected—that the hellish uproar far below the plateau was actually a coordinated action against the German stronghold. That conviction could only be reinforced by the strike wedge of the American helicopters assaulting the plateau.

"They've bought the game!" Stavers exulted, and indeed they had, as the defenders unleashed their own weapons. No sudden helicopters, no barrage of missiles, but the oldest and most reliable defense of any besieged fortress. Patschke and his people had prepared well. Pipes inserted at different levels of the steep slopes opened to pour thousands of gallons of sticky oil and naptha down the vertiginous slopes—and were set aflame. The entire eastern half of the Pasaja mount became a roaring wall of fire. Tributaries of flame splashed in all directions and the river itself far below exploded into a holocaust. The survivors of the booming fires and skin-shriveling heat escaped across the river or fled to the flanks of the mount yet spared the flames.

"Scan the frequencies," Stavers snapped to Gibson. The Indian hit several electronic controls and nodded to Stavers. "Got 'em. They're working UHF." He had the frequency used by the helicopter team.

"Trinity Twenty-Three to Leader."

"Go, Two Three."

"They're finished down here. Between our attack and the fire spilling out of those slopes, these people are wiped out as a force. They're showing white flags and—sir, goddamnit, there are some women with them!"

"I don't care if they're orangutans. If they don't grab for sky, cut them down."

"Yes, sir. There aren't more than a dozen or so left we can see still moving."

"Get down there among them, keep flanking fire ready at all times, and bring them aboard your air-

craft. Keep them covered. Search every last mother down to their jocks and socks. Got that?"

"Got it, sir. We're starting down now."

"Roger that, Two Three, and as soon as able, get your asses up here. We've just run into a hell of a lot of trouble. Be alert for very heavy automatic weapons fire. When you come over the crest, take advantage of the smoke we'll be laying down. Arm your aircraft for chemical agents dispersal. Leader out."

Stavers turned to Marden. "Find a clear spot and put her down. Keep everything running. Logan, get those decals ready. Soon as we're down, you, Toshio, go out with him. Pull the Jewish stars off and get those Blue Light insignias on fast."

Skip Marden found a clearing, dropped in quickly. Matsumara and Logan jumped outside and peeled away the Star of David decals. In their places went large pale blue decals of a crossbow with sniper crosshairs. Neat. Just like that, they were now part of the Fast Deployment Force stationed at Fort Bragg. Logan and Matsumara came back inside. "Everybody get those Blue Light jackets on. Use your flak helmets. And don't forget; we're all part of the 409th Composite Group out of Bragg." Stavers tapped Marden on the shoulder. "Let's move it, Peter Pan."

Marden grinned and the Nighthawk clawed back into the air, headed directly for Pasaja, climbing steadily. "Skip, turn on every light we've got. Landing lights, strobes, beacons, everything. Hoot, punch me into the Trinity frequency."

"You've got it," Hoot confirmed.

"Trinity Leader, this is Peter Pan. Do you read? Over."

He knew there'd be a lot of puzzled looks between the chopper pilots and crews of the Trinity Force. There had been no other helicopters assigned to this mission, and sure as hell no one with the call sign of Peter Pan. Stavers called again in the open. "Peter Pan to Trinity Leader, come in, come in, please. Receiving on your operational frequency. Over."

A suspicious voice came across in a dead monotone. *"This is Trinity Leader. Who the hell are you and where are you, Peter Pan? Over!"*

"Roger, Trinity. Peter Pan is a Nighthawk, three miles east of your position of Pasaja and climbing to plateau height. We've got lights on for you to pick us up. If you're still engaged with enemy forces we'll hold off or we'll come in to help. Your decision, Trinity. Over."

"What's your outfit?"

Stavers didn't answer immediately. He pointed ahead of them. Four of the big Sikorsky choppers breaking away from Pasaja in two pairs to flank them. He pointed for Marden to take the Nighthawk straight ahead.

"Trinity, Peter Pan is from the 409th Composite out of Bragg. Blue Light Four. You copy?"

"Yeah, we copy, Peter Pan. We don't understand what you're—"

"Trinity from Peter Pan, we have your search choppers in sight, two teams each. Confirm they are friendly and will act as escort or we will launch seeker missiles immediately. Over."

He looked at the others, then spoke on the intercom but kept his transmit button down so Trinity would also hear him. "Ready missiles each quadrant. Two seekers each helicopter. On my count-down to zero, launch missiles. Five, four, three—"

"Hold your fire! *Peter Pan, repeat, hold your fire! This is Trinity Leader. Those are friendlies, goddamnit! Confirm!*"

Doug Stavers was all honey and silk. "Ah, Roger that, Trinity. Hold one, please." He paused. "Stand down missile launch to ready alert. But don't trust those mothers. On your toes, people." He clicked his transmitter button several times. "Trinity Leader from Peter Pan, confirm seeker ordnance on standby. We'd like to come in with your group on the plateau." Then he dropped his private little cup of scalding coffee in Trinity's lap. "Have you had any sign yet of Patschke? Over."

He knew the stunned look on Trinity Leader's face that *must* be there. The identification of Ernst Patschke was probably one of their most jealously guarded secrets, and here was a stranger chopper on the loose from the 409th blabbing it all over the airwaves!

"*Peter Pan, observe full transmit security. That's an order. Over.*"

"As you wish, Trinity. I repeat the request for joining up. Over."

"*Our choppers will lead you in, Peter Pan. Be ready for anything. We have heavy autofire from concealed positions and we've lost nine aircraft.*"

"Roger that, Trinity." Stavers decided on the Big Lie. The last thing he wanted was to have Patschke and what he was carrying torn to pieces in a wave of destruction generated by these chop-pers. "We've been on that plateau before, Trinity. Suggest non-persistent Green Ring Three along the upwind rim of the plateau. With that wind it'll be gone in ten minutes. Repeat, we recommend use of—"

"We read you loud and clear, Peter Pan. Stand by. All Trinity crews, don your masks. All Trinity crews, don your masks. Choppers Five, Six, Seven and Eight, get upwind of the plateau rim and launch chemical loads immediately. Go, go."

Four helicopters slewed about, hovered off the edge of the Pasaja plateau, and fired salvos of rockets that exploded with deep crumping sounds along the upwind surface. A greenish-white cloud leaped into being and flowed with the wind-whipped mists along the plateau. The gas would remain effective for only ten minutes and then it would be as harmless as fog. Eleven minutes after the chemical warheads detonated, two helicopters moved slowly along the plateau, sensors sniffing out any trace of the gas. It would have affected only those directly exposed to the gas; it was the least persistent, the least dangerous of all their lethal chemical weapons. With all-clear radioed to all the helicopters, they began landing on the plateau.

There was no defensive fire. The Sikorsky choppers landed in a classical strike-destroy-occupy pattern, rangers leaping to the ground, fanning out with automatic weapons and flamethrowers to every building, to whatever might be inhabited. No opposition. One ranger called in.

"Sir, over here on the north rim. We've found an entrance to an underground complex."

"Stand fast. I'll be right there."

Stavers had Marden bring the Nighthawk down.

He turned to the others. "Hoot, you and Toshio come with me. Skip, as soon as we're out of here, you lift off and hover about a quarter of a mile out. Just ignore anything they say to you. Josh, stand by the salvo triggers. Anybody screws with you, cut him out of the air."

Stavers jumped to the ground, Gibson and Matsumara slightly behind and to one side cradling submachine guns, following Stavers as he went at a steady trot to one helicopter with three orange slashes on its nose. That would be Trinity Leader. Several men clustered by the nose of the helicopter. One man gave orders steadily on his radio. They were sending men to occupy all openings to what was clearly a deep complex within the Pasaja mountain. Good move, Stavers thought. They're getting ready to handle anything.

Stavers stopped before the man with colonel's eagles on his collar and snapped out a salute. "Colonel, I'm Major Douglas Stavers, commanding the 409th Composite."

"Larry Rawlings," came the reply, with a salute so crisp it could have sliced bacon. "Major, what the hell are you people doing here anyway? This is a secret mission, and I'd like to know how you even *found out* about us!"

"Begging the colonel's pardon, we didn't 'find out' anything, sir. We're here on orders. There are thirty more Blackhawks dispersed to the east of this area awaiting my orders. There's been a bad security leak in this program, Colonel. A lot of people knew about Colonel-General Ernst Patschke and the fact that he's got his hands on three fission bombs. The people, ah, on top felt it would be wiser if we backed you up without *anyone*, including yourself, being told of the operation." Stavers looked about him and forced an expression of admiration to his face. "But I must say it's obvious you didn't need any help."

Rawlings knew how to cut the mustard, and he didn't waste time on useless conversation. "Major, we're about to move into that complex beneath us. First, who the hell are those civilians? Or mercenaries or whatever they are that attacked us by the river?"

"That's part of the problem, Colonel. You were hit by two separate forces and they're not working with each other. The ones that opened fire from north of this place are from an Israeli team that—"

"Israeli!" Rawlings shook his head. "What the hell are *they* doing here?"

"Simple, Colonel. They want those bombs. Their cover story is that they were after Patschke as a war criminal."

"That's a crock of shit and you know it, Major."

"I didn't say I believed it, sir. I said that was their cover story. From the looks of things, however, just about all of them were killed."

Rawlings nodded, gestured to Stavers to hold his words. He went to his radio. "Trinity Leader here. Murphy, you pick up any survivors from that group north of this place? Over."

"Trinity Eleven here to Leader. Yes, sir. Four, all wounded. The rest of them were wasted. Over."

Stavers gestured. "Colonel, ask them if Stan Havorth is among the survivors."

"And who is Havorth?"

"Their leader. He's a captain in the Israeli army."

"You sure know a hell of a lot for someone I've never even heard of." Rawlings shook his head, passed on the query. The reply came at once. "Leader from Eleven. Sir, one of the survivors says that Havorth was killed in the fighting."

Stavers didn't wait to discuss it. "Get that confirmed," he snapped.

Rawlings looked at him in open surprise. The major's remark wasn't a request. Rawlings put it aside for the moment. "I want positive ID on that individual. Get identification of some kind or bring the body up here. Move it, Eleven. Leader out." Rawlings turned back to Stavers.

"You got any more surprises for me?"

"Yes, sir. You were hit by two separate forces, like I said. You've taken care of the Israelis. There's that second force and that's the one we're most interested in. An Italian paramilitary strike team."

Rawlings felt his mouth open and he closed it with an effort. "This whole thing is getting insane," he said with mounting displeasure.

"Colonel, I follow them. I don't pick them."

"You're right," Rawlings said by way of apology. "But— *Italians?* They're part of NATO, man! They've got nukes in their arsenal through us. Why would they—"

Always tell a bigger lie. "Colonel, it's a communist underground team. They're financed by OPEC to disrupt the European community, *and* to get at least one of those three nukes Patschke somehow got hold of. Look, Colonel, I even know their leader. It's a woman. Rosa Montini. She looks as nice as the young girl living next door but she's hell on wheels and meaner than a wolverine. We want her. Special orders; right to Washington. We get her to talk and we open up a whole hornet's nest of undercover operations against our people."

Rawlings showed his suspicions. "Where the hell did you get your information? I've been on this whole program from the word go, and I—"

"Colonel, damnit, I don't want to be disrespectful but you're wasting one hell of a lot of time," Stavers said sharply. "Now why don't we stop all this jawing, and get down to the nitty gritty? You get on that radio of yours through direct military comsat and you talk to Washington and—"

Rawlings stiffened. "You didn't answer my question, Major. I asked you *where* you got your information."

"You won't believe me," Stavers said with a shrug. "From the KGB."

"That's a crock of—"

"Damn you, Colonel, *check it out.* Call your people, I don't care. The contact is Vernon Kovanowicz. I'd suggest you also use the name of Jack North. He was special forces—"

"Was?"

"He was burned to death, Colonel, if that helps any."

Rawlings hesitated. "No, no; there's no question. You know *too* much. Shit, I knew North. How did he get it?"

"One of those things," Stavers said tiredly. "In a commercial crash in Philadelphia. On landing."

Rawlings shook his head. "He had a reputation of being untouchable. You just never know." The colonel had obviously come to his decision. "All right, Major. Let's see if this Montini devil of yours is still alive. If she is, you can have her. I'm not after prisoners. Just bombs."

"Thanks."

Rawlings conferred with two of his officers; they went to their radios and Stavers saw heavily armed rangers herding a group of prisoners toward them. Even from a distance he spotted Rosa Montini. There couldn't be any mistake. She wore combat fatigues and paratrooper boots; everything no-nonsense. She'd been stripped of weapons, but from the way she moved, as lithe and graceful as a cat, she still showed signs of being dangerous. The side of her cheek was bloodied and she walked with a slight limp. Stavers had never seen her before, but he *knew*. He was also surprised with her beauty. Face smeared with dust and dirt, weary, wounded, limping; none of it mattered. Something extraordinary came through. He imagined her at another time and place and knew he'd be seeing one of the most beautiful women he'd ever known. Beauty within as much as without.

And dangerous as hell.

The group reached them. Stavers nodded to Rawlings. "That's her. With your permission, Colonel, I'd like to take her off your hands."

"You've got it. What about the others with her?"

"They're yours."

"We'll let them find their own way out of here."

Rosa Montini stared fixedly at Doug Stavers. She showed no sign of open recognition, but Stavers knew she had seen many pictures of him—and possibly observed him—without his knowledge of those moments. He had to make a move that would let her comprehend everything that was happen-

ing and convince her that her only right move
would be to go along with whatever he presented.
He nodded to her. "Havorth is dead," he said
quietly.

She picked up on his meaning immediately. *This
man had no reason to tell her anything.* She understood all too well he knew of her operation and
had figured who'd been behind the killings. No
secret involving as many people as did the existence and the mission of the Six Hundred could
long remain secret to any determined and skilled
man. She knew he'd been questioned by Tony
Casarotto and many others. He knew too much,
and he had quite thoroughly pinned down her
movements and then anticipated what she would
be doing. She looked at the tall, powerful man
before her. She knew authority, quiet confidence,
the skilled and untouchable killer. God knew she
had tried through her own people to eliminate this
one. How many times now? It was ridiculous, and
it was a credit to herself, she mused, that she
didn't show any sign of surprise that he was *alive*.
For like so many other people, she "knew" Stavers
had died in that flaming wreckage in Philadelphia
and had been buried in Arizona and—

She forced a halt to mental wanderings. What
had he said? *"Havorth is dead."* Why would he tell
her that? Why would he tell her *anything*? She
expected immediate death from this man. So he
was giving her a message. He had eliminated a
powerful competitor in Havorth; the Israelis would
not be so quick to replace their strike force once
they learned the size of the American effort involved here. New comprehension began to dawn.

She knew the Americans had been involved in this effort to find the fabled diamond, what they called the Godstone, its name cursed by Butto Giovanni, insisting in his last moments of life that it was instead the true Star of Bethlehem. Little matter at this moment. Stavers had more in mind than her death, and that meant death might not be at hand. He had also given her several moments in which to use her own wit.

Then she saw the subtleties of the situation. The uniforms. *Stavers, and the two men with him, they are not wearing the same uniforms.* Her eyes shifted and she saw the Nighthawk hovering beyond the rim of the plateau. So they did not come together! *All the American machines are of the Sikorsky type and that one is different.* She cursed herself for childish myopia. All she needed to do was think. Stavers was playing a role here, duping the American colonel! And giving her a heaven-sent opportunity to move with him, away from these Americans, where her life would most likely end before she ever left this windswept mountain. She turned to the American colonel.

"I hope what you came for was worth the deaths you inflicted on my people. And one thing I don't understand, Colonel," she added, gesturing. "This is *not* your country or your people. What right do you have to be here? To kill so many?"

She did not upset the colonel. He was perfectly sure of his position. "The name's Montini, isn't it? Yeah, that's what the major said. Rosa Montini. And you're one of those stinking Eyetie communists. I'll tell you something, lady. When people like you try to get their hands on atomic bombs, then you all deserve to be cut down right where you're found. As far as I'm concerned, you're alive only because the major, here, has need for you that I don't."

He doesn't know about the diamond. She held her breath, feared her expression would give away her sudden inner torment and looked at the ground to avoid the colonel's eyes. *Stavers hasn't told him a thing. They're looking for bombs and the colonel knows nothing of why we're here. This is—* She saw the clump of grass lifting slowly, then another, and all across the plateau grass was coming up from the fields and in an instant she knew what was happening and there was no time to shout a warning and moving instinctively, wasting not a split-second she spun sideways and threw herself at Stavers, locking a leg behind his heel and throwing all her weight against his body. He fell backwards, twisting away from her, but she kept her leg locked tightly and clung to his clothing with two hands that were steel claws. She pressed her face against his. *"Stay down!"* she screamed. *"They're—"*

A deafening roar of machine guns drowned out her words. She pressed her body and face hard against the earth, the chugging staccato sounds hammering at her, tearing into her ears, and above that awful sound was the closer cry of death, bullets slicing air with that unmistakable hissing whine just over their bodies. She'd had only that momentary warning. The old trick of the Japanese in the second world war, repeated again and again in the savage fighting of southeast Asia. Let the enemy pass by while you remain huddled in small holes covered with grass and leaves and *then*, when they are behind you, all about you, everyone rises from concealment and fires machine guns at pointblank range, sweeping in all directions.

The opening thunder of guns brought on sudden screams of wounded and dying men, the deep crumping blast of helicopter fuel tanks exploding. Heat and shock waves rolled over them; dust and thick, acrid smoke, men shouting and the Americans firing back with heavier weapons, those still able to move hurling themselves physically against the brown-skinned natives who had waited so patiently for their moment. The Americans had been caught by surprise but their reaction was swift. Several helicopters burned fiercely but others thrust violently upwards to give their gunners clearer fields of fire. Death sprayed the fields. It was over quickly, Americans with faces twisted in hatred killing with knives and other weapons, wanting no prisoners and taking none.

She rose slowly, Stavers already towering over her, his face a death mask. She turned to see where he stared and she knew at this instant this man was totally, completely unpredictable. His cheek twitched from muscle spasms and shock was stamped deeply into his eyes. He ignored the shouting men and exploding fuel tanks of helicopters, the commands to move into the fortress below them. He sank slowly to his knees and his face turned to stone as he reached down to touch the bloody pulp that had been the face of his friend.

The top half of Hoot Gibson's face and head had been blown away.

Toshio Matsumara lay nearby, biting his lips to

keep from crying out. Rosa Montini went to him immediately, snapped free her belt and applied a tourniquet to a blood-soaked leg. He'd taken hits in both legs; white bone showed through his trousers. She pulled his belt free, tightened it about the second leg for another tourniquet. Toshio gasped with pain. "Flare gun ... right side ... *fire* ..." She grabbed the signal gun from its holster, turned to face the Nighthawk hovering in the distance, and fired. A flare burst away with a hissing bellow and exploded with bright blue flame. The Nighthawk was already coming in, flaring to touch down. It hit hard and two men came out fast. The first was giant. He snarled at his companion. "Get the medical kit. *Move!*" Then he went to Stavers. He didn't touch him.

"Doug." No reaction. "Doug, *please*, Hoot's gone."

Stavers looked up with tears streaming down his face.

The big man spoke quickly. "Doug, we got *all* of them. Us and the Air Force teams. We killed every fucking one of Patschke's men."

Stavers stared at him. His hand caressed Gibson's mutilated form. He ignored the salty liquid from his eyes. "Hoot was worth more than all of them put together." He shook his head, forcing away the misery, getting back to the moment. Reality returned with its own blow as he saw Toshio, Logan bending over him, a needle stabbing into an arm. "He'll make it," Rosa Montini said. "He'll need a hospital soon, but he'll make it."

The giant from the helicopter turned to her. He was curious, as if seeing a strange bug for the first time. Then his face hardened and his eyes nar-

rowed to pinpoints. "So this is the bitch we're
looking for," he said in a voice that rumbled from
his huge chest. Rosa Montini held his gaze and
looked straight into certain death.

"She saved my life," Stavers said. Marden turned
to him with disbelief. "That's right. She knocked
me flat, under the same burst that took Hoot. I
owe her. We take her with us."

"But—"

"No questions."

"You got it, Doug."

Stavers turned to her. "Go aboard the chopper
with Toshio. You have medical training?"

"Paramedic," she said quietly.

"Then save his life. If you do, it pays a lot of
debts. Get moving. He's bleeding to death." Marden
and Logan carried Matsumara into the chopper.
Stavers watched from outside. He picked up a
compact flamethrower rifle and a bandolier of grenades to augment the Uzi in one hand. "Keep this
thing turning," he said to Marden. "I'm going down
below with the colonel."

"Bullshit," Marden snapped. He came out of the
chopper with a bandolier of grenades tossed over
one shoulder, the Uzi jammed into his belt and a
riot gun in his right hand. "We're playing games
at close quarters; *this* is the baby."

"I told you to stay with the chopper, damnit."

"Yeah, I heard you. Let's not miss the party."

Stavers didn't have time to argue. They took off
at a steady run, following the band of men running to answer Rawling's radio summons. They
pushed their way through the group to find Rawlings and his top men standing before crumpled

steel blast doors. Anti-tank charges are the best can openers going. "Colonel!" Stavers called. Rawlings waved him through.

"The old bastard is somewhere down there. I think he blew his wad up here. Most of his people are dead."

Stavers shook his head. "You go down there after him and you're going to walk into pure hell. Damnit, Colonel, he's been surviving everything and a lot of people trying to nail him for thirty years. Think he hasn't got a few tricks up his sleeve? He *wants* you to come after him. What would *you* do in his place? Exploding mines, collapsing tunnels, rivers of burning oil. You're dead ducks down there. It's *his* rabbit warren."

Rawlings rubbed his chin, looked at dried blood and ignored it. "Everybody!" he shouted. "Get your masks on!" He turned to a ranger. "Get me two masks for these officers, fast." They donned the masks as Rawlings continued snapping out orders. "Okay, get me a couple of pressure cannisters up here. Let's have the NP nerve stuff with a good sink rate."

Marden raised an eyebrow to Stavers. "It's nonpersistent, with a chemical added to make it much heavier than air. It keeps sinking downward. It'll finish off anybody down below who's still breathing."

"Sure, sure," Marden said. He was unimpressed. "You thinking what I'm thinking, baby? We been up here holding a caucus just like whoever's down below has nothing better to do than wait around for this idiot conference to come to a conclusion. So they just wait, they don't resist, they let most of our people get deep into whatever it is down there, and *then* they pull the switch. It stinks."

"You're right."

"Then what the hell are we doing waiting *here?* You *want* to get blown up?"

"Not quite. I want to find out how Patschke got out of here. Every one of those men who popped up from their foxholes before knew he was going to die. That was a diversion. My bet is the old Kraut has already flown the coop or he's about to make his move. *Then* we beat it."

"I don't like it."

"I've *got* to know, Skip."

"Let's not wait *here* to find out. Damnit, my balls are crawling up to my navel. We're sitting ducks! You want to wait, let's get in the chopper and back off a mile or so and watch everything from *there*. We can be back on the ground in less than a minute."

Stavers turned abruptly as a shock wave slammed into them. A bright flash boomed upward from the tunnel they'd split open. Rawlings's men were firing more anti-tank rockets down the tunnel. Whatever they hit would be torn apart. Men began to spill into the sloping ramp that led within the mountain. And suddenly, just like that, Stavers knew that Marden was right. Damn; he hadn't been thinking. Seeing Hoot like that—

He shut it off. "You got it," he said quietly to Marden, and started trotting back toward the Nighthawk. "Keep your mask on until we're aboard. When we're inside, don't wait. Take off and head for a hover position on the west side of the mountain. Nothing's going to happen on the opposite side. Not with all that fire they turned loose there."

They lifted up gently and Marden backed the Nighthawk from the plateau surface, keeping their nose pointed toward the mess strewn across the top of Pasaja. Then he wheeled slowly, taking the powerful helicopter to a point about a mile from the mountain edge. What happened next was almost too fast for them to follow.

A dull flash speared across the steep slope of the mountain, followed by a roiling cloud of dust and smoke. They saw large flat surfaces falling and tumbling away. "What the hell is *that?*" Logan shouted.

No one answered. It all happened too fast. Seconds later, the wind whipped away the smoke to reveal a wide and flat tunnel leading straight back within the mountain. A bright light glowed within the shaft, flickered and became even brighter. Shockingly abrupt, totally unexpected, a small twin-engine jet snapped into view, rushing away from within the mountain, brilliant flames spewing back from rocket bottles hurling the jet to flying speed. The rockets snapped off and the jet pulled up its nose and disappeared within the clouds just above Pasaja.

"Patschke," Rosa Montini said hoarsely.

Stavers was already on the radio. "Trinity Leader, Trinity Leader, get the hell off that mountain! I repeat, get off that mountain! It's going to blow any—"

A terrible gout of flame gushed upward from the entrance to the underground chambers.

"Get out of here!" Stavers yelled to Marden. "Everybody hang on!"

Marden had just completed his turn and was diving as fast as the Nighthawk would fly when the shock waves hit them. For long seconds the helicopter shook and trembled from the repeated blows—and then they were safe. Stavers leaned back, exhausted. Toshio lay unconscious, the morephine they'd pumped into him warding off the pain of his shattered legs. Stavers looked at the woman who sat quietly, holding his gaze with unflinching eyes, her expression saying nothing. He'd wanted to kill her for a long time.

And he couldn't do it, no matter what she'd done in the past. *He was alive because of her.* Stavers turned to Marden. "Set up two four seven on the ADF. That'll take us to a big tanker thirty miles offshore. It's one of ours and they're expecting us. They've got a doctor aboard for Toshio."

He sat back, his eyes returning again to Rosa Montini. He'd wanted to kill her and now he couldn't and what the hell was he going to do with her?

And why did she remind him so strongly of Tracy!

Chapter   XVIII

Stavers sprawled on a deck chair behind the great curving prow of the tanker. They carried a load of ship's fuel and their helicopters, aircraft, and weapons. Otherwise they were empty, the main holds safetied with inert nitrogen gas. Stavers rested his feet on the rail, smoking a cigar and doing permanent damage to a bottle of fine cognac. He wanted to get drunk, but knew he couldn't. Thoughts surged relentlessly through his skull. He was still fighting off the loss of the big Indian who'd been his closest friend. Tracy eased from his consciousness with slow and willingly protracted pain. He'd swept his emotions clean of her father, of Jesús Ferrer and the others, and of so many more before them. Death was more than companion to his way of life; it was a constant presence. It wasn't always bad. He'd seen too many men with their intestines held dumbly in their hands, looking up mutely at close friends, eyes beseeching the single bullet to the back of the head to end immediately the slow, agonized dying. There was nothing wrong with the dying; it was the way you went. He'd fired a burst from a machine gun into a man who'd saved his life twice in Rhodesia, when that friend was trapped beneath a blazing truck and was starting to burn to death. "In the name of God, if you love me, *kill me!*" His last words, will and testament, and cry of love and request for same.

All this put Rosa Montini in perspective. She leaned against the rail, wearing fresh clothing of her size collected from the crew. Incredibly, even without the cosmetics the most beautiful women affected with just the right touch, she was still captivatingly beautiful, her lips full and red, her black hair blowing with the wind. Her full breasts pushed tightly against the shirt she had tucked into bell bottoms. *Wrong place, wrong time*, he murmured to himself.

They'd sent the Nighthawk, Marden flying and Josh Logan attending to Toshio Matsumara, to Lima. He needed major surgery if he was going to keep his legs. Stavers had made a radio call to a Peruvian general with whom he'd worked in the past. Yes, they would attend to everything for Matsumara. The best doctors and the best hospital. "Put my other men on an airliner for the States, will you, General? I'd appreciate that. The Nighthawk? Yes, it's a beautiful machine, and it's yours. Consider it a present for your personal needs."

That took care of that. It cleaned up a great deal. Toshio would have his surgery and recuperate in complete obscurity. Josh would pick up whatever he was doing before, remembering nothing of the wild commotion at Pasaja. Stavers didn't want Skip Marden out of his grasp. The big rawboned bastard was worth any four men and he had the ability to think swiftly of the right answers when everything was wrong. "Go to Indian Bluff, Arizona. When you get there, go to the sheriff's office. Just tell them that Gibson died in a plane crash and you'll be getting the details later. Ask the deputy there for Kathy Sloan. She'll meet you in town. Give her this note, tell her everything that happened, and she'll take you to my office. Wait for me. Do whatever the hell you think is right, but wait for me there. I'd appreciate it if you didn't ask me any questions."

"You know how to make it tough. I hate puzzles."

"You'll have time to work it out."

They shook hands and twenty minutes later the black helicopter swung off to the southeast. Stavers decided to ride the tanker back to California. He'd have passports and money brought aboard the big ship before they made port. He'd also have time to think, to ask a lot of questions and get the answers he needed from Rosa Montini. There was only one fly in the ointment.

He was getting too damned fond of her. It astonished him. For too long she'd been a nonperson representing a powerful and lethal force. She had through that organization tried several times to kill him. The results were bodies strewn in all directions; some were his people, others were from her own group. Right now the odds were devastatingly in his favor, if that was the way you figured it. First they had ripped her strike force at the base of Pasaja, slaughtering them in that terrible pass of the Nighthawk. Those who survived died in the flaming explosions along the top of the plateau and within the hollowed chambers just beneath.

No one lived through the explosions and the deliberate holocaust. Not a soul. Italian, Israeli, American, German or Ecuadorian. The only human beings who'd survived that searing finale to the confrontation had left in the Nighthawk helicopter only because it was already clear of Pasaja. *And that jet; never forget Patschke's jet.*

Stacking up points for people dead was stupid. He'd learned a great deal about Rosa Montini, and at the head of the list was that she was truly a professional. She separated herself personally from her mission. People engaged in crusades often get killed. The Church had a long history of that. Martyrdom was a blessing, not a curse. She did her job and the American who had always proven so formidable and terrible did his. She had saved his life. Period. *He owed.*

He asked her about that. She was brutally honest. "Reflex," she said. "I saw what was happening, and for whatever reason it was to keep you from being killed."

"Subconscious?" he asked.

"You question what it is impossible for me to *know,* my friend," she smiled. "If it was subconscious, then we have proof of it because you are here talking with me and you are not dead. If it was a conscious move on my part, a deliberate act, I don't understand it. You were an opponent about whom I had been warned and was instructed to kill. You did not know Butto Giovanni. A cardinal of Rome. An old and a wise man, even if he was severely structured in his vision of the world beyond the Church. To him, you were Judas. He had heard me describe the diamond as the Messiah Stone. He cursed; anger swept his body like a terrible wind. Did you call it by that name?"

Stavers shook his head. "No. Someone else who knew about the gem long before I'd ever heard of it. That's how they described it to me. Messiah, Godstone; it's all the same to me. And you, Rosa? What is that diamond to you?"

"The same as to the Papacy. The Star of Bethlehem."

"That's sort of far out."

She stood with the sun bright in her face, the wind doing incredible things with her body. "No more than the chalice. No more than the resurrection. No more than any of the miracles. Do you mind if I tell you *why* the old man, Giovanni, was so violently upset when he heard the name the Messiah Stone?"

"I don't mind."

"It began two thousand years ago when men first became aware of its existence, even if they hadn't the faintest conception of what really appeared in the heavens at that time." Rosa went on in detail. The computer studies, the research trips to where the Manturu had once ruled, the myths and the legends; and the slow, growing belief, against all dogma of those established in power in Rome, that what they sought might well be ordained by heaven, and that if this were so, they must bring the jeweled message of the Lord to

Rome. "Somehow, in some way," she concluded, "the Roumanians were involved. Hitler was part of it all. As was Patschke. We're still putting together those pieces. But one thing appears certain. The great yellow diamond, as described with its icy flame, *does* seem to affect people in its presence. Its wearer gains the ability to convince people he or she is right. It's not a matter of *controlling* people. It is affecting them so that they follow of their own accord."

She had been honest with him, and he would do no less with her. He related his conversation with Kurt Mueller.

"That's why he had to be eliminated," she said, as calmly as if discussing a business arrangement. "You see, he refused to talk with us. He threatened to call the secret police. We had no choice."

"That's what most people on crusades claim," he said quietly.

"Then it is what I claim," she told him with disarming candor. "But I wonder if the involvement of the Roumanians is real."

"It is." She sat by his side, fascinated, almost overwhelmed, as he told of his visit with Simeon Tuleca, the films he had seen, the sudden interference of Roumanian state police. She was almost mesmerized by his words.

"Why did your people kill Georgieff?" he asked abruptly. "He wasn't any danger to you."

Again she held his eyes level with hers. It was disconcerting because he saw more than a person. He kept seeing the woman within. "We didn't kill Georgieff," she said quietly. "Your friend Havorth did that. They knew he had a description of the diamond. They wanted it. They caught up with him and tortured him to get the papers or to get him to talk. He refused. They became, as you would say, overzealous. But us? No, Doug, he was valuable to us alive and well."

The pieces were fitting together. Now he had to work out what happened next.

"Why did you keep me on this ship?" she asked, again taking him by surprise.

"The same reason I'm here, Rosa. Everybody on that mountain died, remember? *Everybody*. At least as far as the world knows, everybody died. The flames and the explosions make a body count impossible. They won't be able to identify pieces of bodies. I'm dead and most important of all, right now *you're* dead. No one is looking for us. I need time to think, to make decisions."

"Including about me?"

"Including about you."

"Are you going to kill me, Doug?"

"No."

She laughed, the sound crystal clear, a young girl in high hills and a fresh breeze. "Just like that. No other words, no reasons, no explanations. Just 'no.' "

"That's it."

"And our Star of Bethlehem? Your Messiah Stone? What about that?"

He turned to her, deadly serious. "We'd better get some things in perspective. First, no matter what your Pope says one way or the other, it's not *your* Star, it's not *their* Star, no more than it's *my* Godstone. That's the first thing to understand. The true owners of that diamond are long dead and buried."

"You mean the Manturu."

"You bet your sweet ass, lady. They were cut to pieces when it was taken from them by Bibesco. Hitler got stolen property, although I'm sure that didn't bother him any more than it did the Pope when the Crusaders came home staggering with all the loot they could carry."

She gasped. "You'd equate Hitler with a *Pope?*"

"Don't go missionary on *me*, Rosa. I don't want an exchange on this subject. But more people died for and under your cross than all the people Hitler ever killed. Knock it off. We're professionals in this business and we know which end is up. Let's stay with what we started talking about."

She nodded, keeping her silence.

"Patschke, from what we can determine, is given the diamond by Hitler, who's about to enter his own private Valhalla. Which also means that while the diamond helped him get where it did, it couldn't help him against other people at a distance. Hitler *did* lose, if you'll recall. Anyway, Patschke leaves Germany at the end of the war and flies nonstop with a fortune in diamonds and other things to South America. He sets up housekeeping with his passport and business papers, courtesy of a private bureau in your own little Vatican, which made a fortune doing numbers like that for mass murderers, butchers, sadists and—"

She kept her eyes down. "I know."

"Good. Score one for a proper entry in the history books. So Patschke has the diamond now. We're pretty sure of that. The Israelis want it desperately. They set up a dummy operation with the word out they want Patschke as a war criminal, but the story is so transparent the only people who believe it are the idiot lawyers in the United Nations, and they don't amount to anything, anyway."

He shook his head. "Everybody is so damned rightous about this. Along comes Rosa Montini and her infamous Six Hundred, very well trained and fired up with the same fervor that sent so many millions to their death in the Crusades. The Papacy learns about the diamond and makes *its* own decision that Rome is the rightful owner of something they haven't known about for some two thousand years and which they've never even *seen*. Cute; real cute. They'll do anything to get it. Lie, steal, cheat, torture, murder; anything, because some guy in a skull cap and a long silk robe chanted over a silver bowl filled with tap water he's ordained as holy. Real neat. The ultimate confessional to clear the decks for the crime."

She looked up finally. "And your own people? Your government. They are any different?"

He laughed. "Well, you fooled me that time. You didn't defend the Vatican, which is the usual response. You mean Rawlings and that strike force on Pasaja? *They didn't even know about the diamond.* They were after three atomic bombs they believe were being kept by Patschke in the mountain."

She shook her head. "That is very hard to believe."

"So is the Holy Ghost."

Her lips pressed together. "You may be sure that if they didn't know before, they'll know by now. You Americans are strange people, even brutish in your ways, and you are often crazy, but not that stupid. Your government will add many small things together but they will come up with a large answer. And then *they* will consider the diamond to be rightfully theirs."

"Sure. Just like everybody else."

"What about the Soviets? Surely they've heard the stories by now?" Rosa said.

"The Russians equate stories about diamonds with strange powers right along with astrology and getting rid of warts by swinging a dead cat by its tail around your head in a graveyard. In other words, a loud *nyet*. To them it's all bullshit. Except that they believe people want the stone for its financial value. The Horovitz group in Switzerland places its value at somewhere between six and ten million dollars—and it's escalating all the time."

"That leaves only you, doesn't it."

He flipped his cigar butt over the rail and took a long, slow swallow of cognac, then lit a fresh cigar, doing everything slowly and deliberately. Finally he nodded. "You're right. That sort of clears everybody out of the way except me. *And* Patschke. Don't forget Patschke. Don't *ever* forget him. He's the ultimate survivor, and if I know my Germans, he's got a lot more going for him than just seeing how long he can continue breathing."

"But what about you, Doug? You and the Star?"

He laughed. "You know why it's so hard to figure me in this whole caper, Rosa? Because I'm the only one *who's being honest*, who's been straight from the beginning. I'm a mercenary for hire, and I was hired. Period. No shattering theological con-

cepts, no nationalistic drive, no goodies for man-
kind or any of that rot. Gun for hire. That's me."
He chuckled anew. "I'm the only one anyone else
can trust, because I'm not interested in pleasing
God, in political gain, or in power. I'm the only
one who's *safe* around the diamond. I can't be
bought, I can't be bribed, and I'm not fucked up in
my head seeking never-never nirvana."

"How can you say you *can't be bought?*" Rosa
cried aloud. "You admit you've been hired, you're
a mercenary, you're—"

His hand shot out to grasp her wrist in a clutch
of steel. "Never forget that, Rosa. *Hired.* There's
all the difference in the world between being hired
and *being bought.* I made a deal and we all went in
with our eyes open, and—"

"You made a deal," she sneered. "You're dealing
with criminals! How can you insist on loyalty to
that!"

He smiled at her. "Because I gave my word and
my word is good. You don't understand that. If I'd
been hired by your Pope *he'd* have my word just as
strong. And I'll tell you something else. Right now
your little gang in the Vatican wishes they *had*
hired me. As I'm certain the Tel Aviv crowd does
and just as much." He released his grip on her.
"Don't preach to me, Rosa. Not now, not ever."

"Are you in love with me, Doug?"

"What?"

"I asked you if you were in love with me, you
idiot. You can't hide that you're deeply attracted, I
fascinate you. Just as I'm drawn so strongly to you
and more than a little overwhelmed by you. Not
because you're big or you're strong or a fighting

man or anything like that. There's something inside you—"

"Sure. A little boy who needs to be mothered."

"That *would* be far-fetched, but I come from a
people who believe in miracles. However, it's not
the child that draws me to you. It's the man. *You*.
Whoever and whatever you are. As someone steeped
in logic, I personally detest your loyalty to a criminal cause rather than adherence or fealty to *some*
ideal, but—"

"Hold it, hold it. I consider keeping my word as
pretty damned logical and realistic. If that's ideal-
istic, who cares?"

"That's what I mean," she sighed, her hand moving slowly along his arm. "Utterly unmoving. Committed to honesty even if it's all wrapped up in
self. *Mamma Mia*, what a priest you'd make!"

"Spare me," he grinned at her.

"I will not do any such thing. You avoid my
question, Douglas Stavers."

"I suppose I do." His huge hand reached up to
hold hers, a child's hand in the grip of a giant.
"But then, I think your education has been somewhat lacking." He laughed at the stupefied look on
her face. "Ever listen to yourself, Rosa? Your ideas
of romance would trample the stoutest heart.
Steeped in logic; that was really deep and warm.
And that bit about detesting my loyalty; now, *there's*
a real charmer. But I think you outdid yourself. I
could hear the massed violins and the soft voices
of angels when you ran off with that song-and-
dance about adherence and fealty to ideals."

She snatched her hand from his. To her surprise,
he didn't trap her. The sudden motion impelled

her backwards and for the moment she was lost for words. She gazed at him, unsure, but before she could react that huge hand whipped forward to snatch her bodily to him in a fierce embrace. He moved his lips to hers slowly, deliberately, and she knew he'd given her every opportunity to resist. There was nothing she could do physically against this human engine of death, but death was not what she feared. This was her time to indicate her preference. They kissed long and deep and she did something she had never done before in her life. She let go. As simple as that. Physically and emotionally and sexually she let go within those extraordinary arms, and she knew she was as astonished as her heart was overwhelmed at how strong yet gentle was their kiss. Finally she withdrew. She moved from him, sat on the deck with her knees together and drawn up tightly so that she rested the side of her face on her knees and arms and looked at him quietly and for a long time.

"Still you have never answered me," she said at last.

"Yes, damnit, Rosa, I'm in love with you."

Her eyes widened, then she squeezed them shut for several minutes. A tear trickled down one cheek. "A Rosa I do not yet know is singing at your words," she told him slowly, her voice barely carrying above the wind off the bow. "It is a new experience, this love. It is yet beyond me to understand, and—"

"Don't try."

She went on as if he hadn't spoken. "The other Rosa, who I know so well, is like that part of yourself of which you are so proud. You have given your word; I have given mine. You have sworn to uphold your word; I swore my soul. What do we do, man whom I also love? It would seem we have different masters."

"Right now, right here, I don't give a damn, Rosa."

"You are right. We will face tomorrow," she hesitated, "when tomorrow is here. It is almost night and we are at sea and something new and wonderful is happening to me." She smiled shyly. "It will be nothing I've ever known," she said.

"You mean—"

"Yes. I am still virgin."

His face darkened. "I wish you hadn't said that."

She was astonished. "Sweet Mary, *why not?*"

He wanted to bite his tongue but the words refused to stay inside. "So was Tracy," he said with a terrible anguish. "Goddamn you, Rosa, so was Tracy!"

Chapter   XIX

He needed someone *very* special. Not another mercenary. Not even one of the truly skilled killers, nor a pilot or a demolitions man or a linguist. Something else. Deadlier in his work than all the others, but who wouldn't kill ... *because he'd be so good at what he was doing he wouldn't need to.* He, or she. It didn't matter. He needed a brain of extraordinary cunning and understanding in human affairs. Someone truly global in that scope of comprehension. He needed a priest, a rabbi, and a guru rolled into one and—

He remembered him. No one knew his real name anymore. Well, almost no one. He'd been an outcast as a kid, scorned and kicked around and pushed aside like the dirty little brat he was. Stavers knew him then. They'd taken their lumps together. His name was Joey.

Joey knew it was Joey because that's what they'd called him, but no one had ever told him a second name, and before he could find it out his drunken whore of a mother abandoned him in a dirty mining town in Arizona. He was half-starved and he ate from garbage cans, fighting the cats and the rib-showing dogs, but somehow he got along even with these civilized predators. Stavers lived with a packrat of unwanted Hispanic, Indian, and gutter white kids who'd been taken in by a warm, wonderful group of old men who'd formed an orphanage within their Gospel Ministry ... or perhaps the orphanage had found them. In their instincts of hunger, misery, fear, and privation, the kids managed to spread the word through their packs and they began to collect about the Fathers of the ministry, who were simply overwhelmed by the needs of these youngsters. The ministry had no money and only ramshackle buildings, and the only food and clothing and medicine they could obtain came from begging donations or having the ministers work seven days a week and most of the nights attending to their wide-eyed, thin-limbed orphans. Including Joey and his friend, the Stavers kid.

The permanent bond had formed in a filthy, dust-caked alley when they were ten years old. They'd been backed in the alley by a crowd of smartass rancher kids out for sport. Sport was to set a big hunting dog on Joey and Doug, backs to a fence, no place to run, watching the animal with long teeth exposed and growling horribly. You don't *need* to be more than ten years old to know when there's no more place to run, when it's time to quit being afraid, when whatever childish phrases you know say fuck the consequences. A dozen well-fed kids screaming for the dog to chew them up and Joey white with the fear and sick through his trembling body, and Stavers found a beer bottle. He'd seen enough fights. He knew what to do. It was actually *doing* it that was everything. He broke the bottle and held it by the neck, silent, unmoving, waiting, and the big damned dog made its move and charged. Stavers didn't move the bottle more than an inch up or down or left or right but he did shove it straight forward and the dog took the sharp splintered glass in his nose and one eye and set up a demon howl you could hear a mile away. Blood sprayed as the animal thrashed wildly and the boy stepped forward quickly, raking sideways with the bottle, and tore off the dog's ear and got the other eye. The animal went mad and raced back through the now-terrified gang and Stavers hurled forth a primal scream and ran *at* them, wild and mindless. He heard a screech of rubber and an abrupt howl of agony and then silence. The damned dog had run in his pain before a car that killed him. There was blood everywhere. Stavers dragged Joey to his feet with one hand and with the other he put the bloody, jagged bottle in Joey's hand.

"We're going. Don't be afraid. Don't you ever be afraid of nobody or nothing no more." They walked out onto the sidewalk and the other kids melted away before them and Joey was never again afraid. Not of nobody or nothing no more. He'd stepped across that invisible line. His friend Doug had shown him the way. Never be afraid to die. They can't hurt you that way. Shit, they can't *reach* you that way. Look upon death with a glorious delight and fascination.

You'll find death stepping aside for you, and if he doesn't, who the shit cares?

They stayed together until they were fifteen, when Stavers left the Gospel Ministry. Joey was staying. Joey had changed and Stavers hardly knew him. It wasn't a bad change, but Joey was searching for something and it was nothing he could really identify.

Stavers left and the years melted away in hard combat training and earning his paratrooper wings, learning to fly and how to kill a hundred different ways, and learning also through one war after another that he was blessed, if that was the word— and he believed it was—with that deep primal instinct of both killing and surviving anything that might be thrown at him. He went back to the Gospel Ministry with some familiar faces that were a lot more lined and tired, and the place had decent barracks and all new young faces; they were still on the social shitlist but things were better. He found Father Jim Garvey running the place now, clumsy with a limp and a cane. Cancer had chewed up a leg and a drunken doctor cut it off just above the knee. Garvey shrugged and figured the Lord wanted him to remain at the Ministry and attend to the new kids spilling in.

"Where's Joey?"

"I'll need a better name than that, Douglas."

"He didn't have a better name, remember? We called him Joey. Joey No-name. I left here when I was about fifteen and Joey decided to stay here a while longer. I think he was trying to learn why you old fools devoted your lives to taking care of outcasts like we were."

Garvey smiled. "Never thought I'd see the day when being called an old fool was a compliment."

"What about Joey?" Stavers persisted.

"I'm trying, I'm trying. You said yourself I was an old fool. It takes time to poke through all the cobwebs in a head, Douglas." He scratched a stubbled chin. "You say he remained here to learn more about compassion?"

"No. You're saying that. He was trying to figure out why you people gave everything you had to kids you didn't know."

"Ah, but we're all brothers under the—"

"Stop it, old man. You gave me your help and your love and my life. Forget the words. Do you remember what Joey did? Where he went? Anything?"

"Yes, I remember now." Garvey's eyes widened. "Oh, yes, how could I have forgotten? He became one of the most remarkable people we've ever known. An incredible spirit! Do you know what he did?"

Stavers remained patient, quiet. "No, sir."

"He memorized the Bible. *Memorized it.* He could quote from anywhere about anything."

Stavers didn't figure that one. "Then what?" he said.

"*Then* he memorized the Old Testament as well. *Both* Bibles. The Old and the New. It was a miracle, Douglas."

"And after that?"

"He left here. He said he had a mission in life, I

recall. He went to Salt Lake City. Said he had business with the Mormons. He was going to re-member the Book of the Mormons, their teachings, and he would, to use his own words, bloody well commit everything *they* had to mind."

"Did he?"

"He did."

"Where did he go after that?"

"We received some cards from Burma. Yes; it was Burma." Before Stavers could wonder aloud at that, Garvey's memory was going full tilt. "Then there was a letter from China. He was learning languages by then. He had a lot to say about Bud-dha and he wrote us about Shinto. He could speak all the languages, he told us. He was on his way to Japan."

"And?"

"He gave himself a name."

Patience, patience. "Do you remember it, Father?"

"It would be impossible to forget. We have a picture of him he sent us from Tibet."

Stavers felt his head spinning. He went with Garvey into a spartan apartment and with age-trembling hands the old man handed him a photo-graph. Stavers could barely recognize Joey. He had a deeply-sunk look about him, gaunt with deep, dark eyes. Not body-hunger look. This man was searching for soul food. To feed what magic sprang from the mind, from wondering. "What's his name?" Stavers asked of the man with the shaven skull and toga-like garment wrapped about his body.

"Akim Asid."

"You're putting me on."

"I don't understand."

"Nothing, Father. This was taken in Tibet?"

"We don't know. Tibet, perhaps India or somewhere like that. We know it was Asia. We can't find the envelope. The stamps could have told us. There was also a letter but we can't find it any more. Joey said he had been deep into Shinto and he had learned much from the Bhagavadgita." The word slurred from the old lips.

"What the devil is that?"

"Devil might be a good word, but maybe I'm wrong. I don't know much about the Hindu scriptures. There was something he said about Islamic studies. Is that Moslem or Muslim?"

"Damned if I know," Stavers said. "I suppose it's a point of view. But where did Joey get the name of Akim Asid? And *why?* It sounds like he's on a religious drunk of some kind."

"I fed him," Garvey smiled. "You were his friend. You can answer that better than I."

That's where it ended, and now Doug Stavers had need for Joey No-name. Change that; for the cadaverous, haunting man in the robes he'd seen in that photograph with the name of Akim Asid. Well, apparently Joey—damnit; *Akim*—was making waves, and when you made waves, certain people could always find you. And one of those people was Josh Logan.

They still had two days to go on the tanker. Wisely, and selfishly, Stavers pushed from his mind the turbulent thoughts demanding so many answers. He might never have this moment again. Two days with Rosa, unbothered, uninterrupted, the crew walking on glass splinters about them. A luxurious cabin. Freedom with one another.

Rosa accepted his decision to put aside the world. She had never known how to do that. And what conscience needled at her, she dismissed with her own logic. This man, whom I tried to kill, whose lover I did kill, has me completely in his power for him to end my life any time he chooses. Instead, he makes love to me, and only with my consent. *Heavenly Father, abide a while. I am still with you.* This was love, utter bliss, incredible and exquisite feelings. *But you know all that is to be. This will end. One day it will end, and Heaven will be waiting.*

She felt better for this communion with God. For she had found another heaven, right here, *now*, beneath her fingers, pouring forth from his body into her. Revelation was a word inadequate to describe the wonder coursing through every fiber of her being. She responded with a naked-soul fury of pure passion.

She was too engrossed in the miracle of the flesh to see the devastating impact her release had on the man making love to her.

Chapter XX

He spent a long day briefing Skip Marden and Kathy Sloan on new plans and schedules he'd worked out for the immediate future. Deep within the sprawling underground complex beneath the service station in Indian Bluff, Stavers ran through a litany of details so extensive and complex that by mutual consent Kathy recorded every word and gesture on videotape. At any time in the future when a question arose in Stavers's absence, she could best determine his orders by reference to Stavers on that tape.

Indian Bluff remained his electronic fortress. He moved Ken Longbow into Hoot Gibson's office as sheriff. Longbow had served him well as a deputy and his entire family lived off Stavers's land. There'd be no compromise with the exacting security he'd built into Indian Bluff. To be certain his people would never run short of hard money in his absence, he transferred four million dollars to his local operational account to be dispensed by Kathy Sloan as needs or orders came in. The details seemed endless, and Stavers chafed to get on with the more important details of what lay ahead.

Above all, new and foolproof identification. Passports, licenses, credit cards, checking accounts, business contacts, and a flawless record of school, jobs, and family. Computers eased that need for himself, for Rosa and Marden. They'd be traveling soon, and moving to other countries under their own names was insanely dangerous. The death toll behind them was becoming a full-scale war casualty list and they had the alarmed attention of a dozen governments. Setting up that routine with the missing atomic bombs was having its own backlash. Governments everywhere were alarmed at what terrorists could do with such weapons, and terrorist groups were intensely intrigued for the same reasons. Too many people were starting to pay really serious attention to them. So they became different people with different names, and they were in the import-export business. There were still more details. Stavers had a Grumman G-III assigned to them along with a double crew so they could fly anywhere at any time and for whatever time might be required. He hand-picked the crews who found themselves heavily armed, paid triple wages, ready to go anywhere and absolutely disinterested in anything that went on about them. The G-III with swept wings and new engines could reach any continent or ocean with its special tanks and it could do so ten miles above the Earth. It was registered to a Saudi Arabian oil billionaire.

He couldn't find Akim Asid. He got in touch with Josh Logan who in turn flew to Salt Lake City to rummage amidst the Mormon hierarchy. They did indeed remember a most unusual man who'd buried himself in their archives. He had spent eight months with them, an austere man with incredibly blue, deep, penetrating eyes. Where had he lived all that time?

"You're not going to believe this," Josh told him, somewhat awkward about the matter.

"I'm ready to believe *anything* at this point," Stavers said impatiently. Marden and Rosa sat together with them. "Just *tell* me and let me decide, will you?"

Josh nodded. "First, you couldn't forget his name. Joseph. They kept asking him for his full name and he kept insisting it was Joseph. That's all. If they needed a name for their records then they could use his initials. JNN. Naturally, they asked him what that meant and he told him it was for Joseph No-Name. He never cracked a smile about that. He *meant* it."

Stavers nearly broke up laughing. Joey was pulling it off! He was making the world respond on *his* own terms. God, that was great. He thought of the terrified kid and that snarling dog in the alley and he felt better the more he bridged the gap between long ago and now. "Okay, back to where he lived," Stavers prompted.

"At a small boarding house. I spoke to the old woman myself. Miriam Crane. She's frightened stiff at the whole thing. It seems this Joey with no name showed up and asked for room and board and at the same time told her he had no money. He was wearing this crazy robe, like an Indian—Hindu—wraparound or whatever it is, and sandals. She figured him for some kind of religious nut and was about to politely send him away when he fixed his eyes on her and began to speak. From that moment on she was a goner."

"How? Why?"

"It was what he said. He looked at her in such a way that she couldn't divert her eyes from his, and then he spoke to her from the Book of Ether, which is also a record of the people of Jared. I'm telling you now what *he* said to *her.* As best I could understand, it was that he asked her to recall from the Book of Mormon that the people of Jared were scattered at that time the Lord confounded the language of the people, when they were building a tower to get to heaven. They were not to forget what great things the Lord had done for the fathers of the House of Israel, and this Joseph told the woman that the only way to build the tower that would take anyone to heaven and eternal life was through the tower of words. He stood there and then he began to quote the Book of Mormon. Not passages from the book, but from the *beginning,* he started out with the numbers and the words of Nephi, and he talked without stopping for an hour *and he was reciting the entire book from memory*. Mrs. Crane managed to stop him then. She said she had to struggle to get out the words. She told him he must be hungry, she fixed him dinner, and, well, she put him up for the eight months he was in Salt Lake City, and never charged him a dime and when he left, he blessed her, and Doug, as far as Miriam Crane is concerned, that blessing came from the hand of the Lord right through that of Joseph. Only," Josh said with reflection, "now she calls him *Saint* Joseph."

"That it?" Stavers said.

"What do you want? A chorus of angels and massed trumpets?"

Stavers shook his head. "No, of course not. And thanks for coming down. Only I haven't solved my problem. I still need to reach this man."

Rosa smiled. "The man you call Joseph No-Name."

"No, Rosa, that's what *he* calls himself. He goes by another name, however."

"Tell me," Josh said, a bit petulant, for he didn't like to come to Stavers with loose strings on a request.

"Akim Asid."

Behind him Skip Marden guffawed. "Hell, I know *him!*" he said loudly.

Stavers turned with disbelief. Marden gestured with both hands. "I don't mean I know him personally, or talked with him, but I saw him, oh, maybe a week before we made our little trip south. It was in San Francisco."

"Man, you are leaving me on a fence," Stavers said acidly.

"I was on a charter job flying choppers out of San Fran airport. I met a broad. Really far out, an absolute hammer. Beautiful. She knows ways of—"

"Stay with it," Stavers growled.

"Sure. Anyway, she was far out in more ways than one. Frisco is filled with religious cults. Divine

Light Mission, International Society for Krishna
Consciousness, the Light of Armegeddon, a whole
slew of others. The biggest was the Unification
Church run by Sun Myung Moon. The Reverend
Moon and his weirdo Moonies. This broad, Samantha, was all hung up on Sun Myung Moon. To me
it sounds like a main course in a Chinese restaurant. But she talked me into going to one of their
mass meetings. You never heard so much moaning
and praying and wailing in all your life, but this
round-faced Korean had ten thousand people there.
He also had something *I* recognize right away.
Guards. A whole damn passel of guards. Pros. Martial arts types. Apparently he's worth millions now
from his adoring flock who can't wait to give him
everything they own."

Skip shook his head with his recollections. "I
don't know how it happened, but this guy with a
shaved head—and there were lots of them—but
this one walks up to the stage, stands quietly until
the guards check him out, and right in front of ten
thousand people he bows to the chief Moonie, you
could hear him on the loudspeakers, and he asks
Moon to ask him anything from any of the holy
books. I mean, he said *anything*. I guess Moon
figured he had some devout asshole on his hands
so he played along with it and asked a few questions. The answers came rolling out in a voice that
wouldn't let go of you and they were perfect quotes.
Moon started on some remote religions of Asia. It
didn't matter. Buddhist or Shinto or Islamic. It
didn't matter. He asked, this Akim Asid answered.
The crowd went mad, screaming and yelling and
cheering. And then Asid turns to the crowd and

holds both hands up and the place is instant silence. I'll never forget it. He stands there and his voice booms out. 'I come to you as the voice through which the Lord God speaks and I bring to you from Him the word.' He hangs in there, you can hear a pin drop, and then, I swear his eyes were on fire the way he looked, he says one word. 'Bullshit.' "

"Is that what you thought of what he said or what he *did* say?" Stavers asked.

"That's what he said. *Bullshit.* Then he just walked down from the stage and out an exit and he was gone. You ever see ten thousand people left like sheep clobbered over the head by a sledge-hammer? That's what it was like. Samantha looked like her pet mule had died, crying like a baby. I couldn't figure it out and I couldn't take any more so I split. That's it."

It made sense only to Stavers. He got Ken Longbow on the phone, gave him the different names, the description, and where he might be found in San Francisco if he were still in that city, and requested an All Points Bulletin from the local police on Akim Asid. "Then you get up there yourself, Ken. Go find this Akim character and tell him *I* want to see him. He probably won't pay any attention to you. Tell him the kid in the alley with the broken beer bottle needs him."

"You sure of all this, Mr. Stavers?"

"Just do it, Ken." He hesitated. "And bring him back."

"Yes, sir."

It was all falling into place now. Stavers remembered a lot more about Joey, the way he concentrated so intently on whatever he got into, and the rest became a matter of deduction. There was Alberto Grazzi, who sat with the Board of Directors in the Hotel El Cid; Grazzi, the man who never forgot numbers. The computerized memory. The billion fingers and toes always digitizing their way through his skull. Instant, total recall of anything to do with numbers and figures. But he didn't have any more brains than the guy pushing a broom in the men's room. He had memory but little else between the ears. He was a recall wizard and an intellectual flop. There were people like that. A man who worked in a change booth in the subway of New York couldn't remember to pour piss out of a boot before leaving for work every morning, but he could tell you the complete performance record of every baseball player of every team, dead or alive. And he did so instantly upon being questioned. They were so mutated in their memory process they came under the heading of freak.

Not Joey. He had brains, cunning, survival instincts. Street sense. He was brilliant. *And* he had total recall of anything he read if he so willed it. Which was just what he was doing. He was memorizing every theological text and document he could find. He *would* be the voice of the Lord; that's what he would tell people, and they'd believe him because no ordinary human being could recite chapter and verse the voice of *any* God you might care to name. It was an incredible gimmick, a wonder, and Joey was going to play it to the hilt. He watched the Moonies and studied all the cults and he was learning how and what to do . . . and when he was ready, why, he'd whip up a cult that would spread like a prairie fire and be just as unquenchable.

The scared kid had come a long way from a scummy whoring mother and his own shaking legs in that filthy alley. Stavers grinned: long live Akim Asid! Then his brow knitted. Not yet, though. Not until Joey No-Name paid off an old debt written in blood with a broken beer bottle. Stavers had just selected the fourth member of his team to find Colonel-General Ernst Patschke.

And the Messiah Stone.

Chapter   XXI

Rosa's expression was carved marble: blank and unseeing. Not a facial muscle twitched. Stavers nearly laughed aloud. He knew Rosa was barely concealing her astonished reactions to the appearance of Akim Asid. *This* was Joey? Joey No-Name? It was unthinkable! Akim Asid stepped through the doorway to the underground chamber. He stopped to take the measure of all about him. Good, thought Stavers, he's learned his survival lessons well. Joey was taller and, Stavers judged carefully, not simply bigger, but huge, compared to his last sight of Joey-become-Akim.

If this was what a holy man should be, then Akim Asid was *it*. His head was shaved and browned by the sun, although the wide dome of skin had a startling golden hue. Bushy, pure-white eyebrows were disconcerting, resting as they did in the form

of a bridge with pale blue eyes so piercing and
deep as to appear artificial. A diamond hung from
his left ear, a heavy gold necklace lay about his
neck and rested against his chest, and wrapped
about his body was his own creation of sari and
toga, yards of some fine material with a rustle of
silk and some unrecognized synthetic. Three rings
on his left hand and two on his right. Fine sandals,
leather and burnished gold, on his feet.

Rosa remained silent because she had spent a
lifetime in acquiesence to holy men; not even a
two-headed creature with green horns would have
changed that. If there was to be doubt, then a
frozen face and a silent tongue was infinitely better to some possible insult, no matter if never intended. A deep-red ruby lay in the center of his
forehead; contrasted with those startling blue eyes
and the salt-white of bushy eyebrows, it had its
intended effect of diverting attention while its
wearer had the opportunity to do his own study of
whoever appeared before him. Akim Asid bowed
to Rosa; Stavers watched Rosa trying to find something *right* to do, bow or curtsy or shake hands, or
what. Finally she chose the safe way. She bowed
her head briefly and acknowledged the imposing
figure before her with a single word.

"Father."

He bowed again, his hand sweeping easily through
a salaam of greeting and respect. He turned slightly
to face Skip Marden. As tall and as wide the girth
of Akim Asid, Marden was taller, and where he
lacked the belly girth of Asid, Marden's shoulders
were like the yoke to which one harnessed a team
of oxen. Each nodded briefly to the other, and

finally Akim Asid turned to Doug Stavers. They
stared into each other's eyes and finally Asid bowed
deeply, his hand sweeping through another elaborate salaam before he straightened. His right hand
extended before him.

"How are you, you motherless son of a bitch!"
he bellowed and threw his arms about Stavers.
They pounded one another on the back, standing
at arm's length, holding one another's forearms
like ancient gladiators.

"You've come a long way since that goddamned
alley, Joey. You ever going to make yourself decent and figure out some kind of full name?"

"Akim Asid is at your service, your worship.
Knock off the crap about names. This one is doing
just fine."

"I don't think I'd have recognized you," Stavers
admitted.

"You weren't supposed to," Akim glanced at
Marden. "You're a big bastard. I've seen you
before."

"We never met." Skip glanced from Akim Asid
to Stavers. "What the hell do I call him?"

"Joey will do fine," the big man with the jeweled forehead told him. "And we did meet. In San
Francisco. You were with a girl with long blonde
hair. One of those loonies who wanted nothing
more than to have the Reverend Moon take a dump
in her mouth."

Marden was open-mouthed. "How the hell could
he know all *that*? There were ten thousand people
there!"

"You have a very distinctive hook to your nose,"
Joey told him. Marden shook his head in wonder.

Joey walked to an easy chair and sprawled comfortably. "It's hot, it was a long trip, and I dropped everything when Geronimo gave me your rather personal message," he said to Stavers. "So please get me something tall and cold. I'll take one of those excellent cigars of yours, and be good enough to let me have something for my feet—these fucking sandals; no wonder Christ stumbled on the way to the mount—to rest on. And then you can lay it on me, Doug."

Stavers pressed his desk call button. "Kathy, you get all that?"

"Yes, sir," came her voice through the speaker.

"Make the drink Silver Smirnoff, three ice cubes, a very tall glass, a couple of cigars and he uses matches only. Bring in something that will work as a hassock. If his feet were any bigger I'd call in the blacksmith."

They heard the start of laughter before she cut the switch. Stavers looked at Rosa, who seemed to be in a state of shock. "Rosa, sit down before you fall down."

She sat heavily on the couch by Marden. "I don't believe *any* of this. He's supposed to be a holy man!"

A white eyebrow went up. "What did you expect? Vinegar and scourging? What are you? Some kind of religious fanatic? You have the look about you, that's for certain."

She gasped. "I hardly think a life of training in the private schools of the Vatican could be called fanatic!"

He fixed his eyes upon her and with all her strength she almost pulled back. "I didn't drop everything I was doing and come here to see the only man in this world I call friend to be bothered with theological shit from *anybody*, including you. And to answer your insipid remark, yes, a life of training in the Vatican certainly does qualify you for the category of flaming fanatic. Now just butt out, bitch. If Doug wants you in, he'll tell me." With those words he casually and utterly dismissed her as nothing more than a biological entity who happened to be in the room. Like a small dog, perhaps. And he meant it, and Rosa knew it, and she was completely at a loss. But no longer flustered. Catholicism has one great advantage to it. If you can't love a man, or even like him a little, then hate him. She knew right then she hated this man, and she knew as well, by her judgement of him and especially his relationship with Doug, to conceal that fact.

She felt stupid. She also knew the three men in the room had already judged her feelings and were ignoring them. She was grateful when Kathy came into the room with the drink and cigars and the hassock and fussed over him.

"Thank you, child," Joey said in a deep, sonorous voice as different from his conversational tone as if he were a totally different person. "The Lord find favor with you. Put your bread on Snowbird in the fifth at Belmont."

Kathy jerked upward, startled. "What?"

"Simply a riposte of angels, my dear. You can go now." She left the room as if something were nipping at her heels.

"Whoever the hell you are," Marden said with admiration, "I like your style."

"Of course," Joey told him after sipping at his drink. "In a man of your obvious caliber I would expect to find a keen sense of the superior. I congratulate you on your breeding."

Marden turned to Stavers. "Does this go on all the time?"

Stavers grinned. "You're on your own with him. But I think he's already measured you for size and you have a friend you didn't have before," Stavers told him.

Marden tossed a sloppy salute to Joey, and the great imposing figure of Akim Asid winked back. Joey looked to Stavers. "Let's have it, man. I got a whole new religion to launch out there in the big, bad world and you're keeping millions from being saved."

"I need to find someone," Stavers said. "He's ex-military from the second big war to end all wars. He left by plane while Hitler was swallowing poison. He was a captain and with a small force he chewed up a couple of thousand Russians and an everlastingly grateful Hitler made him a Colonel-General. He flew nonstop to South America as the Russians took Berlin. He probably had some jewels with him, one especially, and from what we understand, some chemical formulas and industrial documents worth an absolute fortune today. I'm interested in one diamond only. His name is Ernst Patschke."

"And you just about burned down a mountain trying to nab him," Joey said quietly. He saw the startled movement of Marden and Rosa Montini. "They provide immediate confirmation, anyway. Hardly a secret, Doug. That place went off with a bang big enough to register on the Richter scale and it burned two days and nights. They could see it for three hundred miles at night."

Rosa motioned without thought of her hand. "But how could you know these things?"

"I have contacts, woman. I'm converting hapless Catholics to souls permitted to lust freely in the hereafter. They keep me informed of what occurs in most places of the world. Will you just shut up?" Before she could utter a sound he was back with Stavers.

"How bad you want the rock this Patschke has?"

"I contracted to get it. My word."

"That's big medicine, then."

"It is that," Stavers said calmly.

"Got a name for the rock?"

"It goes under different names. My people refer to it as the Messiah Stone. Godstone is good enough for me. Rosa's people have a different aspect on the issue. To them it may well be the actual Star of Bethlehem. Part of a bolide."

"That figures," Joey said. "I talked to my oracle. He said the night the kid was born it was cloudy and raining. Anything God arranged to shine a couple of thousand light years away wouldn't have been visible. Lousy timing, but the disciples had to say *something*." He took a long pull on his cigar. "What's so special about the diamond? Aside from the fact that the Pope is squeezing his nuts he wants it so badly, that is." He glanced at Rosa and blew her a kiss. She was turning purple.

"You need to know that." Stavers made it a conclusion stated aloud rather than a question.

"Nobody ever got gin with only nine cards, Doug."

"Yeah. There are stories. One is that bit about being the Star of Bethlehem. Who knows? But no matter where it came from, it's reputed to have the power to affect the minds of men in the vicinity of the man wearing or holding the diamond. It was with an African tribe called the Manturu for about two thousand years." Stavers started at the beginning in a tight but fully informative capsulization of events, names, dates and places. "So that's it," he concluded.

Joey nodded. "Question. Do you believe the Hope Diamond's curse is real? That it does bring on death?"

"Tough to answer, because I never gave it much thought. In the physical sense I'd have to give you a negative response."

"Do you believe this great yellow diamond can affect the minds of men? Cloud their judgement, so to speak. Or even closer to the issue, dim their ability to function with cognitive reality. They're being bullied between the lobes without knowing its source. How does all that fit, Doug?"

"Same category answer. I admit readily that nothing logical accounts for Hitler's incredible sway over other people, his domination of skilled diplomats and his crushing grip on the German general staff. But the logic may not be in the diamond. I don't know. It didn't work—Hitler's aura, that is—on all people. After the war was in full swing he did everything he could to get Franco to join the war on his side. That would have given him Gibralter and locked up the Mediterranean and

North Africa. I know that Franco resisted him. Something went wrong there. I didn't know Franco or anyone that did know him. He must have been something special to resist Hitler."

"Franco promised him a holy war if he invaded Spain," Joey said quietly. "He also promised to bring in the Turks and the Portuguese with him against Hitler and Mussolini."

"He was also a devout Catholic!" Rosa snapped, the words leaping unbidden from her lips.

"I was hoping you'd say that," Joey smiled at her. "You're right, of course. The monument to him, the cross, the marble edifice carved into the mountain that is his tomb, is indeed magnificent. So is the fact that Franco was half-Jewish and that he hated Hitler." Joey was back with Stavers. "The end shot is that you need me to find your precious Ernst."

"You got it, Joey."

"You look much yet?"

"Very much. The Israelis have been searching for him for years. Their program is, well, somewhat delayed now."

"I know. Pasaja."

Stavers showed admiration for Joey's sources. "Then the Vatican has to be considered. They—"

Rosa shot to her feet. "Doug, *please*. He doesn't *need* to know!"

"I think I'll call you Joan of Arc," Joey said. "I've never seen such burning desire to be a fool. Doug's not breaking any secrets, woman. The Six Hundred is the worst kept secret in the world of religious cultism. For some reason the Papacy has the idea that if they mumble incantations over large and foul candles their secrets remain forever hidden from the rest of the world. And—" A finger with a jeweled ring stabbed at her. "So *you're* the one!" he said with quiet triumph. "The girl missing and presumed dead. The ultimate soldier for the Holy See. The modern crusader, as it were. And you really believe your stumbling Six Hundred remain a secret? Rosa Montini, have you never heard of the U-2 or the RB-57B or the RS-71 or the K11 reconnaissance satellites? They have everything but color movies of your vaunted Italian commandos in training. And since they're looking so hard for you, obviously they must pass on the word. Thank you. I always prefer to reach conclusions myself. Having someone else read the last page of a whodunnit to me is always a bummer."

Joey finished his drink, lit a fresh cigar, and watched Kathy enter the room with replacement drinks all around. He waited until she'd left the room.

"I know where Patschke is," he said quietly. He let his words sink in, then looked at Rosa and from her to Stavers. "The next question is whether you want *her* to have that information. Obviously you two have been tumbling in the sack. She has that teenage shine on her cheeks that comes from a good lay. But she'll also cut your throat when the right time comes, because while you're a good piece of ass, my friend, Jehoshua promises her eternal love, and that beats you coming and going, if you'll pardon the pun."

Marden blinked. "Who the hell is Jehoshua?"

"That's Christ's name. His title was Jesus the Christ. It got screwed up in translations from

Aramaic into Greek and back into our language. Let's not get sidetracked on bad historicity. What about it, Doug?"

Stavers didn't hesitate. "She hears it all."

"Good. It's been a while since I've remained for any time in the company of a female Judas. See? She *can* learn. She's been quiet for a while."

"Where is Patschke, Joey?"

"Where *you* would never expect to find him, but where *I* know he must be. Now, if I know you, my friend, you've had thousands of photographs of him sent throughout the world. Which, of course, is a worthless gesture because no one has a picture of him taken less than thirty-five years or so ago. Your rewards to police forces about the world are equally as useless, because a man like Patschke, on the immediate scene, can control his movements and his visibility. Finally, if that yellow ice he carries with him *does* have the power it's reputed to have, who's going to fight him? Or reveal him? Now, at the same time, he will *not* remain obscure. *He can't.*"

"I figured the same way," Stavers said. "He's running out of time. He doesn't have that much longer to live."

"Right on, Holmes, right on."

"You still haven't told me where he is," Stavers repeated, quietly but with great emphasis.

"I'm not playing a game," he was told. "It's just as important for you to know *why* he's where he is as it is for you to know where. Because that in turn affects our chances for finding him. And if I know my messiahs and their followers, we'll get the hoary old bastard. Never forget that he's under that time constraint. The only way he can make the move he wants for power, and I'm assuming he wants that more than anything else in the world because his psyche pattern is unmistakable, is to become the messiah. *All* messiahs *plan*. All religious leaders while they're alive are cultists. The religion forms *only after* the messiah or prophet has gone to the happy hunting grounds. It was that way for the man we call Christ. Mohammed followed in the same footsteps and willingly paid tribute to his forebears, and so on. Each of those men who finally donned the cloak of messiah survived to be elevated to godhead status because they were smart enough and tough enough to realize that a lot of nonbelievers and other would-be messiahs were doing their damndest to wax their asses. This is the reality behind the chorus of angels. Murder, assassination, plotting, scheming, cheating, lying—*all* the bibles are dripping with it. The beatitudes that filter down to us are so cleansed by the goody-two-shoes filled with saintly fervor as they *re*write the good books that we forget a man is pretty vulnerable when he's holding his dork in his hand and taking a piss against a cactus."

Joey reached within the multiple folds of his wraparound cloak and withdrew a heavy prayer necklace, a thickly braided rope-like material studded with oval shapes of different colors. His action was reflex and he drew no special attention to the beads; the whole thing might have been a giant-sized rosary and without deliberate thought he moved his fingers from one bead to another. "All right, it's time to fish or cut bait," he said, looking up beneath those incredible eyebrows and the glow-

ing ruby in his forehead. "Doug, dim the lights in
the room. I'm going to find Patschke for us now."

Stavers shrugged and turned off several lights.
Joey sat with eyes closed, making a steeple of his
hands with fingertips of each hand against the
others. Marden stared; he could swear *that ruby
was brighter than before, was actually glowing.*
Marden looked at Rosa and she looked back with a
face as blank as stone.

"He cannot remain obscured from us." Stavers
wondered for a moment whether he was listening
to Joey or Akim Asid. "Those about him offer total
devotion. There is the awesome, the overwhelming
effect of aura. There is an inevitable outward rip-
pling effect of human affairs. Consciousness is em-
battled. Sodom and Gomorrah face us once again.
The saviour is needed. The people about him believe! He disturbs the ether, he raises great waves
in the turbulence of human affairs. The son of a
bitch is holding court without all this mumbo
jumbo just where I thought he was."

Joey opened one eye and winked at Stavers. "Do
you know how much money people make selling
plastic crosses with that hungup little doll every
year? Lights, please."

Marden shook his head in wonder. Stavers wasn't
surprised at anything, but Rosa couldn't contain
herself again. "Don't expect *me* to believe you found
Patschke through that ridiculous trance of yours!"

"Shit, no. I knew where Patschke was before I
ever came here. Go take a cold douche or something." Again he switched off his recognition of
her. "Doug, he has to move pretty fast now. What
happened in Colombia and Ecuador was that you

brought his house of cards tumbling down around his ears. He can't work through the industrialists as he'd been planning all this time. As far as they're concerned, he lit out for parts unknown because that diamond, or whatever his talisman is, wasn't doing him a bit of good. If, as you say, it requires a physical immediacy, a body relationship within a certain distance, then he has to forget everything he was doing before and go for the big one. He needs a mass audience within which he can mix, create a slow-building hysteria of love for him— and baby, believe me, it has *got* to be love, Christ was right on that score—and from that hysteria he can get a frenzy. Things start squaring themselves then and they go outward from a small core, like a grenade going off in a room, starting with the heat of the explosion creating great shock waves that pour outward in all directions, hit the walls and bounce back. Goddamn, what a speech. I need a drink."

"Joey, you son of a bitch," Stavers said. *"Where?"*

Joey looked up with honest surprise. "You mean you haven't figured it out yet? It's so bloody obvious, man!" Joey looked at his audience one by one. "Any of you people see the movie *Close Encounters of the Third Kind?"*

Marden nodded. "I did."

"Then *think*, you big clod!"

"Of course," Marden said softly. *"Of course . . .* Doug, we're blind. *Patschke is in India."*

Joey took a long swallow of his vodka. "Sure as God made little pink testicles it ain't Patagonia."

"There's no question?" Stavers said.

"Of course not."

Rosa was almost frantic to speak. "But how could you—"

"Quiet, woman. Jesus is a prisoner in the Vatican and we've got to figure a way to bust him out of the joint." Joey cocked his head and tapped a finger against his temple. "The all-seeing eye never fails. Insight, that's what it is. Insight!" He turned back to Stavers. "What's the opposite of insight, anyway? I never really did find out. By the way— Marden, pay attention. Just so you won't strain your imagination, you *did* see the ruby glow. It works wonders on infidels and searching for new beliefs. Look, ma, no hands and no electricity. A microminiaturized circuitry built into the ruby with a battery the size of a pencil dot and good for almost two years of continuous glow for God. The transmitter is in one of my rings, also powered with the same system. When you're whacked out of your gourd on acid or quaaludes, believe me, this forehead glowing navel is a convincer beyond dispute. Now, back to business."

And just like *that*, the snap of a cerebral finger, he changed. The flippant tone was gone, the ersatz guru dismissed, and a very professional judge of human character and foibles was looking at them. "Doug, Patschke went to India because there, more than anywhere else in the world, holy cults and religions and emotional fervor is not only a way of life, but *the* way of life. You have six hundred million people in India alone; in the contiguous area, those lands and people and languages they touch directly or almost directly, the total number is something like two billion, nearly half the people on this entire planet. And the whole of it foments with religions like wine bubbling in a vat. Holy cults and castes, holy men and the anointed, sacred monkeys and cows and those who are venerated and those unclean, where millions starve to death but permit rats to swarm through the grain storage bins because the dominant caste in that particular area believes it's a no-no to kill living creatures. It would offend God. Nothing's changed from the ancient biblical times when the God of Moses slaughtered innocent babes wholesale and made people eat breadcakes wrapped about human dung as punishment. Hell, that's all *in* the good book. Things are just drastic in different ways in India. The main thing to understand is that India is a vast force of cults that almost overnight can assume a frenzied and definitely dangerous explosive growth. There have been so many messiahs and prophets, so many gurus and soothsayers, so many priests and all-knowing, that in that kind of theological swamp and ravishing religious hunger Ernst Patschke would be invisible even if you looked directly at him."

Stavers lit his own cigar and leaned against his desk. "But he's not invisible. We both know that. And he's going to become more and more visible until he's ready to explode like a bomb, but in the theological sense."

"Like an atomic bomb going off underwater," Joey added. "You don't even see the fireball until it punches out its shock wave and vaporizes everything around it and comes roaring and screaming from nowhere." Joey looked surprised with himself. "That's passably good. I ought to use it as a sermon. Anyway, it applies to Patschke. He's not only *not* invisible, he's already building an enormous cult about him. Our problem is that we can't see the cult. It's tough to find a forest when the whole planet is covered with trees. We've got to get in there among them, Doug. It's going to have to be reasonably quick, before he becomes too powerful, and it's going to cost a hell of a lot of shekels. Travel—"

"We have our own heavy iron, Joey. Double crews. The works."

"Bribes. *Lots* of bribes. We're going into the land of Shiva, among others. Now there's a god for you. Screws his brains out as the lord of reproduction and also is kept busy as the lord of destruction. Never a dull day. But bribery is the way of life over there. The more places you want to go, the more officials you need to see, and the more officials you see, the higher the price."

"No sweat."

"We'll need local transport, and if you want to keep your skins from rotting away, you'll need—"

"You'll need our experience more than yours for that," Marden said after his long silence. "Meaning no insult, Joey, but even that devil's barb of a tongue that you have won't get you through where our experience will."

Joey looked at Marden. "Your points are well made. I appreciate that. I also yield to superior experience."

"That's one of the best ways of staying alive when the natives are restless," Marden said.

"The logistics are in your hands, then. Thank you." Joey looked at Stavers. "You have the contacts you need with the proper government offi-

cials? I would have thought so. Very good. *I* have
the contacts with the army of gurus, temple leaders and holy men, which also means the police of
various localities. With all this and an open check-
book, we'll find him."

"Not for a moment do I doubt we'll find him,"
Stavers said quietly, but with a lethal authority
unmistakable in the room.

"Questions, Doug, if you don't mind?"

"Shoot."

"Who goes?"

"The four of us in this room."

"You're taking *her?*"

"The four of us in this room. You never asked
me to repeat myself when we were kids, Joey.
Don't start now, please?"

Joey didn't miss *any* of that. He'd just been reminded in the barest of subtleties who was running this show. "Very good," he went on smoothly.
"How many in your flight crews?"

"Four pilots, two navigators, two stewards, and
an additional two men who will fill different needs
as they arise. The G-III has international communications capability at any time, is linked to my
own computer system here at any time. All satellite links and *very* reliable."

"Who are we?"

"The four of us have worked for the past six
years for the Archeological and Anthropological
Institute of Arizona. AAIA for short. All records are
attended to. You are Joseph Akim Asid Sharif, for
the record, so any crossup of names won't be a
problem. All we need are some mug shots and
fingerprints for identification papers and we'll take

care of that as soon as this meeting ends. You also are the expert in anthropological cultures and above all our Ph.D. of theological studies."

"Excellent. Do I do all this for fun or is there compensation? Before you concern yourself with my having gone to the cashier's desk in Hades, if you're short I can well attend to my own needs and not burden you."

"You," Stavers said with a grin, "are slicker than owl snot on a brass doorknob."

"One hopes one does well." He offered a salaam to Stavers, who offered a finger in return.

"No problem with the money. You have an account?"

"What do you think?"

"At least a dozen."

"I prefer the even thirteen as a personal choice."

"Tell Kathy your favorite and we'll donate an even hundred thou to your cause."

"When do we leave?"

"Three days from right now. We've got a great many things already cleared up and now it's time to wrap up details. You've got to know Marden better, and I *am* going to ask you to drop the needles-under-the-eyeballs routine with Rosa."

Joey looked crestfallen. "I was just getting warmed up."

"Never mind. I need a *team*."

"All right. It's done."

"Rosa?"

Her eyes said one thing and her words another. "*Anything* to find that German devil and the diamond. Including full cooperation."

"I'm satisfied," Stavers said. "We'll work together as a team day and night starting tomorrow. Tonight, Joey, it's just you and me. We have a lot of catching up to do."

It had been a hell of a meeting. Joey was a lying son of a bitch. He'd learned that since they had last met, but he'd learned very, very well, indeed. Nobody who's acting out the role of a religious cultist or a guru or whatever the hell he was supposed to be was also a walking arsenal. The trick with the glowing ruby was nice vaudeville and it would stimulate the libido of those freaked out on acid or whatever.

But Joey clanked when he walked. He wore, among other things, a zodiac necklace, each sign of the zodiac neatly embossed in a wheel about three inches in diameter. Stavers had taken a very good look at that necklace. The rims showed the barest hairline along their circular edge, which meant that were intended to snap apart and release the deadly shuriken within, those eight-pointed stars that could be thrown with incredible accuracy and would imbed themselves two inches deep in a man's forehead. So what was his pal Joey, priestly garments and all, doing with a kind of weapon with which he could stand off people, or nail someone going the other way? Stavers had heard more, seen more. When Joey eased his great body into the chair the folds of his robe fell away to one side and Stavers knew why he wore such a garment. It concealed a lot and it also dampened sounds, which is why Stavers hadn't heard the wooden thunk of the nunchaku. They were advanced and deadlier cousins of nunchucks, made of rosewood and with a swivel chain connecting the wood. That flexible connection meant more speed and hitting impact than a nunchuck, which in the hands of a good man would let him smack unconscious or kill a half-dozen men closing on him.

And those rings. Stavers had thought long and hard about them. Joey's cover story with the glowing ruby was just that—a perfect cover story for a cheap-shot parlor trick that wouldn't fool a has-been magician. The cover was that he had more batteries, more micro-electronic chips and systems secreted within that all-enveloping drapery he'd hung on his body. Transmitters? Two-way transceivers? Was he also carrying explosives on him? Stavers didn't know, but he'd find out tonight when Joey went to sleep. An x-ray machine with a focus would go right through the wall of Joey's room and tell Stavers about things he couldn't see.

There were two more points that troubled Stavers. The first was that for a smart dude who was looking ahead and covering all bases, Joey had played awfully dumb about what was painfully obvious. If they were successful, then they would meet up with Patschke. They still had time to figure out how to take care of the wily old German and get their hands on that diamond.

But—*what happened then?*

Who would try to kill who? Marden was the only other person Stavers trusted completely. Rosa was in love with him. He felt it, he knew it, and he didn't need Pal Joey to remind him that Rosa believed utterly and implicitly that she was married for all time to Christ, had since she was a child. What she had to do with earthly pleasures to carry out her mission for the Papacy absolved her of all sins. Confession would dismiss such trivia. She would be a saint if she succeeded, so she let her emotions go along for the ride. Stavers saw no reason not to let her do so. He loved the girl and cursed himself for it, because he knew there would come the day when Rosa would draw down on him and he would have to kill her. And Rosa would lose because Stavers didn't underestimate her faith or her skills, and he had long before now warned Marden to keep an eye on the girl and at the first truly suspicious move to kill her. Rosa knew that but she didn't believe it. That would be her downfall.

That night he and Joey went to an out-of-the-way Mexican restaurant. It was ramshackle and dusty but the food was brilliant to the taste and the tequila excellent, and they were secreted away from the whole world. Stavers knew every man and woman and child in the place on a first-name basis. They were served and attended to and otherwise left alone, and Stavers began to wonder just when Joey would drop the great-old-days routine and break his shell.

He waited until after dinner. "You picked up on what I'm carrying," he said without preamble. Stavers allowed as how he had done just that. "And you're wondering who I'm working for, right?"

Stavers swallowed tequila and lemon and salt and acknowledged that he was. "I'm paid two hundred grand a year to build a master file on the cults and religions in the country today. They're powerful and getting more so all the time."

"Who's paying?"

"The National Council of Churches."

"You're kidding."

"Hell I am. Think I'm decked out like this because I light candles and count rosaries and sing psalms? Come on, Doug, this is *me*."

"I'd never know it."

"Two hundred thousand a year plus expenses helps."

"I guess so. Why is the Council paying all this loot?"

"Because the cults are getting so big they're taking the kids away from the churches. And if the churches don't have their infusion of young blood and young minds, they lose power. They lose power, then like *all* churches in history they start coming apart at the seams. Hell, look at Rosa Montini. She hasn't got a thing to do with the group I work for, but look at the way the Vatican is going at the same problem. They've got to increase their strength, dig in deeper, give the people something to offset the growing strength in other areas." Joey grinned. "I don't think the Vatican has ever gotten over Stalin's remark when someone discussed the Pope with him. Remember that? 'How many divisions does the Pope have?' That's all he wanted to know. Well, the old-time religions are building their muscle."

"And you're one of the shock troops."

"Right on, brother."

"I'm glad you told me, Joey."

"I figured, and I was right, that you knew something didn't lay right. Okay, the next question we've been avoiding. Do I need to make a speech about the Montini girl?"

"Nope."

"Who kills her?"

"*You* don't."

Joey shrugged. "You call 'em, Doug, like you always did."

"Right. Now, where are we going?"

"I've put a lot of thought to that. The best place to find out what we need to know, and I've already had some vibrations about this, is a small city near Bhagalpur. As you might have anticipated, it's on the Ganges, since that river is holy to the Hindus. West of Bhagalpur there's a north branch of the Ganges, the Kosi, which is fed by the snows melting off the Himalayas. And there is a town called Bhuj, where religious freedom is not only tolerated, but venerated as a source. That's where I believe we'll find Patschke. The town, or small city, is mainly temples. It's the perfect place from where Patschke can grow, because all India—in fact, that whole part of the world—believes a new prophet or messiah will spring from the temples of Bhuj."

"Where's the nearest main airfield?"

"Bhagalpur. In fact, it's got two. One is Indian Air Force and the other a sort of commercial hodge-podge, but it has some airlines and facilities for other planes."

"Where the hell did you get all this information so quickly?"

"While I was in my room."

"Who'd you call?"

"Oral Roberts."

"Stop crapping me, Joey."

Joey boomed with laughter. "That's our pet name

for the master computer that's maintained by the church council. They, or I should say the computer, told me everything I needed to know and," he snapped his fingers, "like *that*."

Everything fitted. It was a great dinner and a great evening and they had a lot of tequila in them as the Mexican waiter drove them back to the garage in Indian Bluff, let them off, and didn't wait around to ask any questions. Stavers didn't bother trying to keep quiet as he crashed into his apartment, and Rosa didn't bother to feign sleep as he sat heavily on the bed, slowly removing his boots. She pushed him back onto the bed to finish the job for him. He wasn't talking and she didn't pursue anything.

She got him onto the pillows and he sprawled comfortably. She stripped him naked and her hand slid between his legs. "Lock up," he said to her. "All alarms."

"They're on. Relax."

"With you squeezing my balls? You're kidding."

Her fingers caressed him. "Never."

When they finished making love, he slipped easily into a half-world of wakefulness and sleep. He snored lightly. She lay by his side to hear his murmuring as he slid down into a deep sleep. *"He's still a lying son of a bitch . . ."*

She lay awake a long time thinking about Joey.

Chapter   XXII

Four days later the sleek Grumman soared above the mountain ridges rising to each side of Indian Bluff Airport. They were on their way. One day's delay went into assuring their clearances in remote airports, being certain all palms were well greased and that all paperwork was in order and ground facilities were ready. Nothing was more maddening than to be screwed tightly against a fly-infested wall of a piss-ant airport while a seedy official stumbled through papers he'd never find until the local currency fattened his pocket. Except to have all *that* neatly out of the way, only to find the field was short of fuel or had the wrong fuel or the fuel truck didn't work or *something*. There was only one sensible way to avoid that, and Stavers took the expensive but most reliable route. He sent an advance man by commercial jet to every stop they planned to make. The advance man would pay off the officials, get ten copies of all paperwork, pay for and then tag-and-seal with police notice the fuel truck in question, and generally make sure the snags were paid for and out of the way before the Grumman with AIAA painted on its tail showed up.

They stopped in Los Angeles to top off fuel, pick up food and supplies, and check their final clearances and then headed across the Pacific to Hawaii. The crew rotation would work out perfectly. Roger Janca had left seat into Hawaii and decided to take her all the way along the next leg. "Mr. Stavers, it's a hop of some five thousand miles, a little less, nonstop into Manila. The winds look good and we should land with a thousand miles left in the tanks. Anything goes wrong along the way we can divert to Guam."

"I'm just along for the ride," Stavers told him, although both men knew that was nonsense. Neither Janca nor any other crewmen made that kind of decision without getting a personal authorization from Douglas Stavers. The long flight went well. Rosa dozed on and off, Stavers did a lot of heavy thinking, and Marden and Joey played gin rummy nonstop across most of the Pacific Ocean. They hit Manila three minutes ahead of schedule and called it quits for a while to soak in tubs and enjoy Filipino cuisine.

From Manila they had an easy straight shot to Calcutta, but the charts didn't reflect the bloodthirsty unhappiness on the ground below, and there was no way they'd fly through airspace controlled by North Vietnam and its contentious neighbors.

Janca took the airplane into Singapore in an easy hop of less than three hours. Heavy thunderstorms lined their route but the G-III sailed on up to 51,000 feet and had plenty of room to ignore the angry violence below. Singapore gave them a good opportunity to check with the advance man. Phil Nelson met privately with Stavers. "It's all set," he told him. "You'll be met by a Major Barsi Shahpur and a Mr. Sirpur Rajkot in Calcutta. They'll come aboard the aircraft before any of you depart. That way there'll be no chance for error."

"Who's waiting for us in Calcutta?"

"Gary Cowart, sir. I talked with him an hour ago. Everything is in order."

"What do you hear from that pesthole at Bhuj?"

"It's hot, the insects are horrendous, the local population like lemmings, the streets are jammed, and there's absolutely no place for visitors to stay. Something's up in that area, Mr. Stavers, but we've no idea what it is yet. Either a religious festival or a holy day, we don't know. Cowart informed me that Larry Vincent, he's your point man in Bhagalpur, went on to Bhuj personally with a heavy load of tents and equipment. You'll have to live at the airfield there unless you can make other arrangements. He's getting everything you need. Hired local helpers, that sort of thing. Then he'll hotfoot it back to Bhagalpur to meet you. I imagine that the Indians who'll meet you in Calcutta ought to fetch things a bit smarter than they seem right now."

"Nelson, you seem to have it pretty much in hand."

"Thank you, sir. Have a good flight."

They lifted through steaming heat from Singapore and turned northwest along the Strait of Malacca, Sumatra below the left wing and the Malaya Peninsula on their right. They cruised at 48,000 feet over the Andaman Sea, crossed the chain of Andaman Islands, and started down in a long descent with the pilots turning long and lazy to avoid scattered cumulus buildups. The Mouths of the Ganges appeared before them and they sandwiched in between a huge 747 and a DC-10, rolling along a Calcutta runway baking in oppressive heat. Money does wonderful things. A FOLLOW ME truck led them within a large hangar and the doors closed behind them as they taxied inside and shut down. A rumble filled the hangar as huge air conditioners poured relief into the metal structure.

Stavers stepped out of the airplane to be met by two Indians who might have emerged from the pages of their nation's history. Major Barsi Shahpur stood six feet three inches tall with a bristling handlebar moustache, an impeccable tailored uniform, white leggings and the inevitable swagger stick, clearly in use for a long time, judging from the polished and well-worn leather along the staff. Shahpur was of light brown skin and clearly he had learned his military bearings under British service. He snapped to attention before Stavers, his heels clicking together as if he were on parade, with a salute so crisp it seemed unreal and a booming voice. "Welcome to Calcutta, Mr. Stavers!" The major's hand shot out in personal greeting and Stavers took it. "We are at your service, sir. May I present Mr. Sirpur Rajkot of the Royal Indian National Police."

Rajkot was cut of different cloth, a man accustomed to slow thinking, great patience, and making his moves only when everything was neatly arranged to his satisfaction. He was of a darker skin and with a thinner moustache and wearing a suit of dark Italian silk. He was very sure of himself, wore pale sunglasses, and his jacket was just that extra large touch not to reveal the shoulder holster. He, too, was a very obvious professional, and there was no doubt but that he'd trained with Interpol and likely also in the United States. Stavers couldn't place his accent when he spoke; it lacked the British so clear in Shahpur's words. Whatever it was, it had been cultivated with great care. Rajkot greeted Stavers warmly, if with the inevitable police restraint. That figured also; Stavers had never heard of the Royal Indian National Police, and that meant a new secret police organization with far-reaching powers. Someone was cutting himself a slice of power in Indian politics. Stavers introduced his party and they wasted no more time in getting down to the business at hand.

"How long before we leave for Bhagalpur, Major?" Stavers asked. "We've come a long way and the University is short on both people and funds. If this airplane hadn't been placed on loan to us from Arizona Mines, we wouldn't have been able to make this trip at all."

"We understand," Shahpur said in agreement. "The paperwork is in order. We can dismiss customs and other such problems, but because of the speed we wish to offer you, may we ask that each member of your party submit to a photograph and a thumbprint from the right hand? It will take no more than an hour to provide each of you with a sealed identification card from Mr. Rajkot's office, a copy of which will be kept on file here, and in that manner there will never be any question of your status here, which is both of the honored guest and visiting scientists."

"Excellent, Major, and you have our gratitude for all your efforts, and Mr. Rajkot also, for what you've done for us. Can you tell me when our contact man will be able to see us?"

"Ah, Gary Cowart. We are good friends, Gary and I. He is an Anzac, you know. He prefers to consider himself both Australian and New Zealander. Did you know that when he was a young man he fought right here in India with the British Army? It seems a hundred wars ago. He's waiting for you now in our reception suite."

It all went smoothly. The fingerprints and photographs eased off any pressure Rajkot might be getting from his superiors, and it indicated complete cooperation on the part of the Americans to meet whatever the Indians required. Cowart greeted Stavers warmly. "Did Nelson give you the word on what's going on up at Bhuj? They're going crackers up there, I'll tell you that. A madhouse. People pouring in from everywhere. A great new prophet, an oracle. You can hardly move about. I hope Nelson informed you we'll all be staying at the airport. It's not much but a lot better than the constant rush hour in the town. We'll leave your new machine in Bhagalpur, of course, and continue on to Bhuj by several helicopters. You can thank the good major, here, for that. He cut a thick wad of red tape to bring that one off."

Stavers didn't need to mention that a small fortune had been paid to slice that red tape. Any mention of the machinations and payoffs behind the scenes would have wrecked everything they were doing. The more Stavers thought of that, the more he decided to follow instincts clamoring for attention at the back of his head.

"Major Shahpur, Mr. Rajkot, I would consider it an honor if you two gentlemen could accompany us to Bhuj," he said with as much openness as he could present. "There may be language difficulties where local dialects are concerned, and the last thing we wish to do is through ignorance offend any of the local people there. There have been times when Americans have blundered rather than walking the right paths."

The major smiled at him. "That took a bit of saying, Mr. Stavers. I commend you warmly for it." He glanced at the secret police official, and right then and there Stavers knew his instincts had been right. "I would be delighted to join your group. I can make a call and have whatever personal effects I need brought here immediately."

"My sincere apologies," Rajkot said with a slight bow. "I have other pressing duties. However, the major is more than up to the task of helping you thread your way through our customs."

That was it, then. If Stavers hadn't asked, then *both* men would have gone along. And Stavers was doubly glad he had made a last-moment change before leaving Arizona and decided to stay with everybody's real name. He had changed their association and business references, but that didn't matter at all. A neat little trick, that bit with the

thumbprints. They were already being fired by
computer printout via satellite to Interpol and
checked against file prints, and there was no way
they'd miss Stavers or Marden. The flight crew
would also be on file; most of them had military
backgrounds and their prints were strictly routine.
Rosa Montini and Joey Akim Asid Sharif were
clean; their prints would be going into the computers for the first time. And if Stavers proved to
be right, then Rajkot would show a sudden and
very piercing interest in one large student of theol-
ogy wrapped in his robes and clanking with holy
pendants. Because Indians just did not believe
Americans were *that* learned or serious on religious matters. Quite the opposite; they were plastic dullards who would *never* understand the true
meanings of life. Stavers suppressed a smile as
Rajkot made his move, smooth and pleasant, and
even Joey didn't miss it. *This* was the test, to
engage this large and strange American in conversation and ferret out whatever nonsense might be
behind his ridiculous posture.

Thirty minutes later Sirpur Rajkot was a stunned
and shocked believer. He had opened his own conversation coyly and he had a mountain of snares
with which to entrap the American with the strange
mixture of names. India was a land of many major
religions and hundreds of sects, but no matter
what Rajkot might say, Joey broke into the conversation and completed not only the thoughts but
the sentences of the Indian police official. When
Rajkot mentioned the holy books, Joey recited them
in a marvelous blend of piety and strength and the
words flowed from him as honey would pour from

an upended jar. By the time they were through, it was Rajkot who felt as if something were missing in his knowledge of his own people.

The end of their conversation was the signal to release the Grumman and they went aboard the aircraft in good spirits, Major Barsi Shahpur aware that something strange, perhaps even mystifying, had taken place between the robed American and Rajkot. He had never before seen the policeman at a loss for words and with his face more blank than deeply aware of those about him. The major decided that at his first opportunity he would meet this American directly on subjects of which he, as a native, could not be bested. Stavers anticipated just such a confrontation. The two days and nights before they left Indian Bluff, Joey had closeted himself in the computer room and gone through nine extensive volumes of the Bhagalpur and Bhuj areas, down to streets, names of temples, local deities and native customs. The good major was in for the surprise of his life, and he would stay neatly off balance while they were in Bhuj seeking out the ever-elusive Ernst Patschke.

Chapter   XXIII

It took a damned good pilot to put the Grumman down safely at the miserable pisspot they called an airfield at Bhagalpur. No one told them the field was hard packed clay instead of concrete or macadam. The dust atop the clay meant lousy traction for braking—and in landing a sweptwing heavy jet, barely good enough can mean a fast trip to the cemetery.

Bhagalpur didn't present merely a challenge, it was an hysterical dare. The temperature stood at 115 degrees, and that raised the effective altitude of the airstrip to about seven thousand feet. A clay surface, roiling dust, short runway and thin air presented a vicious mixture. Janca set up the Grumman for a long and flat power approach, riding just above the edge of the stall and holding her aloft with screaming engines. He slammed the main gear down at the very edge of usable runway, instantly went to full reverse thrust with the engines and stomped on the brakes and to his own surprise came to a stop with a few hundred feet still before them. Stavers kept an eye on Gary Cowart through the bumpy descent and hard, precision touchdown. The slender man remained aloof from the proceedings and Stavers realized that Cowart must have gone into dozens of remote airstrips far worse than this when he fought the Japanese in the northern reaches of India and in neighboring Burma.

They parked on a hardstand beneath high trees. Natives pushed the airplane back until foliage sheltered it from the worst of the sun. Within minutes a bamboo scaffolding rose in place and long strips of cloth stretched from one bracket to another, an effective sunshield entirely around the airplane. The major stepped outside into oppressive heat, Stavers with him.

"I will call ahead to Bhuj," Shahpur explained. "I want to be certain an area of the airfield is prepared for us." He shrugged, as if future problems might be somewhat on the overwhelming side.

"I didn't know you had an airfield at Bhuj," Stavers said.

"I abuse the word, Mr. Stavers. It is an old strip fit only for small airplanes and helicopters. The problem, as Mr. Rajkot reminded me before we left, is that Bhuj has suddenly become the most sought-after place in all my country. Mr. Cowart mentioned that to you, I believe. Hundreds of thousands of people flock there. Bhuj is inundated.

When something like this occurs, it is understandable."

"I seem to be the only one who doesn't understand, Major."

"A holy man," Shahpur said, "comes from a distant place he will not reveal. The multitudes do not care *where* he originated, at least in the physical sense. He is a prophet, of which we have many. He is a holy man, of which we have more. But our people seek a truth and he offers something *different*, which I do not yet understand, from all those who have come and gone. We will find out soon enough."

Stavers remained aboard the Grumman, in the aft conference area. Outside the plane an old truck banged and wheezed to provide power for air-conditioning within the cabin. Stavers sprawled out on the couch, Rosa Montini in an easy chair across from him. She waited for the cigar. When Doug was deep in thought, the cigar appeared inevitably. "Did you hear what Shahpur said?" he asked.

"Him, and also Cowart," Rosa replied. "Cowart told me more, and then I had the opportunity to speak with Joey for a while. Bhuj is an area of ancient temples. Many towns in India have such temples, of course, but Bhuj is where the true holy men visit when it is their time to speak the words from on high." She was uncomfortable. "All this is different from the high walls of a school in Rome," she said after a pause. "I can *feel* something from the major. Rajkot gave me the same feeling. They are men beyond fast and easy convictions. Men who know all sides of life, clearly. Yet even they react to something they have not experienced personally." Abruptly Rosa shifted her conversation. "This holy man," she went on. "What do you think?"

"I haven't been there, Rosa."

"I didn't ask you that."

"No, you didn't," he admitted. "I'm waiting to see for myself."

"Gary Cowart says that the feeling from Bhuj is spreading like a mist before the wind. That's poetic and perhaps said with some license, but he is an elderly man with vast experience, and frankly, I was surprised to hear that from him. I expected cynicism, or no less than amused, even understanding, tolerance."

"And he's rattling your cage."

"I don't understand."

"You can't figure out why these people are acting this way."

"Of course not. I don't understand it. All this talk of a holy man is—"

"I imagine, Rosa, that this same conversation took place two thousand years ago. What was the name Joey used? Jehoshua. The Hebrew name, the original name of Christ, before its translation by the Greeks."

"Yes," she said simply.

"You know the holy books far better than I, Rosa. Wasn't Christ ridiculed and vilified? Wasn't he called false prophet? Didn't his own people call for his death because he *claimed* to be the true messiah? Or the son of God. I'm not that up on the scriptures," Stavers said. "But if this man claims to be *precisely* what Christ claimed two thousand years ago, you're not going to believe him. Disbelief will be through every fibre of your being. And if you had lived two thousand years ago, you would act in just the same way."

To his surprise, she didn't answer immediately. "The Church believes in its miracles. In our saints—"

"Including St. Joseph who, according to your own records, before the Pope and the entire College of Cardinals *and* several thousand eyewitnesses, all of whom swore to the event, *levitated* across St. Peter's Square. Not once, but a number of times. Do you believe *that?*"

She shifted uncomfortably and avoided his eyes. "If it is in the records of the Church, then I—"

"To coin your own phrase, Rosa, I didn't ask you that. Do you, personally, *you*, believe that a man had the telekinetic power to levitate?"

"*You* use the word telekinetic!" she flared suddenly. "The Church shows it as a miracle!"

He smiled, thin and cutting. "And miracles *must* be sanctioned by the *Catholic* church, right?"

"I—"

She showed instant relief as Gary Cowart came into the aft section. "Oh, sorry. I didn't mean to interrupt anything personal."

"Not at all, Mr. Cowart," Rosa said, smiling. "Please, join us. We were talking about what is going on at Bhuj. What seems to be an extraordinary holy man, from what little we know."

Cowart settled comfortably into a seat. He rubbed his hands briskly. "Well, I can't tell you much, of course, although the grapevine, which is the most reliable indicator of any sort here, is positively humming. We'll know soon enough, of course. But from what I understand, we have something completely different on our hands. For decades now I've seen the holy men come and go. I've *seen* them do utterly fantastic things. Place themselves beyond any pain. Stare down a cobra. Go into trances—astral projections, I believe you'd call them—and return with extraordinary descriptions of places they in no way could know, in minute detail, without ever having been within thousands of miles of that particular place."

Rosa spoke impulsively. "Have you ever seen any miracles by these holy men?"

He smiled, an expression of acceptance of things beyond his ken. "I have watched a holy man touch the blind and make them see." He let his words hang. "I have seen a holy man make a withered, crippled leg whole and the cripple walk straight and true from his presence. And I have seen a holy man sitting with his legs crossed several feet above the ground." He held up a hand to forestall any reaction. "Before we go any further, I can't tell you whether I *saw* the man levitate, or whether somehow he affected my mind. I don't know. But I do know what I saw, I know what I believe, and I daresay I would pass any polygraph as to telling the truth. May I make a suggestion? Wait. Simply wait until we are at Bhuj and we can see for ourselves." He looked at Stavers. "That is our purpose for going, isn't it? I mean, I have arranged in Bhuj for the proper clothing, for local guides, and they will be all the more reliable because of the major going with us, and all that."

Stavers nodded. "That's why we're going. In part, anyway. We do have some studies of temples, things

like that." He smiled. "Besides, there *is* Joey Akim
Asid Sharif. Whatever he sees, whatever he hears,
whatever he reads in those temples, he will remember in every detail."

Cowart shook his head to express his wonder.
"I've talked to that jolly bloke. The most extraordinary mind I've ever run into. It's like a computer."

"His mind *is* a computer," Stavers said.

"Well, yes," Cowart said, not really saying anything because he couldn't cope with that mon-
strous idea of a human mind soaking up and
retaining *everything* it witnessed like some giant
electronic blotter crammed tightly between two
human ears. He was saved from further reflection
by the major's appearance.

"We are ready!" he boomed at them. "Four helicopters, all from our air force." He looked directly
at Stavers. "Everything you, ah, need." He had
almost said "requested," but that was part of the
arrangements. Nothing voiced, nothing committed
to paper. The money had long before changed
hands.

They left the Grumman and walked several hundred yards in thick heat and swirls of dust. Behind
them a military truck brought personal effects and
their equipment. Stavers noted without comment
that Skip Marden was wearing his steel-toed jump
boots. *So he was feeling something also.* If he was
wearing those boots, he was preparing himself for
a fight; for *anything*. Stavers motioned for Marden
to let the others board the personnel helicopter
first. They stood a short distance away for a quick
exchange to themselves.

"Don't think about your answer," Stavers said quietly. "Just let it come out. What's in your head?"

Marden fixed his eyes on Stavers. "It's in the back of my neck," he said cautiously. "Not in my mind. It's in the back of my neck and it's cold and I don't understand it and I don't *like* it. Everybody is on edge. From what I gather, it gets worse the farther north we go."

"To Bhuj, you mean."

"I don't give a shit what they call it." He gestured idly to the north. "It comes from up there, whatever happens to be there."

"You loaded?"

Marden nodded. "Christ, like a walking arsenal. It's all built-in stuff."

"I should hope so. Keep the major happy, Skip. *He's* on edge. Don't let that big moustache and ho-ho-ho fool you. He's been looking over his shoulder, too."

Marden didn't move his eyes. "They're waiting for us."

"Let's go." They boarded the helicopter and closed the sliding door. Batteries whined and the engines spooled up and great blades turned as the big British chopper came alive. They might be in the midst of ancient Indian life, but these were modern jet-powered machines. The helicopter rolled forward in a huge duststorm and lifted, rotors thundering and jet exhausts filling the world with a powerful whining roar. Behind them the other three helicopters, the same Westland models, rose like giant locusts and slid into a loose formation. They flew west along the Ganges and then swung in a wide turn, low over the surface, up the Kosi River on a northerly heading.

"The river's filled with boats," Stavers mentioned to Major Shahpur.

The major looked down with him. The muddy stream was barely visible as boats of every size and shape pushed and shoved in a crowded mass. "Yes, and they're all going north. Can you see that road, through the trees to our right?"

He had no need to say more. A road jam needs no language. It appeared as a horde of refugees pushing their way to survival from some great catastrophe behind them. But like the boats, the traffic on that road, and every road over which they crossed or that came into view, all the trucks, buses, wagons, and people on foot headed northward.

"To Bhuj," the major said aloud to reflect their mutual conclusion.

"Your holy man is a magnet."

The major closed his eyes, opened them slowly. "Please, Mr. Stavers. He is not *my* holy man. I don't know even if he is India's holy man. No one ever heard of him before, and I don't even know his name. I'm pleased to be here with you. Our government wants more information. It is not easy to obtain. In Bhuj a delirium rules. Joy and wonder and . . . well, for the first time in *my* life even I am somewhat at a loss. This will be most interesting," he reflected aloud.

Stavers patted him lightly on the shoulder. "That it will be," he said with a half-smile, moving to the back bulkhead of the cabin. He sat alone with Rosa. The others were at windows, fascinated with the sights unrolling beneath them. Stavers decided this was the right moment.

"Rosa, why haven't you told me what's on your mind?" he asked with a brusqueness that caught her by surprise.

"Why, I haven't, I mean, I haven't lied to you, Doug," she forced out in reply.

"Didn't say you lied, Rosa, but that's enough to tell me you're about as close to it as possible. We've exchanged, we've shared, we've pursued the same goal together."

"Why, yes, yes; of course we've done that," she said, forcing the words, afraid of what he might know.

"Then tell me something, lover."

Her cheeks reddened. It was one thing to be alone with this man and hurl herself at his body, but that was *alone*. She didn't care what people thought, she didn't want them as witness to anything; and even this familiarity threw her off balance. Just as much as *why* he was doing this. "Of course," she said quickly, hating the repetition of the phrase but unsure of herself or what to say.

"You've never said a word to me about our precious holy man who's got the countryside turned upside down being Ernst Patschke." His huge hands squeezed her thigh gently. She wanted to pull away but found herself fearing any such move. "And here I was beginning to believe that even the Catholic hierarchy could play their cards straight."

"Doug, I said I *haven't lied* to you!" she hissed fiercely.

"Do you know the difference between commission and omission?"

Her face reddened. "You know I do," she said, her eyes averted.

"Then, for your *own* sake, Rosa, don't ever again try to send off a coded telegram, as you did in Calcutta, that you were nearing your quarry. Rajkot intercepted your wire. He couldn't figure it out, but he's got a keen sense of smell. For your information, the Catholic missionary in Bhagalpur is now under house arrest. The phone lines are cut and the place is sealed off." He looked at her as if from a great distance. "I want you to know. You've almost wrecked everything we've done these past weeks. If you try it again I'm going to give Rosa Montini to Rajkot for a present." He rose to his feet and looked down on her and suddenly she realized she *didn't* know this man, not with all the times he had entered her body and they had embraced; she didn't know him at all.

"Unable to tell him anything," he added just before turning away. And she knew he had passed his death sentence on her. She leaned back, her white teeth pulling at her lower lip. Would she have the chance to kill him before he made his decision to eliminate *her?* It was unlikely. The crazy one who was mad and a genius at the same time, Joey, was as dangerous as any of them. And there was the giant, Marden, totally and always faithful to Stavers. One blow of his giant fist would crack her skull.

What would Butto Giovanni have to say *now,* she wondered. What miracle of wise decision would he bring forth from his old mind and vast experience and fierce convictions that would do her a shred of good? Old man, she thought, you expired too early, and I am sure you are harassing the angels with your convoluted logic even now. And she was all the more surprised with herself because she had *never* before questioned that old Giovanni had been anything but absolutely right.

And if this were so, then this cold, bloody barbarian with whom she had discovered such fantastic animal love might yet prove the one who was right. She closed her eyes, hot, weary, and utterly confused.

Implore as she might, God would not answer her call for help.

Chapter   XXIV

"Major, circle the town, please."

Shahpur nodded to Stavers, placed a headset and microphone about his head. "Circle the town," he ordered the pilot "First around the hills, then in closer, and stand off slowly from the large white temple. Don't fly directly over the temple until I tell you to do so."

The major removed the headgear. "Over there," he pointed. "The hills. Do you notice anything strange about them?"

"The color," Stavers said at once.

"That is so. The color comes from tens of thousands of people encamped in these hills. The blue haze is from their cooking fires. All those colors; their clothes, tents, their belongings. Tens upon tens of thousands of them."

The roadsides were the same. Packed with humanity, and then they discerned order below. Indian policemen on horseback and on motorcycles, herding the teeming masses, maintaining order because the packed throngs needed and instinctively sought order. "They move slowly," the major observed. "That long snaking line. People in a path eight feet wide. Like a warm glacier. The centipede of a million legs, torpid, moving slowly but always closer to the temple." He studied the mobs below. "I wonder what is so different this time," he mused.

Stavers steadied himself as the helicopter rocked in choppy thermals. "The difference is that this holy man has science behind him," he said without any warning that he had knowledge of what might be taking place below them. Shahpur's head snapped about like the movement of a striking snake. The jolly ruddiness of British influence in that same instant vanished.

"Just what the hell do you mean by that?" he demanded.

Stavers smiled at Shahpur. "I mean that India has moved into the twentieth century. Modern science. Her own atomic bomb. She has universities and medicine and the whole shooting match. But by and large the people of India are unchanged over thousands of years. Those people down there, Major," he said, pointing from the helicopter window. "You tell me. They're *your* people. Take away a few of their trappings, the rayon and nylon clothing, the meaningless transistor radios, those ancient trucks; all of that meaningless crap. If you did that, wouldn't those people be the same as they were two thousand years ago?"

"I fail to get your point," Shahpur said stiffly.

"And you didn't answer me, man! *The answer!*"

Shahpur took a deep breath. "The same. Their beliefs, the way they—"

"None of that means shit," Stavers said coldly. "Right now those people are flocking to a prophet, a man of holy wonder, a beseecher of heaven to their side. If that same man in whatever temple he's in down there were to have appeared two thousand years ago, *he would be Christ.* Or at any time in history he would be Buddha or Mohammed or any of the prophets, or messiahs, or gods."

Stavers was punching as neatly as he could with words instead of rapier thrusts. He wanted to get Barsi Shahpur off balance, especially on his own turf, in a shocking few moments. If he could do that, then Shahpur would work *with* him. And the way to do that was to convince the major that an all-time snow job was being pulled off on *his* own people, who were being made emotionally hysterical by a false prophet— No, Stavers corrected himself. "But you know what, Major? He's no prophet, he's no messiah, he's no god. *He's a fucking charlatan*, a snake oil man, a sideshow freak of incredible talent. He's screwing those people down there, he's screwing India, and before he's through he's going to make India and its people, good and honest people like yourself, let alone those religious zealots down in Bhuj, the laughing stock of the whole goddamned world."

Major Barsi Shahpur swallowed, his face showing sudden perspiration. His hands shook as he looked at the mobs below, and then turned back to Stavers. "We know such a thing is always possible," he said slowly, so low that Stavers could barely hear him. Then Shahpur revealed his consternation. "You say all this with such conviction!" He glared at Stavers. "How can you know such things? And what if you are *wrong*? Are you some prophet yourself that you have miraculous insight? I have spoken to people from Bhuj. They say there is no error, this man is truly holy, they say that—"

"Don't crap me, Major."

Shahpur turned white and then crimson. "You go too far," he warned.

"Oh, come off it," Stavers said with disdain. "If you were that certain, you would have joined those people down there long ago. Is a true man of India ever going to let pass the chance to meet with one of God's true appointed? Stop it, man, just stop it. If you weren't riddled with doubts, you wouldn't be in this eggbeater with me. If Rajkot didn't have all the warning flags flying in his little secret police head, he wouldn't have been pulling fingerprint checks on all of us, he wouldn't have sealed off that Catholic group in Calcutta, he wouldn't have planned for one or the both of you to be here with us, he—"

"Then who is the imposter?" Shahpur demanded suddenly.

"I never said he was an imposter."

"You are mad!" Shahpur shouted.

"He's not a holy man and he's not an imposter. He's been pursuing a goal for years and he *believes* he's a holy man, and he has the ability to convince hundreds of thousands of people he's their new

messiah. To him the fact of conviction is what
Christ had to do. It was his challenge, God's gaunt-
let; if he were worthy, then he would prevail. Down
there an old man who's been dreaming such a
dream for decades is putting everything to the
acid test. He's been planning and planning. He's
put everything together. And if it works, he'll be so
powerful no one will be able to stop him. Not you,
not me, not your whole country. He'll be like a
tidal wave of fire. The world is ready for his kind.
The world is scared shitless of nuclear war and
biological war and industrial slavery and the rest
of all that good crap. We're living in the atomic
age and the space age and the age of agricultural
miracles and you've still got seven to ten million
people dying every year of starvation in *this country alone*, and one to two hundred million dying of
hunger every goddamned year, and half the whole
fucking world lives on a substandard diet and
they're ready to embrace *any* god who comes along
they can believe. And you know what's down there,
Major? A man who's found the way to make them
believe."

"What do you want, Stavers?"

"I want his ass, that's what I want."

"You expect me to *give* that to you? Hand him
over to you on a silver platter?" Shahpur laughed
humorlessly, then sobered. "As you say in your
quaint idiom, Stavers, no deal. Maybe I'm hedging
my bets, but—" He shrugged, then picked up his
thoughts. "One never knows. He just *may* be a
prophet."

*"He's a fucking Nazi officer from Hitler's head-
quarters!"*

Shahpur looked as if he'd been hit in the face with an iron bar. He recoiled physically, his eyes wide. "You can't mean that," he said, his voice suddenly hoarse.

Stavers hammered at Shahpur. "Goddamnit, I've been chasing that son of a bitch for years," he snapped, adding a bit of embroidery. "Rosa Montini's been after him. The Israelis have been after him. We've been following him around the goddamned world because he's the next Hitler, *that's why*. Damnit, Major, *think*. Just *think* of everything you've learned from history: how Hitler could sway the masses, that bungling idiot who didn't finish high school, who was gassed into blind, hysterical convulsions, who was a goddamned incestuous pervert; think of all those things and tell me he didn't have some incredible power, magnetism or aura or whatever you call it, and *that's* why he made it to where he did. Well, the man you're calling your new prophet or messiah is Colonel-General Ernst Patschke, and that's why I want him."

Stavers was thinking as fast as he could speak. The truth was an incredibly effective bludgeon, and he was making decisions as he went along. He had to stay one step ahead of Major Barsi Shahpur, keep him off balance. So he would tell him the truth but not the entire truth, and even as he parried and thrust with the major the plan was forming in his mind, and if he were right, then Shahpur would answer as though Stavers had written the script himself.

And he did.

"I'm what in your own language would be called between a rock and a hard place," Shahpur said slowly. "Even if what you say is true, do you know what would happen to me if I listened to you and brought on the downfall or the removal of what all those people down there *believe* is the prophet of all prophets? Stavers, we'd be torn limb from limb."

Stavers felt his own domination of Shahpur falling away from that grim reality. "I hate to say it, but you're right," he told the Indian officer.

"Then what in the name of all that's holy do you suggest we do?" Shahpur whispered fiercely. "You have so much information, damn you, give me *that* answer!"

Stavers rested a powerful arm on Shahpur's shoulder. "I can't. Not yet. But I will. I want only one thing from you."

"Which is?"

"If I prove to you I'm right ―"

"That's not enough," Shahpur said with sudden coldness.

"And I can keep the status quo, will you help me get that Nazi officer out of there?"

"That is one very large order, Stavers."

"I know that. Will you go along on that basis?" Stavers squeezed Shahpur's shoulder and looked directly into his eyes. "If nothing else, you won't wreck the emotional state of *your* people. What happens if Patschke sweeps all of India with his new holy call and *then* they find out the truth?"

"I'd rather not think about that."

"Sure, sure, but you've got to, and we both know it."

"Do you want him dead or alive?"

"It doesn't matter to me."

"If you could carry out a change and no one would know any better—"

"Is there, in all of India, a man, *any man*, who can quote every holy book of every religion, every caste, every belief?"

"Never."

"But there is."

Shahpur was shocked, utterly disbelieving. "Who is such a man?"

Stavers had made his decision in these past moments. "Don't turn around to stare at him. Joey Akim Asid Sharif. *He* can quote every holy book in the whole freaking *world*."

"I have listened to him. I can believe that."

"Then, if the change could be made, and we had our friend chanting day after day, week after week, every holy word ever put into print, wouldn't this be miracle enough to cover us?"

"It *might*. But that's still a long way from accomplishing what you're after."

"Well, then let's do it on the basis of another quaint expression from our language. We'll play it by ear."

"That's a dangerous game."

"We have another saying. Nobody promised you or me a rose garden."

"A condition, Stavers. Even if everything you say is true, I insist on one condition."

"Which is?"

"He must not be harmed. In no way."

"That's a bitch and you know it."

"Break that condition, Douglas Stavers, and you will never leave India alive."

Stavers nodded. "Fair enough." They clasped hands.

Now all I have to do, Stavers groaned inwardly, *is figure out how to do the impossible. I need my own miracle. . . .*

Chapter   XXV

They dropped with screaming exhausts onto the dusty open field that passed for an airstrip at Bhuj. Sacred cows with ribs jutting like iron grates bellowed and ran from dust howled upon them by the rotor downwash. Finally the helicopter settled with hard bumps in a maelstrom of animals and people shrouded in dust and scattering from the tornado winds. Shahpur seemed relieved to face direct physical problems. Immediately upon leaving the helicopter he encountered a squad of local militia and police, and just as quickly the major established himself as the new and dominant authority. Several policemen took off at a dead run as Shahpur's voice thundered orders, and they returned within minutes accompanied by at least fifty natives. Within the hour their tents were in place, stakes pounded deeply into the ground, a generator whined for radio communications and electricity for the tents, a power line had been dragged to the scene for haphazard telephone contact for Shahpur, and they had their living and working quarters established.

That night they changed, and not simply their clothing. Skin dye to conceal the unmistakable pallor of white skin. Yard upon yard of linen for their bodies. Sandals and head wrappings. And standing outside the tents, ready to obey every order and every whim of Major Barsi Shahpur, were four local militia who looked scruffy and disreputable and who would melt into any crowd in any city in the land. Gary Cowart would remain behind in their small tent conclave, and he was relieved to learn of that decision. He had no desire to shuffle interminably in line to watch some mythical mumbling from within a temple. He'd spent too many years in this part of the world, watching the prophets and messiahs and holy men come and go. He'd seen *wars* come and go, and he'd seen powerful governments toppled and men of equal ambition and power replace those of power and ambition. He was utterly beyond interest in these events.

"We will travel by ox cart," Shahpur announced after night fell.

"What for?" asked the astonished Marden.

"There are people here from all across India," Shahpur explained, "as well as from neighboring lands. Strangers are not unusual. Americans or Europeans in modern vehicles would be the worst insult to these people who have come in answer to a holy call. You would be looked upon as taunters of the truth, on a lark to see something of interest to tourists. You might not live through the hour. These people can be extremely faithful to an idea, an emotion. Strangers are welcome enough, but not those who come from a plastic world with false ideas and a contempt for God." He looked at Rosa as he finished his words. "Even those who think theirs is the only true God in this world." He pointed to the two large wagons with a team of oxen at the head of each. "There is straw. Make yourself comfortable. And understand that if you need to relieve yourselves, you will do as these people do. The roadside, anywhere it is convenient and not insulting to those about you." He again looked sharply at Rosa. "If you hesitate, it will be dangerous. Be certain before you leave the privacy of these tents."

She nodded. "In the eyes of the Lord a believer is beyond all insult."

"For your sake, I hope so," he told her.

They spent most of the night in the creaking, rocking wagons, for the first few hours feeling their astonishment at the multitudes about them. The road carried a steady procession, but one much lighter than during daylight hours. The forested areas to each side of the road, in the hills beyond, were speckled with glowing eyes, some dim, others brighter or fiercer than others, and the cooking fires of the devout resting for the night, families and friends and strangers all swimming together in this enormous tide moving slowly down an emotional stream. The air hung heavy and fetid with smoke from the fires, with the dung of animals and the sharp ammonia smell of tens of thousands of human beings urinating and leaving their waste in ditches or on hillsides, wherever they could find room to relieve themselves.

"Holy Jesus," Marden swore. "It smells like a prison camp out here."

"You have a suggestion for solving the problem, Mr. Marden? An overnight miracle of sewage lines and plumbing and water? Anything along that line?"

Marden didn't blink as he returned Shahpur's hard gaze. "You're too sensitive, major. I was *in* a prison camp in Africa. We were all thrown together. Whites, blacks, browns; it didn't matter. The ground was hard and the only tools we had to dig latrines were our fingernails. There's nothing here that I haven't known for a long time. What I find so surprising is that these people," he gestured to take in the great crowds spreading to either side of the road, "are so willing to endure anything to reach that temple. If you'll think about it, Major, I wasn't criticizing. I was *recognizing* a great human drive."

Shahpur found it impossible to conceal his surprise. "You are more than you seem," he said by way of oblique compliment. Marden nodded; all the words necessary had been spoken.

Joey looked about him with a growing wonder in his face. His eyes darted constantly at the people who trudged slowly along the road, even more slowly than the steady plodding of their wagons. He saw people sleeping in rows on the hillsides, naked men with their legs crossed and in some strange trance, asleep—if that were the word—with their eyes open. He understood these men. They were here and they were not here. They could be spoken to and they might hear, but their minds were removed, gone somewhere, disassociated from their flesh. He studied the people all about them and judged them and he felt as if all his posturing, all the years of moving through the plastic, greedy nonsense of the cults he had known were being washed from his body by this incredible experience. Several times he started to remark on such things to Stavers, but something held his tongue, and when he realized what was happening to him, he knew a quiet and wondering astonishment that shook him to the roots of his being. *He no longer cared what they thought.* For years he had planned and schemed and plotted, he had worked within an organization within an organization, always structuring every move, always setting up the future scenario. He held more power than anyone in his group, although he was the only one aware of such enormous strength . . . and, quite as suddenly as everything else, even *that* no longer truly interested him. He had a deep-lying allegiance, a sworn oath to uphold, and it was falling away from him like dead skin sloughing from a leper. He was intimidated by a thought that kept ringing through his mind.

His was an incredible gift, this power of total recall. He had read every holy book and document and record he could find and he knew them all, he could summon them to mind and— Why was he thinking *that*; here, now? The thought he would not admit kept hammering at him, clamoring for recognition, and he did his best to push it aside, for it frightened him. *Maybe this was the whole*

idea from the beginning. Maybe from the very mo-
ment that whore brought you into this world, lower
than the low, you were destined to be here at this
time in this place, for you are a fount of wisdom, the
chalice of man's recorded dreams and soul, and—

A chill swept through him. He forced his thoughts
to quiet, for he recognized the danger. He was
convincing himself. Something was pushing up from
the deep recesses of his mind, something huddled
there for all his time of life, something he had
shoved down and refused to recognize, and now it
eroded the foundations of his cynicism and his
lethal role in life. Troubled, he fell into a deeper
silence.

Rosa leaned against Stavers, sought refuge within
the strength of his powerful arm about her. "You've
been quiet a long time," he said finally to her over
the creaking and groaning of the wagons, the low
buzz of the enormous numbers of people from all
about them. "I don't know, Rosa. Maybe I was too
hard on you before."

She shook her head, pushed her body closer to
his. "What you said was true. But that's not it."
She looked up at him. "I'm frightened, Doug. Truly
frightened."

"You?" He could hardly believe her words.
"You're a trained professional. You're a—"

She placed a finger over his lips. "None of that
means anything now. Not *here*. I have never felt so
small, so insignificant in all my life. These people,
Doug! They're believers, all of them. I feel lost
among them, as if even *I* were answering a call.
Look at them. Just *look* at them. I do, and I think

that this is what it must have been like in the Holy Land so very long ago."

His voice became harsh. "We're going to see Ernst Patschke, not Jesus Christ," he said, the words almost a snarl.

"It's not *him* I'm talking about. It's these people. I can *feel* their emotions. It overwhelms and frightens me."

"How would you feel, Rosa, if you were to *know*, and I mean to know beyond question, that Christ was a fraud?"

"Oh, Doug." The disappointment was heavy in her voice and she felt like crying. Would he never get off her back?

"Hon, you don't understand. You missed the point. I wasn't talking about you. I'm talking about them too, all these people. Don't forget for a second to whom they're going, and what he has that's drawing these people to him."

She stared at him. "My God, I'd forgotten that. What happens to them, I mean."

"The same thing that happens to Rosa Montini if she discovers that the son of God was a fake, a charlatan, and that the whole marvelous, wonderful truth was a hollow mockery."

"That would kill me. I can't even admit to any such possibility. You know that!"

He nodded. "I know, I know. I'd also like to know what you would say to all these people, if you could?"

A tear fell slowly along her cheek. "That's why I feel so *helpless*. I want to tell them; I *do*. But I can't, I simply can't. To break so many hearts . . ." Her voice fell away.

"You'd let them believe even while you know it's false," he said to her.

She nodded slowly. "I'd have to. Yes. I couldn't be that cruel."

"Rosa, I wonder if someone a long time ago faced this same problem and made the same decision you just made."

She stared at him, afraid, unable to talk. A figure loomed out of the dim light of reflected fires, and she was grateful for the sudden appearance of Barsi Shahpur. He settled down next to them, offered a leather flask of wine. Rosa shook her head, but Stavers drank deeply, wiped his mouth with the back of his hand, returned the flask to Shahpur. "I know a reconnaissance when I see one," he told the major. "Tell us what you've learned."

"I think I am grateful for your very blunt, insulting talk we had in the helicopter," Shahpur told him, leaning back against a pile of straw. "If it were not for what you told me —" He shook his head. "What would be the words, my American friend? As your Indians would say, there is powerful medicine out there." He waved an arm to take in the multitudes.

"How much does he know?" Rosa demanded suddenly, bringing an amused smile to Shahpur's face.

"He knows it's Ernst Patschke we're after," Stavers replied. "We have an, ah, arrangement. We must prove to him everything I've told him about Colonel-General Patschke, and then we can't harm the old bastard. We've got to keep the status quo among these people so we don't break their hearts."

"And they don't break our necks, yours and mine," Shahpur concluded. "Aside from the impossible demands that would have disturbed even Hercules, that is what I know, Rosa Montini."

Rosa nodded, visibly penitent, her eyes downcast. *He didn't mention the diamond. He's still playing it straight with me. He didn't tell Shahpur about the Star of Bethlehem. Just the man* . . . She glanced up at Stavers. *So even in the midst of all this, he continues to plan.* She made up her mind not to assume powers that lay beyond her, not to rock any boats, to go along. She really had no other choice. But she felt weight removed from her soul.

"I spoke with many people," the major said slowly, now sitting cross-legged before them. "If I didn't talk to you, Stavers, well, the people with whom I spoke, you understand, there is no way they talk with me except through their heart."

"I understand."

"Several have already seen the holy man."

Stavers felt his body tighten, moving to a fine edge. "They describe an aura about the holy one." Stavers and Rosa exchanged glances; they remembered what they had heard about the diamond. "They say the aura is *visible*. I am aware that the mind can bring on such an aura. Also that with certain electronic devices it is possible to affect the senses and even create such an aura."

"Very good," Stavers said quietly.

"But the *feeling* they have. That is what is so dominant," Shahpur continued. "They are overwhelmed. They explain that their tongues become knots, their limbs weak, as if all their own strength of body and soul is totally embraced by this person."

"Description, Major; damnit, tell me that," Stavers said impatiently.

"They see only his eyes."

"I don't understand," Rosa said.

"He wears a long robe with a hood. Only his eyes are visible. And his eyes gleam. One man said they were like the eyes of a great cat in near darkness. Like the eyes of a tiger, unblinking, gleaming."

"By what name," Rosa asked, "is he known?"

"That is a stroke of wisdom on his part," Shahpur said. "Those who spoke to me say that only God in His infinite wisdom will proclaim the name of His prophet when the time is ready. Until then the name has emerged from amidst the people. They call him simply the Holy One."

"Neat," Stavers said, his sarcasm unhidden. "He wears a hooded robe. No way to tell if he's wearing sandals or raised shoes of some kind. The hood conceals his actual height. The robe can also have a shoulder brace, so his general appearance can be anything he wants. No one sees his face except, I'm sure, those closest to him, and they've never *heard* of anyone named Patschke. Besides, if he looks like a winner they're going to climb aboard his bandwagon. Few things in this world are better than being the high temple priests of a new cult that's off and running. And then," Stavers looked directly at Shahpur, "he's learned how, from the world's best teacher, to sway his audience."

Rosa took in that line with the greatest interest, for it confirmed her earlier beliefs. Stavers had said nothing about the great yellow diamond. Not a word of that chilling golden fire. The name *Hitler* would do well enough for Shahpur to believe that whatever he was capable of accomplishing, Patschke had tutored beneath the most compelling—if not perhaps the worst—orater in history. Outside of his calling foreign officials "little worms" after an encounter with English diplomats, no one could bring to mind *anything* ever spoken by Hitler that endured in the mind. The name would suffice for the major.

"Can you come up with anything else?" Stavers was asking Shahpur.

The major nodded. "If there is one phrase, it would be total conversion. No person has gone through the lines in the temple without emerging convinced absolutely, beyond all question, that he was in the presence of a holy man."

"No proclamations of a messiah or prophet?"

"No one to whom I spoke recalled such words."

"Fits the pattern, anyway," Stavers grunted.

It required another twenty-four hours to reach the temple, where the local police sequestered the oxen and the wagons. Stavers, Marden, Rosa, Joey, and the major joined the long, shuffling line that ever so slowly, albeit steadily, approached the ancient temple. They remained hooded and wrapped in linen, shapeless except for their height, talking in whispers.

The effect of Patschke was growing. The believers were increasing in leaps and bounds, for many of the holy men of the countryside, after *their* exposure to the hooded prophet, were spreading the word, the new gospel voiced by the self-appointed disciples. These were the preachers of the new coming, fiery in their belief, humble in their closeness, effective in their imprecations. From the hills and the countryside, from the buildings surrounding the temple, all through the parks and along the river that flowed behind the temple, a low chanting had begun, a paean that increased in volume, that filled the air like sound with wings, the musical cry of gladness, unrelentless, constant, through day and night.

"It's spooky," Marden growled, all his instincts aroused to their peak. "It's like a phantom army all around us."

"It is truth," Joey said, his smile barely visible beneath his turbanned wrappings.

"*What* the hell do you call truth?" Marden hissed angrily. "That Nazi—"

"Cool it," Stavers said, moving between them. He turned to Joey. "Have you gone crazy? Don't pull this shit on me, Joey."

"He misunderstood. What these people believe; *that* is what I referred to."

Stavers nodded, clapped him gently on the shoulder. As he turned away he leaned close to Marden's head. "Watch him like a hawk. He's cracking. He's starting to believe *he's* the new choice of God, or something."

"I got it," Marden said simply. He was almost grateful for something to do. He had already learned to keep one eye on Rosa Montini like a radar lock. Now he'd have Joey to contend with. He liked that. He didn't underestimate the big man who babbled and told tales in his glib, silvery tongue.

That son of a bitch was as dangerous as a wolverine in close quarters.

Finally they moved in the long shuffling line to the overhang of the temple. Stavers and the others looked about them with practiced eyes. The all-faithful, weeping in their glory and truth, would not see the television scanners artfully placed within statuary which meant there were watchers in back rooms and side rooms, always ready to make their move to protect Patschke. The more he saw the more convinced became Stavers that the wily old German had brought with him a few hardcore adherents, that they were all gambling on Patschke pulling off his new messiah role. The Germans would be out of sight of the thousands coursing slowly through the temple. Indians would herald the new day, usher the crowds through. Nothing untoward would be seen.

Several more hours, and before them the stone hallway broadened into an arch. The walls glowed softly. A nice touch, there. No lights to stab into the eyes. An ethereal illumination, done with fibre optics and other electronics. Not a word was being spoken by the crowd before or behind them and Stavers decided to keep his counsel to himself. He knew Marden and Joey well enough to know they were also picking up on what he'd seen; the TV scanners, the dandy little touches with electronics. Music drifted to them. It was almost impossible to define. It touched upon the senses, caressed the ears. And then Stavers recognized it: the same kind of music most medical hypnotists use. Perfect mathematical chords, designed to relax the listener into complete contentment. Music created

by a computer and issued from a synthesizer. No
speakers anywhere. That meant overhead and possibly some well beneath the flooring, intended for
multiple-phonic effect as if the music ebbed and
swelled from everywhere. After a few moments the
listener no longer consciously heard the music,
but it had already created its effect. It was like
aural Valium.

The hallway dimmed in lighting. Shadows mostly,
now, the crowd moving slowly. The effect was
perfect. People strained to see ahead of them and
anticipation reached new heights. A master had
planned all this. They kept shuffling forward, and
then before them Stavers saw a new glow. That
must be the main chamber. If he knew these old
temples, it would be a great curving dome overhead. He wondered what they might do within—
He cut off his own anticipation. They'd know soon
enough.

Then they were inside. The crowd was tightly
controlled. No ropes, no walls. A line of living blue
fire stretched alongside the crowd, from wall to
wall of the great chamber along that side where
the awestruck throng moved. A laser beam: completely harmless, but glowing and twisting within
itself, frightening as hell. It came from solid rock
and vanished into solid rock and it was nothing
more than a beam of coherent light, but devilishly
clever. He'd been right. The inside of the ancient
temple was a great dome.

At the center of the temple dome stood a massive throne of pure marble, and seated on that
throne was the Holy One. Stavers and the others
stared. The hooded robe was a soft grey and the

face within the hood only partially visible. Stavers made out long platinum hair, the shadowed edge of a sharp nose; he could barely see the chin and lips but—

The eyes. They glowed softly. An incredible faint lavender glowing from within that face. All about him Stavers heard gasps, moans, prayerful chants. The effect of that hooded figure was devastating. Stavers turned to look about him, quickly, so as not to attract attention. He found what he sought: a slight recess in the stone wall immediately behind him. If he could climb up and behind that wall, he'd find a projector for ultraviolet light that struck and reflected from the contact lenses on the eyes of the hooded figure and cast forth a *reflected* glow. An old Hollywood trick, to be sure. But here? Who would question what these people saw, and—

His vision seemed to blur. Not much, but enough for the hooded figure on the throne to appear to ripple slightly before his eyes. His brain felt squeezed as though an invisible wire were being tightened about his skull. He felt overwhelmed by the incredible personality of the hooded man, felt insignificant in the presence of this greatness. There could be no question but that this was from the All High, that God had not forgotten His people. The crowd behind them kept pushing, prodding them forward and they stumbled through the corridor exiting the temple, unable to speak. He saw tears on Rosa's face; awe and bewilderment and fear mixed together. Barsi Shahpur had a face of stone. Not a muscle moved. Stavers looked at Marden and saw the signs of a great struggle within; he was fighting his way out. Joey was something else.

A beatific smile adorned his face, made it seem as if this man had just glimpsed the eternal truth.

Doug Stavers knew otherwise. Joey Akim Asid Sharif had glimpsed something, all right, but it was a twisted truth and not at all eternal. *Later, later*, Stavers promised himself.

Barsi Shahpur shook his head repeatedly, kept striking himself on the temple with the heel of his hand as if trying to rid his brain of some rasping influence. He leaned against a tree, cursing to himself, and suddenly withdrew a slim knife from a leather boot. Before anyone could move he slashed a furrow along the inside of his forearm. Blood flowed across the arm and to their astonishment he looked up, a grim smile on his face. "That broke it," he said with quiet triumph. "The sudden pain, even though it felt far distant from me." He looked to Stavers. "All right, now you tell me. What happened in there? Do you have some scientific answer or do we accept the miracle? Because in all my life, my American friend, in all my years of temples and monasteries and all that has happened, never has my mind and soul been so assailed."

Stavers nodded. "Rape would be more like it, Barsi. Not here. Where can we talk?"

Shahpur nodded. "Down that street to our right. There is a large private residence. Formerly the property of a wealthy man. It is now our field headquarters. We go there."

They moved in pain, befuddled, heads aching, to the high walls and high iron gate. Armed guards stared at them. Shahpur loosed a volley of angry words and expressions and immediately the gate opened wide for them. They moved to a private garden and fell into seats and benches. Marden sprawled on the ground, breathing deeply. Shahpur barked orders to a soldier, and men ran to bring them fruit, bread and strong brandy. It helped.

Barsi Shahpur let out a long sigh. "It is all right now," he said, as much to himself as the others. He took the time to wash away the dried blood and to pour alcohol where he had slashed his forearm. "It took this," he said to the others, "to free myself from the fog that swallowed my mind in that temple. Stavers, it is time for your answers."

Stavers nodded. "His eyes. You saw them glowing?"

"Yes."

"Contact lenses and a reflection of ultraviolet lighting. The beams came from the wall to our left as we were in the dome. It has no harmful effect on the wearer."

"I recall music like none other. It would fit well the description of music of the spheres. It had a celestial lilt to—"

"It was born in a computer, Barsi. It was played by a snythesizer. Extreme high-fidelity speakers scattered through the dome so the music seemed to come from everywhere. It's used by medical hypnotists and also for brain-wave experiments in the alpha, beta, and theta frequencies. It leaves your mind open for suggestion. Unless you're prepared for it you can't fight it—and you were not only prepared for it, you were ready for punishment. You recall you seemed to lose your vision? A keening sound that became so intense you felt as if you had broken glass behind your eyeballs, icepicks in your ears?"

Barsi Shahpur smiled a death's head grin. "I commend your eloquence, but I can do without such stark reminders. How was this done?"

"Ultrasonic generators. You can't hear them; they're above normal hearing frequency. Didn't you notice that on the streets near this temple there were no animals? No cows, no dogs, no monkeys? *None* at all. As badly as you felt that sound— and I stress that you *feel* it, you don't hear it—it's worse for the animals. You won't even find any rats in that temple. It drives them out and it near drove us wild."

Shahpur sat in silence, reflective. Rosa had withdrawn. What Stavers had said to her earlier about her own admitted failure to tell all these people the truth, even if she could, was disturbing her profoundly. Rather than the deadly, well-trained agent of the Papacy, she felt like a small girl, in a boat without oars.

But not Joey. He was doing everything but beaming. Stavers watched him carefully; and he observed Marden, who had made Joey a personal, constant subject. Barsi Shahpur also had come to notice this astonishing mood of the strange American, and it puzzled him. Unable to fault such obvious joy, he had kept his silence until now. "I still never know how to address you," Shahpur said. "Joey sounds so grating against your miraculous talents." Stavers nodded to himself; Barsi Shahpur had picked a good opener, had turned the conversation directly to Joey.

"Talent is an ethereal gift," Joey said with an enigmatic smile. "In that temple I found greatness."

Stavers exchanged a glance with Marden and Rosa. Still there had not been a word said about the great diamond which he was convinced that Ernst Patschke, beneath that hooded robe and all, wore about his neck. And it was the Godstone that had given them their worst problems in the domed temple. All else, the music, the effect of the glowing eyes, most especially the ultrasonics, all this had been to weaken them, to leave them naked to whatever effect the man and that diamond could have on them. Patschke had indeed learned well from his former master ... but it was not eloquence he had learned from Hitler. The former Nazi leader used bombast and ridicule and threats to push and prod and bully a nation and then other nations, and with the first advantage at his disposal he had added crushing military and secret-police savagery. Patschke had learned both from Hitler and from history. He was to be a quiet occupation, a spreading of the robes of Godhood to his chosen. You didn't need mechanized armies when you had the army of the faithful. There was an old saw taught by the Germans in their command and staff schools. Von Clausewitz, the Prussian genius who reduced the complexities of geopolitics and militarism to their basics, first propounded it. He had pounded into his students, who would one day become the military leaders of Germany, the axiom that "War is an expression of political failure." It was that basic and that simple and utterly realistic.

And if there were a political failure? Von Clausewitz sailed on to his next and even more pertinent axiom. "The ultimate goal of war is to make the enemy change his mind." *Change his mind*. You don't have to beat the enemy; you don't have to win, if you prevent the battle from ever starting.

That's what Ernst Patschke was doing. Following the dictates of the great von Clausewitz and going right for the jugular of history. Grab the minds, squeeze the souls, win the hearts, and do it all with gentle love and utter devotion.

Christ lasted a lot longer than Hitler.

Barsi Shahpur looked with renewed interest at Joey. "I fail to see that greatness." He gestured to the others. "After what they have explained, you seem to find wonder and greatness in parlor magic? In a charlatan who deceives?"

"That is the test!" Joey said with sudden, unexpected heat. "Major, let me ask you something." He didn't wait, but rushed on. "Do you believe in Buddha? In Shiva? Do you believe in the sanctity of Christ? In the only true prophet, Mohammed? Do you believe in God? Don't even bother to answer, because your beliefs may or may not have anything at all to do with the truth. *We both know that*. You believe what you believe because it was drummed into your soul from the day you were old enough to think. This Montini woman; she *knows* her God, her Christ, are the only true measures of some undefined heaven. She *knows*, absolutely and implicitly. What if all these great ancients who have ascended to godhood and sainthood had used precisely the same methods, if not the same equipment, as Patschke in that temple? What if they had used drugs and fear and psychology and magic tricks? Do you *know* this didn't happen? And even if it did—and this is what you little people never learn from history, and what *I* have learned from having in my head the wisdom of every religion on this planet ever committed to paper—*it doesn't matter how a human being becomes sainted or a god.* If it happens, and millions of people believe these things to be true, *they become true.*"

"Three cheers for Saint Joey," Stavers said acidly.

Joey spun about as if struck, his eyes glaring at his childhood friend. "And what the hell do you mean by that!" he shouted angrily.

"You think that line of reasoning is original? Shit," Stavers said with disarming casualness, "that's the oldest debating-society gimmick in history. If the stars are in the sky, it's only because I'm here to see it, and that's what makes them real. If I'm not here, the stars ain't there. B follows right behind A. If enough people can be brought to believe in something, that makes it real. And if Joey Akim Asid Sharif has his way, he's going to keep the oath he's been carrying around in the back of his skull all his life."

Rosa looked bewildered. "Doug, I don't understand any of this."

"It's not that complicated, Rosa. Joey, here, wants the job."

They stared at Joey, who stood full height before them, arms folded, eyes almost aglow with the fervor running through him. "And that's wrong, Doug? Think of this incredible opportunity we have! In me we have one man who *knows* all the world's religions, who can bring them together, who can bring their strength to bear on the nations even now standing on the edge of nuclear holocaust. *I can prevent all that!*"

Stavers leaned back in his chair, hands beneath the cotton folds of his garment. "Is that why you killed Kurt Mueller?" he asked quietly.

The only sounds they heard was Joey's heavy, fast breathing and the constant chant and singing from the thousands of people about them. Rosa stared in shocked disbelief at Joey, then to the completely relaxed Stavers and back to Joey, who was quickly regaining his self control.

Joey found a seat and lowered himself slowly. Finally he nodded. "How did you know? More important, *when* did you find out?"

The others were shocked to hear no denial.

"You were in Berlin and you killed Mueller, but not before he spoke with us and led us on our way. Then you arranged to have Georgieff killed, and you had your people go after Charlie Erickson on his way out of England. You tried to kill us in that hotel. The rest of the killings you left up to your staff." Stavers sighed. He removed a small notebook and a pen from his clothing, opened the pen and made some notes. He didn't look up from the paper. "You blew your cover when you were giving Rosa the old razzle-dazzle in Indian Bluff. You chewed on her pretty good about everybody who was somebody in our business knowing about the Six Hundred, and you yapped about U-2 and other reconnaissance aircraft and everything you said was common knowledge. Except one thing, Colonel Joseph Mitchell of APTO."

"What the hell is APTO?" Marden said from the side.

"Advanced Political Team Operations," Stavers said. "Established as an emergency measure by the White House and answerable only to them ever since the fiasco of the rescue mission in Iran, which was about the biggest special operations fuckup in history. The White House decided at that time it couldn't trust CIA or FBI or NSA or anybody else when it came to special operations. So it created its own palace guard, the elite of the elite, and Joe Mitchell, here, has been its lead field agent ever since the day it started."

"You didn't say how you found out," Colonel Joseph Mitchell said in a low, dangerous voice.

"K11 is the Q-secret code symbol for the reconnaissance satellites which send all their photography and other data directly to the White House. No in-betweens. No military intelligence or Strategic Air Command people to screw it up. The pictures come back and go straight to the White House. Right to the vice president, who, I might say, is quite willing to hasten the demise of the president, who is seventy-six years old and doddering about the Oval Room. Joey, here, was his ticket to the number one seat." Stavers emphasized his words with the pen in his hand, pointing it at the robed figure before him. "You see, the only way you could have known about K11 was to be the man heading that team."

Stavers pressed the clip of his fountain pen. They heard a brief spitting sound. Joseph Mitchell crashed backwards in his seat, fell head over heels and lay on the ground, thrashing madly for several seconds. His body twitched and then he slumped and lay still.

"Mother of God," Rosa whispered.

"What did you do!" Shahpur demanded, his face a mixture of anger and confusion. Everything had been taken from his hands and he was feeling more and more like a pawn in the grip of this strange American.

"He's not dead. Relax," Stavers told them. "The pen is a dart gun, Barsi. He took a load of diluted etorphin; when he comes to he'll be a hypnotized dummy. Etorphin is a super morphine. He won't be able to think on his own for a month. But it won't matter. He's got advanced cholera. It's already all through his system."

Shahpur stared in complete disbelief at Stavers. *"Cholera?* Are you sure? In this country that is a death sentence for millions!"

Stavers nodded. "I know. And he's got it very, very bad. That was in the second dart he took. The most virulent cholera agent turned out by the biological warfare laboratories at the Aberdeen Proving Grounds. When he comes to, an hour will have passed. Those special agents in that second dart will have more than enough time to do their job. The normal cholera microorganism is *Vibrio comma.* This is a hundred times more effective. Or deadlier, as the case may be. When he regains consciousness, he'll be a walking plague . . . *and* he'll go where we tell him to go. The etorphin is the most potent mind-altering drug in the world; don't forget that. Joey has about three days to live. Right now the microorganisms are going through his system with super speed. When he stands up, *if* he can stand up for a while, he's going to have horrible diarrhea, he'll be puking up his guts, cramps are going to tear him apart, and his bladder is going to be squeezed absolutely shut. He won't be able to take a leak even if it kills him. And that it most certainly will do."

"But we can't leave him here to spread cholera like that!" Barsi Shahpur was shouting. "We've got to get him out of here!"

"I agree," Stavers said calmly. "So you'd better get on a radio immediately, Major. Call Gary Cowart at the field. Have him get a helicopter here at once. The machine can land in the clearing behind this house. Do it right away, please."

Shahpur took off at a dead run for the main house. Rosa and Marden stared at Stavers in near shock.

"Relax," they heard. "Those inoculations you received before you left Indian Bluff? You received the antidote for this special cholera agent. It won't bother the three of us. Joey didn't get it, as you may have expected. Now, until the major gets back here, he still doesn't know about the diamond. Patschke's got to be wearing it under his robe. Whatever happens, you go along with me. We get to Patschke. Skip, you cover me. Rosa, you do the same. *I'll* get the damned stone off Patschke and then we get the hell out of here."

"How?" Marden demanded. "We're right in the middle of a million or more of the faithful. You know what'll happen to us if we try a crazy stunt like that?"

"Nothing. They're going to be too busy. Okay, knock it off. Here comes the major."

Shahpur was winded. He fell into a chair. "I've spoken by radio with Cowart. They'll be taking off with two helicopters any moment now."

"Two? Why two?" Rosa asked.

"One may break down. You've never seen cholera as an epidemic. I have," Shahpur said, his face pale with the thought. "So we will have two helicopters, the second as a backup."

"You've forgotten only one thing," Stavers told him. "If something happens to you, you'll be leaving a walking epidemic behind you. No way to stop this stuff from spreading like crazy. I think you'd better tell your staff that I'm your second-in-command. That way, no matter what happens, we can get Mitchell the hell out of here."

Shahpur turned to his side. "Captain!" he roared. An officer ran at once to them. "Captain, that is Major Douglas Stavers," he said, pointing to Stavers. "He is on special assignment to our army and our government. If I am not available or I am indisposed, you will follow his orders to the letter. Do you understand?"

"Yes, sir."

"Good. Inform all your men immediately of my orders."

"Yes, sir." The captain saluted and beat a hasty retreat.

Shahpur seemed to collapse even deeper into his chair. "I simply cannot believe you would be so insane as to bring cholera, any type of cholera, into this land," he said icily to Stavers.

"That all depends," Stavers told him.

"On what?" Shahpur asked in amazement.

"On what we intend to do with him, of course."

"Do with him? We get him away from here, away from this mob of helpless people, Stavers, and we kill him, and we burn his body at once."

"That's ridiculous."

Shahpur's eyes narrowed. "And what did you have in mind?"

"Simple. You lead Mitchell back into the temple. That way we guarantee the danger of a cholera epidemic. Of course, we also spread the word, we get a panic on our hands, and everybody bails out to leave us with a free shot at Patschke."

"I am truly stunned by you, Stavers. What could even lead you to believe I would do such a thing? It is madness even to—"

The first dart caught him in the throat. He didn't even move. He froze in his seat, his eyes rolled back to show only the whites; and before he slumped, the second dart with the violent cholera agent disappeared within the skin of the exposed throat. Stavers closed the pen and replaced it within his clothing. "When he comes to, he'll be in the same shape as Mitchell. The choppers ought to be here in fifteen minutes or so. I want these two people aboard the lead chopper right away. We head for the temple and we land on the prayer grounds in the back. Then, when these two come out of it, they'll be puking their guts out and staining their clothes. You can't stop it. The anal muscles, the sphincter, are rendered useless by this type of cholera agent. Once these people get a look at these two, puking and staining themselves, staggering about with cramps and the sweat bursting from their faces, *they'll know*. All hell will break loose. Even Patschke's hand-picked Indian guards will bug out."

"I can't believe you'd do something like this," Rosa said in a hoarse, throat-constricted voice. "You could kill hundreds of thousands of innocent people!"

Stavers turned a smile of death on her. "You, of all people. Who would have believed it? The same woman who's been trained all her life to kill. The same woman who tried several times to kill *me*. The same woman who led a full-scale attack on Pasaja. The woman married to Jesus Christ, who has sworn against burning for everlasting torment in Hell if she fails in her duty—*you're* faulting me for this?"

"These are innocent people!" she screamed.

His eyes bored into hers. "Rosa, damn you, *think*. Patschke is the new Hitler. He's on his way to dominating the world, to starting the holy war to end all wars. You'd better remember that the body count of the second world war stood at two hundred million people dead. Don't ever forget it. Not for a moment. This cholera is short-lived. Maybe a hundred thousand people will die and it'll be all over. So get off my ass. And while you're wringing your hands for all those innocents around us, you'd better ring up your memory of the Crusades and the Inquisition, all in the name of your Holier than Holy Church and your only true God. Now, shut your goddamn mouth before you make me sick. Here come the choppers."

They thundered down from the night sky like messengers of death. Precisely as Stavers had planned all along.

Chapter   XXVI

"Captain! Over here!" Stavers yelled.

The Indian officer ran to where Stavers was bending over the slumped form of Major Barsi Shahpur. "What happened to him?" he demanded.

Stavers pointed to the sprawled figure of Mitchell. "The same as him. They've both got it. Do you have a doctor here?"

"A doctor? I insist on knowing what's wrong with them!"

Stavers shrugged. "You're in command here. *You* do it. You'll have to isolate them immediately. They've got cholera. It's already in an advanced stage."

The captain recoiled, a hand coming up as if the gesture could avoid the deadly disease. "Ch-cholera?" he stammered.

"The worst kind," Stavers said. "Get some men,

Captain. I need help getting them into those helicopters." He looked toward the two machines. Gary Cowart stood by the sliding door of the first big chopper, waiting.

"Major! I recall Shahpur's orders to me! *Orders!* If anything happened to him *you* were to be in command, and I, uh, I am following my orders. You do it, sir!" He spun on his heel and dashed away.

Stavers grinned at Marden. "I'll take the major and you take Joey." He pulled the unconscious form of Major Shahpur to a vertical position and tossed him like a great sack of meal over his shoulder. Marden did the same with Joey. "Let's get with it," Stavers said. They went directly to the first helicopter, Rosa following, her face white. They dumped the two bodies into the cabin, climbed after them, dragged them away from the door. Marden helped Rosa into the cabin, Cowart following, closing the door.

"Gary, don't ask any questions. There's no time to waste. Get the crew to get these two things into the air at once. Have them fly to the prayer gardens behind the temple. Where the new holy man is holding his seance."

"They may balk," Cowart said quickly. "Give me something to tell the pilots."

"The major and the other man are very ill. We've been asked to bring them to the holy man to save their lives."

"That'll do it," Cowart said. He went forward, spoke rapidly and earnestly to the pilots, who looked back at the two unconscious forms being tended carefully by Stavers and Marden. The engines spooled up and moments later they were in the air, swinging in the direction of the temple. Cowart moved back to Stavers.

"It's set. What happens after we land?"

"We'll take these two into the temple. The pilots can either wait for us or—" Stavers stopped as a new thought came to him. "Tell them they can wait for us or they can leave in the other helicopter. Tell them, *but only after we're on the ground*, that these two men have cholera."

"I say, that's going a bit far, isn't it?"

"Just tell them, goddamnit. You're paid to follow orders, Cowart. It doesn't matter if they're here when we get back or not. Marden can fly this thing blindfolded. In fact, if they believe there's cholera aboard this chopper they'll get the hell away as fast as they can."

"So would I, old man, so would I," Cowart said reflectively. "By the way, they don't really have it, do they?"

"Cowart, are you crazy? Do you think we'd be hauling them around the way we did if they had cholera? I just don't want any interference after we're on the ground, that's all. Oh: if they do leave, make sure they keep this thing running. We may not have time to go through a whole engine start. You stay aboard and wait for us. Got it?"

"Got it."

The helicopter flight to the temple grounds took only minutes. Stavers sat by the still-unconscious major, talking with Marden and Rosa. "Listen to me. We don't have much time. I've already started things at the temple. A lot of people down there are sick as Hogan's goat, throwing up all over the place."

"How did you do that?" Rosa asked, amazed but ready to believe anything of this incredible man.

Stavers grinned. "On the way into the temple I left two small aerosol cans with a timer release in the bushes. They went off after we left. Slow release. Very slow, in fact. They've been spraying vomiting gas into the air. By now the place should be ankle-deep in puke. They won't know what's doing it. When we show up with our two prize specimens and drop the word on that crowd, it's every man for himself."

He reached again into his linens. Rosa shrank back. "For Christ's sake, woman, if I intended you any harm you'd have been dead weeks ago." He removed his hand to show them three sets of earplugs. "Put them in your ears. They'll kill most of the ultrasonic frequency waves in there. We may hurt a bit, but they won't bother us that badly." His hand again went into the robes, came out again with three Red Cross armbands. "Put these on also. Everybody knows what they mean. People will look before they ask. Okay, get ready. They're coming out of it now."

Joey was still unconscious when his body went through its first spasms. He threw up wildly, choking. "Get him sitting up!" Stavers snapped to Marden. "The bastard'll choke himself to death lying down."

The helicopter rocked as it settled, then thumped onto the grassy surface behind the temple. The shock of the hard landing started Shahpur out of his torpid state. He tried to sit up, felt bile squeezing bitterly up his throat. Stavers helped him up. "Just hang on, Major, hang on. You're sick. We're getting you inside to a doctor now. Cowart, open the goddamned door. Skip, you got the grenades with you?"

"Just move it. I'm set," Marden snapped back. He was in action again, in his element. They half dragged the two men from the helicopter, got them groggily on their feet, supported them as they started for the temple. Behind them Cowart was talking to the pilots. Stavers glanced behind him. As he had anticipated, both pilots were running to the second helicopter to throw themselves on board, shouting for the other pilots to leave immediately.

"Cowart!" Stavers yelled. "Get over here!"

Cowart ran to them, almost at the same time as temple guards approached them warily. Then Stavers saw the reason for their caution. Bodies were sprawled everywhere, people dry-heaving, their bodies convulsing from cramps. The vomiting gas had done its work effectively. "You know the language," Stavers told Cowart. "Tell them who Shahpur is, that it's a matter of life and death to bring these two straight to the holy man."

Cowart went ahead of them, engaged in a brief but intense conversation with the guards. He turned and nodded to Stavers. "Good. Get back to the chopper and wait for us there."

They went ahead, following the guards, half-dragging the stupefied, drugged men, who were now throwing up every step of the way. A foul smell spread from Joey and the major as their sphincters went completely lax and their bowels emptied within their clothing. Stavers shook Shahpur violently. "Can you hear me, Barsi? Damnit, listen to me!"

Shahpur nodded, gagging, weak, soaked in perspiration. "Those men, there. Tell them you must see the Holy Man. Tell them you have cholera and you're dying. *Tell them*, you bastard!"

Two guards came back to the strange scene. Barsi Shahpur lifted his head. Under the effects of the etorphin he would do anything he was ordered. He blurted out what he'd been told to say. Stavers knew the ploy was working. The moment they heard *cholera* in their own language and took a hard look at Shahpur, choking and spewing bile from his lips, drooling uncontrollably, fouling himself, they ran for their lives.

Stavers and Marden pushed on, the way clear, Rosa following. The mobs that had jammed into the temple before were gone. Bodies lay everywhere, twitching or unconscious. Screams and shouts rent the air as the guards shouted the terrible warning of cholera. They pushed down the stone corridor and moments later entered the great domed temple. People were dashing madly away before them. The hooded and robed figure rose slowly to his feet from the marble throne, studying them intently. Stavers and Marden flung the two bodies away from them. Stavers didn't take his eyes from Patschke.

"Watch that hallway to the right of that throne. His own people will be coming through there."

"You handle your end," Marden told him, reaching within the folds of his clothing. His huge hands held four small grenades, three in the left, the fourth in his right. He pulled the ring with his teeth, kept the timed detonator down ready to use. They didn't have long to wait. Several burly men came running through the hallway entrance behind the raised throne. Marden released the detonator handle. He timed it exactly. One second for the release, one second to throw, two seconds for the grenade to be in the air directly before the men rushing them—and the white phosphorus grenade exploded in a savage glare of light. Blazing phosphorus spattered outward, searing the men, burning everything it touched, their skin and their clothing. White smoke boiled into the air. The men fell back, screaming, and Marden let fly with another grenade. This one hurled two men violently against the stone wall. The other two writhed on the floor, their clothing burning fiercely.

"Get him!" Marden shouted above the uproar.

Stavers looked at the hooded figure walking slowly, almost regally from the throne, *toward him*. "Patschke, you son of a bitch, stop right there!" Stavers yelled. One hand was within his clothing, poised.

He couldn't believe it. Patschke stood still, looking at them; and then slowly, every move measured, he loosened his robe, shrugged his shoulders, and let it fall from his body.

Rosa Montini screamed, so long and piercing it seemed torn from her heart. Again and again the scream stabbed at them.

Chapter   XXVII

Stavers stared in stunned disbelief at a beautiful old woman with long, straight platinum hair. She stood proud and erect before him, a burning yellow flame at her throat just above her breast. Her skin was a coppery gold, old but softly, and slowly she raised one hand and pointed an accusing finger at Stavers. Behind him Rosa had gone slowly to her knees, fingers clasped tightly in prayer, and he could hear her voice whimpering. "Mother of God, Mother of God," she repeated over and over.

Stavers felt something twisting inside his head and he knew there was no time to think, no time left for reasoning, no time for anything but what he had planned for this moment. He heard a voice of music calling out to him. "Child of faithlessness, you have sinned. You have—"

His hand came whipping from within his garment, lifted up and snapped forward. They barely heard the whistle of wind as the eight-pointed *shuriken* hurtled from his hand to sink deeply between the eyes of the incredible woman before them. For a long moment she stood unmoving, shocked, eyes widening. The hand with the pointed finger convulsed in a claw of dying, and in slow motion the beautiful figure folded like a collapsing doll to crumple to the floor.

Rosa threw herself with nails outstretched at Stavers's face. She didn't make it. Marden smashed the side of her head with a wicked backhand and she spun wildly around, blood flying from her cheek. "Bring her with us," Stavers ordered.

He ran forward to the dead woman, knelt down. The incredible diamond hung from her neck on a heavy golden chain. Stavers gripped the chain in his powerful hand, placed a foot against the woman's head, and yanked with all his strength. Skin tore, but the chain snapped. His hand clamped around the diamond. "Move out!" he shouted to Marden. The big man carried Rosa like an unconscious child over one shoulder and they ran from the temple, down the corridor, stepping over and around the bodies. Screams and shouts filled the night air; the cries were of the dreaded cholera plague, and Stavers felt a chill wind as he saw a crowd milling about the helicopter, fighting like animals to get aboard. "Grenades," he said calmly to Marden as they ran. Marden tossed him two grenades, Stavers pulled the pins and hurled them directly into the mob. The white phosphorus stabbed into bodies and in moments the panicky mob was screaming in pain from this terrible new enemy. They fell aside like wheat before a scythe as Stavers and Marden sailed into them, kicking and hurling them away from the helicopter. "Get inside!" Stavers bellowed to Marden. The big man tossed Rosa into the cabin, went for the pilot's seat. Cowart had no idea what was happening, but he was a cool head. Stavers vaulted past him into the cabin of the helicopter. "Hold them off until we're ready!" he shouted to Cowart.

Cowart nodded, turned to face a new mob running toward them. He heard the helicopter engines rising to a scream, poised himself to climb aboard, had time only to hear Stavers calling above the engine roar to Marden. "Jump takeoff! *Go!*" And before Gary Cowart could turn for his own escape, the big chopper lunged forward and away, out of reach. The last view Stavers had of Cowart was his body falling beneath the raging, terrified crowd that watched their escape from certain death rising away into the darkened sky.

Stavers turned to Rosa. She was just regaining consciousness, the side of her face bloody. She moaned as Stavers raised her to a sitting position. Marden glanced back. "Where the hell are we going?" he yelled.

"Take her straight to Bhagalpur. Get on that radio. Use Shahpur's name. Tell them to get the Grumman ready for immediate takeoff. When we get there, you park this thing alongside the Grumman, leave everything running, and then get the hell out and into the Grumman. Got it?"

Marden gestured his acknowledgement. Stavers moved Rosa to where she could lean against the side of the cabin. He went to the rear and turned on a small light, then removed a knife from his pocket. He had planned long and well for this moment. The diamond rested in his palm, flashing its icy yellow fire into his eyes. He brought the knife to the great gem, and slowly and carefully pried away the gold prongs. He threw away the chain. There was only the incredible stone, even in this dim light brilliant and commanding. He studied it a moment longer, taking its measure. About one and a quarter inches long and an inch wide and three-quarters of an inch deep. He reached into the pockets within the long yards of linen and brought out a small vial of vaseline jelly. He coated the diamond with the jelly, steeled himself, and pushed it into his mouth and as far down his throat as his fingers would reach. He started to gag, fought off the choking sensation, forced himself to swallow. The great diamond slid into his stomach.

He returned to Rosa. In the dim light from the rear of the cabin she was a ghastly white, blood caked along the side of her face, her body bent over in terrible cramps. One leg twitched convulsively. She forced herself back to a sitting position, her eyes begging help from the man with her. Marden had turned to look back into the cabin. "What the hell's wrong with her?" he shouted above the engine roar.

Stavers looked directly at Marden. "She has cholera," he said simply.

Marden's face went grim. "You said we were given the antidote," he said coldly.

"We were. Only hers *wasn't* the antidote. You and I are the only ones who are safe."

"Doug, you're making me ask questions. How do I—"

"Don't be stupid, Marden. If you had cholera, you'd be puking your guts out by now. Shut up and fly. I want to get there while it's still dark."

He turned back to look at Rosa. Through the spasms of nausea and the bile trickling through her lips she began to understand. Her eyes were pained and accusing. "You would do this to me?" she asked, still disbelieving the ultimate truth.

"You swore to kill me in order to get the diamond," he said simply. "I took you at your word."

She tried to laugh and spewed up bile instead. She managed to speak. "And you failed. *You failed!* There was no Patschke! You killed a beautiful old woman. Oh, you filth! A holy woman! You—"

He laughed and reached out for her, grasped her arm to pull her closer to him. He brought his face next to hers. He wanted direct, intimate eye contact with Rosa Montini.

"An old woman? A holy woman?" His laughter boomed out. "That's why no one ever saw Patschke," he said, almost with a distant triumph. "He had transsexual surgery, made himself into a woman and had plastic surgery to make him, *her*, so very beautiful. But it was Patschke, all right. No one else could have had the diamond."

Her eyes widened. "And you . . . now you have . . ."

His smile was ice, hard. "That's right, Rosa. I have it."

She pulled herself closer, her head against his arm, looking up at him. "How could you do this to me, Doug? For the sake of God, we were *lovers*," she implored him. "No matter what, I—" Blood bubbled from her mouth and she fought off a body-wrenching convulsion. "Oh, hold me, Doug, *hold me*, my lover, my sweet . . ." She made a valiant effort to get closer, he helped her up, it would be different, if nothing else, to kiss her one last time on her bloody lips, and—

The knife came out of her boot and slammed like liquid fire between his ribs. In the sudden horror of what she had done she convulsed again, and he felt steel grating along a rib. He gasped, not uttering a sound, and hurled her away from him. Almost at once he realized his mistake. He'd thrown her toward the front of the helicopter. Maddened now, blood spurting from her mouth, she shrieked like a demented animal—and in one final spasm of remaining strength she fell against the back of the pilot's seat and shoved the knife at Marden. The sharp blade went into his shoulder, and as her arm fell away with weakness she sliced a furrow down his arm. The helicopter jerked wildly.

Her eyes mad, summoning the energy from some impossible reservoir, she climbed shakily to her feet, bracing with one hand on the side of the cabin, beseeching her God for the last burst of strength to jam the knife into Marden's neck. With both hands, trembling, she brought the blade up, blood burst from her lips and she struck.

A steel bar smashed into her arm. She thought this to be so. The steel was human: Stavers's hand, crashing against her arm. Over the roar of engines and wind they all heard the bone snap. He grasped her wrist, jerked her violently, and white bone pierced her skin. He laughed, pulled her to him by the broken, torn arm and lifted her from the floor of the helicopter.

"Like you said, Rosa," he spoke close to her eyes, "we were lovers." His face jerked down, lips drawn back in a feral snarl, and he kissed her, then his teeth tore open her lips. Laughing, he spat away her flesh and hurled her body through the open door into the dark night.

Chapter   XXVIII

Sirpur Rajkot arrived at Bhagalpur an hour after the American jet took off. In its place on the dusty airstrip was an Indian Air Force helicopter, its cabin stinking from blood and vomit.

Two of the flight crew were trained paramedics, and the Grumman had an extensive field medical kit aboard. The medics cleansed their wounds and bandaged them with skill, shot them both full of antibiotics, and completed their tasks without making the mistake of telling Stavers and Marden to take things easy for a while. By the time the Grumman landed in Singapore both men were dressed in business suits and were clean-shaven. They emerged with the crew at Singapore Customs, showing no sign of having been stabbed savagely and deeply the night before. Neither man gave any clue of the pain he endured.

Their papers were in order. "Will you be leaving soon?" an official queried.

Stavers shook his head. Everyone about him was incredibly cooperative, almost anxious to please. He spoke calmly, with an air of confidence that was almost devastating to encounter. "No," he told the customs official. "I'll spend about twenty minutes with my crew. Mr. Marden is getting our bags from the aircraft. He and I will be leaving on Singapore Airlines. There's a 747 flying nonstop to San Francisco, I believe?"

"Yes, sir. I can confirm your reservations immediately."

"I'd appreciate that."

Stavers talked to Roger Janca and the others. "We'll go back commercial. Take the plane to Los Angeles and wait there until you hear from me. Have a good flight. You hit any real weather, sit it out. There's no rush."

"Yes, sir, and thank you. Have a good trip yourself, Mr. Stavers."

Stavers and Marden watched the Grumman take off. Their own plane would leave in twenty minutes. "Everything's set," Marden told him.

"Good. Let's get aboard. I can use a drink."

Thirty-five minutes later the 747 was climbing eastward out of Singapore. Stavers reclined his seat and relaxed with a martini. He glanced at his watch. It was twenty-five minutes from takeoff. One hour after takeoff for the Grumman.

High over the Pacific, three phosphorus grenades in the cabin of the Grumman exploded and blew out the sides of the fuselage. Blazing phoshorus and smoke erupted into the cockpit. The airplane went straight in from forty thousand feet.

Two Wells Fargo armed guards carried the attaché case through a private entrance of Hotel El Cid. In the penthouse suite, five people, the Board of Directors, waited with almost unbearable suspense for the delivery of the case. Stavers had called them from San Francisco. His contract had been fulfilled. He spoke with Vernon Kovanowicz. "It's done. It's being delivered by Wells Fargo directly to your meeting room."

"Where are you calling from, Stavers?"

"St. Catherine's Hospital in San Francisco. I inhaled some white phosphorus."

Kovanowicz chuckled. "We heard about that. Very neatly done, if I say so myself."

"What about the people in Bucharest?"

"There was a terrible fire in the museum. No one quite understands how it got out of control so quickly. Twenty-three people died. It was a tragedy."

"Including?"

"Yes, Stavers. Including them."

"I'll be there tomorrow night to arrange for the rest of my payment."

"You've earned it. I'll see you then. *Prosit*."

They gathered in their group so that they would see the Messiah Stone for the first time, together. Concetta de Luca was given the honor of opening the case with the key from the sealed envelope. She lifted the top of the case with shaking hands. She paused to smile at the others. Kovanowicz gestured impatiently for her to stop her theatrics. She opened the case wide.

Four pounds of plastique explosives went off with a blast that tore heads from torsos, ripped open bodies, and blew out all the windows in the penthouse.

"You're the only one left who knows, Skip."

"Yes."

"You know what's ahead of us?"

"What Hitler started, what Patschke came so close to doing."

"What we're going to do," Stavers said, smiling.

Skip Marden worshiped this man. "Of course we will."

"You know I trust you completely. I'm about to prove that."

"I know you are. Please don't concern yourself about anything."

"Oh, I don't." Stavers smiled. "Everything's set?"

"Yes, everything."

"Then let's get it over with."

In the private sanitarium in Arizona, sealed off except for the people directly involved, two of the finest surgeons in the country, assisted by a staff of nine, took Douglas Stavers into unconsciousness on the operating table. The surgery was quick, simple, and completely successful. The lead surgeon removed the large object from the patient's lower stomach where it had lodged painfully. They followed their instructions to the letter. Immediately upon its removal from his body, the object was sealed in a leaden bag and attached to the arm of the unconscious man. Douglas Stavers was sewn up, checked and rechecked for vital signs, found in excellent condition, and wheeled to the recovery room.

The surgery had been little more complicated than that required for an appendectomy. Stavers sat up the next day, walked the day after, checked out of the hospital the third day. He left behind him the surgical staff, with a total payment for their work and several days of preplanned isolation in the sanitarium of two hundred thousand dollars. With them were the four guards, each of whom had been paid ten thousand dollars for their loyalty and strict obedience to instructions. They would leave on the morning of the fifth day.

That night the small clinic vanished in a roaring, flame-spewing explosion from the charges Marden had set previously. There were no survivors. Marden was very good at his work.

Now only they, the two of them, knew of the great diamond that hung from the neck of Douglas Stavers.

He could feel its extraordinary effect through his body, changing his mind, bringing to him an incredible, an undeniable sense of power and control. He had thought long about this moment, what he would do once all the petty details were behind them. A world waited for him, a world filled with the errors of those who had held the Messiah Stone but who had followed the wrong paths.

He thought of Rosa. What had she said to him? In her search for the Star of Bethlehem, the celestial signal to all the world of the birth of the son of God, all those who sought this sign of heaven were absolved from all sin, from all crime, from all deeds.

A test, so said the Vatican, ordained by heaven itself.

You didn't make it, Rosa. No star shines on you now. No heaven rejoices and the Vatican is gloomy. You're not even real. You were a dream exercised by old men greedy for power, and now they tremble in the dark night, because they know that their sign from heaven is not for them. They must move aside.

But their holy books were right.

There would be a Second Coming.

A new Messiah.

Of whatever God *he* proclaimed.

Stavers looked out upon His world and smiled.

ABOUT THE AUTHOR

Martin Caidin, a prolific and versatile writer with more than 120 books to his credit, is also a world record-breaking commercial and stunt pilot, a warbirds veteran, a parachutist, airshow performer, and a man who has owned everything from sleek fighter planes to a huge three-engined German WW II bomber. Aside from "living all those lives about which he writes," he is a recognized world authority in the fields of aviation, aerospace, astronautics, military science, and related fields. He has revolutionized research in the hard application of psionics research and development, as well as changing the world's thinking in the fields of bionics and biophysiology through his *Cyborg* research and writings.

After military service in the U.S. Maritime Service and Merchant Marine and then the U.S. Army and Air Force in many parts of the world, as well as special studies in the bombed areas of Japan,

Martin Caidin served as Nuclear Warfare Specialist to the State of New York and many other states, as well as the U.S. Government, and as an international consultant on mass destruction weaponry systems. He served as a consultant on aviation physiology to the FAA, on military space systems to the USAF, and worked closely with Wernher von Braun in this nation's most secret pioneering efforts to reach the moon.

As an international consultant, he has analyzed in great detail the effects of nuclear, biological, chemical, and other weapons on various target systems in this and other nations. He has gone face-to-face with top officials of the Soviet and many other governments in his own talk show on issues critical to the survival of the United States, and has hammered out crushing defeats against his TV opponents.

As a commercial multi-engine pilot of both landplanes and seaplanes, he has owned and flown a wide variety of civil and military aircraft and files often throughout the U.S. He has flown "war-weary" bombers and transports across the Atlantic, manned fighters and bombers in motion pictures, and performed as an airshow barnstormer. He earned the permanent title of "Thunderbird 8" from flying with the famous USAF aerobatic team, is a member of and jump pilot for the US Army's Golden Knights championship jump team. Among the more spectacular events of his career is the world wingwalking record, set when Martin Caidin flew a German Ju-52 bomber *with 19 wingwalkers on his left wing!*

Mr. Caidin's first novel, *Marooned*, a thrilling account of a space rescue, became an internationally acclaimed major motion picture. Many of his novels have been bought for filming for movies and TV series. *Cyborg*, published in 1972, became the world-famous TV series *The Six Million Dollar Man* and *The Bionic Woman*. His more recent works of fiction, notably *Killer Station* and *The Messiah Stone*, moved into national prominence even before their release. He is also the author of more than 80 authoritative books on military air history. Many of them, including *Samurai!* and *The Ragged, Rugged Warriors*, are judged internationally as classics in their field. His books on space flight have been printed worldwide in dozens of languages.

Martin Caidin is a Charter Member of the Congressional Aviation Hall of Fame, a Fellow of the British Interplanetary Society, a Knight of the Mark Twain Society, the founder of the American Astronautical Society, a recipient of the Silver Wings' Carl Fromhagen Award honoring Martin Caidin as a "Pioneer and Master Aviator and Distinguished Author," and many more international awards and honors. He and his wife, Dee Dee, who is also a pilot, balloonist, former parachutist, TV and film producer, and professional model, maintain studio homes in both Gainesville and in Cocoa Beach, Florida, where Martin Caidin is also a visiting professor at several universities. Martin and Dee Dee Caidin devote much of their time as a tightly knit team, in addition to flying and writing, to advanced scientific projects, the making of action-adventure movies, and applying their extraordinary experience to the problems we have fashioned for ourselves with advanced weapons. But most of all, Martin Caidin makes our world exciting, and shares with us that excitement in his books.

Author's Afterword

I have wrestled with the problem of properly describing this book. Is is a nonfiction novel? Or a dramatization which binds together the incredible and startling events that race through nearly two thousand years of turbulent, spellbinding adventure and challenge?

Most of what you read in *The Messiah Stone* is true. Because the passage of time and the wickedly complex diversity of events render it patently impossible to be specifically true on all counts, I have chosen the novel as my vessel to carry this amazing story to you, the reader.

First, what is called the Messian Stone, or the Godstone, or the Star of Bethlehem—the great, flawless diamond of icy fire—*is real*. It exists. I have been familiar with it for many years. There is a name that does not appear in what we offer to you as a work of fiction: Kelley Phillips. His relationship with the Messiah Stone—what he has also called the Stone of Prometheus (for reasons which become strikingly evident in these pages)—would add much to the spinning of this tale, but for many reasons (which also manifest themselves as you read on) his name is absent from these pages.

Almost every event and most of the people in

The Messiah Stone are real. The story of the Roumanians, their great aircraft and their forays through Africa and Europe; these are real. These people existed, held internationally recognized positions, went to the places described and participated in the events that are told. The role of Adolf Hitler and the young captain he promoted on the spot to Colonel-General of the *Wermacht*; all this is *real*, as are the events in the Berlin bunker in those horrific days of 1945.

And the people, the characters who form the main tapestry of the book . . . *even some of their names are real*. Not all, but some; we will not and cannot tell you more than that, again for reasons made clear in the adventure that is *The Messiah Stone*.

It is a journey you are not likely to forget easily.

—Martin Caidin

Announcing one hell of a shared universe!

OF COURSE IT'S A FANTASY . . . ISN'T IT?

Alexander the Great teams up with Julius Caesar and Achilles to refight the Trojan War—with Machiavelli as their intelligence officer and Cleopatra in charge of R&R . . . Yuri Andropov learns to Love the Bomb with the aid of The Blond Bombshell (she is the Devil's *very* private secretary) . . . Che Guevara Ups the Revolution with the help of Isaac Newton, Hemingway, and Confucius . . . And no less a bard than Homer records their adventures for posterity: of *course* it's a fantasy. It has to be, if you don't believe in Hell.

ALL YOU REALLY NEED IS FAITH . . .

But award-winning authors Gregory Benford, C. J. Cherryh, Janet Morris, and David Drake, co-creators of this multi-volume epic, insist that *Heroes in Hell* ® is something more. They say that all you really need is Faith, that if you accept the single postulate that Hell exists, your imagination will soar, taking you to a realm more magical and strangely satisfying than you would have believed possible.

COME TO HELL . . .

. . . where the battle of Good and Evil goes on apace in the most biased possible venue. There's no rougher, tougher place in the Known Universe of Discourse, and you *wouldn't* want to live there, but . . .

IT'S BRIGHT . . . FRESH . . . LIBERATING . . . AS HELL!

Co-created by some of the finest, most imaginative

—

talents writing today, *Heroes in Hell* ® offers a milieu more exciting than anything in American fiction since *A Connecticut Yankee in King Arthur's Court*. As bright and fresh a vision as any conceived by Borges, it's as accessible—and American—as apple pie.

EVERYONE WHO WAS ANYONE DOES IT

In fact, Janet Morris's Hell is so liberating to the imaginations of the authors involved that nearly a dozen major talents have vowed to join her for at least eight subsequent excursions to the Underworld, where—even as you read this—everyone who was anyone is meeting to hatch new plots, conquer new empires, and test the very limits of creation.

YOU'VE HEARD ABOUT IT—NOW GO THERE!

Join the finest writers, scientists, statesmen, strategists, and villains of history in Morris's Hell. The first volume, co-created by Janet Morris with C. J. Cherryh, Gregory Benford, and David Drake, will be on sale in March as the mass-market lead from Baen Books, and in April Baen will publish in hardcover the first *Heroes in Hell* spin-off novel, *The Gates of Hell*, by C. J. Cherryh and Janet Morris. We can promise you one Hell of a good time.

FOR A DOSE OF THAT OLD-TIME RELIGION (TO A MODERN BEAT), READ—

HEROES IN HELL®
March 1986
65555-8 • 288 pp. • $3.50

THE GATES OF HELL
April 1986 Hardcover
65561-2 • 256 pp. • $14.95

A giant space station orbiting the Earth can be a scientific boon ... or a terrible sword of Damocles hanging over our heads. In Martin Caidin's *Killer Station*, one brief moment of sabotage transforms Station *Pleiades* into an instrument of death and destruction for millions of people. The massive space station is heading relentlessly toward Earth, and its point of impact is New York City, where it will strike with the impact of the Hiroshima Bomb. Station Commander Rush Cantrell must battle impossible odds to save his station and his crew, and put his life on the line that millions may live.

This high-tech tale of the near future is written in the tradition of Caidin's *Marooned* (which inspired the Soviet-American Apollo/Soyuz Project and became a film classic) and *Cyborg* (the basis for the hit TV series "The Six Million Dollar Man"). Barely fictional, *Killer Station* is an intensely *real* moment of the future, packed with excitement, human drama, and adventure.

Caidin's record for forecasting (and inspiring) developments in space is well-known. *Killer Station* provides another glimpse of what *may* happen with and to all of us in the next few years.

Available December 1985 from Baen Books
55996-6 • 384 pp. • $3.50